FIRE IN THE HILL

H. Fred Neale

Llumina
Press

This book is a work of fiction. Names, characters, places, and incidents either are the product of the author's imagination or are used fictitiously, and any resemblance to actual persons, living or dead, business establishments, events, or locales is entirely coincidental.

ISBN: 978-1-62550-522-4 (PB)

"Dedication"

This book is dedicated to my wife Patsy who always convinces me I can do something I can't, and my sister Dixie who never grew up, and still believes in Santa Claus, ghosts and UFO's.

Short Description of "Fire in the Hill"

There is something strange hidden underneath the small Texas town of Tejas Hill, but not for long. Perched on top of a limestone bluff, like an island floating in the flat Texas blackland prairie, Tejas Hill appears to be like a thousand other small towns, but looks are deceiving. The townsfolk are eccentric, and in some cases, downright threatening.

Set against the backdrop of a small town caught in a legal struggle with a huge mining conglomerate, a strange group of people converges on the town, searching for something they don't understand, only to find they are searching for the same phenomenon.

There is Abra Avant, respected archaeologist, seeking an answer as to why the same person appears unchanged in family photos generations apart and still operates an antiquity shop in town. Skippy Beto, career college student and soon-to-be heir to a broadcasting fortune, seeks an explanation for a rare meteorological event after a misfired mining blast. Finally, there is Dennis Smith, a promising young scientist hired by the mining company to investigate geological anomalies inside the bluff while the company tries to steal the amazing machine he has invented.

Against the backdrop of these seemingly unrelated quests, an eccentric local snoop best known for making pornographic gestures to citizens and inspecting houses when no one is home is found murdered on top of the local abandoned university tower. The body, wrapped in steel reinforcing rods like a statue, is posed in one last gesture of defiance.

Enter two FBI agents, one seasoned and jaded, and the other fresh out of the academy, sent to investigate why a ham radio post card from a local radio operator has appeared on a Mars rover during a presidential press conference.

Throw in a nasty little gray alien named Klatoo and a half-alien beauty named Yasha, and the stage is set for mischief and adventure. This strange cast of characters, events, and investigations converge for a climatic showdown in a prehistoric cave inside the bluff, where the secret everyone seeks is finally revealed, changing the life of all who have sought the answer and ultimately, everyone else as well.

Welcome to the strange and deliciously different town of Tejas Hill.

"Prologue"

The big limestone hill had already been there so long, for so far back in time, that even the night, with all its stars looking down, seeing all, could not remember the event that thrust the bluff up out of the black dirt prairie. Little Eagle climbed to the edge of the limestone bluff and sat down on his heels. It was cold and crisp, the kind of still night that makes the air feel stiff and frozen. The kind of night where your breath hangs above your head, unable to move.

Little Eagle did not come to the bluff for the usual reasons. He did not come that night to watch for herds of bison or mammoth. Not for the pictures that moved across the sky and told stories, shadowing the seasons and telling the people where the game would be. No, he came for something no one else came for. He came to see the burning fires that fell from the sky.

He was not the only one who saw them, but he was the only one who cared to watch for them. The shaman did not like them, probably because he could not predict them. Little Eagle understood that you could not control others with something you could not predict. He was wise enough to keep that observation and his curiosity about strange events in the sky to himself.

He did not know if this night would be the night, but he had seen the lights in the sky falling three years in a row during the month of the Dipper. He knew where to look, but not why he was looking. What good could come from the flames that lit up the sky with their crossing? The people had fire. Anyway, the lights never seemed to reach the ground. It did not matter. It only mattered that this was something different in a life where all that really mattered to living was known—the animals, the signs, the weather, the grass, the seasons.

As the Dipper crossed the north horizon, the fires came streaking across the sky. First a few, then more. Then a torrent, more than he had ever seen. Most died on the way down. And then he saw the rolling ball of flame that would change his life. It was bigger than the others, and it came from low on the horizon. It started low across the sky, rolling slowly like a large stone, fiery pieces falling off its sides. It almost lit the entire sky. As it came across, one glowing piece came loose and fell toward the hilltop, so close he could see flames coming off the side and hear a distant roar growing in his ears.

Complacent, Little Eagle sat still, sure that this one would go out like the rest, something to remember when he was doing something he wanted to forget. Closer it fell, until he realized that this ball of fire was not going out. Out of the corner of his eye, the larger fireball it had broken off from roared by overhead. It would have been the sight of his lifetime, but just now, Little Eagle had a problem to deal with and legs that could not move in time to save him.

The orange glowing mass hit the side of the bluff the length of two giant bison below his feet. On impact, it shattered into a thousand pieces, so bright it took his sight away as they showered over him. The dark rock at the core of the fireball buried itself deep inside the hill, hitting a vein of water that ran through a fault in the center of the bluff. It flowed in the water, strangely buoyant, falling deeper inside the hill until it reached a pool in the bottom of a large cave hidden under the bluff.

Little Eagle did not know this and would never know this. At that moment, he was glad to have his sight back and astonished to see a small piece from the flaming stone lying on the ground by his foot. He knew what it was by the glow. Black as night, but pulsing light like it was lit from within. He wanted to clutch the stone, but he knew what happened when you touched the coals from the fire. No, he waited, waited until he knew the stone could no longer be hot. Strangely, the glow within subsided, but did not go out altogether, and the stone never lost its warmth, even in the depths of winter. Amazingly heavy for its small size, Little Eagle always carried it in his fur knapsack, never far from him.

Little Eagle would keep that secret to himself. Although he would keep the stone near him the rest of his long life, he never let anyone see it at night, never let anyone see the eerie glow inside the stone that never went out. The bluff kept its secret, too, never letting anyone see the large piece laying in the pool deep down, never cooling despite the cold water that pulsed around it for millennia. Unseen, but working its magic on the bluff and all who lived there and drank the water that came from the springs that flowed from the pool.

For you see, the stone that fell that night was special beyond belief—a freak of events that had never occurred and would probably not occur again. The planet that spawned the rock lived far beyond the

Dipper. It had been an old world before the moon formed over the earth and the first rains fell from the sky. It had harbored life, different and strange, and peoples who looked nothing like our people, and whose civilizations were great and lived long. But it had long since been overtaken by the old, tired, and swollen sun. A gas giant captured by the gravity of another galaxy that swung too close, pulling it and many other suns and worlds out into the great black.

When the old sun could no longer expand, and would not go out, it exploded, traveling light years in seconds and just as fast, imploded back on itself, tearing the rock apart so that it did not become a part of the burned-out hulk that rotated, sending out radiation like the light in a lighthouse. Instead, it slingshot its way through the cloth of the universe into a black hole, deep into another universe.

Through the hole, rare elements and pressures, matter and antimatter, things that never came in contact, and could not exist together under any other circumstance, came together long enough to change the rock, to forge a fire in its core that could not go out. Creating an energy that altered deadly radiation into a force that changed all living things it contacted, but in odd ways.

Little Eagle's family never left the bluff and buried his body under rock slabs in the cleft left by the meteor in the side of the bluff, just as he had asked. The strange rock was still in his knapsack, casting an eerie faint glow within the tomb. His descendants were still on the bluff generations later when a granddaughter, many times removed, married a young settler with red hair, descended from the Vikings, and founded the town of Tejas Hill.

"Cast of Characters"
(in order of appearance)

1. LITTLE EAGLE - PALEO- INDIAN

2. DEBORAH MENDEZ - WIFE OF DR. DIRK MENDEZ

3. DR. DIRK MENDEZ - NEW LOCAL SURGEON

4. CONNIE - CAFE/GENERAL STORE OWNER

5. EARL - BOYFRIEND OF CAFE/GENERAL STORE OWNER

6. SHADE MCCAIN - LOCAL BIGWIG

7. DAN DAHONEY - ANOTHER LOCAL BIGWIG

8. JAINIE PLUMBER - STEELY EYED RETIRED TEACHER

9. SANDY NORTHCUTT - MINING COMPANY EXECUTIVE

10. DENNIS SMITH - PROMISING YOUNG SCIENTIST

11. JOHNNY BROWN - CHILD WITH STRANGE ABILITIES

12. BETSY BROWN - OVERWEIGHT TWINKIE EATING MOTHER

13. BILLY BURKHART - PREACHER WITH PAST TO HIDE AND MONKEY ON BACK

14. KINNERD IRVIN - LOCAL SNOOP WITH STRANGE HABITS

15. LARRY CLAKEY - LOCAL JACK OF ALL TRADES

16. LEON NEALY - LARRY'S GIANT HALF-WIT SIDEKICK

17. CHARLES LATIMER - LOCAL ARCHITECT SHOOK BY BLAST

18. DAVE LUMPKIN - WEATHERMAN EXTRAORDINAIRE

19. GEORGE LUMPKIN - DAVE'S FARMER FATHER

20. EVELYN LUMPKIN - DAVE'S DEPRESSED MOTHER

21. PATTY LUMPKIN - DAVE'S KID SISTER

22. SHANNA - ASST. WEATHER WOMAN WITH AMPLE FIGURE

23. SKIPPY BETO - BROADCAST MAGNATE'S SON AND TRUST FUND HEIR

24. ABRA AVANT - ARCHEOLOGIST SEEKING ANSWER TO MYSTERY

25. LANNIE OLSON - TEJAS HILL CITY SECRETARY

26. LINTON EGGLESTON - ANTIQUE STORE OWNER WITH MANY SECRETS

27. JOHN ELVIN WRIGHT - HAM OPERATOR WITH POSTCARD ON MARS ROVER

28. MATILDA - GOOD NATURED MAID WITH A HEART OF GOLD

29. JOAN WRIGHT - SUCCESSFUL MOTHER WITH ODD PARENTING SKILLS

30. KLATOO - NASTY LITTLE GRAY ALIEN

31. MADGE BURKHART - BRAZEN WIFE OF TRAVELING EVANGELIST

32. WILLIAM CALVIN BURKHART - TRAVELING EVANGELIST

33. HARDY HARRINGTON - RICH GULLIBLE WIDOWER

34. YASHA - GOOD LOOKING HALF-ALIEN WOMAN

35. GENERAL ANDY "ICEMAN" ANDERSON - WASHED UP ASTRONAUT

36. RANDY STUCKEY - BROWN NOSING AIDE TO THE GENERAL

37. THE PRESIDENT OF THE U.S. - YOU FIGURE OUT WHICH ONE

38. DON SAMUALSON - HARD NOSED TV REPORTER

39. BUDDY EISNER - FILLING STATION/GARAGE OWNER

40. GLYNNIS EISNER - BUDDY'S DEVOTED WIFE

41. JASON FELLS - IDIOT SAVANT WITH PHOTOGRAPHIC MEMORY

42. NATHANIEL HENRY - YOUNG GREEN FBI AGENT

43. SAM NIKOSIA - OLDER JADED FBI AGENT

44. DAN RUMSDELL - U. S. SECRETARY OF DEFENSE

45. EVELYN - RUNS SALVATION ARMY RE-SALE SHOP

Chapter One

"A NEW START"

Deborah Mendez sat deep in the beige, leather passenger seat of the Mercedes Benz. Her perfectly coordinated outfit was an odd shade of lemon, which miraculously matched her high heel shoes exactly. Her expression became pained as the long car made the turn off Highway 68 onto the edge of the bluff. Deborah had "pained" expressions down to a science, and on a scale of one to ten, this one rated about a four.

"Dirk, are you absolutely sure that this is where the realtor told you to go?" she asked as the road began to wind past a number of odd little houses with old cars and motorcycles in the front yards, metal barns with old cow skulls nailed to the side, and too many other Texas white trash clichés to mention.

"She told me to go eight miles out of town and to take the first right at the top of the big hill, and I believe that is just what we did." Dirk did not like to be questioned. That came from being a doctor. No one questioned a surgeon other than another physician, and that was something that had been happening far too often lately. Though he was perturbed, he made sure not to show it too much. Deborah knew she could not push him too far, and he knew she could make his life pure hell for short periods with her displeasure. "Don't worry, she also told me to ignore the white trash on this side of the hill and hold my judgment until we reached the bluff on the other side."

Deborah relaxed somewhat as she melted back into the plush leather seat. She fanned herself with the county map they had purchased at a convenience grocery. Deborah sighed, as if wistfully remembering a future lost. "It's too hot to be house hunting. I wish we could have stayed in Longview."

The statement hung in the air unchallenged. It was never meant to be bait for a fight anyway. They both understood exactly why Dirk

1

could not stay in Longview any longer. Neither of them would ever directly mention Dirk's loss of privileges at the hospital, or the unfortunate death of the young woman that broke the camel's proverbial back. It was the same thing that happened in Tyler and in Dallas before that and in Atlanta before that—all the way back to his residency in Boston.

Dirk had accumulated a phenomenal record in Harvard Medical School and had shown great promise as a surgeon. So much promise that one hospital after another coveted the brilliance he showed for short periods of time. He possessed a mind like a steel trap, but with a fatal flaw that was only discovered through day-to-day contact with him. That flaw was an attention span like a laser with a ten-minute life. He was brilliant when he was interested, but his interest level deteriorated as he gradually encountered the situations a surgeon normally encountered. Once he experienced a difficult medical problem during a surgery, that situation no longer challenged his ego.

That might not have been so bad, except that Dirk had no head or temperament for the mundane details and observations necessary to treat patients in the days before and after surgery, and that is where tragedy always struck. It usually involved a condition going bad, easily recognized, but just as easily overlooked by a surgeon too uninterested to notice.

"Dirk, is that a store up ahead? Stop and see if they have any Avion. I'm dying from this heat."

The big S-class sedan glided gracefully into one of the three parking spaces in front of the small brick building that comprised a significant part of the entire downtown district of Tejas Hill. Dirk had started to undo his seatbelt when to his utter surprise, Deborah stated, "No, I'll go. If we're going to live in this one-horse town, I want to see what the crackers are like." In keeping with her total disregard for the needs of others, she did not ask if he wanted anything, and he didn't notice.

Inside the store, Connie was pondering the menu for the lunch special. She couldn't decide whether to have pintos again or fried squash with the corn on the cob and the salmon croquettes. Out of the corner of her eye, she spotted the big four-door Mercedes, not a sight one usually saw amid the GMCs and the Dodge diesel crew cabs with multiple toolboxes on the back.

Idle interest turned to downright gawking as the car door opened and the long slender leg in the yellow high heel appeared below the bottom of the door. The creature that lifted out of the car was too perfect, too tall, too shapely, too everything to be coming into the Tejas Hill General Store. Unconsciously, Connie wondered if the WD40 that Earl had just sprayed on the screen door latch would be dry.

I'd hate to have to lie to that woman if WD40 ended up on that outfit, and I'm damn sure not going to buy her another, Connie thought as she raced to open the door first.

"Come on in, I was just going to get the mail" came out of Connie's mouth as the door flew open, startling Deborah as she tried to determine how to make a graceful entrance through the screen door with an RC Cola emblem in the middle of the front and "Come back to see us" on the back. Connie held the door open for the startled Deborah until she was safely past the door handle. Seeing the telltale drips of oil on the wood floor, Connie made a mental note to tear Earl's ass up when she got the chance. If she had told Earl once, she had told him a thousand times that WD40 was not the cure for everything, and it did not work better if you sprayed enough on to drip.

Deborah was already performing her ten-second survey of the store. She was an expert at instant surveys, and could spot a real boutique from a "want to be" within five feet of the door. This wasn't the same, but old habits were hard to break. Her eyes gazed out from under the perfectly matched and frosted bangs that had been trying to wilt in the heat all morning and performed a 180 on the store. Opinions came instantly and without self-inspection. Clean and organized, with all the merchandise neatly on the shelves. Out front was the prime money-maker—the chip and cracker display—with the candy on the left side, and the small array of Vienna sausage, potted meat, Beanie Weenies, and little cans of Spam on the right side.

To the right was some kind of tank with a slightly fishy smell and a pump blowing bubbles in the water. Deborah sensed the cool breeze emanating from the concrete tank and moved away from the bright sun in the door nearer to the source of the breeze. It reminded her of an old-time water fan, an analogy she would never acknowledge since doing so would reveal she knew what a water fan was. People like Deborah should never know what a water fan was and would certainly never know that the cool draft coming from the minnow tank felt and smelled a lot like putting your head close to a water fan.

Behind that was the ice and soft drink counter with an assortment of cups and caps and straws. In the back were the two obligatory bathroom doors with "Women" on one and "Everything Else" on the other. To the right were shelves with small containers of sandwich spread, A-1 Steak Sauce, bread, motor oil, personal items, and a large display with individual packages of every pain reliever known to man, priced at about ten times the price per pill in a thirty-pill bottle. The short-order counter with cash register was in front of the kitchen, and a small hall to the dining room rounded out the vista.

"You all right today?" Connie asked as she came back in and walked by Deborah, heading for the counter. A faint smile escaped the corner of Deborah's mouth, acknowledging the question with as little involvement as possible. An insecure person might have felt miffed by the response, but Connie was not an insecure person. What Connie appeared to be was the exact opposite of Deborah. They both had short hair, but Connie's was spiked and red this week. Not red like real people's hair, but red like the teenagers used to outrage their parents. Her jeans had seen better days, and so had the Indian Paint Festival T-shirt that she was wearing. Without missing a step, Connie maneuvered the sharp turn around the counter and was facing Deborah with a smile when she reached the counter.

"What can I get you?"

"I don't suppose you would have any Avion, would you?" asked Deborah with a defeated tone intended to both telegraph her assumption that they did not and her disappointment all in one. That tone could wither the most seasoned and jaded clerk at Neimans or Dillards and bring a manager running from thirty feet away. If Deborah was waiting for the usual apologetic response, she was going to be disappointed.

"Hell, no. We used to stock it, but the grocery supply charged an arm and a leg for that stuff. After that, we stocked a generic brand from Sam's warehouse for a while. Between you and me, I couldn't tell the difference anyway, but I couldn't give that stuff away."

Connie leaned over the counter close enough Deborah could smell the salmon croquette batter on her hands as she wiped them on her apron. "Between you and me, I think some people care more about the label than they do the water," Connie opined with a conspiratorial nod, looking around as if there were someone else in the store and she was telling some personal, embarrassing family secret. "You know the kind I mean?" said Connie. "Too much money and not enough sense."

This confidential disclosure must have shaken Deborah more than she realized, and her face must have shown it, too. Just as quick, Connie leaned back and laughed easily, "Oh, I'm not talking about you, honey. I can tell you probably would know the difference. I was talking about the local folks trying to act as if they're from out of town. Anyway, the water is so good here we finally gave it up and started giving away cups of ice with Tejas Hill city well water. Here, you look hot; let me get you some."

Before Deborah could get out the "no," as in "No, I only drink bottled water," Connie had bounded around the counter again and was busily pouring water into a foam cup with ice. She looked out at the car and made another one, handing both to the startled Deborah. "Take one to your husband. He looks mighty hot out in that big old car." Connie's expression turned wistful as she stared at the handsome man in the shiny car. "If I had a husband that good-looking, I'd sure want to keep him happy," she said, glaring at Earl as he passed by outside. "By the way," Connie stuck her hand out. "My name's Connie."

Startled, Deborah could only take it and utter, "Deborah—my name is Deborah."

About that time, Earl rounded the corner on his way back, walking at a pace measured to cover as little space in as much time as possible, a habit cultivated over years of working menial jobs for governmental agencies that were just proud to have a body to do whatever job Earl seemed happy to do and no one else would. "I sure could use some water," Earl stated in a loud voice to the room in general and Connie in particular.

The response was instant. "If you're thirsty, you might try some of that WD40 you've been splashing all over the place."

Earl never broke stride as he drifted by and headed out the screen door. In his hand was a pipe wrench covered with dripping oil and grease.

Before Connie could divulge any more personal information, Deborah turned around and headed for the door, wondering how she was going to open the door without touching the handle after Earl. She made it halfway when Connie's voice stopped her cold.

"It's none of my business, honey, but if I gave as much for that out-fit as I bet you did, I'd want someone to tell me the sweater was a knock-off."

The statement hung in the air like a challenge for a long second. Deborah was used to dishing it out, and she damn well wasn't going to be bested by a forty-year-old café owner in worn-out Wal-Mart jeans.

In one fluid motion, Deborah turned and faced Connie, looking her dead in the eye. "And just what is that supposed to mean?"

"Look," said Connie. "That's a Chanel outfit, right?"

"Yes, and?" Deborah responded.

"And you didn't buy it at an authorized Chanel dealer, did you?"

Long pause, then, "No."

"And that is the new lemon chiffon color they introduced last year, isn't it?"

"Yes, but what has that got to do with it?" asked Deborah, wonder-ing how this person would know that.

"Well," started Connie, "you wouldn't know if you weren't in the business, but that sweater is from a knock-off collection by Nauvoo Textiles out of New Jersey. The color's a little off if you look at it in direct sunlight, and the V-neck is too shallow. The symmetry is all off. That's where the cut-rate places make their money—selling you the knock-off sweater for the designer price."

"And just how would somcone in a place like this know that, even if it were true?" asked Deborah without ever blinking or taking her eyes off Connie.

"Well, that's one of their latest colors, and I worked on the design of that sweater when I lived in New York. It's been around awhile in several different forms since then." Connie waved her hand toward Deborah, as if to brush off the entire matter. "But don't worry; no one outside the busi-ness would know. And anyway," said Connie, dropping her voice and leaning forward so that Deborah leaned in before realizing it. "I won't tell anyone." She finished the sentence with an impish grin that brought a smile to Deborah's face in spite of her best efforts to look aloof.

Confounded, Deborah managed to say, "Thanks," as she turned around and headed for the door in disbelief. *I've been had*, she thought, too stunned to notice Dirk opening the door for her as she got in.

"What's that?" he asked as he got back in the driver's side. The question broke through her stunned disbelief. "City well water, I think," said Deborah as she handed the cup to Dirk, drinking from her own cup to find something to do rather than explain to Dirk what had just happened.

Dreading the first taste, she was surprised to find the water was smooth, refreshing, and had an odd tingle as it went down her throat. It had an indefinable flavor, almost like lemon or lime in ice tea, but not any fruit she could identify. Before she knew it, the cup was empty, and she felt better.

"I don't believe it; you just drank water that didn't have Perrier or Avion on the label. That must be some water." He took a sip and stopped, looking straight at Deborah. "You know, I could swear I smell salmon patties with onion. I haven't smelled salmon patties with onion since Grand died."

Deborah quietly wiped her hand on her monogrammed handkerchief, saying nothing as Dirk backed out and glided toward the tallest part of the bluff. She couldn't help glancing at the sweater and skirt as the bright sun dappled through the trees, and now she could see the slight difference. They didn't match.

Chapter Two

"Same Song, Nineteenth Verse"

The auditorium in the old college was shaded and unusually cool for July in Tejas Hill. The four-story limestone facade with the bell tower and a silver dome lying on the ground on one side seemed almost surreal in the small community. It was the type of building that could weather decades of abuse and neglect with little effect, constructed with a care and quality unheard of today.

Even though the college had turned into a seminary, and the seminary had closed decades ago, it was still known as the college to everyone—a source of pride and history in a community that had no claim to fame other than having the highest elevation within a hundred miles in any direction.

In the center of the huge room sat an odd assortment of people, mostly upper-middle age to downright ancient, huddled in folding chairs set in a circle almost like a wagon train circled against the Indians. Although the voices were often raised in anger and insult during these meetings, the members of the Bell Tower Erection Club seemed to understand that they were nearing the last stand. They did not always like each other, but this was all they had left in the way of doing something productive. Their kids were mostly in their 50s and 60s. The grandkids barely knew them unless they lived close enough to see them on a daily basis.

Their goal was always the same. Raise money and restore the college, as if doing so would make them young again, back to the ball players and thespians in the faded college pictures on Connie's dining room walls. Full of muscles, hormones and promise. Before the operations, deaths, and illnesses that had gradually taken their spouses, happiness, and in small pieces, their freedom and health. Putting the tall silver dome back on so the college would reflect sunlight like a beacon again to anyone within thirty miles of the town seemed an almost sacred duty to them.

Truth be told, almost any of them could have written a check and done the job, but doing so would put them out of the last real business they were likely to have. They lived for the never-ending feuds over petty city affairs that pitted them against each other at one meeting and brought them together as allies at another, sometimes in the same day. The issue was nothing more than a way to keep the fire of life alive and worth living. Underneath the rancor, they truly loved and treasured each other in an odd way, relishing their idiosyncrasies.

The hidden observer in the rafters was quietly watching two particularly large men, different in appearance and demeanor, but alike in a determination that often controlled the meetings, sometimes circling each other like two old bulls in a small pasture. This day, Shade McCain had the floor. He was a tall man and almost half as wide as he was tall. His overalls carried a freckled round face with large lips, nose, and eyes and little neck, topped by a full head of coarse, sandy-blonde hair. A beauty he was not, and just now, he was mad.

"I don't see what all the fuss is about. I just thought Goliath ought to contribute to the Indian Paint Festival. After all, they sure don't mind shaking all our houses every time they blast. Am I right?" He paused to make his point. "And anyway, what can it hurt if they give us $1,000.00 for the Bell Tower Erection Fund?"

Shade delivered the statement as if the answer was obvious and he was as innocent as he wanted them to believe. In truth, he was as shrewd as they came. A Depression child, he knew what hunger meant, and he knew what a man would do to feed his family in hard times. He had done it all to feed himself and his mother. He'd boasted, buffaloed, and intimidated his way into one job after another. Shade learned early when a smile and a good line would work and knew how to finish a fight when it wouldn't.

With hard work and luck, he had taken a job turning wrenches in a mechanic shop in Houston and turned it into a major heavy-machinery sales and repair chain located in every industrial district in Texas. He knew full well that he was coarse, loud, and overbearing, and he used that knowledge to his benefit. He could bulldoze and bullshit his way over most people who dared to stand in his path. However, this game had been played in this room many times before, and these people were not most people.

Dan Dahoney, the other old bull in the room, knew the answer to the innocent question. His silver hair waved as he reared back in the chair, taking a large lungful of air to deliver the intelligent, articulate barrage that would shoot holes in Shade's argument like BBs through Swiss cheese. Everything about him was big and tall. His resume read like a who's who in publishing—from grammar school teacher, professor, author, editor, to finally editor-in-chief and owner of a well-respected publishing house in New York State.

Much like an aging Richard Burton, he could read the phonebook and make it sound like Shakespeare, and that was the problem. Whatever he said seemed overblown, too large, and complex for the small stage he had chosen for his retirement. His fierce eloquence about Tejas Hill was well known to everyone of note within fifty miles and caused many people to avoid him if the opportunity existed. Seemingly oblivious, he was actually aware of this effect. Behind the feigned surprise when someone mumbled some excuse or another to escape one of his street-corner lectures, he reveled in his knowledge and power.

"Shade, you know better than that, so don't try to insult our intelligence." Shocked, Dan looked around to see who had stolen his thunder and found Jainie Plumber, of the historic "Plumber's Mill" Plumbers. The indictment was delivered in the calmest, quietest voice imaginable. Jainie was somewhere north of sixty-five. She was an educator who had spent decades putting adolescent boys who acted much like Shade in their place. She had eyes of steel that told you in a heartbeat that this woman would not brook any crap from anyone.

"That limestone quarry has been a thorn in this town's side since they blasted the first shovelful of rock. They dried up artesian springs all over the bluff that had been flowing for the hundred and fifty years that my family has been there. They have scared citizens half to death with their blasting. If you let them start financing every club and civic project, they will buy their way inside the city limits. You ought to be ashamed, and you know it, you old pirate."

Delivered without a discernable change of expression other than one slightly raised eyebrow, the contempt Jainie's tone heaped on Shade damn near melted the people who sat next to him. Shade appeared unimpressed, having been her target at various meetings for many years. Yet he dared not argue or dispute her statement. Of all people, not her. Under his anger, he could not help thinking about the soft beauty that he alone had seen in her face. He could not help thinking that if he had not left, they might have married, and she might not

10

have turned into the flint rock of a woman she was now. But most of all, he could not help thinking that she was the one who refused him. She was the only thing he had ever wanted badly that he could not get.

Shade grinned his broadest cracker grin at her, making him look more like Mr. Magoo through his thick glasses. "Jainie, you could at least smile while you insult me." Shade delivered the statement with a leer.

While the words had no effect, the leer did. No one in the room knew about the romance so many decades ago, and she wasn't going to do anything to let that cat out of the bag. That had been their secret. Back then, Jainie hid the romance because Shade was considered coarse and unacceptable by her parents. Shade hid the romance because he dared not let his mother know he was wasting precious time and money on something as frivolous as romance when he could be working. Jainie was the pearl he would never be good enough to own, and he was the wild seed that she would never be allowed to marry. In all her life, he was the only lover she ever had, and it broke her heart when he told her he was leaving to find work in Houston. She would have gone with him in a heartbeat, chucked it all for him, braved the indignation and shame of family and friends, but he did not ask her to come. He just told her he was leaving.

When he came back, well on the way to being successful, she did the only thing her wounded heart would allow her to do—turn him down. She was so busy with her teaching, so full of her duties that she failed to notice that all her friends were young married women with children. She never thought about the fact that bachelors were few in Tejas Hill, and any man who was not already married by twenty-five either had some terrible personal problem, was unusually ugly, or was not interested in women.

By the time she did realize it, it was too late. Her reputation and grim demeanor scared potential suitors the same way they scared the eighth-grade boys she taught. They both knew they loved each other and had cheated themselves out of true happiness, but no one else did. For decades, they made sure they attended the same meetings, unconsciously stood as close as possible, even touched hands or brushed against each other during the brief encounters that social situations always seem to provide. Insults and arguments became the way they showed each other they still cared. Bitter enemies to the outside world, bitter lovers to each other.

In a move that shocked the watchers of these ongoing wars, Jainie dropped her eyes, sat down, and began looking for something in her small, neat pocketbook. Much like a cat that has bested another, Shade continued to stare at her for several long seconds, the visual equivalent of circling the vanquished foe to make sure he is not going to get up again. The discussion moved on around the table, but the outcome was already clear. Shade would protest, swell up and huff, then grudgingly return the donation to Goliath that he himself had sought.

Chapter Three

"What's an Interocetor, Anyway?"

Dennis Smith looked for all the world like one of those twenty-something geeks that always seem to have the latest electronics and no real life as he wandered the manicured green plateau that was Bluff City Park with what appeared to be a metal detector. At twenty-nine, he was too old to be a child prodigy. Having earned his doctorate, he had graduated to overeducated, unemployed genius status. But for the odd machine in his hands, he would probably have been just another guy designing computers for some corporation or running a small internet service.

And what an odd machine it was—part metal detector, density recorder, ground penetrating 3-D radar, Geiger counter, liquid and flow detector, gravity tester, along with more arcane measurements. A love of geology and a fixation on means of measurements had led him through eight years of Texas A & M University in engineering.

Goliath regional vice-president, Sandy Northcutt, had happened on him during a PR lecture at A&M University. During the question and answer section, one student asked a question that intrigued Sandy.

"Mr. Northcutt, has Goliath ever been able to develop a machine that would measure the sub-strata in every possible way without drilling, blasting, or large machinery?"

Sandy laughed, "No, we haven't, but we sure would be interested in someone who could. That person would have a great future at Goliath, Mr. Ah-h-h?"

"Dennis. Dennis Smith," said the young man with the mismatched outfit.

"Well, Mr. Smith, maybe we can discuss the idea later."

Corporations like Goliath needed a certain number of innovative people on the cutting edge, just in case. At the reception following the lecture, he sought out Dennis.

"Dennis, I see by your name tag you're with the engineering department?"

"Yes, sir. I've been working to combine geology and technology on a new level. So far, no one is much interested." Dennis seemed almost apologetic, used to rejection.

"Well, I don't know how much I'm interested in that, but I was interested in the question you asked," Sandy said. "Obviously, no one could fill that order at the present, could they?" Sandy asked, taking a sip from a glass of mediocre Texas wine.

"Actually, I have." The statement from Dennis was as bold as it was short. Sandy slowly lowered his glass and looked at his face to see if it was a joke. Surely, he was just another graduate student who had reinvented the same old wheel in another form.

"That's a bold statement, Dennis. What exactly can your machine measure?"

Dennis took a deep breath. He no longer appeared gawky and unsure. He was warming up to a subject that was near and dear to his heart. "Well, it can measure density, composition, depth, strata formations, radiation, magnetic draw, gravity, and seismic activity in 3-D. It took me eight years to develop it."

"What's this machine called?" asked Sandy, stalling to observe this odd young man.

"I call it the Interocetor," he said, "after a machine in an old science fiction movie my dad used to like called *This Island Earth*. You probably wouldn't remember it. It had giant insects that looked like wasps and a fantastic flying saucer that crashes into the ocean at the end of the movie."

"Actually, I do know that movie; it had a big guy with a forehead like Frankenstein." Sandy wasn't going to get excited yet. String the little geek along slowly; don't show any real enthusiasm. "That sounds interesting, but how could one machine do all of that, and how big would it be?"

Almost as if he had read his mind, Dennis said, "With all due respect, sir, I may be a geek, but how the machine does it is my domain, and the machine itself is no larger than a metal detector."

"I wouldn't want to insult you, Dennis, but what you're describing sounds a little like those infomercials I see on TV on Sunday morning that claim to do everything in one small package."

"Well, that's been the reaction I've gotten so far," replied Dennis, "but I keep hoping that I'll find a company smart enough to give me a chance. Do you think Goliath might be that smart?" The question was direct, and this time, it was Dennis looking into Sandy's eyes, watching for reaction. Sandy didn't flinch or blink. In his mind, he was thinking, "This guy is a lot more than he appears—a player with a mathematician's mind."

"We just might be, Dennis, we just might be." Sandy reached for his wallet and pulled out his card. "Tell you what—why don't you come round to my office in Memphis next Monday? Give me your address and phone, and I'll have my office arrange for the airline tickets and transportation. You don't need to worry about any expense, and you don't need to bring anything, except for that machine." He saw Dennis begin to stiffen. "And don't worry, we'll sign an agreement not to pirate any technical information or copy your machine. I want you to feel free to show off your prize."

The necessary information having been swapped, Dennis and Sandy bid farewell, leaving Sandy to ponder a potential test for this young oxymoron. He had never seen that much timing and raw instinct coupled with that much sheer intellect, if the machine was all Dennis claimed it was, and somehow, he bet it was. As his mind went over various sites and questions related to the many properties Goliath operated in the United States and abroad, he suddenly thought about that little town in Texas. What was the name of that place? The district manager had been talking forever about mining inside the city on a big bluff. Sandy remembered their geologist raving about how the place was odd, the water was odd, and measurements never seemed to be right around the bluff.

Further investigation never seemed reasonable with the expense of multiple disciplines, especially just to indulge a geologist's hunch about a normal limestone bluff with a small town on top. Later, Sandy e-mailed a memo to his office while somewhere over Arkansas in the company jet to gather all the information and testing on Tejas Hill and have it in his office before Monday morning. He also left word to have the district manager in his office Friday. What was that guy's name? Winston something—Winston Raymond. Yeah, that's him.

That was six months ago. Back on Tejas Hill, Dennis had a hard time believing what the Interocetor was telling him. He had never seen anything like the readings he was getting. The density was right where it ought to be for a big limestone hill, except where the spring ran out of the rocks at the tip of the bluff, just above a strange indention with smooth edges.

The indention was about twenty feet around, right under the edge, and seemed to glisten with the western sun going down. It was almost as if diamonds had been impaled in that circle. The strange part was that when you crawled over the edge and climbed down, expecting to see crystals as big as marbles, you didn't. The only thing you could see were grains, as small as coarse sand, black, impenetrable up close, but brilliant at a distance, with a fire as if lit from within.

Above the spring, the Interocetor went crazy. First, the density jumped off the scale, far past iron, far past iridium, far past any heavy metal he knew. And that was just the beginning. Temperature changed, fluctuating by as much as six degrees, seeming to pulse with the water coming out of the rock. *Impossible*, thought Dennis. And gravity. Gravity had been an afterthought, a constant that never changed significantly. But here, over the hole, it was twenty-five percent less than normal.

Just for fun, he switched to radiation, and that is when Dennis Smith first felt fear. The needle went off the scale. More radiation than Chernobyl at twenty feet. Enough to kill a person in minutes. Enough to leave the whole hill dead, with people burned with mutations and horrible birth defects for miles around. Without thinking, he started running, tripping over a bicycle lying in the path.

"Momma, that man ran over my bicycle," six-year-old Johnny Brown observed calmly.

"I saw it, honey. Don't worry; he didn't hurt it." Betsy Brown, Johnny's momma, weighed in, without missing a bite of the Twinkie she was sucking down. It wasn't that she didn't care; it was just that it was hard to get her large mass moving, and the bike was okay.

"Why did he look so scared?" asked Johnny, used to his mother's inaction.

She watched Dennis run the rest of the way down the path to his car, throw the strange machine in the backseat, and gun the engine, peeling out down the road. Putting down the Twinkie, she began to think. Johnny's question was a fair one, and she always tried to answer fair questions. Not always the stupid ones, but always the fair ones.

She looked around the hill slowly, taking in the setting sun, the green grass, and the wildflowers. No snakes, no mad dogs, no hoodlums, nothing out of place she could see. Satisfied, she picked the half-eaten Twinkie back up and carefully wiped off a blade of grass stuck in the filling. Johnny sat there, patiently watching her and waiting for her answer. She was his window to understanding the world, and they both took each other seriously. Satisfied the Twinkie was fine, she took her next bite and made eye contact with Johnny. "I don't know, honey; there doesn't seem to be anything to be scared of. Maybe he just wants to get the Tuesday special hamburger at Connie's store before she closes."

Johnny pondered the answer, probing her face to see if it was a real answer, or just something to say to get him to move on to something else. Under his pudgy body, sandy hair, and fat neck, Johnny was a strangely perceptive six-year-old. He saw words in his mind in colors and tasted some like food. Although Johnny did not yet know if other children did this, he instinctively knew not to discuss it, fearing that if he did so, his mother might stop saying the words that tasted the best or looked the most beautiful in his mind.

Johnny also had another ability that seemed perfectly normal to him. He could tell good and bad people by their colors. Good people were colorful greens, blues, and yellows. Bad people were red to gray to black. Old people were the same, only in paler shades. Babies were usually white, and other kids ran the spectrum, changing with each mood. To Johnny, it seemed that the older you were, the more the color seemed to stay the shade that matched the person.

Satisfied with her answer, Johnny nodded solemnly and ran to the natural spring pool, scattering the turtles sunning on the large rock in the middle, happy with the minor mayhem he wreaked on the local reptile population and enjoying the prism explosion of light that the ripples on the water created in the eye inside his mind, the one he saw with beyond his two eyes.

As they left the park, they passed Brother Billy Burkhart. "Evening, Betsy." Brother Billy smiled with a slightly deprecating drop of the head as they passed. Johnny veered around his crimson aura, pulling his mother in a wide sweep around the reverend.

"Evening, Brother Billy," replied Betsy, trying to move her considerable bulk a little quicker to get by him. Betsy couldn't see colors, but she sure as hell could feel his eyes probing her butt once she got by him. *Pervert*, she thought to herself.

Fat. Fat and lonesome, thought Billy, remembering that Betsy was single. Women to him were much like sheep. Too bad times had changed with all this freedom. *Back to the Old Testament, back to where women understood their place and needed a strong hand to tell them what to do*, thought Billy.

Down the bluff, Dennis slid his new Saab into one of Connie's three parking spaces with his hands trembling and his skin sweaty.

"Think," he told himself. "That can't be right. If it was, the whole town would have been cooked in minutes." He felt better, logic over panic, brains over impulse, a regular scientific Sherlock Holmes. *Hell, I'm starting to believe all the crap the locals keep saying about this hill*, he thought, laughing quietly to himself.

Oh, well, long as I'm here, I might as well eat, he thought, smelling the exhaust from Connie's grill fan, rich with grilled ground beef and onions.

"You still cooking?" he asked, talking before the screen door closed behind him.

"The door is still open, isn't it?" asked Connie.

"Yeah," came the reply.

"Then I'm cooking. You want your usual cheeseburger with Texas toothpicks?" asked Connie.

"Sure" he said, emptying some of the ice out of the large Styrofoam cup he had just filled and switching between the Coke and Dr. Pepper buttons as he filled the cup, adding a shot of cherry flavor at the bottom and top.

"You finding anything strange with that little machine of yours?" Connie eyed him intently as she moved about the kitchen.

"No, not really," lied Dennis nonchalantly as he poured over the chip rack looking for the Tom's Vinegar and Dill potato chips.

"Well, I know you're lying," said Connie, slapping the meat on the grill. "But I guess you'll tell me someday, along with what that machine of yours really is."

"What do you mean?" The question drifted up—full of the surprise that Dennis tried to hide.

"Look," Connie said, as she set down his silverware and napkin, "I may not be a genius, but I never saw anyone caress a Wal-Mart metal detector like you caress that machine of yours. I've watched you in the park. You play that thing like B.B. King plays 'Lucille.' You love that machine, and I know that. I just want to know why. So you can tell me when you get ready. In the meantime, your secret is my secret." Connie winked as she brought over the ketchup and set it on the table.

Dennis relaxed. He knew he could trust Connie. Hell, Helen Keller could have told you that you could trust Connie.

Chapter Four

"Maybe You'll Get Gas, Maybe Not"

K innerd Irvin confidently drove his fire engine red Ford tool truck down the middle of Bowie Street toward the fancy neighborhood at the top of the bluff. His gray coveralls did not carry any emblem or company name. In fact, strangers often wondered who the odd-looking man in the red truck was and what he was doing. As he neared the turn to the cemetery, he saw Jainie Plumber's white Oldsmobile 98 making the turn.

Hot damn, he thought. *I'll have some fun now.*

As the Olds neared, Kinnerd looked into the windshield until he saw her eyes on him, and then shot her the finger. Jainie, used to the insult, never flinched, glaring at him steadily as she drove by with the same look she reserved for a nasty eighth-grader. Come to think of it, he had been one of her nasty eighth-graders thirty years ago.

Most of the time, Jainie did not think about her life in terms of what might have been. She was respected in her community, almost revered by the many students she had led to see life beyond the bluff. Few things could upset her, but Kinnerd was one of those few things. When he shot her the finger, his eyes full of insult and carnal lust, it cut to her soul in a way nothing else could, and it filled her with a rage that only a spurned woman could understand.

It seemed to her that he knew her innermost thoughts and was laughing at her. As Kinnerd passed, she made sure not to look away. *Someone ought to kill that sorry son of a bitch*, she thought to herself, in terms that were really worse than that and that she would never utter aloud. *We'd all be better off if he was just dead.* Jainie let herself think about that prospect for a minute. The thought filled her with such calm satisfaction that he was completely out of her mind in five minutes.

Jainie was not Kinnerd's only target. He prided himself on insulting everyone he perceived as being better than him, which included most of the Bell Tower Erection Club. Kinnerd couldn't figure out how a town like Tejas Hill could have so many smart-ass, artsy-fartsy people—musicians, writers, doctors, lecturers, professors—all in less than 400 people. Hell, he couldn't even stand to drink the water in town. Whenever possible, Kinnerd had avoided the city well water all his life. Although he would never admit it, when he drank the water for very long, he found himself starting to have strange thoughts, doubting he was normal, thinking his actions were strange, and beginning to question his motives.

Bullshit on that; smart people have it coming, and I'm not gonna go soft and introspective like them, he thought, suddenly wondering what the word introspective meant and why he would even think about using a word like that.

Kinnerd knew he could get away with his little pranks for two reasons. First, his father was a prominent gas producer who sold natural gas to the city at an extremely low price in return for an exclusive franchise. Highly inflated service fees made up the profit and were designed to provide Kinnerd with a steady income. Second, the exclusive contract made sure Kinnerd was the only natural gas man in the city, and no one wanted their gas turned off.

Kinnerd had suffered a head injury in a teenage car wreck. Although the doctors weren't quite sure how bad his head injury was, they suspected his brain had almost been cut in half. The oddest result of his injuries was that he could move his eyes independently and focus them separately, like a chameleon. When Kinnerd finally got out of the hospital and rehab a year later, he was emaciated, mentally disturbed, and couldn't help the odd and inappropriate things he did. He suffered something sort of like post-traumatic stress disorder coupled with Tourette's syndrome. So what if he occasionally made pornographic gestures, or ended up in someone's house? People forgave him. Hell, he was disabled and couldn't help it.

What people did not know was that Kinnerd gradually learned how to control his behavior, but by then he had figured out that he didn't have to. He could just keep getting away with it. He enjoyed being able to harass the local intelligentsia with immunity and rarely missed an opportunity to do so. Along the way, many of the people in the city figured it out, too. Any sympathy the local townspeople had for him had run out years ago.

Physically, Kinnerd never regained his former stature. At forty-two, he was still gaunt and emaciated, with skin burned and wrinkled from years in the sun digging up gas leaks. Looking for all the world like one of the Ents in *Lord of the Rings* with thick coke-bottle glasses, he appeared years older. The thick glasses made his eyes look twice as big as they were, giving him a menacing look that he exploited by moving his eyes independently whenever he wanted to scare or intimidate someone. Snooping, stalking, and harassment became his chief entertainment.

His hatchet face, burned skin, magnified eyes, and unpredictable behavior kept everyone in the city inclined to overlook his eccentric behavior. After all, it wasn't anything school kids didn't do to each other every day and what would happen to the city if his daddy cut off the cheap gas? Lately, he had become so sure of his immunity that he had taken to new tricks, like showing up unannounced at people's houses, claiming he had a report of a gas leak or some similar excuse to get inside and snoop. No one got gas unless he turned it on, and everyone paid what he asked. Kinnerd's superiority and contempt for his fellow townspeople grew with his brazenness.

One thing Kinnerd liked was to have his ego stroked, and one thing Goliath liked was a dumb-ass insider they could manipulate. Kind of like the organ grinder—give him a good monkey, and the show was on. It all had happened by accident when Kinnerd tried to shake down Sandy Northcutt for the gas meter to the crusher. Kinnerd had humhawed around about the difficulties of putting in a meter sufficient to deal with Goliath's needs and how it might take an engineering study and a couple of months to handle the request. Next, he hinted that he might could shortcut the process if he wanted…long pause…slight wink at Sandy. "I'm sure you know what I mean. After all, two men looking eye to eye can get around any obstacle if they try."

Sandy had to work to keep a straight face. Hell, this village idiot didn't even have the sense to hide the meter sitting in the back of the truck waiting to be dropped in the hole that was already dug. He had a pretty good idea what was coming when the foreman told him some guy from the gas company was at the gate mumbling that there was some kind of problem and that it might be big trouble for Goliath. Sandy's aggravation turned to interest when he saw Kinnerd at the gate. It was common knowledge that Kinnerd knew everything going on in the city, and that he attended every council meeting, offering his view as if he was on the council and lecturing the council members about what they had better do.

Sandy knew Kinnerd was largely ignored. That was good, because Sandy wanted him largely ignored, as long as he kept listening to what went on out front, and more importantly, through the paper-thin city hall walls in the closed meetings, where everyone but Kinnerd got tired and went home.

Sandy remembered the little song and dance that followed when he reached the gate. "I think you might be right, Mr. Irvin. You seem like a bright guy, and I'm sure glad to meet someone from this city with a little sense. Let's go up to my office. It's too damn hot to talk out here. Let me fix you a drink and see if we can't get this wheel a little grease." Long pause…slight wink at Kinnerd. "I bet you know what I mean." Knowing, conspiratorial look.

Hot damn, thought Kinnerd. *This is easier than I thought it would be. I can make some real money off this city slicker.* Kinnerd chuckled to himself. *He's falling right into my little trap.*

Hot damn, this is even easier than I thought it would be; this cracker is falling right into the trap, thought Sandy as they climbed into his Escalade, settled into the plush leather upholstery, and closed the darkly tinted windows.

One hour, two glasses of Crown Royal, and $500.00 later, Sandy had an ally for life, one with an ear right into those damn closed meetings. Rumor had it Kinnerd could even get access to the tape recordings of the closed meetings. Sandy didn't want to know how he could do that. It would just be the icing on the cake if he could.

Sandy had been trying to get around the ordinance that kept Goliath's mine out of the city ever since that third-rate lawyer down on Austin Street had drafted that confounded ordinance outlawing mining inside the city. Up to now, that ordinance had withstood over two hundred and fifty thousand dollars worth of lawsuit and been upheld one court short of the United States Supreme Court. It had not gone unnoticed at corporate headquarters that Goliath was getting its butt whipped by a legal team financed with stew and cornbread suppers. Goliath's first two law firms had already been fired, and Sandy knew this was one battle he better win, or he could spend the next ten years at home with Madge, enduring her never ending remodel of the mansion and trying to find novel ways to spend the interest on his mega 401K complete with floating stock options. The thought of that was enough to make him try anything, and Kinnerd was as near to "anything" as he had right now.

Chapter Five

"Lights, Camera, Action"

The Ford crew cab bounced along the dirt road to the edge of the old quarry just inside the city limits. Larry Clakey slid the truck to a stop so fast the dust flying behind him swelled into the cab. He reached across the greasy front seat, and brushed a pile of coke cans, cracker wrappers, and sardine cans to the floor and grabbed the clipboard. His swamper, Leon, burped, took a deep breath, and asked, "Now, just what the hell is it those idiots up at the cwusher want us to do?"

Leon talked with a slight lisp. He was prone to make his L's and R's sound like W's.

They looked a lot like the two guys in *Of Men and Mice*. Larry average size, but with a quiet forcefulness and personality that could move bigger men. Leon was huge, the victim of an overactive adrenalin gland that left him 6' 8" at age fourteen. He looked scary as hell, and knew enough to act mad when he had to, but he was harmless. In his mind, almost everyone else was bigger and smarter. If it hadn't been for Larry hiring him, he probably would still be sweeping at Wal-Mart. *That Warry's a smart man*, thought Leon for about the fourteenth time that day.

"You watch your mouth and don't be calling them idiots," scolded Larry. He didn't care if Leon called them idiots, except he might forget and do it to their face. Satisfied he had gotten Leon's attention by the hurt pout on his face, Larry moved on to answering the question as if it had just been asked. "I never heard anything like it. They want us to set off an explosion inside the city limits and videotape it." Larry pulled out the video camera box as if it contained cobras. He fingered the controls, not knowing he had activated the microphone. "They told me to set it up a safe distance away and make sure the blast is a small one." Larry moved ahead of Leon as they headed down the path away from the blast site.

"I hate to pull this kind of bullshit on the town. I just told Connie the other day we wasn't gonna do anything inside the city. I'm gonna feel like shit when I have to go in there and face her after this," frowned Leon, looking worried as he began to run the wire up to the top of the hill they were going to hide behind.

"Yeah, but before you get to feeling too bad, just think about how you'd feel if you had to go home and tell Doris you got fired because you didn't want Connie to feel bad about you." Larry set up the tripod and watched Leon's pea brain take all that in. A small hint of a smile played around his mouth as he watched Leon ponder the risks both ways.

Satisfied that he had the question analyzed correctly, Leon looked up at him and said, "Yeah, you're wight."

Leon had been diagnosed as borderline mentally retarded in childhood. Larry teased Leon in a round-about subtle manner, but no one else in the crew better try it. Leon was his man, and he knew he could trust Leon with his life, money, or kids. Leon would die trying to do whatever he told him to do.

"You ever use one of them video cameras before?" asked Larry as they walked up along the path to set up the camera.

"Naw, I've been sort of leewy of them ever since that fitness twainer and her husband made that sex video with the vegetables and took it back to the video store instead of *Rocky III*."

Larry couldn't help laughing as he remembered his wife telling how everyone at Video Store copied the film and then called the woman. "We think you may have mistakenly left a personal tape here at the video store." Dead silence for about a minute, then, "I'll be right down."

Larry punched Leon on the arm. "Hey, Leon, that's about as funny as when that society wife caught her husband on the eighth hole out at Big Oaks Country Club with that waitress with the big ta-tas after the bar closed."

Leon was already nodding his head. "Yeah, I wemember, she waited 'til he went to sleep and glued his hand to his tallywhacker with Super Glue." They both had to stop working long enough to stop laughing. Leon was warming up to the story now. "I heard the ambulance had to twansport him naked with a blanket wapped awound him. Man, don't you know that was embawwassing?"

Larry grinned back at Leon. "I would have had to just flat-out leave town." Larry's face got semi-serious for a second before busting out laughing again. "I could not believe it when the hardware store put that lighted sign out in front the next week, advertizing Super Glue for half price. The sign actually said, 'Super Glue, just right for those 'special occasions.' I swear, they actually had quotes around the words 'special occasions.' Larry and Leon continued to chuckle to themselves as they made their way down the path.

"Where you gonna set that thing up?" Leon asked after they had walked a little further in silence.

Larry stopped, surveying the hill for a minute, and then started walking again. "Aw, I don't know. I figure pretty close to the blast. When I was welding in Alaska, I took pictures of them mountains. Biggest damn things I ever saw—plum majestic. But when I got the pictures developed, they looked like anthills." Larry stopped about three hundred feet from the charge and looked back. "I figure right here. Just put all that crap down right there, and let's see if we can hook this thing up."

"Why is the charge so woow?" asked Leon.

"Well, they want a video that makes it look like a black cat firecracker, so they can show the townspeople how safe blasting is," said Larry.

Leon looked at Larry to see if he was joking. "You ain't joking, are you? They ain't really gonna twy to pawn off this pee-wee woad as a weal bwast are they?"

"They damn sure are, and you better keep your trap shut down at the store and around town, or I'll have your ass picking up trash at the yard every Saturday for a month." Larry thumped Leon on the back for emphasis. "You did remember to tell that blasting guy to set the charge at one-tenth the normal charge, didn't you?" Larry looked Leon in the eye so he could be sure.

"You bet, Warry; I told him a tenth this time."

Larry had been listening to Leon so many years, that he was used to the hairlip and Leon's tendency to talk fast when he was excited or carrying out an important order. Little wonder the blasting foreman heard, "Ten times this time."

Ten times normal is a lot of load. That must be some solid stone under there. He was concerned enough to ask again. "You did say ten, didn't you?"

The huge guy with the hairlip looked offended at the question. He then said something that sounded a lot like "Yeah, a ten times this time, just like I said before." Leon bowed up as if he was getting ready to be real pissed off. "You got some kind of heawing pwobwem?"

The Blaster guy backed up a little. "Naw, ten, just like you said before. Sorry I didn't hear it right before." He thought, "I don't know what all he said, but I heard 'ten times' again, so that's what they'll get."

Normally, the blasting company would have set off the charge, but the boss told Larry that he and Leon would set this one off. Larry still had a blaster license somewhere from years back. The blaster had set the charge in banks of five, timed to detonate in sequences to break up the formation and drop the rock wall like a curtain in an auditorium.

When timed and sized correctly, a wall of solid rock would simply disintegrate without flying into the air. If done wrong, you could end up with fly rock—chunks of rock big enough to kill a man or go through a roof, accompanied by a shock wave that could move furniture and crack brick walls. Unbeknownst to Larry, Leon, or anyone else, Tejas Hill was fixing to find out what flyrock was in a big way.

"Let's see—got it on the tripod, got it pointed at the blast site, got the volume up," Larry looked puzzled, knowing something was wrong. "Oh, yeah, take the lens cap off."

Leon stifled a laugh, "Yeah, that might be a good idea, Warry." Leon walked away, trying to hide the fun he was having catching Larry doing something wrong.

"Aw, screw you," said Larry, careful not to look at Leon so he wouldn't see the smile he was trying to hide. "What do you say we get into the truck, start the video, light that puppy up, and run like hell?" asked Larry with a wide grin.

"Sounds like a pwan to me, Warry. I got the bwast box right here." Leon was already getting into the truck.

They drove to the top of the hill and parked. Larry opened his Big Red, and Leon opened his Pepsi. Leon bit off the plastic end to some Captain's Wafers and handed the package to Larry for first dibs. They both took a swig, admiring the panoramic view off the hill, spanning a horizon that stretched for thirty visible miles in three directions on a clear day. The surrounding valleys were dappled with green fields punctuated by fence lines filled with trees in every shade of gold and green, softened by the distance like a Grant Wood painting, interrupted mostly by creeks and ponds lit sapphire blue by the sky, diamonds of light skipping on the surface.

Larry and Leon would never think about it or admit it, but that view changed from season to season, day to day, even minute to minute. It was too beautiful to describe. They only knew it was irresistible, the thing that kept them in a second-rate job—just the freedom to ride from place to place, sometimes not talking, but knowing how special it all was and knowing there was less of it and fewer days for them with every day that passed.

A thinking man might have been driven to try to record his feelings in a poem or a painting, but not Larry or Leon. All they knew was they liked to drive around with each other and look at the country. In reality, it didn't matter; they knew how lucky they were already.

"You ready, Leon?" Larry looked over at Leon with the blast box in his lap, his right hand on the lever, and a Captains Wafer halfway in his mouth.

"You bet, Warry. Wight it up!" Leon turned to the windshield with his drink in his hand as if he was at the drive-in as Larry slowly twisted the handle and watched in awe as all hell broke loose in slow motion.

Instead of collapsing curtains of rock falling gracefully, the curtains went straight up in a series, like the walls of a fort blowing up one wall at a time. A person looking through the video camera would have seen the walls shoot up, then an eerie silence. For long seconds, the camera was stricken with rhythmic, fine vibrations as the shot reverberated down through the layers of rock that were stacked like the layers of a buttermilk biscuit. Just as one thought the worst was over, a viewer would have seen what looked like a wall of gray dust coming down, and then realized the wall was advancing toward the camera like a tidal wave.

As the wall approached, the viewer would have seen that the wall was not dust, but rocks. As the sound of them hitting the ground became more audible, the viewer would have realized that the rocks were not rocks, but in fact small boulders, blinding the video in an instant as the wall rolled by, but leaving the audio to record the sound rushing away as quickly as it had come.

In the annals of Tejas Hill, everyone would remember where they were when the old quarry pit blew up.

Billy Carroll and his wife were composing chamber music for the Tejas Hill Chamber Society recital when the front window of their studio blew out.

Spud Pickens was taking an afternoon nap before training his cutting horses when the blast blew the couch into the air and him onto the floor.

Charles Latimer was putting the finishing touches on the front elevation of the plans for a neo-modern residential interpretation of Falling Water on the Big Bluff addition for that new Doctor Mendez when the blast blew the ink well and paints all over the drafting table.

Doris Jones and her brother Henry watched in disbelief from their goat pasture as a wall of rock rose hundreds of feet into the air, and then began to come down like hail, breaking trees and sliding a three-foot boulder gracefully across their yard, stopping feet from the front door. Doris was so upset, she swore off Lone Star Light for a week.

All in all, it was one hell of an afternoon. Leon and Larry were barely recovered and raised up in the pickup seat when the two-way radio blasted alive with the voice of Sandy Northcutt.

"Larry? Larry, if you can hear me, you and that damn halfwit of yours better get your ass back down here and tell me what happened. The phone is lighting up with people complaining, and I almost choked to death on a Texas toothpick when that blast went off. Do you hear me Larry? Larry?"

Leon looked at Larry with real fear in his eyes and said, "Warry, I swear, Warry, I told that guy a tenth this time." Larry paused, looking at Leon carefully to make sure he was telling the truth. He was.

"I know you did, Leon. I know you did."

Larry dusted a rock off Leon's shirt, put his gimme cap back on, and looked out at the horizon with a bored expression, as if nothing had happened. "I tell you, Leon, I was about tired of them son of a bitches, anyway, weren't you?"

Leon nodded yes, not quite sure what was coming next.

"What do you say we find us another job? Screw 'em if they can't take a joke, right?" Larry grinned and punched Leon's arm for emphasis.

Unable to believe his good luck, Leon could only say, "Yeah, Warry, I'm with you."

Larry and Leon pretty much saw the handwriting on the wall. There was no real reason to go back to the yard just to get an ass chewing and fired. Larry made sure their truck was waiting just inside the gate with the keys in it when Sandy got to the yard the next morning.

Luckily, Shade McCain was looking for a couple of ranch hands to work cattle and ferry around the endless pieces of high-dollar equipment he was so fond of tearing up. Larry and Leon could now be seen most days riding the outskirts of town with a big flatbed full of equipment or a cattle trailer full of registered cattle, a Big Red, a Pepsi, and some kind of snack or another.

Chapter Six

"Something Fishy's Going on Down There"

On the day of the blast, Dave Lumpkin was preparing for his afternoon broadcast at KWOW- TV in Athens. After twenty-five years of doing the weather in every major market in North Texas, he was not nervous. He had an instinct for bad weather coupled with a gambler's luck that had allowed him to scoop all those young "weather personalities" that lived and died by the computer models at the competitors' stations.

He did not know or particularly question where his gift came from. He had spent his first twelve years on the family farm in Tejas Hill drinking spring water that flowed from an artesian well on the property. Later, his family moved to Fort Worth where his dad got a factory job building jets at a defense plant. His parents were not a particularly happy couple, and his mother, deep in depression (unnamed then), often sent Dave out with his younger sister to play in the fields until mealtime.

Dave must have inherited his mother's pensive side to a degree, for the two kids often spent afternoons watching clouds form, fronts come in, and rainstorms build. He found shapes, people, and animals in the clouds and predicted rain and storms to amuse his sister. He learned Texas weather by observation, not by books. He was always interested in the weather and assumed he was just lucky at forecasting. Dave was fairly confident and sure of himself. In his mind, he did not have a gift. Rather, his advance knowledge of weather was as normal to him as walking.

The first time he knew he had the gift was when he was ten years old. Things were tough, and his father had borrowed his limit at the First State Bank to plant a grain crop. Even a ten-year-old knew they would be foreclosed on if they didn't make a crop and pay the bank.

The problem was rain; there had been none, and forecasting the weather back then had more to do with almanacs and clichés than science.

That particular Tuesday night, Dave was sitting at the supper table with his father, mother, and six-year-old sister. His parents had argued about money and farming the night before, and you could have cut the tension with a knife. Dave's mother was not a born farmer and put up with the life for her husband. But after four bad years, the dream was crashing to an end, with a job in the city in sight if this crop failed.

As he cut into a center slice of ham next to the pinto beans on his plate, Dave's father looked through the front screen door at the sunset red with clouds and said, as if seeking divine intervention, but in a wistful voice that expected nothing, "I swear, I'd give anything but you and the kids to know when its going to rain on the north field." The north field was four miles out of town. One hundred fertile acres neatly cultivated, rowed, and planted with expensive grain seed waiting for a rain. "I'd just give anything," he said as he put the ham in his mouth and drank from the ice tea glass.

First, Dave looked at his mother to see her reaction. There was none. She simply looked tired and defeated. Dave knew she would clean up the kitchen and go to bed after seeing he and his little sister were in their pajamas and in bed. Thinking about what his father had asked, Dave pictured the north field in his mind just as he had seen it two days before, and wondered when it was going to rain.

That is when the gift happened the first time. In his mind, he saw a large thunderhead approach from the southwest, an odd direction for storms that time of year. Somehow, Dave knew it was Thursday. He could even tell it was late afternoon, probably about the time his Dad came home for supper—about 5:00 p.m. His mind saw the storm come over, as if in fast forward, and the old rain gauge fill up to 1.75 inches.

Anxious to make his father and mother feel better, Dave felt he should share what he knew in his heart was going to happen. Before he could, his mother spoke. "George, I don't know why you don't just give up. You and me and the kids could have so much more if you went to the city and got a real job," his mother pleaded one more time, looking George hard in the eyes.

"Daddy, I know—" Dave was interrupted in mid-stream by his father voice.

32

"Evelyn, you know I can't quit with this crop in the field and a note at the bank."

"Daddy, I know when it's going to—"

Once again, Dave was interrupted, this time by his mother. "To hell with the bank, George. What about Dave and little Patty? What about me?" This time there were tears of frustration in her eyes that George could not face. He looked down at the table just long enough for Dave to get out, in a voice about three times louder than he had intended the first time he tried, "Daddy, I know when it's going to rain on the north field."

The statement stopped everyone cold. Even six-year-old Patty stared at her brother, unable to take in the loudness and certainty of his voice and the way he had interrupted their parents in the middle of a fight.

Evelyn broke the silence. "What did you say, Dave?"

Dave, now not so sure, looked down at the table, swallowed big, looked up at his mother, and spoke in a much lower tone. "I said I know when it's going to rain in the north field." Then, emboldened a little, he looked his mother in the eyes. "And I know how much it's going to rain, too." He nodded quickly to emphasize how sure he was then looked down at his plate, not sure what would happen next.

Maybe it was because the statement made his mother forget the hard question she had asked his father. Maybe his father was simply amused at Dave's bold and ridiculous assertion. Whatever the reason, they both stopped and looked at Dave as his father chuckled and said, "Well, okay, you little Harold Taft, when is it going to rain on north field and how much?" George looked at Evelyn with a hint of a grin. Maybe because she was tired of the same endless fight back and forth, she bought into the joke and said, "Yeah, Harold, when's it going to be?"

Even at ten years old, Dave already had enough pride to not like being the butt of the joke, and he did not like the way both his parents were laughing with each other at his expense, and calling him "Harold Taft" after the legendary Dallas weatherman. With a red face and courage he never knew he had, Dave stood up by the table and said, in as clear and measured a voice as a ten-year-old could handle, "It's going to rain on the north field on this Thursday afternoon at five o'clock, and it's going to rain 1.75 inches. And if you don't believe me, I'll—I'll—"

(Dave had trouble with exactly what came next.) "I'll never tell you when it's going to rain again."

With that dreadful threat, Dave ran to his room, with everyone, Patty included, laughing to tears in the kitchen. The event was forgotten until Thursday afternoon when it rained 1.75 inches exactly on the north field at 5:05 p.m. From that point on, Dave's answers to weather questions became a serious business at home, and later, at the general store and in response to neighbor's questions as word spread. Dave never wanted for a Coke and sack of peanuts at the general store after that.

Later, the CIA would call it "remote viewing." All Dave knew was if he could visualize a place, or see a place on the map, he could predict rain, snow, sleet, even tornadoes and storms within a seven-day window. He simply saw it in his mind in fast forward. Despite that inside advantage, he could not predict a four-year-drought that finally sent his family to Fort Worth and the farm to a renter. Dave went to TCU and studied meteorology.

When he predicted the great Lake Mexia tornado before the thunder head that spawned it was a blip on the big boys' radar in Dallas, he was set. He could smell a rainstorm from fifty miles away, mostly from the hair on the back of his neck when he walked outside the studio each evening to smoke a Salem. That Salem and a few minutes of quiet while visualizing the broadcast area each evening had more to do with his forecast than all the radar and computer models in the studio.

One thing that Dave was big on was equipment. He knew enough to know if anyone ever figured out how he really did his forecast, he was finished. That's why he always insisted on every new gadget that might help a weatherman, even though he rarely relied on them. So it was on that afternoon, he was looking at his new ultra-atmosphere scanner. It really was one hell of a piece of equipment, able to measure and record bursts of various energies and subtle changes in the upper atmosphere, including northern lights and other unusual electrical discharges.

Bored, Dave was reading the instructions and fiddling with the dials, wondering what kind of scientific bullshit he was going to have to sell to the station manager to convince him this had been a good purchase. The screen was tuned to the southwest. It looked similar to one of those night scopes he had seen in those action movies. The horizon coalesced in a never-ending array of Day-Glo colors as electrons fired in the upper atmosphere. Sunspots, northern lights, lightning, thunder-storms, or other atmospheric abnormalities could affect it, but short of an atom bomb, not much on the ground could. Right now, there was nothing of the sort in the area.

That was why Dave was shocked when he saw the sprite. Sprites are bursts of energy recently discovered exploding like spears of dense light from the tops of thunderheads into the edge of space. Their cause and effect were only now being investigated, and they interested Dave greatly as harbingers of particularly bad storms.

The problem was that there was no bad weather in the area. It was a typical Texas afternoon, with soft, puffy cumulus clouds in a turquoise sky. Stunned, he reran the sequence, watching as the radiation spiked up from the ground to somewhere over one hundred thousand feet in the air. Checking his Richter scale, he noticed a series of small tremors at the same time.

"My, my, my, what have we got here?" Dave thought as he recorded the sequence.

Scrambling for ideas over the cause, he thought of an old friend at the military base in Ft. Hood that he stayed in touch with. He dialed the phone. "Hank, Dave Lumpkin here... Yeah, I'm in Athens now... We moved back after Mary's dad got Alzheimer's. Needed to be closer... Yeah, it's really a bitch, but he's doing the best he can... How are Susie and the boys?... Come on now, you got to be kidding me! Ritchie's married with two kids?... Hell, I thought he was about fifteen years old... Yeah, time sure does run... Say, I need a favor. You don't know anything unusual going on in the area, do you? Maybe some kind of explosion or quake... Really, some kind of big blast was reported at Tejas Hill?... A misfire at a quarry?... You don't say... Naw, it's no big deal. Just came up as an anomaly on my equipment... Yeah, I knew if anyone would know, it would be you... Well, you and Susie need to come over; I'll take you to a great seafood place on Lake Palestine... Yeah, they got all the shrimp and crab legs you can eat... You bet, we'll look for you... Come see me now."

Dave hung up quickly as Shanna came in. Smiling the thinnest of smiles, she nodded as she walked by him in the small control room, smoothing her blouse unconsciously over those gorgeous boobs that she was still paying for on the MasterCard to that handsome plastic surgeon in Highland Park. Dave could feel her sniffing him with disgust, like a cat finding another cat's kill as she walked behind his back. Although she was nice enough to his face, he had seen a dozen like her and worked with more than his share.

They were all the same in the beginning. Eager and bright-eyed. So happy to get the chance to work for a weather legend. Yeah. That usually lasted about six months before they started trying to scoop you. First, the skirts got shorter and the blouses got tighter. Then they started trying to hog airtime any time there was something big brewing. They all thought you could transition from weather girl in Podunk, Texas to Oprah or Katy.

In the end, it was always the same. After a few months, they started treating you as if you were yesterday's news with one foot in the nursing home. Dropping little comments about the joys of retirement. No, I don't need more time off to help my wife, but thanks anyway.

"Anything happening?" inquired Shanna, catching a whiff of his excitement.

"No, nothing I can see." Trying to avoid her, Dave headed for the back door. "I'm going to smoke a cigarette. Call me five minutes before air time, okay?"

"Yeah, okay," said Shanna, eyeing him walking out the door.

Out in the courtyard, Dave spotted Skippy sneaking in the back entrance to cover being late again. He looked a little like someone had crossed Brad Pit with Shaggy from *Scooby Doo*, but a lot more handsome. Given that Skippy was the station owner's son, it wasn't as if he was going to be fired. Skippy, at twenty-seven, was coming down from a seven-year-long bachelor's degree in journalism and media at Sam Houston State, yet seemed to have learned nothing about journalism or media.

There was only one way to describe the way Skippy was moving. Weaseling. Right now, Skippy was weaseling up to Dave. He almost looked like your dog when you've come home and found the wet spot on the carpet. If Skippy could have wagged his tail, rolled over, and peed straight up into the air, he would have.

"You're not going to tell the old man, are you, Dave? Please. You know he'll shred my ass if I'm late again," Skippy whined. "I just can't ever get a good story," he said, taking the Salem out of the pack Dave held out.

Dave took a hit off his Salem and handed Skippy a light while scanning the horizon. "Skippy, you're not ever going to get a story unless you're around to get the call. But I may be able to help you. I want you to take the station van and go out to a little town called Tejas Hill. Tell the old man I told you there might be a good story down there." To himself, Dave thought, "The old man will be overjoyed he's actually chasing a story instead of fathering some more grandchildren he won't ever get to meet."

"What am I looking for out in this Tejas Hill?" asked Skippy.

Dave thought to himself, *Your ass in a hole in the ground, if you're lucky, and having a good day*, but out loud he said, "I'm not sure, but there is some kind of radiation source out there. Something strange was going on in the atmosphere around the quarry out there when they blasted today. Just check out the locals, fish around, and see what you can find. If it pans out into a story," Dave paused for effect, "I'll tell the old man what a great job you did."

"You bet, Dave; you can count on me." Skippy almost fell over himself in gratitude as he headed for the station van. Suddenly, he stopped with a puzzled look on his face. "What am I gonna do for expense money?"

"Tell you what—" Dave reached into his back pocket as he walked up to Skippy. "I'll front you three hundred bucks cash, but you bring back your receipts and reimburse me, okay?"

"You bet, Dave. If there's a story there, I'm going to find it." Skippy already had the cash in his pocket and was halfway in the van.

Dave waved, speaking under his breath. "I'll be surprised if you find the town, much less the story."

Just in time, Shanna leaned out the door, holding her blouse closed so her boobs wouldn't fall out. "Five minutes, Dave."

"Thanks." He dropped what was left of the Salem on the grass and headed in. "Showtime!"

Skippy might act dumb on occasion, but he wasn't stupid. At twenty-seven, he knew he had pushed the old man about as far as he could. What Dave didn't know was that he had gotten the big ultimatum. Produce stories or get a job at McDonalds. Too many close calls with professors, fathers, and husbands had taught him you only have so many lives, lies, and luck to go around, and you better know when yours is about up.

Right now, Skippy figured he was about out of lives, lies, and luck, and the trust fund didn't kick in for a while. If he was going to stretch this gig much longer, he needed a score. Dave might not have known it, but this time, Skippy was motivated. Under the bad dog act, Skippy was brilliant at achieving his own ends.

This time, it was his hind end on the line. He was ready to work as hard at saving it as he had at doing nothing for the past seven years. Skippy popped in a CD, and the sweet sounds of Martha Reeves singing "Nowhere to Run, Nowhere to Hide" drifted toward the sunset.

Chapter Seven

"High Noon at Connie's Place"

Skippy pulled into Connie's parking lot at 12:45 p.m. Once he found the hill and made the turn onto the blacktop road, there wasn't much place else to end up. He tucked the station van into a hole between an old Studebaker pick-up and an S-class Mercedes. As he walked through the door, he saw about as close to heaven in a woman standing at the counter in a pair of denim overalls and a T-shirt without a bra. She was talking to a woman with funky red hair running the cash register.

"Connie, tell me again—what was that variety of tomatoes you were telling me about so I won't get screwed at the nursery again."

Connie never missed a beat ringing up a six-pack and a sausage wraparound for the roughneck at the counter. "Rutgers, honey. It's an old variety, and it makes a real sweet tomato, not huge like those Big-boys, but a whole lot better. Be sure and get the Clemson spineless okra, and God help you if you grow a straight-neck yellow squash around here."

"Be sure and come back, now; you'll be out of beer by three o'clock," Connie waved as the roughneck went out the door.

He yelled back, "Only if you promise to go dancing with me tonight."

"Bull," said Connie. "You couldn't stay up with me an hour."

The flirting over with, Connie turned her attention back to Deborah. "How are you hiding the vegetables from old stuck-up Dirk this time?" she grinned as she asked.

"You won't believe it, Connie. You're gonna split a gut when you hear this. I told him that *Bon Appetite* magazine had this article about French herb and vegetable gardens and how they were all the rage in the Hamptons." Deborah had to stop she was laughing so hard. "I told him all his doctor buddies in Dallas would be impressed if we had one, too." Now they were both about to split a gut laughing. "I not only don't have to hide them anymore, he wants weekly status reports on what will be ripe when we have our big bash for the new house."

Connie goosed her in the side. "You brazen little heifer—you didn't?"

"I sure did," bragged Deborah. "Now he's bragging to everyone in the hospital about 'his' vegetables and herbs, like they never saw a tomato. He even asked Latimer how to design a garden spot."

"Oh, God, tell me what Latimer did." Connie couldn't wait for the punch line.

"Well," said Deborah, leaning in close, "he looked Dirk straight in the eye and told him to get a hoe, mark off a square, and dig 'til he dropped! Dirk hasn't spoken to him since."

About that time, Connie and Deborah figured out that Skippy was staring at them. They stopped, turned, and stared back.

Connie broke the silence. "Okay, here it is. She's the queen," pointing at Deborah. "I'm just the queen of the kitchen. Got it?"

"Got it," said Skippy with the smile that had dazzled dozens of young coeds. "How about I just find myself a spot and sit down?"

"Good idea, chief; I'll be right over to take your order."

Skippy made the corner to the little dining room, but all of the eight tables were taken. There was one table for two with a nerdy-looking guy with long hair about Skippy's age nursing a Bud Light longneck.

Hell, thought Skippy. *It's the nerd or nothing.* Strolling over as if he owned the place, he sat down at the same time he stuck out his hand. "Skippy Beto. Mind if I join you?"

Dennis Smith was too surprised to do anything but look at the hand as if it was alien. By the time he recovered enough to extend his hand, the guy was already sitting down and reaching for a menu. "What's good, dude?"

Dennis pulled back his hand and said, "It's Dennis, not dude, okay? And everything is good, except I wouldn't get the fried chicken livers after 12:30 if I were you. They get a little dry."

Even self-absorbed Skippy could tell he had pissed the little guy off. "Look," he said, leaning forward, "I just got frosted by the cook from the truck driving school out there, and all I was doing was gawking at the angel in the overalls. I just had to have a place to sit. I promise I'll leave you alone if you just let me eat lunch here. How about it?" Skippy goosed Dennis on the arm, nodding his head and grinning at the same time.

Dennis couldn't help it; this guy had a smile you couldn't resist. "What the hell, knock yourself out." Dennis stuck his hand out. "Dennis Smith, and welcome to Tejas Hill."

Handshakes done, Skippy settled right in as if they were old buddies. "Yeah, and ain't this place a kick in the butt? I didn't know they still made towns like this. Who are those two women anyway?"

"Well, the one that isn't the angel is Connie. She owns the place, and I wouldn't try to screw around with her. She's tougher than Don Rickles. The other one is Deborah Mendez, as in the wife of Doctor Mendez, the local surgeon. She's as tough as Connie, but she doesn't have to talk. She can freeze you with a look. I wouldn't mess with either of 'em." Dennis took a swig off the Bud, sizing up Skippy now that he had the time.

Connie walked up, took out her order pad, and looked at Skippy as if she was looking at a pile of day-old dog shit on a white carpet. "What can I get you?"

Skippy sized Connie up. "Look, Connie, I'm real sorry. I could tell you I was looking at you, but you look like you can smell a lie a mile away. I just couldn't take my eyes off little Ellie Mae over there. I'm real sorry, so how about you get me whatever Dennis here usually has, okay?" Big smile, lots of white teeth.

Connie didn't miss a beat. "I'm sure glad you said that." Connie slid over a spare chair and sat down at the table. "Because if you had said you were looking at me, I would have had to tell my boyfriend Earl over there," Connie smiled and waved at Earl, who was chopping onions in the kitchen with a big butcher knife. Earl waved back with a big grin, giving Connie a big okay sign. Connie looked back at Skippy and said in a quiet, serious voice, "He hasn't been out of the State School for very long, and he's real jealous. If his medicine were working, he'd probably just kick your ass. If not, you might end up on a hamburger. Capiche?"

Skippy looked over at Dennis to see if she was joking. Dennis just stared back with a blank expression and took another swig of his Bud.

"So," said Connie, getting up as if nothing had been said, "You want a Bud with those fried chicken livers?" Skippy grinned his best. "Yea, and bring my new friend here another Bud, if you don't mind, Miss Connie."

"I don't mind at all," said Connie, letting just the hint of a smile cross her face as she turned around and headed for the kitchen.

"Man, I see what you mean." Skippy looked like he had just been baptized. "The women around here are tough if they're all like that." Moving on, Skippy looked Dennis over one more time and said, "So, what does a suave guy like you do around Tejas Hill?"

Dennis let the backhanded insult slide off. After all, it was a slow day, and he was bored. Why not talk?

"Well, I'm a scientist for an outfit called Goliath Construction Materials; they're the biggest provider of rock for industrial use in the world."

"A scientist? You got to be kidding!" Skippy fell back in the chair as if he had just been told his mother was a lesbian. "I never would have figured you for a scientist. I thought you were some kind of computer geek."

"I am some kind of computer geek. That's one of the kinds of science I do." Dennis wasn't smiling, but luckily, Connie brought two Buds, and everyone got distracted long enough to forget the little faux-paux.

"That's pretty weird, because Goliath is why I'm here, too." Skippy was beginning to pay a lot more attention to the conversation. "What kind of science are you doing for Goliath, anyway?"

Dennis took a measured sip of his beer and gave Skippy the same look that he had impressed Sandy Northcutt with months ago. "Look, Skippy, or whoever you are, I may look like a nerd, but I'm not stupid. What are you doing here, and why are you so interested in Goliath?"

"Easy, big boy." Skippy threw his hands up as if Dennis had thrown down on him with a .038 pistol. "I'm just a cub reporter for a little station called KWOW in Athens. You might have heard of it?" Dennis indicated that he hadn't. "Anyway, our weatherman is a guy named Dave Lumpkin. He's kind of a creepy old dude, but he can smell weather like your dog can smell a can of sardines in a hot garbage bag." Skippy was warming up to being the storyteller. "Anyway, he has this new machine that scans all kinds of energy in the upper atmosphere, and when Goliath blasted yesterday, the thing registered some kind of radiation. I think he called it a sprit."

"It's a sprite, not a sprit," said Dennis with a deadpan look that belied his rapidly increasing interest.

"Okay, sprit, sprite, what the hell, right? Anyway, this thing registered this radiation clear into lower outer space. Dave told me if I came out and found out what the deal was, he would put in a good word for me, and man, you can believe I need a good word with the old man right about now."

Finished, Skippy took a long draw and finished his beer. Looking around, he caught Connie's eye and held up an empty longneck, "Hey, Miss Connie, could we have two more?"

"You got five bucks?" asked Connie. Skippy gave her his "you don't really expect me to dignify that with an answer" look, and Connie reached into the cooler for two more Buds.

"So—your turn." Skippy took a drag off the new beer and looked at Dennis, waiting for the story.

Dennis didn't really have to ask who the old man was. Skippy might as well have worn a T-shirt saying, "My old man owns the company, and I ain't worth shit!" Be that as it may, Dennis knew the town was weird beyond description, and he was getting tired of being the resident "outsider." It might be nice to have an ally connected enough to be used, and too dumb to know he was being used, especially with a rich daddy and a TV station's resources. Goliath had the money, but so far, all they were interested in was keeping Dennis busy with make-work to keep the leash on his magic machine. Dennis wasn't telling Sandy Northcutt half of what he suspected, and he wasn't going to start now.

"Well, funny you should ask. Goliath hired me to do a little light prospecting about the physical properties of the bluff. There might be some non-confidential information available from my research, but I need to be sure we don't screw up each other's nest. That was a hell of a blast yesterday, and I can't get too curious working for the company, but I would like to know more about it."

Dennis could make up his mind real quick, and he had already made up his mind about Skippy. "Tell you what—let's team up, and you share what you can with me, and I'll share what I can with you, and neither of us uses the other's name without permission, okay?"

"Man, you're singing my song. A poor dumbass like me needs all the help he can get. Where do we start?" Dennis smiled an easy smile, took another drag off his Bud, and leaned in, lowering his voice so only the first few words could be heard. "Okay, this is the deal—first, we—"

The booming voice of Dan Dahoney drowned out the conversation from two tables over, where he was regaling a thirty-something lady with premature white hair and a large briefcase with some well known Tejas Hill history. "Did you know that at its peak, the college had 460 students and was recognized as one of the great universities of Texas?"

All around the room, a silent "not again" shudder went up from every local in the place. Connie yelled from the kitchen, "Now, Dan, don't bore that pretty lady to death with all that dead old history before she has a chance to find out we still have real live people around here."

In keeping with her usual "know it all before anyone else does," Connie already knew the young woman with the striking hair was Abra Avant, a recognized archeologist from New Orleans with family ties to the hill. She was supposed to be here working on family genealogy, but Connie wasn't so sure. That just didn't quite ring true, with no family left alive, all the genealogy in the world on the Internet, and no library in Tejas Hill. Still, she had bought lunch and a dessert, and that was enough for Connie.

Chapter Eight

"THE CURIO SHOP"

T he corner building was north of Connie's store. It was your typical, small-town brick party wall building. The front had two huge plate glass windows, where mannequins with the latest clothes had been displayed in the fifties when the store was a thriving dry goods store. Now the windows were clouded with dust and cobwebs. Above the door was a glass transom with the words:

Eggleston
Artifacts and Curiosity Shop

In large typewriter-letter style in black with gold leaf shadows to the left of each letter.

A person walking or driving by might have thought it was closed except for a sign hung on a string in the middle of the recessed front door that said, "Open, Please Come In." The other side read, "Sorry, Closed." The white-haired young woman opened the door, setting off a small bell on a spring on top of the door. "Is anyone here?" she asked, peering tentatively around shelves full of antiques and artifacts from numerous cultures.

"Of course, my dear, come in." The voice was clear as a bell, with an odd accent that did not seem as comfortable with vowels as with consonants—not quite European, but certainly not American, either. It seemed to come from the back, where several head-high bookcases blocked the view.

Making her way into a sitting area hidden by the bookcases, Abra saw a man sitting in a mahogany Empire-style chair inlaid with yew wood and gold leaf, with marquetry decorations on the slender legs. He was impeccably dressed in slacks, a dark sports coat, and an honest-to-God burgundy ascot. At a distance, in the low light cast by the oversize

Ralph Lauren lamp on a matching table beside him, his body seemed that of a male model, long and lean. He had auburn hair pushed straight back over his head with a white streak slightly off center, long legs in expensive wool slacks, delicate hands, and long fingers wrapped around an oversize volume with drawings of Mezo-American glyphs on the pages. Abra noted that he had not lain the book down, only lowered it.

"May I help you?" It was only then that the man laid the book aside, as if he regretted doing so. In one fluid motion, he stood up to his full height of well over six feet.

To this point, Abra had believed the man was in his forties or fifties. As her eyes adjusted to the low light and he reached out his hand, she saw his skin and piercing green eyes clearly and sensed he was ancient. He reminded her of Michael Renne in *The Day the Earth Stood Still*, but much older. His deeply tanned skin was smooth, but up close, almost translucent. The eyes were piercing, clear, and seemed to see through her, almost like searchlights. He was a contradiction—old, but seemingly much younger than any older man she had ever seen.

Disconcerted, she took the extended hand. Unlike most people in Texas, he did not shake her hand or try to squeeze her with a death grip. Neither did he let it go quickly, but continued to hold it as if the position was as natural as breathing to both of them. "Linton Eggleston," he said with a slight smile. "What may I help you with today, Miss—?"

Regaining her senses, Abra held his gaze as she said, "Abra Avant, Mr. Eggleston. A pleasure to meet you."

Satisfied with the exchange, his hand was suddenly gone, leaving hers dangling in the air. "I must apologize in advance; my shop is somewhat boring for the tourist trade. We don't have much in the way of the usual trinkets and scented candles. If that is what you are looking for, you might find Trash and Treasures, down the street, a little more exciting." The veiled put-down coupled with the way he turned away to reach for his book again was about like someone throwing cold water on her. She was not some trailer park queen, and he was not hosting *Masterpiece Theater,* even if his get-up did look like that Russell Baker guy.

"Actually, I don't care for trinkets, and I absolutely cannot tolerate potpourri or scented candles. I heard that your shop was a source for out-of-print books on archeology and history."

Eggleston paused and turned around in another fluid motion.

Damn, he moves more like a cat than a man, she thought as he smiled at her and surveyed her face again.

"Now I really must apologize. Not only have I underestimated you, I have also offended you, and those are two things I rarely do in the same breath." He quickly slid a chair from a corner and placed it in front of him. "Please, sit down, and tell me what I can do for you."

"First off, I would not have thought I would find the nation's best-known authenticator of ancient American artifacts in a backwater town like this. I've read about you in Southebys and Christies' auction catalogs for years." Abra took in more of this man, wishing he were thirty years younger. His eyes never left hers as his face flashed from intense attention to embarrassment, then to pride, all in the space of her sentence.

"Thank you for the complement, but the answer to the question is very simple. This is my home. Where I came from. As much as I love the luxury of my New York apartment, I find myself missing the endless vistas changing colors with the seasons and the sky. My God, that must have sounded balmy." Looking down, Linton laughed at himself easily. "I guess one gets that way with too much solitude and too little company. Enough about me. What type of history are you interested in?"

Abra found it hard to do, but she lied anyway. The lie came easily since he had provided the subject when she first arrived. "I'm looking for literature documenting nineteenth-century and early twentieth-century expeditions in Mexico and South America. Maya, Aztec, Toltec, Olmec, Inca—it doesn't matter to me. I'm really interested in the illustrations of glyphs and decorations drawn on site. Also, any Egyptian hieroglyph sources you might have."

Linton's face, which had been full of polite interest, began to freeze over, as if she had asked him for a vanilla-scented candle. "I'm sorry, Miss Avant, but you really must be making fun of me. No serious student of Pre-Columbian glyphs would be asking me for books on Egyptian hieroglyphics in the same breath. You'll probably be asking me for books on ancient astronaut pyramid builders next."

This time, she held his gaze so he could not turn away to reach for his book and dismiss her. Satisfied he was not going to turn away, she reached for his hand. "Please, listen." She paused. "I am not making fun of you. My specialty is in linguistics as they relate to tracking populations and cultures. I recently began to suspect that glyphs and signs from a number of cultures have related connections and origins that might rewrite several accepted theories. But sources are hard to come by, and some of the best illustrations are in the old volumes like the ones published by the early explorers. I may be wrong, but I am serious."

He appraised her carefully as she spoke, admiring her nerve and odd beauty. She was not a woman that all men would be attracted to, with many nice features that did not exactly fit together. Her looks took a second and even a third glance before you began to see the unique way her features worked together. She was a woman he found attractive and would notice. "So, then, you would be conversant in Native American languages?" he smiled as he asked the question.

"Of course. That was my specialty."

Without missing a beat, he spoke quickly and fluently in a Native American dialect she should know. "A ge yv-a gv du lo (Young woman know words?)"

As quickly, Abra responded in the same language, "Yes, old man, young woman knows words."

Linton chuckled, replying, "Touché, and well done. Now, let's go see what an old man has in his stacks to interest the bright young student." With that, he turned away, moving so fast she could hardly keep up.

Yes, old man, she thought, *I'm looking for a historic mystery; and you're the mystery.*

As he wound through shelves of artifacts and books, she could not see his face go cold, with the full concentration of a warrior tracking game. Linton knew the way of animals, and people were animals, especially to him. *What does she really want, and how am I involved*? he wondered. He did not know the nature of her deception, but he knew there was deception, and in that deception, danger to him. He saw it in her pupils as they dilated. He saw it in the color in her cheeks and changes in her breathing when she lied. He could easily distinguish simple flirtation and polite interest from outright manipulation. *Let her think what she will*, he thought. *The hunt is on.* The outcome was certain in his mind as to who would win. The winner was always known. The question was the prize and the price. There was always a prize and a price for the winner. Always. It had been so long since the game was this good.

Sadly, like most modern people, Abra retained little of the raw instinct upon which many of her ancestors had survived to produce her. Had Abra possessed those instincts as she followed Linton through the stacks of books, she would have sensed one overriding emotion rising in her. One that she could have smelled, sensed, and felt all at the same time. Raw fear.

Chapter Nine

"Welcome to City Hall!"

City Hall in Tejas Hill was a small metal building about twenty-five feet by fifty feet. Inside, Lannie Olson, city secretary, was nominally in charge. The better question would have been in charge of what? Normally, the counter-person in a city office was a facilitator, someone to help you or guide you to someone who could help you. Not so in Tejas Hill.

At city hall, Lannie's main job was to see that you got as little information as possible until she could notify the mayor who you were and what you were asking for. Only then were you likely to get what you wanted. Since dispensing information was the only thing she was actually authorized to do, that meant that she had little to do, and since the citizens of the city knew better than to ask her for anything, it was a real rarity to have someone actually enter city hall.

Lannie was in her late thirties, with a nice figure, nice knit outfit, nice hair, nice makeup, and nice degree. She was, well, nice. It took about two minutes to figure out she was one of those insecure women that tried too hard; she was too friendly, too helpful, too quick to laugh and overreact. A perpetual victim. In some perverse way, that willingness to try too hard to please made her the perfect person to be city secretary. She could rarely give people what they wanted, but no one could get mad at her because she was so sincere, tried so hard to please, and then apologized as if it were her fault that she could not deliver.

A sign in front said "City Hall." Underneath was a handwritten note wrapped in plastic and taped to the door that said, "Hours: 8 a.m. to 12 noon, Monday and Thursday." Skippy stared at the sign as if it were written in Chinese.

"Damn, I sure hope no one has any important city business on any day other than Monday or Thursday."

"It's no big deal. It's not like the big city." Dennis was already opening the door as he talked. "You just call the mayor or whoever you need if the office is closed. It's not like they've got a lot to do."

Inside, Lannie, taken totally by surprise at someone actually coming into city hall, was hurriedly trying to hide the current issue of *Cosmo* under a metal desk that had been discarded from the grammar school when it closed twenty-eight years before. Embarrassed, she looked about as guilty as an eighth-grader caught with a *Penthouse* magazine. Unable to find a place to hide the magazine, she simply turned it face down on the desk.

"May I help you?" she blurted, standing quickly and wiping her hands on her gray tailored slacks.

"Yeah," said Skippy, pointing at the back cover with the picture of an anorexic model wearing skimpy bikini panties standing with her legs wide apart, her hands over her flat chest and a surprised look on her face. With his most disarming smile, he asked, "Is that the latest issue of *Cosmo* that's got that fashion layout with Carmen Hezzera? I heard it's hotter than a pistol." Too embarrassed and surprised, Lannie looked at the magazine on the desk as if it were a snowball that had dropped out of a clear blue sky in the Sahara.

"Oh, that," she said, with a big pause and crinkled nose, as if she had just smelled month-old milk in the icebox. "I wouldn't know. Someone must have left it here; I was just on my way to throw it out."

Lannie always felt slightly naughty reading *Cosmo*, even when she was alone. After all, it always had all those beautiful models wearing all that skimpy underwear and posing in those odd positions that always looked like they were having some kind of kinky sex, only with the man missing. And those articles—always something like "Ten things you can do to make your man go wild in bed." Lannie could think of only two things to do in bed that would drive a man wild, and one of them was something she wasn't ever planning to do. She always figured she must not be too good at the other one because her husband had walked out after ten years, telling her, "You're a real nice woman, Lannie, and I wish you the best, but you really need to loosen up if you want to keep someone around." He had run off with a twenty-year-old checker at Wal-Mart with big boobs and a mouth full of Double Bubble. They had two kids, lived in a doublewide at the edge of town, and really seemed to be happy.

Seeing her obvious embarrassment, and having been the butt of the joke too much in his own life, Dennis shifted the conversation, "Actually, Lannie, we need a permit to do some testing on city property."

"Oh, a permit. That's wonderful." She began to flounder around the desk, looking for her permit form. Finding it, she took a new Bic from the creamed corn can wrapped in contact paper and assumed an official pose. "Okay—name?"

"Dennis Smith."

"Company?"

"Goliath."

"Reason?"

"Geological survey."

"Area?"

"Bald Hill."

"Type of equipment?"

"Backhoe, electronic and hand equipment."

Lannie put the pen down and looked straight at Dennis. "Dennis, you know everyone here likes you, but that last blast about scared everyone in town half to death. You're not going to try to start regular blasting in town are you?" Lannie still lived in a world where a man would tell you the truth if you looked him in the eye. She looked him straight in the eye.

"Actually, what I'm trying to do is find out why that blast was so bad. Goliath doesn't want that kind of incident any more than the town does." Satisfied, and feeling more in control, Lannie turned her gaze to the irrepressible Skippy, who was giving her his best "bad puppy dog" smile.

"Who's your friend here? I don't recognize him." It was delivered with all the seriousness of a guard at a Nazi checkpoint.

Not waiting for an intro, Skippy stuck his hand out. "Skippy Beto, ma'am. Reporter with KWOW, Athens, Texas. I'm here doing a little piece on Tejas Hill. I'm thinking of naming it "Tejas Hill, Past, Present, and Future." He spread his arms across the air as if he were pointing to a banner on which the words were written. "What do you think?" asked Skippy, looking at Lannie intently as if he really cared what she thought.

Warming quickly to someone who actually cared about her opinion (God knows the mayor and council sure didn't), she smiled and said, "I think that sounds great. We could use some publicity."

Warming to his own bullshit, Skippy added, "I can see it now. City hall, the nerve center of town, presided over by none other than Lannie, capable city secretary. What do you think?"

Lannie straightened her jacket and smoothed her hair as if the photographers were fixing to arrive to do a photo shoot. But before she could answer, Dennis kicked Skippy on the side of his leg, gave him a probing look, and said, "Skippy, aren't we in a hurry to get that work done?"

"Huh? Oh, yeah, yeah," said Skippy, catching on, and looking back at Lannie. "Gee, Lannie," he said in his best Eddie Haskell style, "I guess I got kind of carried away, but we really must be getting out there to the job site." Actually, Skippy had no earthly idea where Bald Hill was or why they were going there.

"So, how about that permit?" Dennis smiled hopefully at Lannie, to no avail.

"Oh, gee, I can't possibly give you a permit today."

"You've got to be kidding, right?" Dennis looked surprised.

"No, no, I'm not kidding." Lannie seemed perplexed that anyone expected anything the same day they asked. "We have protocols here. First, you have to fill out the application. Second, I have to deliver the application to the mayor. Third, he has to consult with Kinnerd Irvin to make sure no gas lines will be affected. Then, if everything is okay, the mayor tells me to issue the permit." She smiled apologetically, "But since this is Thursday, I won't be back until next Monday, and by the time I see the mayor, and he sees Kinnerd, it will probably be next Thursday at the earliest, and maybe the following Monday."

"But won't you be seeing the mayor today? I just saw him coming out of the post office across the street," Dennis asked, "and Kinnerd is always driving up and down shooting everyone the finger. Can't they get together today?"

"Well, yes, that's possible, but I have to make a copy of the permit and the application." Lannie looked at Dennis and smiled, as if that explained everything.

"I must be missing something." Dennis seemed genuinely confused. "Can't you just make a copy after the mayor signs it?"

Now Lannie seemed genuinely perplexed. "Oh, no, we don't have a copy machine here, and the city only pays me to go to the office supply company once a week to make copies. That would be next Thursday."

Satisfied, once again, that she had explained everything, Lannie smiled at Dennis, waiting for him to go away, but Dennis wasn't ready to go quite yet.

"Yeah, but can't you just run it through the fax, or fax it to yourself from your computer and make a copy?"

"Oh." Lannie looked surprised. "I thought you knew; we don't have a fax or a computer. I keep all the city records on a typewriter." Sensing that more explanation was required, or maybe just trying to fill the stunned silence and shut the open mouths that Dennis and Skippy couldn't seem to close, Lannie babbled on. "Several of the citizens offered to buy the city a computer, copier, and fax, but the mayor said the city had done just fine with that old Underwood for a lot of years, the expense of the additional upkeep and electricity weren't in this year's budget, and we've already adopted next year's budget, so it would be three years before we could consider getting any of those items. Anyway, I don't know if I'd be smart enough to operate them if we had them."

The last sentence ended with that same self-deprecating laugh. Then Lannie simply stopped and looked at them, as if surely that was all they needed to leave. She waited for them to leave with the smile glued to her face.

Looking on in disbelief, Skippy almost said, "I'm not sure you could operate them, either. In fact, I'm not sure you're smart enough to operate toilet paper."

"Tell you what." Dennis held his finger up in the air as if he had just gotten a brainstorm. "What if I take the permit to the office supply myself, or pay you to go to the office supply yourself, and then you get some time out of the office, and I get the permit."

"Oh." Lannie started backing up, holding her hands up as if Dennis had just asked her to sell heroin to a fifth-grader. "I couldn't take any type of bribe. The mayor tells me almost everyday that it would violate the Open Meetings and Open Records Act for me to give special treatment to anyone so they could get anything the same day. He said I could be arrested and charged with a crime." She delivered the statement with a firm shake of her head to emphasize the "get arrested" part.

"Now, I think the two of you had better leave before the mayor gets here and I have to tell him what you tried to do." She wasn't smiling. Dennis and Skippy backed out the front door like two bank robbers that just found the vault open and empty. Too stunned to speak, they hastily got into Dennis' Saab and drove off.

It was probably the preoccupation of mulling over the events that had just transpired at city hall that caused Dennis to cross the centerline in the curve at the bottom of Mesquite Street in front of the rented minivan driven by Abra Avant. Trying to avoid a collision, Abra swerved into the ditch, hitting her head on the roof. Strangely, as she lost consciousness, she saw Linton Eggleston's face smiling at her, as if he knew the answer to the secret she was looking for.

Chapter Ten

"What Are We All Doing Here?"

A bra woke up slowly, aware that she was laying on something soft, with a cool, wet towel on her forehead. She thought about trying to sit up, but the effort seemed beyond her. Instead, she began to move each arm and leg slowly, trying to feel if anything was broken. At a distance, she heard a voice say, "You think she's gonna croak on us? My old man will kill me if we kill someone and I don't even get a story."

Dennis stopped rubbing the towel across Abra's head and looked into Skippy's face. "Listen, dumbass, if you spent as much time looking for your story as you do worrying about your old man and covering your ass, you might find something."

"Yeah, well, I may be a dumbass, but at least I'm not some kind of geek who never had a date." Skippy wasn't gonna let Dennis get a cheap shot like that one in unscathed.

"Who told you I never had a date?" Unwittingly, Dennis had just told Skippy his rough guess had hit the mark. "Do you know someone who went to school with me?"

Having regained her focus and hearing everything beginning with the first insult, Abra couldn't help but laugh. Even at an odd angle, she could tell that the little fellow that looked like a scholar had probably never had a real date.

Startled, Skippy blurted out, "Hey, dude, I don't think she's dead. She's laughing at you."

Still off balance from the direct hit, with his junior high paranoia in full swing, Dennis blurted, "Why? Does she know someone who went to school with me? Well, does she?"

Looking back and forth between Skippy and Abra, who by now was sitting up, laughing and holding her head in pain, Dennis seemed genuinely confused why they were falling back on the couch, slapping each other and laughing harder.

56

"Ain't this little dude a real Beaver Cleaver?" Skippy slapped Abra's shoulder for emphasis, putting them both into another laughing fit.

Too mad for words, Dennis got up, heading for the kitchen, yanking the dishtowel off Abra's forehead for punishment. "Well, I guess you're all right." As he left the room, he looked back at the couch, just in time to see Abra falling into Skippy's arms, hugging him in laughter as if they were old friends. As she did, her skirt pulled up over her thigh. Too honest and well behaved, Dennis turned away before he saw any more, but wished he hadn't.

It all seemed so natural, and you could tell this wasn't the first time a woman had fallen into Skippy's arms. Skippy hardly seemed to notice. Dennis found himself hating Skippy just as he had hated every high school stud that always seemed to have women hanging on him with no effort. Hell, the few times a woman had hugged Dennis, it was for something nice he had done, or because she was too drunk to notice who she was hugging, or just too plain to care.

Dennis got a glass of water and stood at the sink, wishing someone would bottle some of what Skippy had so he could buy it, yet knowing all the intelligence and money in the world would never buy that for him. Never in a million years. For just that second, he knew he would trade all his considerable intellect, and probably his future, to have what Skippy had and so obviously took for granted.

From the living room, he heard Skippy calling, "Hey, Dennis, come on back. We didn't mean anything, honest. Come on, man, don't be mad."

Skippy begging was hard to take. Dennis wasn't about to go back. He stayed at the sink drinking water, determined not to back down, and then he felt a soft hand touch his arm. He turned to see Abra looking into his eyes, standing very close to him, her hand touching his arm as if to prevent him from running away. Honestly, Dennis wasn't used to having a woman he didn't know this close to him, and his natural inclination was to move away. Unfortunately, the kitchen cabinet and sink prevented that, so he did the next best thing and looked at the floor.

"I know I don't know your name, and I sure didn't have any right to laugh at you." Abra paused, dropping her head until she caught his gaze again and lifted his face with her eyes. "If it makes you feel any better, I didn't have many dates in school either with this white hair. The boys used to call me the great white witch, sometimes worse." With that, he couldn't help but chuckle with her. "Let's start over, okay? My name is Abra Avant."

Somehow, her look took all the anger out of Dennis, and suddenly, he felt like a fool. "Dennis. My name is Dennis Smith, and I'm sorry I took it so seriously. You know how it is, you think you've outgrown all that junior high bullshit, and then somebody says something that brings it all back."

Abra gave him a "Boy, do I know!" look, and Dennis felt so much better he almost didn't notice that she was holding his hand as she led him back into the living room to the couch. It felt pretty good, and Dennis really hated when she let go.

"Okay, I know who Dennis is, so why don't you introduce yourself, and somebody tell me why I'm here instead of a clinic."

Skippy jumped right in, with a semi-serious look for a change. "Skippy Beto, KWOW News, at your service. It's like this. Tejas Hill doesn't have a doctor or a hospital, and the nearest hospital is twenty-five miles away. Anyway, Dennis here seemed to know what he was doing, and he said we better get you somewhere you could lay down until we could see if you were hurt bad."

Skippy grinned his most disarming grin. "Luckily, it looks like the only thing that really got hurt bad is the Beaver's feelings." Skippy grinned at Dennis, and despite his best efforts, Dennis laughed, too, watching Abra try to stifle a laugh herself. The air was cleared, and everyone seemed relaxed.

Skippy seemed out of explanations, so Dennis jumped in. "Your car isn't hurt, just stuck. Why don't you lay back and relax, and I'll fix some supper, and we'll all go and get your car out in a little while."

Abra started to protest and ask them to just carry her to her car, but her head really didn't feel that great. "Yeah, that might be a good idea. You got any ibuprofen?"

Dennis was on his feet. "How about a Darvocet, instead?"

"That sounds great. I'll just lie back on the couch, if you don't mind, and let you guys surprise me for dinner."

Skippy followed Dennis into the kitchen. "You cook too?" Skippy looked at Dennis as if he had just mentioned that he tamed lions.

"Yeah, I can cook. Can't you?" Dennis asked as he opened the cabinet to check out the choices.

"Hell, no, I can barely open a can of beanie weenies, and that's if it's got a pop top. What are we gonna cook, anyway?" Skippy was standing behind Dennis, holding the cabinet door open and peering intently at the cans and items on the shelf.

"Tell you what," Dennis said as he reached into the icebox. "I've got some chicken breasts, fresh garlic, and basil, so find me a can of mushroom soup and then get that box of long grain and wild rice in the cabinet, and we'll make some French baked chicken breasts." At the same time, he closed the icebox door with butter, milk, celery, carrots, and mushrooms in his hand.

"Damn, are you some kind of chef?" Skippy seemed genuinely impressed.

Dennis liked having the upper hand again, and still smarting over the date thing, he couldn't resist a small dig. "Well, some of us didn't have an old man who owned the business. My mother was a cook and Daddy left when I was pretty little. She couldn't always afford a sitter when I was in school, so I'd hang out in the diner after school and help. It beat sitting around, and it was really kind of fun."

While Dennis was putting the ingredients on the counter, Skippy opened up two Bud Lights. When Dennis turned back to see the reaction, Skippy held out a longneck in a gesture of good will, "Look, I'm sorry. I didn't mean anything. Being the boss's son ain't what it's cracked up to be. You never are good enough." A rare frown crossed Skippy's face for the briefest of moments then he was his old grinning self again. "Friends?" Skippy held the longneck out a little further.

"Yeah, friends, and I'm sorry about the dumbass crack." Dennis took the beer, and they both took a few swigs, enjoying the moment. Truth be known, Skippy had a lot of friends, but not the kind you could trust. Most of his were the Highland Park kind. You know, the kind that only associates with their kind of money.

Skippy felt like he could trust Dennis. Dennis was so gratified that he didn't even realize that the beer Skippy had just given him was his.

"Do me a favor—get that cutting board and cut me up some of the celery and carrots and crush about four big cloves of garlic." Dennis handed the butcher knife to Skippy, who looked at it as if it was a scalpel. "It's real simple. Just wash everything, pull the strings out of the back of the celery before you slice it, and crush the garlic under the flat edge of the knife to get the paper skin off."

Skippy took a long draw off his beer and wandered off to the far corner of the kitchen cabinet with a confused look on his face. A man on a mission.

Almost exactly one hour later, Abra woke to the heavenly smell of the combination of garlic, Marsala wine, and chicken. Dennis and Skippy were sitting at the table, drinking beer, and obviously waiting for her to wake up. As soon as she moved, Dennis's face lit up. "Hey, I sure hope you feel like eating."

Abra sat up, amazed to find her headache gone and feeling entirely rested. "Listen, if I could have two guys fix a gourmet meal while I take a nap, I might be willing to wreck my car every day." Drawn by the smell, Abra sat down in the empty chair at the kitchen table.

Abra had to admit that all the attention was flattering. Skippy and Dennis were like two awkward puppies falling over themselves trying to impress her. She couldn't help but laugh at the obvious competition that was going on to be the first to serve her. Somehow, a plate of food and a cold beer appeared in front of her without anyone being blocked or tackled.

"Guys, settle down and get a plate. I'm not going anywhere until after you feed me. Just relax!" Abra waited while they both got a plate full of food and sat down. She was fixing to take a bite when she noticed they were both looking at her intently, as if something momentous was going to happen when she took a bite. Amused, Abra slowly took a bite, began to chew slowly, and then began to quietly choke, as if she were going to barf on the table.

Dennis looked stricken, almost in disbelief, as he leaned forward and said, "Is something wrong? Are you all right?"

Skippy turned to Dennis and shook the back of an open hand at Dennis in a purely Italian move. "Aw, shit, look what you've done now. I thought you said you could cook." Torn between Skippy's disgusted look and caustic accusation and Abra's choking, Dennis didn't know whether to jump or run.

Having milked all the fun and human emotion out of the situation, Abra quit choking, smiled, swallowed the bite, and took a long draw off her beer. "Tastes good to me," she said, as if nothing had happened. The relief on Dennis' face was replaced with a long, nasty stare at Skippy, who suddenly seemed inordinately interested in the foam in his longneck and the loose end on the label.

Sensing someone needed to break the silence, Abra put her fork down and placed her elbows on the table and her chin in her cupped hands. Looking at Skippy and then at Dennis, she said, "Okay, so what are two bright guys like you doing in a one-dog town like this?"

Caught by surprise, Skippy and Dennis gave each other a "you go first" look. When no one jumped in, Abra looked at each again with a smile and said, "Come on guys, with two cool dudes like you, there must be a good story here."

Dennis could not stand to be rude and broke the silence. "Well, I'm here working for Goliath's science department running geological tests on the bluff." Dennis paused, sipping his Bud and looking at Abra to see if she was going to be duly impressed. Before she could respond, he saw Skippy grinning and pointing a wagging finger at him out of the corner of his eye. "He's lying. Mr. Wizard here is lying to you."

Aggravated, Dennis said, "How many of my Buds have you drunk anyway?"

The reply was instant. "Not enough so I don't know when you're lying."

Abra caught Dennis' eye with a "let me take over" look and shifted her gaze to Skippy. "Okay, Skippy, why don't you tell me what Dennis is really doing since you seem to know so much."

Skippy paused long enough to take a deep drag off the Bud as if this was going to take a lot of energy. "Well, I'll tell you, I really don't understand it all, not being a geek—uh, I mean, not being a real scientific kind of guy—but Beaver here has got some kind of magic machine he keeps in the trunk of that Volvo he drives."

"It's a Saab, dumbass, not a Volvo, which you would know if you weren't so damn provincial," said Dennis with the slightest hint of amusement.

"Provincial?" Skippy reared up from his slouch. "Who you calling provincial?"

Seeing the grins going back and forth between Abra and Dennis, Skippy took on a questioning tone as he asked, "Hey, what does provincial mean anyway? Is that some kind of insult?"

Now it was Dennis who took a slow drag off his Bud. "Naw, Skippy, it ain't no insult if you're from Texas. Just a normal state of being."

Skippy looked down, as if deep in thought, nodded to himself as if he had digested the idea, and then looked back at Dennis. "Well, I guess that's okay, so long as it wasn't an insult." He pointed his finger again at Dennis with a "you better not be jacking me" look.

Having made his point (at least in his own mind), Skippy turned what was left of his attention back to Abra. "Anyway, like I was saying, Beaver here has this magic box that looks like a metal detector made with a dashboard out of a '59 Buick. It has a bunch of gauges that measure all kinds of weird stuff like gravity and density. Anyway, he's been trying to act cool, but I can tell this hill is really freaking him out. The other night, he came home so upset that he looked like he discovered an atomic bomb under the city park."

Abra looked back at Dennis and said, "Well, how about it, Dennis? Is Skippy right? Do you really have a magic machine in the trunk of your Saab?"

"Not really magic, just a machine no one else has. To be honest, Goliath hired me to get to see my machine in action. That's why I'm keeping my readings to myself as much as possible."

"So they won't let you go?" asked Abra.

Dennis paused a minute and looked her in the eye with a serious look. "No, so I can hang on long enough to find out what's inside of this hill. There is something here that exists nowhere else anyone knows of."

"Yeah, sure. You guys are just pulling some crap on me, aren't you? You're not really serious? That machine can't do all that, surely!" exclaimed Abra, intrigued by the boldness of Dennis' statements.

Dennis was like many underdogs. You could make fun of him, but he could not stand someone making fun of his invention. He returned her stare for a long second, as if pondering some brash act, then said, "Wait just a minute." Without another word, Dennis got up and walked outside.

"Oh, hell." Skippy rolled his eyes and put his beer on the table. "You've gone and done it now!"

Dumbfounded, Abra and Skippy stared at each other, wondering if they had made Dennis mad again until they heard the trunk on the Saab close. Dennis walked back in with the machine in his hand. He sat down in the vacant dining chair next to Abra.

Abra and Skippy moved over to see better as Dennis began lecturing like they were a class of under-graduate students. He pointed to a round gauge. "Do you know what this is?" he asked, looking from one to the other.

"No," came the response from both.

"This is a radiation gauge. It measures radiation from natural and artificial sources. There is radiation everywhere—in dirt, in dishes, in houses, everywhere—just like background noise on a radio. When I turn this on, you will hear it. It sounds like static, and this gauge will give you the number of radiation units present, which should be about here on the gauge in international units."

Having impressed all present, he hit the power button. The gauge spooled up to the predicted strength, accompanied by a random, but constant static from the speaker.

"Don't worry. That's the normal reading almost anywhere on earth."

Skippy, having surpassed his thirty-second attention span, opined, "Okay, so what's the deal? It's normal." He headed for the icebox for another Bud. "Anyone want another of Dennis's Buds?"

"Tell you what, Skippy—bring me a fresh glass of water, no ice, okay?" Abra and Dennis waited as Skippy fumbled in the cabinet for a glass, ran the water, and returned to the table, setting it down in front of Dennis. Dennis pulled a sensor out of the handle of the machine, paused for effect like David Copperfield about to make the Statue of Liberty disappear, and quietly said, "Watch this," as he moved the sensor over the top of the glass. Without warning, the needle on the gauge leapt off the scale. The random static turned into a sound like a thousand crickets, and a warning beep like the back-up warning on a truck began to sound.

Abra, and even Skippy, had seen enough public television and science fiction movies to know that this was not a good thing. Abra backed her chair away from the table without realizing it. She looked at where Skippy had been sitting, only to find Skippy in the kitchen, peering around the doorway as if the sheet rock wall was going to protect him. Dennis simply sat there with a resigned look on his face, waiting for them to finish whatever involuntary reaction they were having.

With both spectators frozen, Dennis spoke just loud enough so they could hear him over what was now a solid noise. His words were even and gravely serious. "What you see here is enough radiation to cook this entire town and everyone within four miles to a golden-brown within minutes. Even if you tried to leave, you would be throwing up and sick by the time you could drive past the city limits. By the time you were fifteen miles down the road, you would be dead, and your corpse would be radioactive for the next twenty-five thousand years." Allowing enough time for the blood to run from Abra's face, he quietly touched the power button, and all the sound stopped.

The silence hit Abra like a deafening sound. In the sudden quiet, she realized she had not taken a breath since Dennis placed the sensor over the glass. Taking a gulp, she sat frozen, wondering if it was a joke, trying to sense if she was feeling abnormal. Abra was too dumbfounded to speak. She looked up where Skippy had been standing only to hear Skippy throwing up in the bathroom.

There really was only one question Abra could ask. "What's going to happen to us?"

Dennis's face gave nothing away. He paused deliberately, looked at his watch, and said in a quiet voice, "I'll show you in exactly sixty seconds." He continued to look at the face of his watch as the seconds ticked by. Skippy returned, wiping his mouth with a washcloth, and peered intently at the face of Dennis' watch.

When sixty seconds was up, Dennis told Skippy, "Put the sensor over the glass again."

Skippy looked at Dennis as if he had told him to French kiss a tarantula. "Bullshit! Why, so I can hear myself fry?"

"Trust me," said Dennis and held out the sensor to Skippy. Not knowing exactly why, Skippy took it and moved it over the glass of water as if it contained nitroglycerine.

"Now watch." Dennis grinned at the two white faces staring at him and keyed the power switch. Amazingly, the gauge went to normal and stopped, and the static froze at a quiet background level.

"Is this some kind of trick? What does it mean?" Abra reached out and firmly clinched Dennis arm for emphasis. "Are we going to be okay?"

While Skippy and Abra waited, Dennis took a measured sip of his Bud and looked back at them. "I really don't know." He paused for a long second then continued. "Skippy cut up the vegetables, and I'm not sure he washed the celery first. You may get salmonella if you ate the chicken." With that, he grinned.

Abra's relief was real, but she was not joking when she said, "You better tell me real quick what just happened and if we're okay; otherwise, I'm going to kill you before my fifteen minutes runs out."

Dennis lost the 'I know something you don't know' look. Instead, he looked like he was at a loss for words. His voice was measured and serious as he replied, knowing he had gone too far, "I truly don't know, but I know it won't hurt you. I've tested the water with every measurement you can think of in the lab. Every instrument measures the radiation, but the radiation does not have any harmful effects. Something that causes all the bad side affects is missing, but everything else is still there. It's like friendly radiation."

Dennis warmed up to his subject. The more animated he got, the more Skippy's eyes glazed over, until he finally had to get two more of Dennis's longnecks out the fridge. He handed one to Abra, who drank half in one swig and burped like a lumberjack in spite of herself. Amazingly, no one noticed, and she didn't even try to apologize. A bond had been forged that transcended manners and formality. "The funny thing is, the radiation is gone within a couple of minutes once the water is subjected to any type of atmosphere or light."

"I've been quietly taking readings all over the city, and I've come to three conclusions." Dennis still had his audience. Even Skippy hung on his words now that his unending need for cold beer had been temporarily slaked. Abra nodded for Dennis to continue.

"First, whatever is responsible for the radiation in the water and the other anomalies is a solid, concentrated mass that is unbelievably heavy for its size. Second, it is under the city park at a depth of approximately a hundred feet. Finally, there is a void inside this hill. I don't know how big it is, and I don't know for sure how to get inside, but I know it is there from density tests I've run. The problem is Goliath. I don't trust them, so I don't tell them what I find. I'm not sure they would even believe me if I told them." Dennis saw a deep frown cross Abra's face as he finished the sentence. Taken aback, Dennis looked to each side to see if Skippy was picking his nose or doing something else equally obnoxious behind his back. Unfortunately, when he looked back, Abra was still looking at him, still looking disappointed.

"What?" Dennis looked confused. "What? Did I say something?"

Abra appeared annoyed. "Look, Dennis, I don't claim to be a saint, but I thought you were a straight-up guy."

Dennis looked hurt and confused. "I am a straight-up guy. Hell, half my friends want me to raise their kids if they buy it in a plane crash. So, what?"

"Well, isn't Goliath paying you to do those tests? Don't you sort of owe it to them to tell them about this great discovery?"

Dennis looked relieved. "Let me answer you this way. Two things have convinced me that I really should not tell them—or put a better way—that they don't deserve to be told the truth."

Abra waited for the rest of the explanation. Dennis continued after taking a drag off Skippy's beer.

Skippy looked downright offended, moving the bottle slightly out out of Dennis's reach.

"First, I've caught them trying to examine my machine twice, and I know they've tried to tamper with it to get inside. They said it was a mistake, but I know the only reason I'm on the payroll is so they can steal my technology. I don't have the money to patent it, and they know it.

"Second, I know what they intend to do. At the plant, it's no secret. They intend to blast this bluff off the face of the earth. There is enough rock for thousands of miles of highway under our feet and they intend to pave every one of them. I may not be from here, but I think we all realize how strange and special this place is. I don't think I could imagine this town gone. Could you? If they were straight, they would be getting everything I know. The way I see it, they're entitled to all the loyalty and honesty they're giving to me."

Abra thought for a minute. "I guess you're right. They must be a bunch of assholes." Abra smiled back at Dennis. "So, what do you intend to do now?"

Dennis smiled. "You may be sorry you asked. The truth is I need some help, and I can't do everything by myself. I'm going to have to get out there in the middle of the night to find a way into the bluff since they won't give me a permit down at city hall."

Skippy perked up at the sound of something that might be illegal or improper. "Hey, you mean like the Hardy Boys and Nancy Drew, digging in the graveyard at midnight?"

Dennis nodded. "Exactly, Skippy, just like that." He turned to Abra and asked with uncharacteristic bravado, "Well, Nancy Drew, are you up for a good mystery?"

Abra felt a tingle down her back that she hadn't felt since she was fourteen, hiding behind a fig tree on Halloween night, throwing eggs and persimmons at boys in cars from the next town. She liked the feeling. Sometimes, life was just too damn boring. "I'm in," was all she said.

Skippy was ready to celebrate, slapping Dennis on the back. "This calls for a celebration. Fresh beer all around." He was headed for the kitchen. Smiling at Abra, Dennis didn't even turn around. "Hey, Skippy, is there anything you won't celebrate?"

Skippy came back in with the load, paused with a real serious look on his face as he pondered the question for a few long seconds of his precious time. "Naw." A crease appeared in his forehead from all the deep thought. "Naw, I don't think there is."

Everyone settled in, leaning close around the table as if someone might hear. "Okay, here's what I think we ought to do." Dennis started explaining the plan.

Chapter Eleven

"Can You Hear Me Now?"

John Elvin Wright sat alone in the ham radio shack in semi-darkness. The green glow from the dial of the old ham radio transmitter cast an otherworldly glow on his face. His chiseled features seemed exaggerated, his cheek bones sharp and curved in the dim green light.

A throwback to another time, the shack seemed frozen in the fifties. Ham call signs were thumb tacked on the wall to the point they almost seemed a pop culture wallpaper. Truth be told, most of the call signs were from ham operators long gone, their transmissions continuing out into space far beyond the solar system, much like the Voyager space probe sending its weak signals out, no one listening anymore.

Like the shack, Elvin himself was a throwback to another time. Computers and the Internet had all but killed ham radio. Each year, fewer and fewer of the old operators lit up the ether each night, casting their call letters out onto the sky like fishermen casting nets in a contaminated pool.

Like sperm whales, increasingly alone in an ocean with fewer and fewer of their kind each year, the mundane contacts that used to be so common now took on an urgency and intimacy that was tangible in the air. Ham operators as a group had always been loners, usually disconnected from family and friends who rarely understood the allure of the colored dials, tinny speakers, and numbers dotting the multiple bandwidth lines.

Elvin was more disconnected than most. Transmitting and receiving was not an important part of his life. It was his life, and a much fuller life than most would have imagined. The product of a loveless marriage, his father had been an alcoholic, and his mother a porcelain clotheshorse.

They thought a child would warm their home and hearts. Elvin had been nothing more than an experiment for his parents. Little more than a self-help book that offered promise for their miserable relationship, he had been cast aside as soon as his mother realized he was not going to warm her husband or her home, and instead was going to occupy a considerable amount of her preening time.

The Wrights partied deeply in the hard-drinking, hard-living fifties. They had inherited oil boom money and lived in a big brown Tudor mansion on the north side of Corsicana. Their sporting goods and electronics business on Beaton Street placed them in the public view, and on the surface they got along well. They were well liked, well respected for their success and money, and sought after on the country club circuit for their ability to hold their liquor and entertain with the best of them.

Early in his life, before he was old enough to resent or even understand the slight, Elvin was pawned off on a succession of black maids who worked for his mother. His mother made sure he was impeccably dressed each day before she left for the store, confident that no one could say her child did not have the best.

By the age of six, Elvin had not only learned to accept her daily leaving, but to look forward to it. He had his own world, and it existed at the top of the stairs of the large two-story house that they lived in. To make up for their neglect, his parents lavished Elvin with every toy imaginable from the endless supply available at the store.

The neighborhood children, better off than most, were amazed on the rare occasions that Elvin was allowed to have friends over—not friends really, only other children who were curious to see the toy house that was the top floor. The upstairs was one great playroom full of electric trains, highly detailed model boats with motors that worked, finger paints, and metal model soldiers.

Elvin was a lonely child with little athletic ability. He dreamed of being invited to play baseball, football, or whatever game was in season at school or at the park. Sometimes he got a half-hearted invite to play, destined to be a humiliation since he was always the last one chosen, and even then, reluctantly. Somehow, the same ball he could pass or kick with precision in his own yard avoided him as if he and the ball were opposing magnets when other kids were playing with him.

Left to his own devices, he soon began to play board games, then card games with the succession of maids who raised him. One particular maid, Matilda, was a seasoned gambler. Cursed with a husband who was not, she had, early in her marriage, taken to winning back the money her drunken husband had lost the night before at the old lake campgrounds.

Her skill was born of necessity and the need to feed her own children. Her other virtue was a large bosom that hid a heart as big as Dallas. Her big eyes and simple mind saw straight through the farce that was Elvin's life and parents. No amount of money, clothes, makeup, or jewelry could hide the cold sadness of that house or the engine of their lifestyle, fueled on alcohol and money.

Matilda enjoyed Elvin, and marveled at the imagination that hours left alone playing with a small warehouse of props had created. She found him quick to understand all types of games, and she enjoyed coaching him on the tricks and finer points of strategy. It was not long until he could reason, count, and measure the odds like a seasoned gambler.

By age ten, Elvin could hold his own in a straight-up game of poker. Once he had mastered all the games Matilda knew, he taught her chess so he would have someone to play against. "Lord sakes, you are a sneaky little bastard," she would chuckle when he got the best of her. Always detached, Elvin would look off as if distracted and mumble, "Luck. It was only luck, Matilda. You'll win next time." And somehow, she would. Matilda always suspected that he let her win, looking for her approval and affection.

Matilda made sure of one thing. She made sure Elvin did not grow up to be the little sissy he seemed destined to be at an early age. She taught him about being a real boy. "Elvin, don't you take no shit off those boys out there on that playground. If they hassle you, you get 'em like I showed you." And show him she did.

Drawing on experience acquired in a far different neighborhood and background, Matilda showed Elvin a few moves that middle-class boys did not learn at the local grammar school. Elvin was not small, and after the first few times he proved himself, he found he rarely had occasion to fight. There was not enough interest in him at school to make him a target. He was left alone and liked it that way.

At the age of twelve, two days before school started again, Elvin's life changed forever. He was waiting at the table, drinking a cup of coffee while his mother fussed, gathering up her glasses, keys, purse, and adjusting her clothes in front of the mirror on the hall door, admiring her figure.

The phone rang. His mother answered and was quiet. Watching her out of boredom, Elvin heard her say something like, "Well, I'm so sorry to hear that. It certainly puts me in a bad spot, but I'm sure she didn't plan for this." Elvin's interest was already aroused before he heard the word "she." He knew something bad had happened to someone, and he figured out who it was from the way his mother was perturbed, despite the phony protestation of sorrow. "Well, you let me know when the funeral is and if we can do anything for you, okay? Well, goodbye."

By the time the phone hung up, Elvin had put on his best poker face. Whatever was fixing to happen, he was not about to show any concern to his mother. She might get a conscience attack and decide to stay home. At this point in his life, he could accept almost anything without emotion. This one almost pushed him past his limit.

Joan. Elvin's mother was named Joan. Somehow, she had never been mom or mother to Elvin, only Joan. On the rare occasions he had to address her as something, he usually settled for "Mother." It was more of a title. Something she was entitled to by virtue of giving birth to him. He did not dislike her in any way. She was more like a guest in a hotel who stayed down the hall, only she made sure you were taken care of. Sort of like a concierge at a fine hotel.

"Elvin, we have a little problem, and I don't want you to get upset, especially not while we have a big sale starting." Elvin's eyes were wary, but he steeled himself unconsciously as he continued to eat his jelly toast and drink his coffee milk. He waited for the ax to fall, and fall it did, with little ceremony. "Matilda had a stroke last night and died. I don't know why she couldn't have waited two more days until school started."

At that moment, Elvin did something he never had done. Looking straight at Joan, making sure he caught her eyes as she tried to avoid him by pretending to fuss with something inside her purse, he said in a quiet tone, "I'm sure she did it just to inconvenience you."

Joan rarely listened to her son. She thought she did. She acted as if she did. But truthfully, she listened only enough to nod uh-huh, or answer in a more or less appropriate way. Dumbfounded, she could only stare as she realized the depth and maturity of his sarcasm. Mentally, she calculated his age and realized that he was twelve years old.

"Well, that was a terrible thing to say, and I think you should be real sorry for saying it."

"I'm sorry, Mother," he said, and took a bite of his toast, leisurely chewing and washing it down with a swig of coffee milk. "I guess I was just upset." His smile was thin, extremely thin.

Joan seemed relieved at the apology. Maybe she had misunderstood what he said. "Sure you were. After all, she's been with us for— Well, for—"

"Seven years, Mother. She's been with us for seven years." Elvin continued to eat and was startled when his mother hugged him over the back of his chair. Wanting to recoil from such unwanted intimacy, he forced himself to endure the hug, and even worse, the kiss on the cheek that followed, complete with a healthy dose of Chanel Number Five.

Joan took his measure as she began to speak. "Do you think you're big enough to stay by yourself? It's only two days until school starts, and I can't possibly find anyone on this short of notice. Tell you what. If you can, we'll go to the store, and you pick out anything you want to pass the time. What do you think?"

"Sure, Mother; I think I can do that," he answered, relieved as she let him go, having gotten the response she wanted. Elvin knew this was a big opportunity. He had more toys than anyone, but there was an unwritten rule at the store. He was expected to pick something that had been in stock a long time, or that was out of season, or that was a special or floor demonstrator—something not likely to sell soon or make a big markup. His training at Matilda's hands and the many hours listening to the stories of how she turned bad luck into good had taught him to recognize and seize a good opportunity.

Thankfully, Elvin did not have to fake the few tears that rolled down his cheek. They were genuine. Matilda was the dearest human being in his life, and he knew he would never again have a friend and mentor like her. He would mourn her in his own space upstairs, but a few tears were all he would allow himself in front of his mother. After all, greater sympathy meant greater freedom at the store, and he knew exactly what he wanted.

Later that morning, under the glare of his father's disapproval at that many dollars in merchandise leaving the store, Elvin carried out a Grundig short-wave radio and big Jason telescope and put the boxes in the cavernous trunk of the big Buick Electra 225. Comfortable that her son continued to have more of the best, Joan left him a tuna sandwich in the Frigidaire and emergency phone numbers under the magnet on the fridge door.

From that point on, Elvin raised himself and did pretty much what he wanted. He marked time at school, easily made exemplary grades, and appeared mildly interested at the usual school activities. Late at night, he spent his time listening to foreign broadcasts from all over the world on the big shortwave radio with the wire antenna he strung around the eves of the house.

On clear nights, he would view the cold stars and sterile planets visible in the big Jason reflector telescope. He could even see a few galaxies and the belt of Orion and wondered what or who could be out there. Gradually, he began living less in the world of high school, and more in the world of starlight and radio waves.

By the time he graduated from college with a psychology degree and went to work for the state school, both his parents were dead, and his slow inward decline to self-imposed isolation was almost complete. He leased the Corsicana mansion out for the income and moved back to his grandparent's home on the west side of the bluff in Tejas Hill.

Elvin didn't give a rat damn that the neighbors in their big new houses resented his old farmhouse sitting in the middle of the prettiest eighteen acres on the bluff. Unconcerned with his own physical sur- roundings, he valued the sweeping vista off the bluff and the unrestricted view of the heavens much more than the old farm house falling down around him. At work, Elvin spent his days interacting with his fellow employees and patients as little as possible and without any emotional involvement. In a perverse way, his detachment made him the perfect psychologist—able to divine everyone's emotional and mental problems but his own.

Unknown to Elvin, others had watched the hill since the night that changed Little Eagle's life. Time for them was relative—just another force they could manipulate. Their knowledge allowed them to live hours in seconds, or seconds in hours. Time was a highway on which they could go faster or slower. It was their choice, depending on their needs, whims, wants, or goals. For thousands of years, the lights in the sky that ignored gravity had been drawn to the hill with its unbelievable characteristics.

Tesla had it right. It was all magnetism, electricity, and plasma, just like the medicine show. No one on earth had yet mastered the complicated and delicate combination of powers that allowed a craft to make a ninety-degree turn at 5000 miles an hour without vaporizing the passengers into goo against the wall. The watchers had, but they recognized that this hill hid something even they could not understand. Long bored with mutilating cattle and interbreeding experiments with humans, they longed to know the secret in the hill that caused the unbelievable readings on their screens.

Their long, gray, slender fingers and large, dead shark eyes could do much. They could bend gravity and light. They could walk through walls and float above the ground. They could even skip back in time or to the future for brief moments when threatened. But there was one thing they could not do. They could not land, dig, move dirt, and uncover the powerful chunk of outer-space material that lay in the pool at the core of the bluff. They knew only that it was something even they did not understand, and that was a rare thing indeed.

Even if their bodies could have stood the light and the gravity for long periods, they could not hide themselves or their craft. Manual labor was not big with the aliens. Hell, for that matter, neither was eating, sex, or emotion as we understood it. What to do? What to do?

Too bad they could not recruit a human to get the work done, but how would you communicate with or even find such a human? You would have to make contact. It would have to be someone out when you were there at night above the hill. It would have to be someone you could reach in some way or on some band no one else would likely receive. It would have to be someone who was cold and detached enough from human society to first believe, then accept, then help. It would have to be someone like—yeah, someone like Elvin.

They were nothing if not patient. They watched the young boy visiting his grandparents on the hill with his primitive glass scope. They even made sure he saw them enough to be confused, then tantalized. They monitored the primitive communications and mundane messages that passed into and out of his radio. Night after night, year after year, they watched and listened as he became more detached and less of his world, and more of their world of dark skies and cold starlight.

Gradually, they became more comfortable that here was a human that shared their temperament with an intelligence that was enough, with training, just enough for their purposes. But how to contact him? In code? No, he might not believe. How about an abduction? No, that might warp him to the point he could not be used. A real dilemma, and like much in life, one that was solved by accident.

Since the advent of radio, much of their communication was in earth language. Their natural language consisted of clicks, whistles, and consonants, much like the earliest African tribes they taught to communicate millennia before. Those cave and rock paintings showing floating shaman were no accident.

They needed a way to communicate without arousing suspicion on those rare occasions when weather events, such as electrical storms, weather inversions, and severe fronts nullified their stealth equipment, making their communications audible. The translator that was standard equipment on their craft was perfect for transmitting in the appropriate language on any recognized band.

On December 19, at 2:30 a.m., a most unusual event occurred. A freak winter thunderstorm moved in ahead of an arctic front. The temperature inversion was thirty degrees in ten minutes in the middle of the night. Three crafts were in formation over the hill performing a routine survey of readings in yet another attempt to pinpoint the source and depth of the anomaly.

We can call him Klatoo. It would be no use to try to pronounce his real name, as doing so would sound something like a parrot getting a Heimlich maneuver. Klatoo was on the transmitter at low power, on a ham band with an effective width of two miles. He was triangulating the three craft to pinpoint the signal from the anomaly inside the bluff, a tactic as old as navigation. By chance, Elvin was at his radio, looking out the dark window at the three pulsing plasma lights over the city park. Distracted, he was skipping bands, looking for a signal, when he hit the band Klatoo was on.

"On my mark, number three descend three hundred feet and compress bandwidth for an alternating reading. Mark."

Elvin watched as one of the three craft descended on cue, flickered for one second, and then flared in a pulse of pure plasma. "Well done," came the reply. "Now, please project a gravity grid on center for ten seconds on my mark."

"Klatoo," came a reply from one of the other craft, "visual or subliminal warp?"

After a pause came the reply, "Visual. It's better, and no one will be up to see, in any case. Mark."

At that, Elvin witnessed what appeared to be a dome spider web in ethereal green light spread between the craft for ten seconds. Amazed, he watched the storm clouds skud through the light, distorting the web. He knew he was not seeing things, and he now knew he was listening to the craft he had been watching for years.

Elvin's blood ran cold. His arm froze on the rotary fine-tune dial. He was at a crossroad. In a few seconds, he pondered his options. Best leave well enough alone. What would they do if they knew he watched? What could they do if they knew he watched? What an opportunity! What would they say? Friend or foe? The most primitive question on earth.

In that few seconds, he detached, telling himself it was all in his mind—a fluke, some covert government experiment. But he knew better. He knew.

From somewhere, he saw Matilda in his mind. Her round black face, the big bosom, and that smile that came from knowing how to get through damn near anything. She looked at him like she did when he was eleven and said, "Elvin, don't take no shit off them boys out there in that playground. Don't you let old Matilda down. You as good as they are, maybe better."

Elvin sat straight up, keyed the mike, and said in his best Southwest Airline pilot drawl, "This is KJOL, Tejas Hill, calling unidentified survey craft over Tejas Hill Park, come in. This is KJOL, Tejas Hill, calling unidentified survey craft over City Park, do you read me? Over."

Klatoo did not curse often. His kind rarely felt that much amusement or emotion. He did not do so audibly this time. However, in his mind, he cursed himself for his carelessness. Observing standard procedure upon discovery, the three craft slipped one minute into the future and decompressed one hour into ten seconds. Elvin saw the lights flicker then go out for a few seconds, then come back on.

On the craft, one hour of intense conversation and thought had taken place. Once he recognized the voice, Klatoo was daring enough to realize the good fortune of the moment and persuaded his superiors to allow him to capitalize upon it. Disclosure and communication was approved.

Back in real time, the reply came just as Elvin was starting to key the mike for a repeat call. "This is Mogollon survey craft number one to KJOL. How is our signal coming in, Mr. Wright?"

Chapter Twelve

"Good Neighbors"

Linton Eggleston was the picture of relaxation as he came into his store, sat down, and dialed the unlisted number to the genetics lab in Simi Valley, California. The eavesdropper standing behind the bookcase only heard one-half of the conversation, but enough to get the drift.

"Doctor Xing, a pleasure to talk to you again…Yes, I am well, and you and your family? …That's good to hear…Did you get the tissue sample I sent to you? …Yes of course, you would be getting future samples if we sign a contract and you succeed. You already know the quality of samples I can provide you. By the way, how are we progressing on our little Pleistocene mammoth? …Yes, I knew you would find viable DNA. I can assure you that quality of sample is available nowhere else…Yes, we would be partners in a way. Your success with that sample could guarantee both of us a place in the history books and you a lifetime of notoriety and wealth…Come, come, doctor, you really don't expect me to tell you how I get my samples. Suffice to say, I just open up my refrigerator here on Tejas Hill and pull them out to thaw…Yes, I can provide many other species once you convince me you can breathe life into our little pachyderm friend again…Keep me informed; after all, I'm not getting any younger, and my patience is limited. Now, if you will excuse me, I have a city council meeting of some importance to attend. Ciao, Dr. Xing."

Linton hung up the phone, intending to open the small, well-disguised trap door in the wood-paneled wall when he became aware that he was not alone in the shop. Sniffing the air as delicately as a fussy tomcat smelling a rat, he took in the scent of body odor, natural gas, and WD40.

Absent the natural gas, Linton would have been torn between Kinnerd Irvin and Earl at the general store. However, the faint whiff of natural gas coupled with the weasel personality Kinnerd was famous for sealed the choice. Already bent over to open the panel, Linton instead picked up a small scrap of paper off the rug, straightened slowly, sat back down in the wing chair, and picked up a book. Satisfied that Kinnerd was behind the shelves to his back, he spoke in a measured, calm voice.

"Mr. Irvin, could you please shut the back door before my cat gets out? She has a tendency to go where she shouldn't when given too much freedom."

Startled, Kinnerd decided to remain still. Waiting a very long thirty seconds just to make him squirm, Linton spoke once more, softly. "Come now, Kinnerd, must I get up, turn around, walk behind the bookshelf, and lead you into the light? Why not just come around, sit down, and tell me what you're doing here?"

Caught, Kinnerd mentally canned the story he was making up about smelling gas and needing to check the heater connection. Kinnerd hated anyone who was smart and different from him, and that meant he hated Linton Eggleston more than anyone in town. He hated his soft voice and funny accent. He hated the way he could never find out much about Linton's business, no matter how much he eavesdropped and snooped. Hell, he had even picked Linton's trash on several occasions to see who his mail was from—mostly museums and universities Kinnerd knew nothing about.

But most of all, he hated the fear he felt when he was around Linton. He could not figure why the old man spooked him. He only knew he always felt like Linton could see through him and read his thoughts. Not to be outdone, Kinnerd swaggered around the bookcase and sat down in the overstuffed chair across from Linton.

"Screw you, old man. You may fool the rest of the town, but you don't fool me. I heard you talking about all that Pleistocene pachyderm crap, and I know what you were talking about." Proud that he remembered the big words and satisfied that this revelation would make the old man step back, Kinnerd waited for the reaction with a smug smile.

Linton put the book down gently on the table and turned his gaze to Kinnerd's eyes. With a face as hard as steel and the slightest of smiles, Linton spoke as if he were speaking to a kindergarten child. "I'm marginally impressed, Kinnerd. Perhaps now you can tell me what Pleistocene and pachyderm mean and what you think I'm up to, and then I'll really be impressed."

"You think I'm stupid, old man?" Kinnerd sneered, waiting for an answer.

Linton let the obvious answer pass and said nothing.

Kinnerd grew agitated. "You may think I'm stupid, but I'm not. I know what I heard because I've been watching you. I know you've got some kind of rabbit hole in this place, too, 'cause I know you leave without ever going outside. I can tell the mayor and sheriff's department what I know and what I heard you say, and they'll sure know what to do." Kinnerd nodded for emphasis and waited. Now it was Linton's turn.

"Kinnerd, let me explain a few things to you. First, the Pleistocene was a geological epoch during which mammals not only thrived, but also reached gargantuan sizes. Second, pachyderm is the family from which elephants arose. I really can't convey to an in-bred, half-wit like you how unconcerned I would be about you trying to explain the conversation you think you heard and nonsense about rabbit holes to the mayor or sheriff's department. However, if that will make your pea brain happy, by all means, knock yourself out."

Kinnerd's face flushed scarlet as he got out of the chair, fists clinched, wondering what would happen if he jumped the old bastard. Linton waited, never breaking eye contact with Kinnerd until he sensed the time for action had passed. Looking down, he quietly picked up his book and began reading again.

Kinnerd, confused at his own inaction and somewhat ashamed, stuck his finger out and shook it inches from Linton's face. His voice was just short of a scream. "You just wait, you wily old bastard. I'm not gonna forget what I heard. You may be smart, but I know you're up to something, and I won't stop until I find out what. Then you're gonna be sorry as hell. You haven't heard the last of me. I've got my eyes on you." Turning to leave, he clearly heard the soft retort from Linton.

"Nor will I, Kinnerd. I'll have my eyes on you as well. Now, be sure and close the door on your way out."

Kinnerd could not stop a chill running up his back until the door closed behind him. "I'm gonna get that spooky old bastard," he mumbled as he got in the Ford and gunned the engine.

Chapter Thirteen

"Holy Moley"

Billy Burkhart had a problem. He couldn't get his mind off sin and sex, especially sex. Lord knows he tried. He had been trying ever since puberty. Early on, Billy knew he would have to follow his father's footsteps as the resident savior of the Brush Arbor Fundamental Baptist Full Gospel Tabernacle Ministry. Billy's father groomed him for the job from the time he was three, teaching young Billy how to give tearful testimonies at the tent revivals. The more tearful and repentant he was, the more money hit the offering plate.

Some nights, he was called on to witness two or even three times if the crowd was thin. The women loved the cute little boy on his knees, crying with happiness at the rapture that the gospel was giving him. They all wanted to hug him, wishing the little hellions at their house were more like him. Billy learned early on that not only did women smell better than men, they had all kinds of soft spots that men didn't have.

By the time he was ten, Billy had learned to bury his face in those big bosoms every chance he got and hug back with a feeling that left more than a few women staring at the young man with a surprised look on their face. He may not have learned to say, "Yeah, baby" like Keith Richards, but he had the general idea. All the nice women that invited them home after the tent meetings took the place of the mother he never had. Well, that wasn't quite right. He did have a mother, though he was not supposed to mention it, and to this day, denied it if asked.

When asked, it was second nature to tell the sad story of how his mother died of cancer, leaving his father, ever the righteous man, to raise his young child singlehandedly. He told the story so humbly, and with such tearful hesitation, that it was a rare occasion the recipient was not in tears by the time he recalled the funeral scene where his father vowed to raise their son to praise the Lord with every word and deed, much like Scarlett O'Hara vowing she would never be poor again.

In the story, his mother's name was usually Mary, frail and sick, but with a face burning through translucent skin with the Holy Spirit. He had heard and told it so many times, he could almost see it and believe it was true, especially when he was drunk. Yeah, there was that other little problem. In addition to sin and sex, there was the problem of alcohol and occasionally drugs.

When he was drunk, he let himself remember the day Madge (his mother's real name), left when he was four years old. She had been barely fifteen when his dad knocked her up in the revival panel van in which they carried the tent. Too scared to face the wrath of her stern father, and too sick of her mother's constant preaching, she thought she could find a new life on the road with William Calvin Burkhart, the handsome twenty-five-year-old evangelist. All she got was another stern father and a whole lot more preaching.

William Calvin Burkhart didn't have any choice. The revival business was like the circus business, or any other business, for that matter. Whenever you got a couple of stump preachers together with a bottle of whiskey, shoptalk was bound to follow. It usually started with someone bragging about how large the crowd had been in the last town, or how much money they made at the last revival. After that, the talk always turned to what the latest prayer-offering gimmick was.

Every town was different, and word spread about what the people in a town would lay down an offering for. Sometimes, it was a prayer cloth woven in the Middle East on the site of the crucifixion (actually a yard of cheap red cotton cloth bought at the dry goods store in the last town and cut into six-inch by two-inch pieces). Sometimes, it was a chip of ancient wood said to have been taken from Noah's Ark in Turkey by Biblical archeologists funded through the revival (actually, a half petrified cedar fence post pulled up on the side of the road and split into slivers about the size of a railroad spike). Eventually, the talk turned to the ranks of those who strayed and were caught.

It was common knowledge that fervor in young women came in many forms, and it was a short trip from religious fervor to sexual fervor. It didn't take long for a handsome young preacher to learn to recognize those with longing looks for the gospel, as opposed to those with longing looks for something else.

Every town had its share of unfulfilled wives with dull husbands who didn't have a clue that women needed fulfillment, as well as nubile

single girls longing for something more than their fumbling farm boyfriends could provide. The rules were simple, and those who followed
them rarely had trouble, or if they did, they were a month down the
road when the trouble became known. Never pick the woman with a
husband around, only the one with a husband on the road or out of
town. Never pick the girls with big fathers or big brothers, only little
fathers and little brothers. And never, never stay long enough for the
bloom to fall off the rose. It had to be a whirlwind romance. You loved
them, you would stay if you could, but the Lord had other plans.

Unfortunately for William, Madge had plans, too, and somehow,
she had found the itinerary for the rest of the year while laying in the
back of the van waiting for William to wind up the sermon. Unlike
most of the girls, who never expected to get pregnant, she knew exactly
what she wanted.

Smarter than most, she quickly surmised that the one thing a young
evangelist could not have was an underage pregnant girl trailing from
town to town ready to tell one and all how she got that way. When she
tracked him down outside Topeka, Kansas four months later, she made
him an offer he could not refuse. Take her on the road as his wife, or
face her tearful expose every time he got to a new town. William was
graceful in defeat, and Madge was grateful in victory. Madge sure
knew how to be grateful by that time, having absorbed all of William's
considerable experience and experimenting a little on her own.

Billy had been born later that year, and William soon learned that a
beautiful young wife and a heavenly young son were good for business.
Everyone wanted to help the struggling young evangelist and his Chris-
tian family. The offerings got better and better, the tent was replaced by
rented halls, and sleeping in the van gave way to sleeping in nice ho-
tels. Overall, Madge gave more than she took, but she tired of the road
and the young baby as quickly as William tired of her. By the time William returned to the random pleasures of the road, Madge was secreting
a part of every offering and planning her getaway.

Although Billy would never realize the truth, Madge did not mean
to be cold. She was simply no different from her unfeeling tyrannical
parents. Parental detachment was virtually a genetic trait in her family
line.

It all came to a head one afternoon in Benton Harbor, Michigan
when William returned to the hotel early to find Madge in the arms of

Hardy Harrington, the owner of the local funeral home who had just lost his wife and asked for a private prayer session with the beautiful young Mrs. Burkhart. Yes, he was short, had a cowlick like Alfalfa on the *Little Rascals,* and was twenty years older than Madge. He was also rich, had a big house, and did not want kids. He was just plain perfect for Madge, and with the stuff she had laid on his table, he was putty in her hands.

Knowing how to seize an opportunity, and doing his best Laurence Olivier, William feigned surprise, anger, and indignance. He may have even cried a few crocodile tears. He wanted to shame Madge just enough so she would leave and take the kid with her. Billy was in the next room, supposedly taking a nap, but he heard it all. Even the part before his dad came in.

"Madge, how in God's name could you do this to me and little Billy? You've broken my heart; I can't take you back. I'll just have to go on without you and Billy. I can't take a child away from his mother." William looked so heartbroken that even Hardy began to feel sorry for him.

Watching the performance, Madge knew the play was now or never, and her chance was lost if Hardy left the room without her. "You're right; I don't deserve you or Billy, and Hardy loves me and wants to take care of me. Don't you, Hardy?" she said, shoving Hardy out in front of her like a shield. Caught between William and Madge, not knowing what was fixing to happen, he looked from one to the other in desperation, his cowlick twitching like a Western Auto TV antenna in a tornado.

By the second, "Don't you, Hardy?" delivered with much more force, and with a deadly look he had never seen, Hardy knew he couldn't let the beautiful damsel in distress down. He figured he could get rid of her later. "That's right. I love Madge, and I'm going to take care of her." Hardy's Adam's apple bobbed up and down as he delivered the appropriate response. Madge hugged his arm and smiled back at him; he looked in her eyes seeking approval for his performance.

With that, Madge sealed the deal, shoving Hardy toward the door to the room and picking up her suitcase on the way. Stopping in front of William, she hugged him and whispered in a stage falsetto that even Billy could hear in the next room, "Goodbye, William. Take care of Billy, and tell him I love him. I know you'll raise him to be the kind of man you are." Surprising everyone, and no one more than herself, she kissed him square on the lips with a passion she hadn't shown in months.

By the time Hardy recovered, he was downstairs in the Chrysler with Madge and a suitcase in the backseat. By the time William recovered, he was standing in the middle of a hotel room with four-year-old Billy looking up at him, saying, "Daddy, where did Mommy go?" It was several hours later before either of them realized what a coincidence it was that Madge happened to have her suitcase packed and ready and standing by the door, ready for her to pick up on the way out. Even more of a coincidence that all of Billy's clothes and toys were still in his little chest of drawers in the corner of the bedroom.

William was still planning the best way to leave Billy when he left town when he and Billy reached the revival hall that evening. The town was small and word had gotten out from the desk clerk at the hotel that the beautiful young evangelist's wife had run off with the most eligible widower in town. Secretly glad she was gone, William was nevertheless miffed at the way he had been manipulated and desperate to dump Billy.

His desperation must have appeared to be sorrow to the large crowd assembled to hear whatever William had to say. Hell, it didn't matter what he said; it was gonna be a show, and it sure was. William channeled all his rage, anger, and desperation into the sermon of his life. He talked about lust. He talked about carnal sin. He talked about casting the first stone. He talked about redemption and forgiveness. Sensing sympathy for his plight, he talked about how he did not know how he and little Billy could make it alone—how he could raise a son by himself.

The offerings were stupendous, far beyond his imagination. By the time he brought little Billy down in front of the pulpit, crying in confusion and clinging to his father, there was hardly a dollar left in any pocket in the audience. By the next morning, William had decided he just might keep Billy long enough to get everything paid for.

He could call Madge in a few months and send Billy back on the train. Surely, by then, Madge would be homesick for him and want him back. The revival stayed in town three extra days, and word of the heart-wrenching story of the brave young father and his abandoned son preceded them to each new town.

By the time a few months went by, two men realized two things. Hardy realized Madge didn't give a damn how many women in town thought she was a whore; she wasn't about to leave. William realized he was stuck with Billy, and that might be the best thing that ever happened to his ministry.

Billy grew up, learning the Bible word and verse, and how to work a crowd. He was intelligent and gifted, but by the time he was a teenager, the story would not work anymore, and it was becoming obvious that the little towhead boy with the cotton hair that was so cute when he was a child was not going to grow into a handsome, charismatic preacher like his father.

By mutual agreement, William left him at a Baptist seminary down in Texas at age sixteen with forged school records and a story about an aunt off-campus. Actually, Billy lived on the small allowance his father deposited in a checking account each month in a cheap apartment near the college. Tuition was not a problem after his father paid a special visit to the dean, an old friend from the road, and reminded him of a particularly messy mistake who was now a high school senior in Waco. Billy received a full four-year scholarship. Fancy that.

When he graduated at twenty years of age, Billy had never worked a day in his life. He had never even mowed a yard. His idea of work was a two-hour show three times a week. Billy was disillusioned far beyond his years. He wanted to believe, he had always wanted to believe, but he knew the truth.

He knew that no one had a clue what the truth really was, or whether there was any truth at all out there. He knew you could depend on no one but yourself, and some days, that wasn't even a sure thing. He had a craft. He knew the Jesus game like Ann Landers knew advice to the lovelorn.

When the dean recommended him as a temporary summer replacement for the Tejas Hill Baptist Church, Billy made sure no one wanted a replacement by the end of the summer. He studied his parishioners, measured their beliefs, and modeled his personae accordingly.

When the door closed on the small farmhouse that he made sure was shielded from view, with plenty of warning of incoming cars, Billy shed his spiritual skin like a serpent and did whatever the hell he felt like doing. Weekend retreats were actually spent partying in the Metroplex clubs. Friends and lovers of both sexes were met and had, but never invited back.

That particular Saturday night Billy was home recuperating from a hangover with a Shiner Bock when he saw the little headlights of Kinnerd Irvin's Ford coming up the lane. Deliberately setting the Shiner behind the couch, Billy clicked the satellite off the Penthouse channel and onto Pat Robertson. *God, what a stale old bore*, thought Billy as he combed his hair and put on a fresh T-shirt before Kinnerd hit the door.

Billy let the bell ring twice before he opened the door. "Kinnerd, what a surprise. Come on in. Is there something wrong?"

Kinnerd walked in the door, scanning one eye to the left and one to the right, sniffing the scene like a Brangus bull behind a heifer in heat. "Well, I really hate to bother you, preacher, but we got this here report of gas fumes in the area, and I figured I better check everyone's gas lines to see if I can find a leak. You don't mind that, do you?" Kinnerd looked Billy straight in the eye to see if he could detect the customary combination of disgust, fear, and just plain anger that most people tried so hard to hide. Kinnerd knew that he creeped people out—and he loved it.

"Of course not, Kinnerd. All of my parishioners are welcome here anytime, for any reason. People living by the Word have nothing to hide. Why don't you look around, and I'll fix you a nice glass of ice tea while you do." Kinnerd was already out of the living room and headed down the hall, opening closets and drawers that could not possibly have anything to do with a gas leak.

Billy took his time getting ice, knowing that Kinnerd was rummaging through his bedroom by the sounds of drawers being opened. He was too careful to leave anything out where a fool like Kinnerd could find it. When he had two glasses fixed, Billy strolled down the hall, peeking into the bedroom to find Kinnerd on the floor looking under his bed. Leaning down so he could catch his eye, Billy smiled, "Find anything interesting down there, Kinnerd?"

This time it was Kinnerd's turn to be surprised. "Oh, Lord, preacher, this ain't what it looks like. That gas is damn funny. Oh, shit, excuse my French. It likes to pool in low spots like under the bed here."

"Do tell, Kinnerd. I didn't know that." There was a thoughtful nod of the head as if Billy were taking in that bit of gas utility wisdom as law. "Tell you what—when you're through searching, why don't you come in the living room and drink this glass of ice tea I've got for you?" With that, Billy wandered back into the den and sat down on the recliner with the nice crocheted throw that Mrs. Binfield had knitted for him last Christmas.

Kinnerd followed, sitting down in the other chair, and picking up the ice tea left on the table without waiting to be asked. He took a deep drink and reared back, reclining the Barco lounger. Billy was concerned. He was used to Kinnerd acting strange. Hell, everyone was used to that. But this was different. Kinnerd was making himself too damn comfortable, acting like he owned the place. Billy knew "up to something," and Kinnerd was definitely "up to something."

"What you watching, preacher?" Kinnerd actually reached for the clicker and began to flip through the channels.

"Well, Kinnerd, I was watching Pat Robertson. He just inspires me so that I always try to make sure I know when he's on." Billy spoke while thinking, *So I can be sure and find something decent to watch.*

"He's a little deep for me, preacher. Mind if I find something a little more fun?" Kinnerd had a downright leer on his face as he asked the question.

"No, of course not, you find whatever you want to watch, Kinnerd." Billy was downright astonished now. Kinnerd was clearly up to no good, and Billy had a feeling it wasn't going to take long to get to the point. It didn't.

Kinnerd clicked by the Discovery Channel, A&E, the Home and Garden Channel, the movie stations, and then he paused, hit the "favorite" button, and on came the Penthouse Channel. "Well, preacher, ain't that strange? I just hit your "favorite" button, and up comes the Penthouse Channel. You watch that much?"

Billy took his time and responded slowly. "Of course not, Kinnerd, the boy that set the system up must have put that in. I never use that button, so I guess I didn't know it was there."

Looking up at Kinnerd, Billy found him absorbed reading the paper as if the conversation was long gone, until he said, "Sure, preacher, and I guess that boy highlighted the TV guide in yellow for his favorite Saturday night porno fest." Kinnerd punctuated the question by holding up the page with the highlighted program schedule. The highlighter was still sitting on the end table between the lamp and Kinnerd's ice tea.

Billy had seen enough cons and shakedowns to last a lifetime. He had seen them rough, smooth, violent, subtle, and every shade in between. He had never seen one as raw and effective as Kinnerd had just played on him.

How did that stupid son of a bitch know that favorite setting? Then it hit him. Kinnerd had been in the house before. He had heard rumors that Kinnerd occasionally went into houses when people were gone, using a claimed gas leak as an excuse. That's how the sneaky little son of a bitch knew about the button, that and the highlighting, too.

"You know, Kinnerd, you really do have a problem with breaking into houses. You ought to let me counsel you on that."

"Yeah, preacher, we'll see about that some time, but right now, I really could use a beer, so why don't you get us one each, and we'll watch what you were planning to watch anyway until I get ready to tell you why I really came out."

With that, Kinnerd dismissed Billy, seemingly mesmerized by the girls in bikinis playing volleyball while his eyes independently followed two different sets of bouncing breasts. Billy got two Shiners, handed one to Kinnerd, and sat down. There wasn't much to do but wait, so he nursed his beer and waited. Soon enough, the main late night porno event came on.

It was the usual set up. Young coed house-sitting when the owner's friend shows up. One thing leads to another and quicker than you can say, "Hi, my name is Bambi," they're both naked under a sheet that always seems to hide the best parts.

"That's pretty good stuff, isn't it, preacher?" Kinnerd's leer seemed larger with the horn-rimmed glasses magnifying his roving eyeballs.

"I wouldn't know Kinnerd, I don't watch that stuff. I just marked it to study for a seminar I'm giving in Tyler on the harmful effects of pornography."

"Sure you were preacher, sure you were," said Kinnerd with a chuckle. "This stuff's okay, but what do you say we watch some real porno?"

"Whatever you want, Kinnerd; you've got the clicker."

"Yea, I sure do, preacher, and I've got a new flick, too. I picked it up on DVD up at that porno shop on the freeway. You got a DVD player?"

"Sure," Billy replied. "Right inside the cabinet there."

When Kinnerd mentioned a porno flick, Billy felt a wave of fear and nausea in his gut. Then when Kinnerd mentioned DVD, it subsided just as quick. DVDs only came out in the last couple of years. That was okay. Everything was okay. Then Kinnerd popped the DVD in, hit the scan button, and he saw the title—*Young Cheerleaders in Heat*. Billy's

Adam's apple locked up as his throat closed. It was like watching a horror movie where you knew when the monster was going to show up.

Sure enough, about ten minutes into the film, Susie pulled off her cheerleader top, took off her shorts and panties, and climbed onto a man in the bed. The camera scanned into a long close-up of the young stud with a satisfied smile on his face interrupted by the rhythmic movements Susie was making. There was no mistaking the face or the hair. Billy's life just about flashed in front of his face. He sat frozen, waiting for the ax to fall.

Kinnerd was having the time of his life. Preacher Billy was sitting over there as if somebody had rammed a broomstick up his ass to his neck. His face was ashen, and he looked like the beer in his hand was going to fall out when that girl climbed on top of him.

"You know something, preacher?" Kinnerd grinned as he waited for Billy to turn and look at him. "I could have sworn that was you that girl just climbed on. Let's go back and see."

Kinnerd sat the chair up straight, hit the rewind button, and stopped just as the camera panned his face. Then he hit the slow motion button. People having sex look stupid enough. In slow motion, Billy looked so depraved and sinful it almost made him sick.

"That is you, preacher. What you doin' in a cheap porno film like this? Hey, preacher, you hear me? What you doin' with that girl on top of you? Was it good, huh?" This time, Kinnerd reached across and punched Billy in the arm to make sure he got it.

Billy knew this kind of situation had one outcome. You gave them what they wanted until you could do whatever it took to get rid of the problem. Billy remembered the guy who shook down the most famous radio evangelist in the fifties. They found the new car he bought in the river. No one could ever figure out why the accelerator was hung wide open.

"What do you want, Kinnerd?"

Kinnerd seemed to ignore Billy, intent on the oral sex the girl was now performing. "Well, what I want right now is for you to get me another beer and leave me the hell alone while I watch this. We'll figure out what else I want later. By the way, preacher, don't think you can destroy the disc. I bought several, and I know where to order more. You ought to have been more careful when you were in college. Damn, look at that girl go."

The rest of the evening was a blur as he got Kinnerd whatever he wanted and waited for him to leave. When Kinnerd did finally leave, he turned at the door and said, "Preacher, you best get ready to pay, and I don't just mean money. I might want some of what was on that film, if you know what I mean. You might explain your way around that coed. Hell, any man in town would take that, but you ain't going to explain your way around your buddy Bruce, or whatever his name is you're playing with later in the film. I'll be in touch." With that, he strolled over to the Ford and gave a friendly wave as he headed out the drive into the dark.

Billy's mind was seething. He remembered the night. They were all drunk and smoking hash. His friend told him the video was just for fun. He should have known people that do that for fun don't have expensive cameras and lights. Anyway, that was twenty years ago. They must have remastered the film and put it on DVD. "What can I do? What can I do? What would Dad do?"

Suddenly, he knew the answer to that. His dad would have told him to look to the word of the Lord. What would the Lord do? What did the Lord do to his enemies? That was easy. He smote them down. Every time, he just smote them 'til they were dead and gone. The panic subsided. Billy began to think rationally. He just had to be sure he did whatever he decided to do right. It had to be right. Absolutely right.

Later that night, Billy went to bed and slept, dreaming peacefully, seeing Dad behind the pulpit, and thinking about Madge, the crowds, and the flowers. He was on his knees, testifying and crying, and the people gave money, and Dad was happy. Everyone was happy. It was a wonderful dream, and in the morning, it all did seem like a dream. Pretty soon, it would be just that, a bad dream.

Chapter Fourteen

"SMILE FOR THE CAMERA"

Abra opened the door to the antique shop slowly, the heavy hinges squeaking, announcing her presence before she could say a word. The shop felt old. As soon as you were inside, the light seemed to change. Outside, the sun was shining; the air was clear. As soon as the door closed, the air seemed as if in a fog.

The sunlight filtering through the beveled door glass lit thousands of small dust particles, like tiny pieces of flotsam in an ocean of air. The draft from outside turned the dust into small dust tornados, swirling toward the corners of the room. The air had that heavy smell of eternity. The same smell that you remembered from your great-grandmother's living room. You know—the room she never opened except when company came. The smell a room gets when it isn't ever used and rarely cleaned.

Abra was about to announce herself when the now-familiar voice spoke from behind the bookcase. "Come in, Miss Avant. I've been expecting you."

Abra turned to the right, toward the bookcase, expecting to see Linton coming around the end to meet her. When he did not, she turned to the left, only to find Linton standing less than a foot away, smiling at her. Trying to cover the involuntary gasp that escaped her lips, she could not help being angry with herself. This was about the third time he had startled her, and she made a mental notation not to be startled by him again, no matter how fast he could move.

"Mr. Eggleston, you certainly have a way of appearing where you're least expected, but then, I can't help thinking you're well aware of that."

"Oh, goodness, my dear, someone of my age is just glad to be able to move at all." Linton laughed easily as he led her through the stacks to the familiar leather chairs. He waited until she was seated before sitting down himself.

"Now, surely you can't have gone through all the material I gave you the other day. I only have so much in the way of reference material, and I would hate to run out too quickly and lose the pleasure of your visits."

While the words sounded like something an old man would say, the look in his clear green eyes sent a very different message. She could not mistake the meaning, and she could not mistake her reaction. Instead of the revulsion someone her age would normally feel toward someone his age, whatever that was, she felt excitement instead.

"No, that's not why I'm here. I have family ties to Tejas Hill, and part of my inheritance from a great aunt was several volumes of photographs and newspaper articles. I've been trying to identify relatives and related families without much success. It seems that all of the people in my family who might know are dead. Connie at the café told me that you might know since you're—" Abra's voice trailed off as she realized what she was fixing to say.

"I believe the term is 'older than dirt,' my dear, and yes, I might remember some of the older generation." Linton smiled, but he did not look particularly amused.

"I don't want to bother you. If this is a bad time, I can come back later." For some reason, Abra was getting cold feet and wishing she had a graceful way to get out the front door. It had all seemed like such a great idea. A way to trip Linton into facing the reality she was already fully aware of. The same face in two different centuries, four generations removed.

How better to test his reaction than to casually enlist his help under the guise of identifying people in old pictures. Harmless and safe. Yeah, the only problem was she was not feeling harmless or safe right this moment. She was almost on the verge of getting up and rushing out when he stood.

"Just let me get us a nice cup of jasmine tea. I find it very soothing, and you look like you could use a minute to get those volumes organized. Why don't you use the work table over there, and I'll be right back."

He started to walk away, and then did something that almost made her believe he could read her mind. He turned, as if a thought had just occurred to him. Kneeling in front of her, he took her hand for the second time, looked her in the eye and said, "Don't worry, Abra. Whatever it is you think you have found, or whatever it is you think cannot be explained can all be made clear. I have lived on this earth long enough to know there are few real mysteries, and those who truly seek answers usually find them."

With that, he was gone. She heard him in the kitchen area, getting cups and running water. By the time he returned, she had regained her composure and was ready for whatever would happen. She had traveled too far and waited too long for this encounter, and she intended to play it out, whatever the cost and whatever the outcome.

"Here, try this; I added some honey and one crushed mint leaf. I hope you don't mind, but I find the combination irresistible."

Abra picked up the cup. It was warm and comforting. The steam coming off the cup carried the scent of jasmine—almost like honeysuckle in the spring. It made her think of the honeysuckle vines along the church wall in kindergarten, full of small white blossoms. She remembered pulling the blossoms and twisting the center stem out from the bottom to get the small drop of dew that held the essence of the flower. It was like a tiny drop of heaven. Sweet and heavy with the flavor and perfume of the flower. You could never get more than that hint of flavor, no matter how many flowers you picked and peeled.

Wasn't that the way of life? Everything perfect and desired was only available for fleeting moments, in small amounts. Maybe that was best; maybe we couldn't stand too much of those things that are truly precious.

Abra took a sip. Looking up at Linton, she smiled. "This is perfect, it couldn't be better." They sat for a few minutes, drinking their tea in silence punctuated with small comments and snippets of idle conversation. Gone was the tension that had been there, replaced with the comfort of two people enjoying each other's company.

Soon, Abra found herself talking about her life in New Orleans with Linton as if he were an old friend, telling him things she rarely told her closest friends. He listened well, seeming to understand what she said, but more importantly, what she did not say.

That was rare in a man. Most men saw life in black and white, while women saw life in a hundred shades of gray in between the two. Most men had little interest in feelings and instincts; the very things that most women lived by. She could tell that Linton was different, and before she knew it, the tea was gone.

"Well, shall we look at the dusty photographs and see who we can resurrect from the dead?" Linton did not wait for her to answer; moving to the worktable, he turned toward her, as if waiting for her to spring the trap. She moved to the table and picked up the first volume.

"Okay, this is my great-aunt Edith's album. I think she was collecting photos almost before there were photos. Take this photo for instance; this is from the dedication of the college in 1868."

The photo was a panorama, the kind of picture taken to record an important event—everyone in their finest clothes, facing the camera, usually with the somber face expected at that time. Abra wondered what the people really looked like, if they smiled, and what they acted like. Surely, they had a sense of humor. Lord they would have had to, living and raising families in a world without the conveniences we enjoy now.

"This is my great-great-grandfather, Edward Avant. He was from Scotland and was the stonemason in charge of building the college." She pointed out the man in the first row in the center wearing polished black boots reaching almost to his knees kneeling in front of a larger group of workers, masons, and citizens. It seems everyone turned out on that day to be in the picture, kids included. "Unfortunately, I have not been able to identify anyone else in the picture. I know he had his mother and father alive at the time, two brothers, in-laws, and cousins, but I can't be sure who is family and who is not."

"Well, let's see," Linton took out a small magnifier and began to go over the picture, one face at a time. His attention was completely on the picture, and for once, he seemed unaware of her presence as he moved from face to face.

Oblivious to her, he occasionally smiled, as if he were looking at a picture of a family gathering and remembering the occasion. Once, he actually chuckled at a particular face. Abra waited patiently as he moved from the first row to the second row and then to the third, mesmerized at the way he seemed to absorb the scene in his mind.

Finally, Linton spoke, "I believe I can help you. Do you see the third man on the second row from the left? That is your great-great-grandfather's brother, Aldon. Do you see the resemblance? Older, but very similar?" Abra nodded, seeing the face as if for the first time. When Abra looked at the face, it did look similar. "And the woman there on the left side of the first row—that would be their first cousin,

Sylvia. She would have been about fourteen at the time, if my memory is correct, and quite the young vamp. Every young man in town was after her." Abra looked at the picture and then at Linton, amazed.

He kept poring over the picture with the magnifying glass. "Do you see the man on the second row? Right there, do you see him?" Linton broke his concentration long enough to look up at her to see if she was looking at the right person. She nodded, looking back at the face his finger was pointing to.

"That is Robert Wynn, the foreman of the masonry crew. There was quite a controversy at the time. The college board was upset because of cost overruns on the stone and masonry, and refused to pay the workers. There was threat of a strike and worse until your great-great-grandfather intervened and paid the workers himself." Linton chuckled again. "He told the board that they either trusted him to complete the job on time and within budget, or they could find someone they did trust. He paid the workers out of his own pocket until the board decided to stick with him. He was a hell of a man and not someone to be trifled with, I can assure you."

Linton continued to peer through the magnifying glass until he reached the end of the third row. Then he slid the glass to the bell tower, to the man standing in the center of the opening. Looking out over the crowd, his face clear in the picture, his long delicate hands curved over the edge of the columned rail. Abra had been wondering how she would lead him to the face without being too obvious. Linton looked at the face intently through the glass and then looked up at Abra.

"I wonder who that is?" he asked, his face at the same angle as the one in the tower, as if inviting her to compare the face in the picture to his—the white streak in his hair was identical to the streak in the hair of the man in the bell tower.

"I don't know." Abra was telling the truth—she did not know, but she certainly suspected. "I hoped that you could tell me." She looked at Linton. She was not going to flinch.

"Does it look like anybody you would recognize, anyone you know?" Linton's slight smile seemed to mock her, or maybe that was just her imagination. Okay, if he wanted the game, she could play the game.

"Oh, I don't know, does it look like anyone you know?" She smiled back, hoping it looked like she was mocking him as much as he was mocking her.

"Well, I must be honest and admit it looks a lot like me. Do you see any resemblance?"

"Yes, I would have to say there is a definite resemblance."

"How could that be?" Linton's eyes were full of innocent question, with only the slightest hint of a smile.

Abra kept a straight face. "I don't know. I thought perhaps you could tell me."

Linton disengaged, dropping his eyes, seeming to lose interest, and returned to the photograph. Placing it aside, he looked at Abra again.

"Well, do you have any more interesting photographs?"

Abra handed Linton a second photograph. "This is the Fifty-Year Jubilee at the college in 1918. The parade came down Reunion Street." As she spoke, she watched Linton's eyes soak up the picture, lit from within. It was as if his eyes were a movie projector putting the image on the paper.

"Oh, my goodness, I can't believe you have this. God, that was a perfect day. See how the clouds frame the college. It was almost as if we ordered the weather. It was the perfect temperature, the most perfect robin's egg-blue sky you ever saw with clouds like white satin. I think that was the best parade there ever was."

Unconsciously, Linton put his arm around Abra in excitement, pulling her closer to see the picture with him. "The theme of the parade was Greek mythology. Every float had to have a theme from ancient Greek history, literature, or drama," he looked at her in excitement, oblivious to the fact that her excitement was not fueled by memory, but rather by the way he was talking about a parade over eighty years ago, as if he were there.

"Look here, do you see that float? It was modeled after the Trojan horse. The drama and engineering departments cleaned out every old barn in five miles looking for wood to make that horse. It was twenty feet high and held ten guys, with windows and doors to open and look out. Old man Barnes gave the entire engineering class an "A" because of that horse."

Abra began to get caught up in his excitement. She pointed to the next float, asking, "What about this one? Who are those tall girls with the shields and tights?" Linton moved his magnifying glass to the next float and laughed. "Those are tights, but they sure aren't girls. Look close, and I think you'll see the evidence." Linton handed her the magnifying glass with a wry smile. "Check it out for yourself."

Abra looked through the glass to check out the costumes below the waist, already knowing what she would find. "Who are those guys, anyway? That must have taken some nerve in 1918 to dress up in drag, as stilted as things were back then."

She looked at the picture until she realized Linton was no longer looking at the picture, but at her face instead. He waited until she looked up, and Abra could tell that she had somehow offended him. "Do you think it was so different being young then from now? Do you think they didn't think about the same things you did at that age? Guys thinking about girls. Girls thinking about guys. Wondering if you were dressed right. Wondering if you would make it with someone. Do you think we didn't feel the same love, the same heat, the same hardness you felt, and the same softness he felt the first time you found love?"

"Hey, excuse me, I didn't mean to imply that the guys back in 1918 weren't all young studs. I just wondered who had enough nerve to dress up in drag." Abra paused. "Okay?"

It was spoken as a question requiring an answer, and Abra waited until his expression softened and he dropped his head slightly to one side and said, "Fair enough. I guess I read more into your comment than you meant. My apologies." Linton's smile signaled that the uncomfortable episode was over.

"Now in answer to your question, the daring Amazon on the left is none other than Amanda Dahoney's older brother Stewart. Their father had two marriages and two sets of kids twenty years apart. Dan's wife Amanda wasn't even born when Stewart was in college in this picture. The fat, short Amazon in the middle is none other than Billy Carroll's father, William Carroll."

Abra knew Billy Carroll's family from her older sisters, even though she had not grown up in Tejas Hill. She had heard about all the old families from Dana and Sue. Having met Billy Carroll and heard the concert quality of his chamber music family group, she couldn't help but observe, "Gosh, I guess they were in show business even back then, what do you think?" she looked at Linton.

"Looks like it, doesn't it?" was his reply.

Not to be sidetracked, Linton was back on the picture. "Now let's see about the handsome queen on the right. Looks like he's over six feet tall, thin, and has a very distinctive streak in his hair. That would have to be—" With that, Linton paused, knowing that Abra was looking at the same familiar face that had graced the bell tower fifty years before. "Well, I guess we both know who that is, don't we?"

When Abra looked up, she saw that Linton was looking at her with eyes made of steel. Gone was the gentle grandfather figure musing over old memories. Gone was the friendly older confidant she felt she could tell anything to. Instead, it was a visage with eyes as cold and dead as a crocodile and a look that telegraphed one message as clear and serious as the S.O.S. from the Titanic. Tread very, very carefully. Anything can happen to you and may happen any minute.

Moving in one quick, fluid motion, but so smooth that it looked almost like slow motion, Linton stood up and casually placed himself behind her chair, placing his hands on each shoulder, inches from her neck. She felt his long, slender fingers begin to exert a slight pressure on both sides of her shoulders, as if he were going to massage her back. Instead, his hands moved to her neck, then remained still, exerting a slight, but ever increasing pressure.

Abra could hear everything he said at that point because she was holding her breath. Her heartbeat was the only sound for long seconds before he spoke.

"I'm going to ask you a question, Abra, and I will tell you in advance that if you do not tell me the truth, you will not leave this room in this world, do you understand me?" As if to emphasize the point, Linton allowed his long fingernails to dig into the space between each breast and shoulder. "You can just nod yes if you don't want to speak." Abra nodded quickly, finding that much easier than speaking. "Good." The pressure from his fingernails eased off slightly.

"Now, here is the question." He paused and then spoke clearly. "Exactly what do you think you have stumbled onto here, and what do you hope to accomplish with your little charade? Take a little time if you need to, but don't wait too long."

Had Linton been any other man she had ever known, Abra would have laughed, slapped hell out of him, and told him to get real and screw himself. Somehow, she had a feeling that would not work in this particular situation. Intuitively, she realized he was telling the truth about what he wanted—the truth. She took a breath and tried to speak evenly with no waver.

"I think you are the man in the bell tower in the picture taken in 1868. I think you are the man in the Amazon float in the picture from

1918. I also think you are the interpreter in a woodcut of a meeting between Indians and French explorers in the seventeenth century and the
same man in a funeral picture in the cemetery from the 1960s. I don't
know exactly how that could be, but I know it is the truth, especially
after today. You were there when those pictures were taken. I could see
it in your eyes and hear it in your voice." Now she paused to collect her
thoughts and finish her answer carefully. "I don't want anything from
this but to know the truth, to know if I'm right, and if I am, how this
can be possible. I mean you no harm. I don't have any wish to share my
knowledge for money, fame, or any other reason. I just want to know.
Will you tell me?"

Abra went quiet and waited for whatever was coming. She knew
somehow that he could kill her if he wanted to, not because she was
weak, but because he was much stronger than he appeared.

With that knowledge came another startling realization. She had
never felt so alive. Abra felt the veins in her neck beating against Linton's fingers. She waited, knowing they would either slacken, or bear
down. Her fate was not in her hands. She was helpless and totally exposed. After what seemed an eternity, her chair swiveled toward him as
he turned her to face him. She watched his face come into view, and
she looked into his eyes, knowing the answer would be there.

She was disappointed to find no hint of emotion either way. Linton
carefully stepped in closer, and in doing so, slightly parted her knees to
make room for his legs. Abra felt her skirt ride up her leg, making her
feel more exposed than ever. Linton leaned down and cupped her chin
so that her face was inches away from his looking down at her.

"I will tell you part of what you want to know and leave you with a
riddle to solve. I am the man in the three photographs. I am not the man
in the woodcut, but I know exactly who he is and exactly what happened in that meeting with the Indians. I will tell you something else.
That is not the biggest mystery in what you have uncovered. I know the
answer to a much larger mystery. I know why this town is special. I
know the entire history of the place, and I know why the people here
are so different from everywhere else. I tell you this for one reason.
You interest me in a way few people have in a very long time. I ask one
thing. Do not do anything to threaten my world or me. A number of
people over the years have discovered that is not an intelligent thing to
do, if you catch my drift."

Abra definitely caught his drift. Suddenly, his eyes softened, and a slight smile crossed his face as he let his hand leave her chin and brush slightly across her cheek in a light caress. "I will promise you one thing. If you ever ask me, I will tell you the whole truth, but be sure you want it and can handle the consequences. Remember what the serpent did to Eve when he told her the truth."

With that, he did something she never expected. He kissed her gently, but for a long time, on the lips, pausing for more than a moment there as his hands caressed her hair. She should have been repulsed. She should have been angry. Somehow, she wasn't either. Just as quickly, he stepped out from between her legs and walked to the door, leaving her exposed, confused, and suddenly angry. She stood, quickly gathering her photos and folder.

As he opened the door and stood to the side to let her pass, the fading afternoon sun invaded the dusty interior of the shop. Suddenly, Abra wanted to be outside in that sun, in the clear air, among the living, and away from whatever the thing was standing patiently, waiting for her to leave. Once outside, she turned to see Linton disappear gracefully as he strolled back to his chair between the stacks to pick up his book as if nothing special had happened.

Outside, watching the dull autumn sun disappear over the tall oak trees and the house with the gables on the corner, she could almost believe nothing special had happened. Almost.

Chapter Fifteen

"Lets Go for a Ride"

John Elvin Wright felt as free and alive as he had ever felt. Staring into the ghastly green glow of the Halacrafter dial, he waited for a response to his last transmission. Having summoned the courage to call the craft floating over the park, and knowing his message was heard, he felt as if a weight had been lifted off his back. The hard part had been the decision to make himself known and to let the watchers in the craft know their existence was known.

Emboldened with a sense of fearlessness that came from knowing he had done something truly extraordinary and risky, he was about to key the mike and send his call out to the craft again when the speaker came alive. "This is Mogollen survey craft number one to KJOL. How is our signal coming in, Mr. Wright?"

He did not hesitate. The conversation that followed would have sounded very normal to another ham operator accidently crossing the channel.

"Clear and strong, considering the weather, and mine?"

The reply from Klatoo was matter of fact, with just a slight hint of humor. "Quite clear, Mr. Wright. One would almost think we were within a block of each other."

"Yes, I imagine one sure would. By the way, you obviously know who I am, but I don't know who you are." Elvin waited, wondering if information was going to be a one-way street. Apparently, it wasn't.

"Come now, Mr. Wright, you do not give yourself enough credit. You know exactly who and what we are."

"Well, I think I have a pretty clear idea as to what you are, but nothing beats being able to put a name with a face, or a name with a voice, if you know what I mean." Elvin was determined to be treated as an equal.

"You are certainly right, and I did not mean any slight. You can call me Klatoo; all my friends here do." Again, a hint of humor tinted the voice. The translator was good enough to translate emotion and inflection to the extent that Klatoo might as well have been actually speaking the words in English, instead of in the static that was his native tongue.

"Klatoo. How original, given the circumstances, and do you have a lot of friends around here?" This time, the humor was in Elvin's voice.

"Well, as you might imagine, my acquaintances in the area are few. To be specific, I can only think of two, counting you, and the other one is not someone I count as a friend." That was an eye-opener to Elvin, realizing he shared his secret with someone else in town.

"Well," said Elvin, "I guess you count me as a friend or you wouldn't have answered my call."

"That's very perceptive. We do hope to count you as a friend, and that brings up my next question." With that, there was a pause. Elvin waited, and had begun to key the mike when he heard Klatoo.

"Would you be free to go on a little ride tonight? Nothing long, just a little drive around the neighborhood."

The question hung in the air like a concrete block. Surprised, but instantly aware that he was being tested, Elvin knew this was it. He was fixing to be in or out of whatever was going on. In the space of a few seconds, he reviewed his life, and realized that, so far, it hadn't been that great. He was alone and had little in common with his world. He knew that was his fault and not the world's. He would have liked it to be otherwise, but in a funny sort of way, he realized his whole life had been on a road that came down to this one finite point.

He could accept the offer and face the unknown and whatever risk it held, or he could refuse and return to what he had now. Elvin thought, *Damn, I guess that question wouldn't be so easy to answer if I had anything that remotely resembled a life.* The decision was clear.

Elvin replied with feigned boredom, "Well, my dance card isn't booked up right this second, so I guess I could do that. Tell you what— you bring the ride, and I'll bring the beer. You just tell me where to meet you."

"Great. How about we pick you up at your house in about five minutes? By the way, I like Lone Star Light, if you have it. Otherwise, Shiner Bock will do."

"Okay. Great! Just give me a minute for a quick pit stop, and I'll meet you in the front yard. Will I need a jacket or anything?"

"No, we have air conditioning, but there is something that you could bring. Would you happen to have any of those nifty call sign postcards you ham operators used to carry?"

"Yeah, I probably still have a few KJOL cards lying around. Why?" Elvin was caught off-guard at the request.

"Humor me, if you would, Mr. Wright. I think you will be greatly amused if you can bring a couple along."

"Okay, I'll see you in the yard in a minute." Elvin knew he should be scared, excited, amazed—all of the above. Instead, he found himself moving through the house as if he were being picked up to go to a movie. In and out of the bathroom, pausing at the dresser, he picked up his billfold and out of habit checked inside to make sure he had at least twenty dollars. Putting the billfold in his pocket, he picked up his Listerine strips, not wanting to offend anyone. Turning to leave, he remembered his Leatherman tool, a miniature toolbox in the space a pocketknife would normally take. *I might need that*, he thought to himself as he shoved it in the pocket of his jeans. In the kitchen, Elvin pulled a cold six-pack of Shiner Bock out of the fridge and headed toward the front door.

Elvin paused at the door. Suddenly remembering what Klatoo had asked for, he put two of his KJOL postcards in his jacket pocket. Then, without a single look back, he opened the door and walked into the cold blast of wet rain the cold front had brought.

At first, he only saw a shimmer in the air. He saw the crepe myrtle tree in the front yard, the air distorted in front of it. Elvin looked closer, amazed, as the outline of a door appeared, looking like the kitchen door when the garage light is on behind it. The bright outline grew wider as the door dropped down. Elvin saw the bright interior through the door, but on each side and at the top, he could still see the yard and crepe myrtle beyond.

Inside the door, a slight figure in white seemed to move to the door, not exactly walking, but not exactly floating, either. The figure stopped just inside the opening and waved Elvin in with a pale gray arm in a manner intended to hurry him inside, then turned as quickly and more or less floated back to the right and out of sight. Elvin took a deep breath and walked up the narrow ramp, ducking inside a door that was less than six feet tall.

Inside, he was forced to turn to the right by a wall of transparent coils that looked like glass. The coils shimmered with different colors of light pulsing through them. They almost looked like the water-filled glass tubes on an old jukebox, but on steroids. The shimmering wall transfixed him until he heard a burst of static, and the wall disappeared around the curve of the hull of the craft. A split second later, he heard Klatoo saying, "Please clear the door; we cannot remain here for long."

With that, Klatoo impatiently disappeared around the curve, but not before he saw Kinnerd Irvin peeking through the bushes next door and the flash of a disposable camera. Klatoo was familiar with Kinnerd and his nocturnal snooping from their surveillance of the town. Unconsciously, Klatoo vowed to remember to do something definitive about Kinnerd before he became a real problem instead of a harmless crackpot.

Looking back one last time, Elvin watched the door shimmer to a close, becoming solid. He wondered briefly if this would be the last time he would see his home, and just as quickly, realized he didn't give a damn.

Elvin followed the narrow space as it wound around the inside curve of the craft, ducking to avoid hitting his head. The walls were smooth, with strange indentions at various different points, surrounded by symbols vaguely reminiscent of Egyptian hieroglyphics. Eventually, the hall opened into an open space in the center of the craft.

The area resembled a sunken living room from the sixties, tastefully decorated with a seating area similar to a Scandinavian-style circular couch. In the center was a console with numerous controls and pulsing lights. There were three people. Would you call them people? Yes, Elvin felt like they were people. Anyway, there were three of them in sight.

The leader, Klatoo, was seated slightly higher and nearer to the center console. A second "man" was standing, facing the shimmering wall on the other side, adjusting something Elvin could not make out. The third person was female, and she startled Elvin the most. The others looked almost exactly like the aliens on the cover of the supermarket tabloids, to the point that their appearance seemed familiar. Still it was strange to see them move, seeming almost lighter than air. As that thought passed through his mind, Elvin realized he felt eighty pounds lighter. He wanted to jump to see if he was imagining a lighter body, but he couldn't with the ceiling inches above him.

"Does it feel strange?" The voice came from the female and wasn't preceded by the static he had heard when Klatoo spoke.

"You mean the lower gravity?" Elvin asked, and the female nodded yes. "Yes, it feels strange, but good." Elvin focused on the girl. She was human, but different in a hundred subtle ways.

Taking in details without consciously realizing it, he saw that she was much taller than Klatoo, and more pale white than pale gray. Her body, under the shimmering, thin, pleated linen gown was reedy, but shaped in an exquisite manner that seemed healthy. A normal woman would have appeared bulimic with that thin a body, but she did not. She appeared just right for her. To himself, Elvin thought, *Good God all mighty, she looks somewhere way beyond just right*.

Her features were chiseled and thin, like an Audrey Hepburn, but elongated in the vertical plane, looking much like the famous bust of Nefertiti. She was hauntingly beautiful to Elvin, and he was instantly smitten; he was sure his face was red.

She did not look away and continued to gaze at him until he nervously broke eye contact and mumbled, "Uh, where should I sit?"

Klatoo illustrated his answer with a careless wave of long, ghostly fingers. "Anywhere you want, Mr. Wright. We don't stand on ceremony on this ship."

Elvin was beginning to get used to the static, clicks, and whistles that came from Klatoo's black lips a second before the human words came from somewhere on his chest. Klatoo turned back to his console, seemingly happy to leave Elvin to his own devices. Being shy, but not stupid, Elvin chose to sit next to the woman, instead of Klatoo. She seemed to be watching the many hues of plasma pulsing in the wall of glass tubes as the colors increased in intensity and speed.

"It is beautiful, isn't it?" She turned and looked him in the eye as she spoke. "I never get tired of watching the plasma shield when we make space." Elvin could not help thinking how odd the term "make space" was. He would have expected her to say, "When we take off." Elvin tried to think of something clever, or even appropriate, to say under these odd circumstances.

Realizing he was socially challenged and knowing nothing else to do or say, he settled for sticking his hand out and saying, "Hi, my name is Elvin Wright. What's yours?" For a split second, he thought he was back in sixth-grade Spanish class, standing in front of the class opposite Betty Kaye Krownouski, saying, "Como se llama? Mi llamo es Elvin" in a terrible Central Texas drawl. The female seemed startled by the question and looked at his hand as if he had held out a two-pound blue catfish for her to shake.

Sensing his faux paux, Elvin pulled the hand back to his side. She looked relieved, almost smiled, and said in clear voice devoid of any noticeable accent, "My name is Yasha, Mr. Wright." She looked back at the pulsing wall and said, "You might want to fasten the air restraint. With this weather, there might be turbulence."

Elvin looked for a seat belt and could not find anything. Then he saw her touch a small black indention on the cushion near her side. She nodded to him to do the same. Finding one by his side, he touched it and felt a gentle restraint against his stomach and chest. Looking down, he expected to see a belt, but saw only a slight shimmer in the air.

"Don't worry, Mr. Wright; it is a simple matter of density. You can get up if you press slowly but firmly against the restraint, but it will not give if you move quickly."

Klatoo appeared in front of Elvin. "Yasha, do not bore Mr. Wright to death with trivial details before we have even departed." There was humor in his voice, but the statement still had the air of control and warning about it.

Much like a slightly domineering father, Klatoo was clearly in charge of the craft and all inside it. Elvin made a mental note to try to see if he was floating or if his feet were on the ground the next time he got a chance to watch him move.

Klatoo sat down opposite Elvin, and he could finally see that Klatoo did in fact wear leather boots over his tiny feet. He also noted that there were no soles; the sides of the boot blended into bottom and the bottom was as smooth and unmarked as the side. Klatoo seemed to have anticipated and understood his curiosity, and spoke as if Elvin had actually asked the question.

"I really must apologize, but much of what you will see will be familiar if you have read the supermarket tabloids or watched much science fiction. We do come from a place with much less gravity and much less light. We can breathe earth air, but cannot last long under its full gravity. We don't float through walls unless it is absolutely necessary, and no, we are not going to strap you to a table and steal your sperm. But we might have to force you to mate with one of our women if you ask too many dumb questions."

Elvin looked from one to the other and realized Klatoo was joking. Whatever strain or tension he had felt disappeared. Elvin could not help but laugh, and looking at Klatoo's face, he realized the little fellow was actually smiling, or as close to smiling as his strange little mouth and large pale eyes could handle. Yasha was almost howling with laughter for an alien, allowing herself a slight chuckle.

"Well, where would you like to go tonight? The moon, mars, or somewhere further?" Klatoo's question was clearly serious.

Elvin wanted to be accommodating. "Well, I assumed you had something in mind when you asked me to bring my call letter postcards. I'll be happy with wherever you have in mind."

Klatoo seemed pleased with the answer.

Elvin was beginning to unconsciously ignore Klatoo's abrasive static and wait for the words. "Very perceptive and totally appropriate, Mr. Wright. You correctly guessed that I already have a destination in mind, and Mars is it. If you are good at keeping a secret, we can have a little fun at the expense of some of those folks who doubt our existence." Klatoo laid his slender hand on Elvin's forearm. "What do you say, Elvin? Do you mind if we call you Elvin?"

"Sure, I guess I can keep a secret as well as the next guy, so that sounds fine to me." Klatoo's hand was light and cool as he squeezed Elvin's arm slightly. Elvin felt better when it was gone. Elvin did not like to have his space invaded anymore as an adult than he had as a child when Joan hugged him.

"Good, let's get going." With that, Klatoo made a series of clicks and whistles, which were not translated, and things started to happen fast. A three-dimensional holographic display appeared above the console with a guide path much like that in a modern airline landing radar, but tapering up. Elvin became aware of a slight sense of movement as the shimmering wall reached a crescendo of color and pulse. He could not detect any sense of speed or direction. It felt more like a sailboat at anchor, floating on gentle waves. One thing was certain—the craft was no longer on solid ground. As Elvin watched, the air shimmered in front of him, and he was aware that time was passing quickly, although not in the normal manner. He felt as if he were living hours in minutes.

As if reading his mind, Klatoo replied to the unspoken question. "That is correct, Elvin, but it is not hours in minutes, but months in minutes."

107

Elvin chuckled. "Don't tell me, you read minds, just like the *National Enquirer* said."

"Not exactly," Klatoo replied. "A little of that, but also a fair amount of general perception and anticipation. It is rare to pick up exact words, but your excitement makes it much easier than usual." Klatoo turned to the console and then looked back at Elvin. "And yes, Yasha does look a lot like Audrey Hepburn." He seemed to enjoy the obvious embarrassment that caused Elvin and Yasha. "We should be there in about a minute. You may feel a slight increase in gravity, but if you will watch above the console, I will show you the view outside." With that, Klatoo clicked and whistled, and a screen appeared in the air above the console as if it were a life-size picture window. Elvin was mesmerized as he watched the already-large salmon ball of Mars grow. He saw the clouds, features, and vastness of the planet in ever more detail as it grew larger and larger in the screen. No longer a ball surrounded by black space, he could soon make out a large plain with the fan features of a dry river delta.

"Won't gravity burn us up?" Elvin could not help but ask, remembering how the space shuttle heated up when entering the atmosphere.

"Of course not; we are making space. Our craft does not fly through the atmosphere in a continuous motion like a plane. It makes space in the atmosphere, changing position on an atomic level much quicker than you or I can perceive. If you could slow it down and see it, we would appear like a roll of film in which our craft changes position slightly in every frame. This happens at a speed that allows us to move through time and space without actually being in the time or space long enough for the effects of gravity, heat, or other normal phenomenon to affect us. We are here and gone before normal physics can perceive or affect us in any way. That is why you will be gone from home for minutes, not months." Klatoo then turned away, as if he had just informed Elvin how the air vent on his AMC Gremlin worked.

As Elvin watched, he realized they were now hovering about a hundred feet above the plain. In the distance, high, thin orange clouds floated in a sky that was somewhere between salmon and pink. He saw rocks in a ravine and a large mountain in the distance, and then he saw a familiar sight meandering between the small rocks in the dry wash.

Every astronomer and science buff was familiar with the Mars rovers. They were now numerous and patrolled the planet like little ladybugs, rolling along until they found a rock or interesting feature and then stopping to smell, scan, photograph, and drill or collect a specimen if called for. The little fellow below had a small camera mounted at several points so panoramic shots could be made in three hundred-sixty degrees.

"Elvin, would you lend me one of your KJOL postcards?"

Elvin reached into his jacket pocket and pulled one out, said, "Sure," and handed it to Klatoo. Klatoo handed it to the other male and said, "Please treat this for the atmosphere." The male took the postcard to a cabinet and placed it inside. The cabinet hummed for a minute, and the door opened. The male picked up the postcard, which now looked laminated, and handed it back to Klatoo. Klatoo turned to Elvin and said, "Watch the screen."

As Elvin watched the screen, Klatoo touched the console in a spot and the outline of an opening appeared where none had been. The space opened, and Klatoo placed the postcard into the opening as if a hand were waiting for it. Outside, the ground rose up until the craft was floating in synchronized motion with the little rover a foot below, oblivious to their presence.

Klatoo asked, "What do you think, Yasha? Should we put it facing the front or the back?"

Yasha thought for a second and said, "To the back—that way they won't see it until the camera changes direction."

Klatoo seemed pleased. As if on cue, a shaft of shimmering air appeared on the screen above the rover with the postcard floating at the end.

Elvin was getting used to perceiving the edges of the shimmer and could see the postcard was on the end of a nearly invisible arm. A small glob of what appeared to be glue appeared on the back of the front camera arm, right over the S in NASA, and just as quickly, the postcard floated above the glob and then seemed to stick itself dead center over the spot.

"That ought to blow some air up their bloomers down in Houston," Klatoo intoned in a low voice as he floated off to the other side of the craft. Yasha chuckled. Elvin sat dumbfounded as he realized that as soon as the rear camera keyed on, it was going to be filled with a picture of the Tejas Hill College above the words, "You've been talking to KJOL, Tejas Hill, Texas," in red and blue letters.

Klatoo floated leisurely over to Elvin, reached down on the floor beside him, and came up with two Shiner Bocks. Twisting the tops off with his slender gray fingers, Klatoo tapped the two longneck bottles together to get Elvin's attention and spoke to the room. "How about a beer for our new buddy Elvin?" Dutifully, everyone in the crew nodded affirmatively.

Chapter Sixteen

"Houston, We Have a Problem"

Saturday was shaping up to be the biggest day in two decades for General Andy "Ice Man" Anderson. One of the second wave of astronauts who came after the Apollo Project, he had always been in between. First, he was in between Apollo and the space shuttle. Too late for the moon and too early for the shuttle. To make matters worse, he missed all the good wars. A 'copter pilot in 'Nam, he had been decorated for his ability to stay on the ground long enough to get all the wounded out, even though he was a sitting duck in the cockpit. His steel nerves had earned him the nickname Iceman. Like so many others, he came home with a chest full of medals to a country that didn't know whether to be proud or ashamed of him.

Unlike many others, that didn't slow Andy down a bit. He had always believed that he was one of the chosen, destined to make his mark in space. All he had to do was wait for his turn. Unfortunately, his turn never came.

A member of the generation after the glory days of Apollo, he had been on the cutting edge of space science and technology, but by the time the shuttle was old hat, his group of astronauts were an anachronism. The young scientists with their home computers snickered at them behind their backs. One by one, his astronaut peers retired, were furloughed, or reassigned to cushy jobs with defense contractors who owed NASA. That might have been okay for the rest, but Andy was determined to hang on until something great happened for him.

By the time he had thirty years in with NASA, "something great" was a relative term. When the director asked him to be the astronaut liaison in charge of operations at NASA in Houston, he got the message loud and clear—take this or retire. On the face of it, the job description was daunting. Total control and oversight for the operations of NASA control in Houston. The reality was much different.

His job was really PR. After two decades of training for launches and projects that never seemed to happen, he was the best known, most photographed, and most recognized astronaut under the age of sixty-five on the planet. The director delegated the real operation of the center to a cadre of well-trained and well-motivated NASA underlings. They made sure all Andy had to do was approve their suggestions and believe, or at least act as if he believed, that they had been his ideas. Most days were spent in photo sessions and structured tours for groups of snot-nosed fifth-graders from Pasadena or Deer Park, or teachers' groups from places like Panhandle and San Angelo.

Today was going to be different. Today he would be standing on the dais with the president of the United States to showcase NASA's latest group of Mars rovers. There would be cameras and reporters waiting to question him. He had lived for this day for decades. By God, he was going to get one picture worth putting on the mantle. At least he could then take down that picture of him shaking hands with that pussy-whipped Bill Clinton. He never liked that picture anyway.

"Good morning, general." His aid Randy Stuckey saluted as he came in. "Ready for the big day?" Randy really didn't give a tinker's damn either way, but he knew enough to know whose ass to lick, at least until they put the old stud out to pasture.

Andy was busy admiring his profile in the mirror wall in the control center. "Not bad," Andy thought. Not like when he was twenty-five. Hell, back then, he could chase Barbara all night at home, and chase the NASA groupies all afternoon at the motel, then chase Barbara all night again. Although he would never admit it to anyone, he finally had to ask the flight surgeon to give him a sample of Viagra. Probably hitting the scotch too hard before dinner.

"What do you think, Randy?" Andy sucked in his gut and hit his abdomen with a clinched fist.

"Impressive, sir. You must work out to stay in that good a shape." Really, Randy was thinking, *Yeah, you must really work out with that bottle of Johnny Walker Red every night to let yourself go that soft.*

Andy turned from the mirror and sat down at his desk. Randy stood roughly at attention, waiting for whatever inane question the general would ask so he could brief the old fool and make him think all the arrangements that had been in place for days were his idea. "Now,

Randy, I want to make sure everything is ship-shape for the president. Let's go over the arrangements one more time."

"Yes, sir. The president will arrive at exactly 1430 by motorcade from Hobby field."

"Good." Andy gave a measured nod, as if he were approving the time and manner of arrival.

Randy continued, "At 1445, there will be a short meet and greet for local party dignitaries in the main conference room."

Another grave nod.

"At exactly 1500, you will introduce the president with a brief opening remark to set up the live uplink. Then, you and the president will push the button to place the Mars rover online live across the world via satellite and Internet. The president will unveil the first view of the Martian fossil bearing strata and the first concrete evidence of vertebrate life on Mars."

Andy's face was already beaming at the thought.

"Finally, the president will make a few comments on the live broadcast before departing at 1530 sharp." Randy tried hard to look like he really gave a damn. "I know this is going to be a great day for you, sir."

Andy shrugged as if it were nothing. "Hell, son, when you've been an astronaut as long as I have, you've had a lot of great days. Why, I was just thinking of telling you and the staff about something that happened when I was helping design the international space station." Andy stopped to take a deep breath to regale the staff and officers present with one of his many stories when Randy stepped forward. "Sir, I know we all can't wait to hear that story, but it's really important that the staff get ready for the president's arrival. After all, I'm sure you want everything to go perfect."

The "staff" as Andy loved to collectively call them, since he couldn't remember their names individually, held their breath, praying they would not have to gather round the general for one of his historical and lengthy lectures from the days of yesteryear. It was exceedingly hard not to yawn or shift from foot to foot to maintain circulation during Andy's episodic stories.

"You're right, Randy; please give my apologies to the staff. I know how interested they all are in my memoirs."

"Definitely, sir. You can bet they will be disappointed." Randy thought, *Disappointed that you probably won't forget and will eventually tell them one of the same stories they've heard a dozen times.*

"Well, at ease, Randy, and tell my staff to make me proud." He gave a quick salute. Randy saluted back. *Yes, suh, master*, came the reply in his mind as he turned on one foot and left the room.

Andy tried to mentally suppress the look of disgust he saw in Randy's eyes as he turned and left the room. As the door closed on the office full of mementoes and awards from a career that never really got off the ground, Andy let himself ponder the truth for one minute.

For just a minute, he knew he was washed up. He knew he told the same stories repeatedly, and that he made them better and bigger every year. He knew that nearly everything that had mattered to his career was ancient history to ninety percent of his employees. He even let himself admit that Barbara had been faking orgasms for the last ten years and he really was forty pounds overweight despite perfect posture.

In the dim light of the office, his face sank, and he suddenly looked every one of his sixty-four years. Truth was, it was getting hard to find anything or anyone he was important to anymore. Andy reached in the deep drawer on the right, poured himself a shot of Johnnie Walker Red in his coffee cup, and drank it in one gulp.

He might be washed up, he might be old, he might even be obsolete, but one thing kept him going. He had been ready and willing to strap himself into a tin can on top of a glorified bomb and die, if that's what it took to keep America ahead in space. He knew in his heart that he would do it today if they called, and that was no bullshit and no small thing.

Unlike the members of the "me" generation that worked under him, he would give it all for America if they asked, even if he knew that's what the result would be ahead of time, and he would never have a second thought. Nobody could take that away from him.

Andy stood up, put on his coat, stood ramrod straight at attention in front of the full-length mirror on the back of the door, saluted himself, and opened the door to meet the president. As he left, he saw the president's entourage emerge from the side entrance with the press and photographers chasing him as he entered the room. Even a block away, it was easy to see the president.

The first thing that struck you when you saw the president in real life was that he was not tall, and that was being charitable. The second thing that struck you was the way he strutted. Yes, strutted was the only way you could describe it—about like a banty rooster in a small barnyard.

His chest was usually stuck out as if it was supposed to arrive about three seconds before the rest of his body. His shoulders were raised to the point that it caused his arms to swing out from his body as if he had huge arm muscles holding his arms away from his body. The only trouble was that he didn't have big arm muscles.

He was the darling of the defense industry because he ramroded the purchase of any weapon system through Congress, no matter what the cost and no matter how ridiculous and unnecessary the system. If throwing money away could buy security, America had to be the most secure nation in the world under his administration.

Never mind a lackluster stint in the National Guard protecting the border in fighter jets between Louisiana and Texas; in his opinion, he was a great soldier. The phrase "a legend in his own mind" would have been coined for him if it had not already existed.

The president had been briefed on the ride over with the reason for his appearance and the names and pictures of everyone important that he needed to greet. He had a script for his remarks, which his staff always made sure was placed on the podium before he got there, but not so early that it was obvious.

Andy was actually one of the people he did not have to be briefed on to recognize. Dripping with phony sincerity, he worked his way through the line of scientists and minor dignitaries, pausing with the more important people and local party officials for photos along the way. Finally making his way to the end of the line near the stage, he greeted Andy with a brisk salute and handshake, "General, I'm a great fan. It's an honor to be here with you today." That was probably the first honest statement the president had made in public all week, and today was Thursday.

"Mr. President, the honor is all mine. I can't tell you how wonderful it is to have a great patriot and world leader in charge again." People in the president's party loved to use veiled statements with key words like "real conservative," "true world leader," and "great patriot" within their own kind to express their unspoken belief that all who were not like them were the opposite. To him and his handlers, everyone in the other party was a closet communist, weak and without morals.

Secretly, they felt it would be un-American to relinquish power to the likes of Bill Clinton and his party ever again. With the Supreme Court in their back pocket, and control of key states like Texas and

Florida firmly in their hands, there was real talk they would never have to. Like the president loved to say in private, "If you can't win it straight up, you win it anyway you can, and we sure as hell showed 'em we know how to win it." That particular comment always earned him that hard warning look from his wife, who had the good sense to understand how a statement like that could topple his presidency.

Climbing to the podium with Andy and other officials, the president gave everyone a few seconds to be seated as he waved to the audience with a boyish grin that was beginning to wear thin on his sixty-year-old face.

The cameras were close so that no one would be able to tell that the audience consisted mostly of the press from local affiliates and the usual reporters for the majors and cable. After pausing to look down and read the first three lines of his speech, the president jumped right in.

"I'm proud to be here at NASA with a real hero like General Andy Anderson on this historic day. Although we have had rovers on Mars for quite some time, we have only now discovered proof that Mars once harbored complex life forms."

The president looked from side to side with his trademark smug grin, which was really an unconscious expression of pride at delivering the first three lines pretty close to the way they were written. Looking down again, he quickly digested the next paragraph.

"In a few moments, we are going to switch to the live uplink to HOMER, a fifth-generation rover for the first live shot from the planet Mars, showing clear evidence of the existence of vertibur— vertibratal—" The president hated multiple-syllable words and made a mental note to have his staff add vertebrate to the ever-growing list of words like "nuclear" that he had trouble pronouncing.

Continuing, he winged it, hoping it was close enough to fit, "fossils of animals with backbones." By God, all those hours half-asleep at Yale in freshman biology had finally paid off.

"When you see the image, I feel sure you will agree with me that no one from this day forward will be able to deny that higher life forms on Mars are no longer a question, but a fact."

He read the next three lines quick. "So, let's get right to it, general. Will you come help me press this button and allow the entire world, from children in classrooms in Montana to students in universities across the world on the Internet and everyday people in their homes all over this great land watching on TV see this historic moment?"

General Anderson rose from his chair and pressed the large red button with the president as they smiled at each other like two junior high sweethearts getting their picture taken at the eighth-grade dance. The button was actually a fake, and the boys in the control room were holding their breath to hook up to the rover at the exact moment the dummy button was pressed.

On cue, the giant HD theater screen in the background lit up with the odd pink glow of the Martian atmosphere. The detail and quality of the image was impressive to the point of being virtually 3-D. You could almost feel the grit from the sand lightly blowing over the rocks visible in salmon-colored sand.

Looking back to make sure the image was on the screen, the president continued. His staff had told him there would be a slow pan around to the rock with the fossil to give him one final photo opportunity while he showed off his grasp of the rover (acquired five minutes before during his briefing). Turning so he could see the giant screen as he spoke to the audience and time his remarks to end at the highpoint shot, he continued his speech. Making sure his comments matched what the screen showed, he knew that when the front camera panned past the rear camera arm, the fossil would come into view.

"As the front camera of HOMER rotates, you can see the amazing detail shown by this new generation of rovers. Alone in the airless atmosphere of Mars, there is no evidence that life exists now. However, in just a moment, you will see proof that life, much like life on earth, once thrived on this now barren planet."

From his peripheral vision, the president saw the arm of the rear camera coming into view, the "N" of NASA creeping by slowly. Comfortable that his timing was perfect, he abandoned the screen and gave the audience his full attention.

"And now, I give you proof of highly evolved life on Mars." The president paused theatrically, knowing what should be coming on the screen. He expected the usual light applause and audible hum of excitement. He did not expect what happened next.

First, the audience seemed to go completely quiet, as if in amazement. As several long seconds went by, chins actually dropped, as if the people in the audience were truly amazed. The press and camera people got agitated, and he saw the camera operators adjusting their focus to zoom in on the image.

Thinking to himself, "*Damn, this must be a lot better than they told me,*" he figured he might as well get as much mileage out of the moment as he could. Without turning, he ad-libbed off-script, something his staff begged him not to do. "As you can see, this image speaks to us across time and space in the universal language of life. One life form to another," he paused, thinking this was really good, "saying, we are here. We are just like you."

Having waxed about as poetic as his pea brain would allow, he flashed another trademark smug grin. He looked from side to side, about to continue, when he realized that no one was looking at him. The audience and press were staring dumbfounded at the screen behind him.

Sensing movement at his side, he glanced at General Anderson just in time to hear him whisper, "I'm going to kill whoever is responsible for this," as he strolled off the dais, leaving the president on his own.

Still not knowing what was happening, the president finally turned to the screen, only to see a twenty-five by thirty-foot image of what looked like a postcard come into view. On one side was an image of an old building that was somehow vaguely familiar. On the other side, in red and blue letters, was the message, "You've been talking to KJOL, Tejas Hill, Texas."

In the lower right corner, in tiny letters magnified to six inches by the size of the screen, one tiny message had blown every mind present, "Printed at Pound Printing, Houston, Texas" along with a copyright date. The Rover had been launched over two years before the copyright date.

People from the south are familiar with the statement, "He had that deer in the headlight look." You know, that "Oh, shit" look that you get when you realize things have gone hopelessly wrong, and you have absolutely no idea what to do.

In the space of a second, the president reverted to childhood. It was just like when he was twelve and his mother caught him in the bathroom with a *Penthouse*. He swallowed hard, looked at the audience for guidance, but they weren't looking at him.

All of the reporters but one were running toward the back of the room with cell phones out.

There in the front row, he saw Don Samualson, his most hated enemy. Suave, educated, probing, and intelligent, he was all the things the president was not. Don had more contacts in governments all over the world than the CIA and KGB combined.

As a reporter for over thirty years, Don knew how to seize a chance moment in history better than anyone and had the awards to prove it. He had an almost uncanny ability to be in the right place at the right time and then know exactly how to play it. Looking straight at the president, with a cameraman who knew better than to ever leave his reporter, Don said quietly, "Mr. President, could we ask you just one question?"

Normally, the president wouldn't have given Don the time of day and would have taken any question from anyone else, but right now, Don was the only person with the calm to ask one, and he needed the ten seconds a question would give him to think. "Sure, Don, go ahead." The president even smiled hopefully.

With a straight face, Don intoned in his grave, almost funeral voice, "Mr. President, I'm sure everyone watching would like for you to explain how a postcard from Tejas Hill, Texas happens to be attached to the outside of a Mars rover camera." A pregnant pause. "Could you perhaps enlighten those of us here as well as the audience at home?" Don finished the question with the thinnest of smiles.

The president suddenly realized why the building looked so familiar. He had seen that building a dozen times as governor of Texas during campaign and sightseeing stops. It was the old college in Tejas Hill. Struggling to maintain a smile, the president thought to himself, *I'm gonna get that smug son of a bitch audited for the next twenty-five years*, as he foundered for an answer.

Just in the nick of time, Jerrie Hammil, his chief aid and political henchman, came to the rescue. The press said she had balls bigger than a Brangus bull, and she could and would talk to the president like a stepchild when it became necessary.

Right now, it was necessary. Mounting the stage, she whispered in his ear, "Tell them there's been some kind of technical difficulty. Tell them you're needed back in Washington, and get the hell off this stage."

Looking relieved, the president held up his hands to quiet the murmur of a crowd that had largely disappeared except for Don Samualson, standing patiently, waiting for an answer. "Ladies and gentleman, there has obviously been some kind of malfunction. It appears we've picked up a local affiliate instead of the rover. My aid has just reminded me that I'm needed back in Washington for an important function this evening, so I must say goodbye and leave General Anderson and his able staff to finish the presentation. General?"

With that, he tried to exit the stage without running. The last thing he saw as he left the podium was Don Samualson smiling at him with that damn inscrutable look he had.

Halfway to the control room, General Anderson heard the president's statement. He knew an order when he heard one. Without a hitch, he turned and headed for the podium, cool, calm, and in control just as he learned in flight school. His plane might be fixing to crash, but by God, he was going to go down in control.

Smoothing his hairweave across his forehead, Don stepped to the exact right spot in front of his cameraman so that the audience could see the keystone cop mayhem on the stage behind him as everyone struggled to regain order. "Well, there you have it, another fiasco from a space agency in shambles and another example of a president without a clue. This story can best be summed up as 'Houston, we have a problem.'" Don paused theatrically. "Live from NASA Space Center, this is Don Samualson, Independent Cable News." The camera panned out from Don to take in the entire screen. You could see the postcard actually blowing in the thin Martian wind as the screen faded out.

Watching the live feed from far out in the upper atmosphere of earth, Klatoo actually fell off the corner of his control dais onto the floor, his alien laughter sounding like radio static as he beat his little gray arms and feet on the floor of the craft to the amazement of the crew.

Chapter Seventeen

"THINGS AREN'T ALWAYS WHAT THEY SEEM"

Abra stumbled across the street, as if in a dream. Her relief at being free from Linton and the horror she had felt in his shop did not last long. Behind the relief was a fascination and interest she did not understand, and that made her angry and confused. On the one hand, she felt violated, almost as if he had used her in some sexually perverse way.

On the other hand, she knew that along with the fear she had felt, there was stimulation. She had been ready and resigned to let him do whatever he had wanted. He could have killed her, raped her, or done anything in between just as easily a few minutes before. Suddenly, she wanted badly to be around someone, and not just anyone, but another woman. She looked up and down the street, but no one was there. About to give up and find her car, she suddenly saw the neon "Open" sign at Connie's Place. Drawn like a magnet, it seemed it took her an eternity to cross the half-block to the front door. Relieved to see that no one else was in the café as she entered, Abra stumbled into a booth.

Connie had been going through the usual routine, getting ready to close. Put up the ketchup, count the change, that type of thing. When Abra came in and made her way to a booth, she moved like a zombie—white as a ghost and oblivious to everything as she passed Connie at the counter.

Without a word, Connie got a cup of black coffee and carried it to the booth after locking the front door and turning off the "Open" sign. She set the coffee in front of Abra and then sat down across from her in the booth and waited patiently. Abra picked up the coffee and drank deeply without ever looking at the cup. After a long silence, she began to talk as if she and Connie had been in the middle of a long conversation.

"Have you ever felt like you were fixing to die, or fixing to be raped, or both?" She still had not looked at Connie or acknowledged her presence. Connie didn't know what to say, so she just sat there, quietly watching Abra's face as the color slowly returned.

When Connie didn't answer, Abra focused on her, as if seeing her for the first time. "Well, have you?" she asked again, wistfully. Connie thought for a second, and then spoke in an intimate tone that made you think she was sharing a great secret, regardless of what she was talking about.

"Oh, hell, honey, I don't know. Let me think."

Connie appeared deep in thought for a second then her face lit up. "Yeah, yeah, I have. That time Mickey Bailey got the drop on me in the back of his old Fleetwood, I thought he was gonna make a woman out of me until I kneed him in the balls. That'll get 'em every time. That and a Sears and Roebuck girdle are all that saved me." Connie waited.

"That's not what I meant. Not like junior high. I mean for real. I mean the kind of fear where you nearly wet your pants and don't care." Abra was looking off again, unfocused.

"No, honey, I guess I haven't. You want to talk about it?" Connie reached out and placed her hand over Abra's. "You want to talk about it?" she asked again, in a much softer voice.

Abra focused on Connie's face, searching her eyes as if trying to decide whether to tell her or not. Finally, she seemed ready to talk. "Something strange, strange and terrible, just happened to me at Linton Eggleston's shop." Abra stopped, looking to see the effect of the statement on Connie's face. She expected shock and curiosity, but that wasn't what she got. Connie's face seemed to freeze. Amazingly, she almost seemed she was stifling a laugh. "Did you say at Linton's shop?"

Abra nodded. "Yes, I don't know if I can explain exactly what happened to me." Abra looked up at Connie.

This time, Connie was clearly amused. "You don't really have to. Let me guess."

"Guess?" Abra was amazed that another woman, and a new friend at that, could seem so callous. "Guess?" This time, the word was uttered in a louder voice with a hint of anger. Clearly, Abra was fixing to go from pitiful to pissed off. Connie jumped in before that could happen.

"Yeah, let me guess. He got you in a chair. Then he was right over you, and he put his hands around your neck so you couldn't really tell what he was going to do. Am I right so far?" All Abra could do was nod yes. "Then he looked at you with that damn enigmatic smile of his and told you he was going to ask you a question, and if you answered wrong, you wouldn't leave the room alive."

Abra was amazed to the point of disbelief by now. "How do you know? You couldn't know. There was no one there but us." Abra grabbed Connie's hand in a death grip. "You've got to tell me how you know. Am I going crazy?"

"No, it's not that complicated. It's also not the first time that's happened to a woman alone with Linton. Did you ever watch silent movies?"

Abra shook her head, as if to clear it. This day was getting weirder by the moment. "Yeah, I guess I saw a few in film class at UCLA. You know, futuristic stuff like *Metropolis*. Why?"

"Did you ever hear of a series called *Lindon Eggleston, the Eagle of the Sahara*? Kind of like a Rudolph Valentino knockoff."

Abra thought for a minute. "Come to think of it, I think we studied one of those. Didn't they film them in Europe?"

"Yeah, that's him. Knocked up one of his leading ladies in California and got run out of the studios by the morals commission. She lost the kid, but she talked loud and long to anyone who would listen when he refused to marry her. He had to go to France to work."

"Okay, what's that got to do with what happened to me?" Abra wanted to know. She really wanted to know.

"Listen, Abra, I hate to bust your bubble, but you're not the first woman he's done that to, not even in this town. Come back here a minute." Abra followed Connie through the kitchen to her apartment in the back.

Surprisingly, the furniture was expensive and stylish, setting off the delicate frost-green color on the walls. Beautiful pressed flowers on linen behind non-glare glass lined the walls with Audubon bird prints. Abra could tell they weren't copies cut out of a book.

Abra was so shocked by the décor that she wasn't watching Connie thumb through the large rack of CDs and DVDs. "There it is. Watch this." Abra fed the DVD into the player as the wide-screen plasma Sony lit up. Fascinated and somehow soothed by the flickering screen,

Abra watched as the credits flew by in fast forward. She caught *Lindon Eggleston, the Eagle of the Sahara* in "The Mummy of the Burning Sands." Jerky at regular speed, the old silent film was comical as the story unfolded. There was the handsome man on a horse, riding across the desert to the towering fortress, then sliding off the horse at the giant wooden gate, fighting a bunch of men, defeating all with a large curved scimitar. Then he was through to the inner sanctum, striding up to a vaguely Egyptian mummy case with torches burning on each side. He threw open the cover as if it was made of cardboard (it was), and the beautiful princess emerged, seconds from suffocating. In double speed, they paced back and forth across the large room, obviously having a deep discussion. The dialogue in scrolled letters passed by, too quick to follow.

Finally, Connie hit the regular speed and the Eagle strode purposefully up behind the princess as she sat to brush her long, beautiful hair. Abra gasped as she realized she was looking at a face almost identical to Linton's, only more youthful, and frankly, downright handsome and striking. Even through the primitive camera and corny staged shots, it was impossible to miss the muscles rippling, the long lean limbs, and that hair with the same streak of white. Eyes blazing, his fingers wrapped around the side of her neck. He spoke in silence as the dialogue screen came up: "I'm going to ask you a question, and if you lie when you answer, you will never leave this tower alive."

The camera cut to her face, nostrils flaring as his long fingers with perfect nails tightened over her carotid artery, pulsing as her neck flushed. Even through an eighty-year-old image, you could see the effect he had on the actress. "Where is the pharaoh's treasure?"

The girl hesitates, apparently wanting to enjoy the moment a little longer.

"In the dungeon, there's a secret tunnel in the torture chamber behind the torches. Pull the torch to the right of the door."

On screen, Lindon spins the chair around, stepping provocatively between the girl's legs, parting the thin gown above her knees. He caresses her cheek then kisses her long on the mouth and bounds out of the room to the dungeon. The screen goes dark as Connie hits the off button.

"Who is that man? He looks exactly like Linton, but younger. It must be his father." Abra looked to Connie for conformation, but that wasn't forthcoming. Instead, Connie took her hand and led her to a small desk in the corner. After they were both sitting, Connie looked at her, clearly trying to gauge how much to tell.

"Abra, you know how I told you this town was different the first day you got here?"

Abra nodded.

"Well, you don't really have any idea how different I meant. Most people here don't even think about it. I guess they're used to it, and scared to talk about it because they can't explain it anyway. Well, I can. I usually don't, but I sure as hell can talk about it."

Connie paused and took a breath before going on. "I'm going to tell you something, and you're either going to believe me, or think I'm crazy. If you ask Linton who the man on the screen is, he will tell you it was his father, the famous silent film star. I know better. Lindon Eggleston is Linton. I know that seems impossible because Linton would be over a hundred years old if it was, but it's the truth. I knew it the first time I saw that film, but I've confirmed it in other ways since then. All my life, Linton shows up every few decades. My mother told me he has been doing that all of her life, too, and she had me when she was over forty.

"She said her grandmother told her about him, too. So he's been doing it for over a hundred years I know of. It's always the same. He stays until people start to wonder why he doesn't age like everyone else, and then he suddenly leaves. He stays gone until all the people in his generation who know him well are dead or too old to remember, then he just shows up again and heads for the family property. If it's been thirty years, he may look two years older. Anyway, he always claims to be a son, grandson, nephew, brother, some relation to the last person that left."

Abra continued talking as if they were discussing "all things considered" on public radio. "On one level, a lot of people in town know it's bullshit, but they don't know how to explain it any other way, so they act like they believe him, even if they don't. He stays until people start wondering how he never seems to get older, then about the time enough people start talking about it, or some outside person gets wind of the phenomena, he just locks the door and leaves again until next time. He can say what he wants, but the proof is on the screen. Connie turned back to the screen and hit the reverse button. Lindon ran backwards into the room, kissed the girl, twirled the chair, and paused. "There, look on his left wrist, do you see that tattoo?"

Abra strained and saw the faint outline of a stylized hump-backed animal. Unable to make it out, she faintly remembered a faded tattoo on Linton's left arm.

"You're right." Abra nodded, happy to have the mystery solved. "You're right; I've seen that tattoo. It is him. He as much as admitted to me that he was over a hundred and fifty years old. I suspected it before I got here, but now I know. He told me. You've told me, and now, I see the proof with my own eyes."

Suddenly, Abra's anger returned. She wasn't some damn sniveling Victorian child, about to faint. "I'm going to get that son of a bitch." Abra was already getting up to leave. "I'm going back over there, and I'm going to knee that sorry bastard's balls all the way up to his Adam's apple, then I'm going to kiss him and ask him how he likes it." Abra was almost out the door, feeling like Wonder Woman, when Connie grabbed her shoulder and stopped her.

"I wouldn't do that just yet. You need to hear the rest of the story before you do." It was only because Connie's grip was strong enough to stop her that Abra turned around.

"I don't care about the rest of the story. He made a fool out of me, and by God, I'm fixing to make a fool out of him."

Connie looked into Abra's eyes. Gone was the impish, clown waitress. She was as serious as Margaret Thatcher addressing Parliament. She dug her hand into Abra's arm a little harder and shoved her against the wall behind the doorway. "Listen to me. You've got to listen to what else I know about Linton, or you may not be able to come back."

Connie waited until she was sure that Abra wasn't going to try to run and eased up on her arm. "There is something else that most people know but won't face about Linton. Over the years, hell, over the decades, the few people who threatened him with the truth, or threatened to tell have always died. Sometimes it looked like an accident. Sometimes, it was obviously foul play. Always, it was strange and macabre at best. It doesn't matter, because anyone who pieced it together had to face the truth. It only goes from coincidence to suspicion if you are willing to face the truth about Linton."

Connie wanted Abra to understand this was fact, and not just her opinion. "I've watched and listened to the old people when they gossiped about the rumors. I looked at the old press stories and photos. Someone usually comes up dead about the time Linton has to leave. He doesn't kill for fun, only when he feels he has to. But when he does kill, he does it with style. One man fell from the tower and was impaled on the wrought iron fence. A suspicious lover drowned in her goldfish pond. Linton was heartbroken at the funeral, by all accounts." One look at Connie's face left no doubt she did not really think he was heartbroken.

"So, if you want to be superwoman, go on over there and show him how you feel. He won't kill you there. I just wouldn't give a plug nickel for your chances of surviving the week. And don't think you could run away. The goldfish pond incident happened in Galveston, and Galveston was quite a ways away in 1893. Don't let that poor eccentric octogenarian act fool you. I know for a fact from my days in New York that he is fabulously wealthy and keeps his private jet on call in Dallas so he can run off to his penthouse in New York City when he has an auction to appraise or attend. I've seen it. It's jet black with lipstick red ostrich leather seats and crystal flower holders. Have you ever seen a cat play with a mouse he's caught?" Connie asked. "You know the way the cat will let the mouse run and act like it's letting the mouse get away, only to pounce at the last minute?"

Connie waited until Abra nodded. "You're the mouse. You're already in danger enough if he told you half as much of the truth as you say he did. He may let you go if you intrigue him, or he may pounce at the last minute. You had better go home and not let your guard down a minute. Especially at night. That old bastard loves the night like a vampire, and he can move like black silk."

Abra remembered the strange way Linton could move, seeming to appear in front of you before you were aware he had moved. "Yeah, I know how quick he can move." Abra seemed to think a minute. "Okay, okay, I'll go home. I guess I've had enough excitement today anyway." Abra smiled at Connie, realizing the risk Connie had taken by telling her the truth, not to mention the risk of being branded a quack. As she got up to leave, Abra hugged Connie, "Thank you. I don't think I ever had a friend who cared enough about me to do what you just did. I won't forget it."

Maybe because of embarrassment, or maybe out of habit, Connie was back in her "cracker waitress" mode, smacking her gum by the time Abra made it to the front door. Watching Abra go out the front door with a big smile, Connie said, "Ah, hell, it's all part of a café waitress' average day."

Abra could tell Connie wanted to leave it that way, as if the last half hour had not happened. "Yeah, I guess it is, isn't it?" Abra said as she waved at Connie and headed for her car with a determined step. Abra didn't even glance across the block toward Linton's shop. Had Abra looked that way, she would have seen a curious thing. Linton, uncharacteristically standing behind the large glass front door, was staring intently toward the old filling station on the opposite corner.

The old filling station was the convenience store of its time. A place where a fellow in a dark blue uniform would actually pump your gas under the giant green Sinclair brontosaurus painted on the front of the building. A place where you could pull an ice-cold RC cola out of the horizontal cooler with the ice water in the bottom and pour a package of peanuts in the neck of the bottle.

Old man Eisner had opened the business when he came back from World War II. Back then, he wasn't Old Man Eisner, he was Buddy Eisner, a hero of D-Day who had seen too much death and carnage. A local football hero just three years before, a piece of shrapnel in the head, a steel plate, and too many dead comrades had left Buddy a gentle man with a slight lisp who avoided emotional situations.

Unlike many young women who ditched wounded boyfriends before or after their return from the war, his sweetheart Glynnis did not. The night before he left, Glynnis had given Buddy all she had to give. Buddy tried to get her to promise that if something happened to him, or if he came back disabled, she would find someone else. Glynnis would not hear it.

With a maturity and resolve that belied her seventeen inexperienced years, she looked Buddy in the eye and said, "I'll be here for you when you come back. I don't care if you come back with one leg or one arm. I don't care if you come back with amnesia. I don't care if you come back half a man; I'll be here. All you have to do is come back." Then she smiled and gave him all she had to give again.

When he came back, Glynnis kept her word, and they were married in the chapel at the local Baptist church. Her mother and friends cried, and it wasn't all happiness. They did not realize that behind his sometimes-blank stare, Buddy loved Glynnis with all his heart. He understood his flaws and understood the magnitude of her love for him. While many of the young women at her wedding later faced infidelity, divorce, and indifference from smarter men who did not go suddenly blank or look abnormal at times, Glynnis and Buddy remained steadfast, having and raising two daughters and one son.

After the wedding, Glynnis' father, an area petroleum distributor, twisted the arms of the Waco Sinclair office and obtained a franchise for Buddy. He wanted Buddy to have the self-esteem of owning a business he was bright enough to handle and his daughter to have a decent living.

Through the fifties, Glynnis' father made sure no competition moved into Tejas Hill. After the fifties, he didn't have to worry. The town was on the decline, and the local convenience store couldn't compete with someone who would fix your flat, pump your gas, and pull you out of the ditch at midnight on Saturday night.

Anyone who walked into the station now was immediately transported back to the fifties. Nothing had changed. The RC machine was still there, serviced by an antique collector in hopes of getting it when Buddy died. The old rotary phone was still hanging on the wall, next to a wall full of pictures of Buddy with various friends, Buddy with his family at different ages, and Buddy with a new wrecker every ten years.

The funny thing was, Buddy never changed. It seemed like he lived to work, and work kept him going. Glynnis had died with cancer in the late sixties, just after their last child graduated. The kids all went to college. A doctor, teacher, and engineer emerged, all living in distant cities.

Buddy never seemed to age. Other men his age could barely move, but Buddy could hop onto a creeper and slide under your car to check a leaking tailpipe with the same agility that made him a great quarterback in high school. Local people joked that the station kept Buddy young and speculated that if he ever retired, he would die.

Truth was, Buddy's life was the station. It was the only place he felt in control. A world he understood. Problems he could fix. A place where his opinion was sought after and valued. He hated to go home at night, sometimes staying open long past dark, cleaning the shop, hoping someone might come by with a flat or an empty tank.

Along with the antiques inside, there was one particularly conspicuous antique outside. The old public phone booth still sat on the east side of the station, and it still worked. For some reason, cell phones rarely worked on the hill, so it wasn't that hard to get the phone company to service the phone.

All concerned made a little money off the facility, and every salesman and regular visitor to the town knew that you could always depend on a working line and a working light bulb with a clean area phone book inside the booth. Buddy made sure of that when he cleaned the booth out and Windexed the glass every other day.

Had Abra looked at Linton, she would have seen his lips faintly moving, as if he were mouthing dialogue as he watched a movie. Actually, he was lip-reading the part of the phone conversation taking place in the phone booth. Unknown to everyone, Linton left a small gap in the large bookcase that hid his chair and lamp. He used the hole, strategically placed, to allow him to monitor the goings on up and down Main Street.

One of the many unusual skills that Linton had developed over his long life was the ability to read lips. Coupled with eagle-eye vision, he found the ability indispensible. It allowed him access to all kinds of private conversations, no matter how low they were whispered. When he saw Kinnerd Irvin open the booth door, tripping the light inside against the growing dusk, Linton was instantly at the door. Oblivious, Kinnerd did not close the door so the light would stay on, allowing him to get the right change out of his pocket and dial the number. This was one call that Kinnerd did not want anyone to trace back to his home.

For all his feigned indifference back at the shop, Kinnerd troubled Linton. He knew about people like Kinnerd. Ignorant, but possessed with an uncanny ability to poke and snoop and learn things they did not need to know. Kinnerd was a personality that had plagued him many times in the past and caused him to do things he hated to do.

Right now, Linton knew he'd better stay a step ahead of Kinnerd. He had used his money to get Kinnerd's phone tapped by an expensive New York detective agency, and he had been lucky enough to see Kinnerd enter the booth.

The rest was easy for Linton, and Abra could have seen his lips unconsciously tracking one-half of the conversation had she looked. "Preacher, this is Kinnerd. Yeah, surely you didn't think you wouldn't hear from me after our little premier the other night. Yeah, you can wish all you want, but that ain't going to change shit. You and I are going to be doing business for a long time."

The unheard response brought a smug, satisfied smile to Kinnerd's face, "Hey, there ain't no need to get huffy. In fact, that'll only make things worse. Okay, now I want you to just shut up and listen while I tell you what I want, got it? Okay, that's better. First, I think you better meet me tonight, and bring $300.00 with you. I need a new set of tires."

Kinnerd snickered at whatever the preacher said next. "Easy, preacher; if you keep talking like that, I may decide I want some of what you were giving your buddy Bruce in that little film we watched. Tell you what, you just meet me in the bell tower at midnight, and make damn sure you've got the cash." Another pause while the preacher complained, then, "Yeah, screw you, too, preacher. I'll see you later."

Kinnerd looked around, more furtive than usual, as he hung up and left the phone booth. If the light had not hindered his night vision, he might have discerned Linton in the doorway, but he would have had to look quick, as Linton disappeared back inside as quickly as he had appeared.

Linton knew opportunity when it knocked, and this one had simply fallen in his lap. He had never trusted the preacher, and it didn't take a Rhodes Scholar to figure out the deal. Just another example of why poor stupid Kinnerd worried him. Now he just had to decide what to do about it.

Chapter Eighteen

"Strange Things in the Bell Tower"

Jason Fells walked. That was about all you could say. Anytime of the day or night, you might see him walking the streets of Tejas Hill, always with a small knapsack on his back. It was such a common sight that no one in town thought much about him. Maybe he was autistic; maybe he was an idiot savant. No one really knew.

He knew enough to wear the right clothes most of the time. He was tall, gaunt, and walked with a purpose that belied the fact that he had nowhere to go. His family took care of him as much as anyone could take care of a person who left at all hours, walked for hours, and then came in, and ate and slept without regard to the time of day or night.

After his parents died, his brother built a small cabin behind his old Victorian two-story and made sure the fridge had milk and fruit, and that there were canned goods in the cabinet. While a man walking the neighborhoods late at night would normally rate suspicion and run the risk of being branded a pervert, no one thought of Jason that way. He was clearly an innocent.

His manner and speech made it clear he had no aggression in his body and little interest in the goings and comings of people and everyday life. Frankly, it was not clear what his interests were, because he never said. His expression was that of someone on the way to somewhere special, but he never seemed to get there. Much like an Old Testament prophet wandering the wilderness, he simply kept wandering.

If the people on Tejas Hill had known everything that Jason saw and knew, they certainly would have paid more attention to him. Jason was, in fact, an idiot savant's idiot savant. Compared to most savants, who could play music after hearing it once, or calculate what day of the week it would be on June 2, 2098, Jason was an IBM computer. His mind was a motion picture camera that ran every waking second. His eyes were the lenses.

Much like a director, he chose his scenes, sometimes in still pictures recorded in a fraction of a second, sometimes in streaming video. Jason could recall a scene at will and replay hours, even days, at any speed in his mind's eye. He appeared uninterested and distracted only because interaction with real people took away from the satisfaction he derived from making movies and pictures in his mind.

Jason possessed heightened senses, which were magnified by his autism. Jason could hear casual conversations, even small animal sounds, from great distances, and he could tune out unwanted interfering sounds at will. He was like a lighthouse, whose beacon could be cast in any direction. Had he been interested, he could have mimicked love scenes from any house in town. He could have told who was seeing who, where, and when, complete with details.

One of the things that gave Jason great pleasure was repetition—anything with a repeat or a pattern. He timed his walks to coincide with a pleasing repetition—church bells, birdcalls, anything that repeated. So it was that Jason was fond of walking around the old college grounds late on moonlit nights. It was there that he often heard a series of sounds that formed a pattern that occurred over and over on those nights when the moon was so bright that you could see colors and shadows almost as in daylight.

The sounds always occurred after 1:00 a.m., when even the night owls were done and asleep. The sounds would begin with the quiet whoosh of a great weight being swung open on massive, well-oiled hinges. Then there would be sixty-three steps that crossed the green grass from the west into the bowels of the college, but seemingly under the ground, as if on stone.

After a brief pause, another heavy object would rotate on massive hinges, then the sound of one pair of feet traversing another sixty-three steps to the bell tower platform. After a period of time that varied from night to night, the sounds would reverse, always before first light. Jason had no interest in the whom or what of the sounds. He only found the sequence intriguing because someone or something was moving out across the college grounds and then up to the college bell platform without being seen.

On that particular Saturday night, the moon was unbearably bright, and Jason instinctively began to circle the college around midnight. As if on cue, he heard the hinges, then the invisible steps across the grass, followed by the predictable ascension to the bell platform. Satisfied, Jason turned for town when a new variation stopped him cold. From his position a block away, he heard the front door of the college open, steps down the hall, then up the stairs to the tower.

A few minutes later, he heard the west side door open, and more steps down the other side of the hall, then up the stairs. Voices followed, quiet and muted at first, then louder, then a muffled thud, and the sound of a heavy object striking the floor. Then more voices, quiet, then a strange sound, almost like a small firecracker bursting, then one set of feet descending the west staircase and heading out the other side of the college.

Unconcerned with the voices, Jason waited for the repetition, sensing new possibilities. Not to be disappointed, he heard the sound of the platform trap door open, followed by the footsteps descending, with one small change. This time, the sound of a heavy weight being dragged down the stairs accompanied the steps, with a satisfying thud as the weight fell onto each new step. At the bottom, the hinges whooshed open, and the steps crossed the grass slowly, the weight dragging behind. At the end, the final door opened, then closed, and the sounds disappeared.

Satisfied with the new addition of the dragging sound, Jason purposefully began walking toward home. Once there, he ate Dannon yogurt with cherries and went to bed with visions of invisible steps on invisible stones under the green grass of the college grounds.

Chapter Nineteen

"Everyone Likes a Good Story"

The black LTD II looked conspicuous despite every attempt to make it look inconspicuous as it pulled off the highway and headed past the Lions Club's "Welcome to Tejas Hill, a great place to live" sign. The tuna-can hubcaps, exempt license plate, and discreet whip antenna fairly yelled "government." The black color and fleet car look extended throughout the vehicle. There was a total lack of ornamentation that frankly cost more to remove than to leave in the factory state.

The two men inside, Nathaniel "Nathan" Henry and Sam Nikosia, were as devoid of ornamentation as the vehicle they rode in, but different in so many other ways. Young Nathan had the regulation flattop haircut that was the current style throughout law enforcement, while Sam sported a full head of dark hair swept straight back on his head.

Nathan was brand new to the FBI, just out of the academy, at the bottom of the pay grade, and hoping to move up. Sam wasn't. A twenty-year veteran, he had made the mistake of delving too deep into the personal life of a conservative talk show host whose program provided three solid hours of conservative propaganda each day.

Sam still believed in the principle that no one was above the law. He prided himself on the fact that he would take down a celebrity the same way he would take down a drug dealer. His morals were color blind, class blind, and gave no break to anyone. After twenty years, he had become resigned to the fact that most of the people he arrested drove better cars than his, and their kids went to better colleges. As Nathan headed the car up the long hill into town, Sam remembered the day that got him to this place.

When he traced a prescription drug ring to the mistress of the talk show host and found out that host was addicted and the mistress had ties to Russia, he blew the whistle to his superiors. The next afternoon, he received a call to report to the regional head of the agency. Sam was confident that his hard work would be recognized. He had been around long enough to know it would not be compensated, only recognized.

In the outer office, the receptionist was tense. Years of undercover investigation had made him observant at all times. His mind was rarely off duty, and his training made him unconsciously more aware of his surroundings. He mentally noted that she seemed nervous and distracted from the word processing she seemed to be trying to finish. She also dropped several items on the floor and kept looking at the chief agent's door.

When the intercom rang, she picked it up quickly, and seeming to be glad to get rid of him, told Sam he could go in. When he entered the office, Sam knew why she was nervous. Sitting in the chief's desk was the secretary of defense, Dan Rumsdell. Hated by his enemies and feared by his friends, of whom there were few, Rumsdell was a legend in the political and security community. Completely devoid of self-doubt, he ran everything within his considerable power with an iron hand.

Sam had learned to think quickly. "Mr. Secretary, I apologize; I'm here to see the chief. I must have gotten the wrong office." He was already turning to leave when the familiar drawl with the iron hand behind it spoke. "Quite the contrary, Agent Nikosia; you're here to see me, so why don't you get yourself a cup of coffee and sit down." Sam stopped and turned around.

He did not want any coffee, his stomach was already churning with the knowledge that no good could come of this meeting. Still, he knew the high and mighty had to be stroked to the extent one could without compromising one's principals.

"Thank you, Mr. Secretary, I'd love a cup. Would you like one?" Sam asked as he poured six-hour-old coffee into a Styrofoam cup.

"No, thank you. Please sit down. Air Force One is waiting for me, and I must make this meeting short."

Sam sat down and dutifully waited for the secretary to speak.

"I've heard good things about you, Agent Nikosia. You have a solid reputation as a great patriot, and I mean that. I've had your background and career checked out from stem to stern."

"Thank you, sir. I'm glad to hear it." Sam was not glad to hear it. It was clear that something bad was right around the corner, coming on fast.

"That's why I was very disappointed when I received your report on one of the administration's greatest supporters in the media." It was not lost on Sam that the secretary had not named the celebrity, even in a secure office with no one else present.

"Yes, sir. I was disappointed, too. It always amazes me how high corruption reaches in our society, but no one is above the law." Sam didn't know exactly where this was going, but he was beginning to get a real good hunch, and he didn't like it. Not one little bit. Setting his jaw, Sam waited for the axe to fall.

"Of course, Sam; by the way, do you mind if I call you Sam?" the secretary even tried to smile.

Oh, shit, this is really bad, thought Sam, but to the secretary, all he said was, "Sure, everyone calls me Sam." Now it was Sam that tried to smile.

"Of course, you're right, Sam. No one is above the law. But on the other hand, in this time of crisis, the administration needs all the friends it can get, and friends like our friend in this case are especially valuable." The secretary paused and looked into Sam's eyes. "I'm sure you understand." He waited for Sam's response.

"Of course, Mr. Secretary, I listen to him every day." Now Sam waited. His kids were grown, his wife was dead, and he really didn't give enough of a damn to compromise his principals, so long as he managed to make it another five years to retirement and that little cabin he was going to build up on Mangus Pass in Colorado on the fifteen acres he was buying on credit.

"Wonderful. I felt like you of all people would understand the importance of keeping a lid on this." The secretary paused, seemingly relieved, and happy to be winding up the conversation. "So, I take it that I can depend on you to do the right thing and just let this go, correct?"

Sam's face didn't show a thing, but inside, all he could think was, *Is there anyone left on this earth that really has any integrity? Is there anyone else who really believes that you have to do the right thing regardless of the cost?*

The secretary was already starting to get up and usher Sam out, but Sam stayed put and said in a quiet voice. "Sir, you can depend on me to do my job, without regard to who I am investigating, or how many people are hurt, so long as I'm protecting my country the way I was taught. That's the way I've been doing it for twenty years. So if you want this matter to go away, you're going to have to remove me and give it to someone else. Otherwise, I'm going to have arrest warrants issued, no matter how many people will be disappointed when I do it."

Sam didn't know what to expect, but he didn't expect what came next. The secretary sat back down and stared long at Sam. It was obvious that Sam's future was being decided. Finally, the secretary nodded to himself, indicating he had made his decision, and started to talk. "I can't say I'm surprised by your reaction. I knew you were a hard-ass the minute I checked your record, and I really knew it when I saw you. That's why I wanted to come myself."

There was something close to a hint of respect in the secretary's voice, "I thought you might give in if I came in person. Obviously, you're as incorruptible as your superiors told me. I used to be that way myself, but I've learned that sometimes the means really do justify the end, and I just can't allow you to sacrifice a man who may make the difference in the next election."

The secretary paused, measuring Sam with his eyes. "I need an answer to one question before I decide if you keep working for this agency. If I have you transferred off this case and out of this region, can I depend on your discretion in remaining silent about this matter?"

Sam didn't hesitate. "Sir, you can always depend on discretion from me. If it's not my case, I'm not going to be talking about it—to anyone, for any reason, and you can depend on that."

The two men stared at each other for a minute, weighing the integrity and intent of the other. The secretary spoke next. "I believe you, Sam. If I didn't, I'd have your badge before you walked out of this room, and you wouldn't ever see your office again, or that pension, or that cabin on Mangus Pass you want to build."

Sam's eyebrows went up and the hair on the back of his neck bristled, but otherwise, one would never have known how pissed off the threat had made him.

"Now, Agent Nikosia, I have a plane to catch. I hope you have good luck on your new assignment." The secretary did not get up or extend his hand. He simply looked down at the desk and picked up a piece of paper, pretending to read as if it was his desk and he had any idea what was on it.

Sam knew a dismissal when he saw it. Grateful that his integrity had not cost him his job and pension, he got up and walked out the door without looking back. It was fifteen minutes before the hair on the back of his neck stopped itching.

Back on Tejas Hill, Sam realized that Nathan had asked him a question, and he hadn't answered. Back in the present, Sam turned to Nathan. "I'm sorry, I was thinking about something else. What did you say?"

Nathan repeated, "If it's not something I'm not supposed to know, can you tell me what we're doing here in a town like this? It hardly looks like a place where an enemy of the state might be hiding."

Sam looked at Nathan, amazed at how little the boy understood and how much he had to learn. Nathan reminded him of his own son, trying to be a man, but not quite sure about all the ins and outs. Patience and praise were what raised boys into men, in Sam's opinion. Sam used the moment as a tool to teach. Looking at the houses and countryside going by as if he hadn't a care in the world, Sam asked, "Well, what were you told about this assignment?"

"Not much, really. The chief had his secretary tell me to meet an agent at the garage and check out a car, and I'd be told where we were going." Nathan looked at Sam, waiting for some information.

"Ok, so you just did as you were told and didn't ask any questions, right?" Sam almost smiled at Nathan's obvious discomfort.

"Yeah, isn't that what I was supposed to do?" Nathan looked back at Sam, waiting for a response.

"Son, let me ask you a question. What one thing do you think is most likely to keep you alive and ahead of the game in this business?" Sam watched as Nathan pondered the question.

Nathan slowed down slightly and seemed to think. He was obviously taking the question seriously. "Knowledge; knowing what you're doing, and why. Knowing who you're dealing with and why."

Hot damn, Sam thought. This little turd may make it after all. "Bingo, son. Bingo. You have to know who you're dealing with and why, otherwise, you're going to be as clueless as they hopefully are."

Nathan could tell Sam was happy with him, and that made him happy. He allowed himself a smile. But Sam wasn't quite through with him.

"Now that we know what we need, tell me what you could have done to find out what we're doing today that you didn't do?" Sam looked out the side window, giving the young agent a minute to think.

"I don't know what you mean. What could I have done? They just told me where to go and what to do. What would you have done?" Nathan waited for an answer, slightly perturbed at the idea that he had missed something. After all, he was top of his training class at the academy.

"Son, espionage starts at home. The first thing you could have done was to talk to the secretary that gave you the assignment. Act dumb and needy. Women love that. Tell her you sure need to know which way you're going because there are some things you have to pick up if you get a chance, or some reason you have to know because you have to change some plans. See if she knows anything more than she told you. Who you're going to meet, who you're going to question and why. Look at her desk. See if she's looking at any notes when she tells you. Talk to the other agents; see if they know what's going on. And finally, ask me. We've been driving for two hours, and you haven't asked me a thing about what we're doing. I'd have told you if you asked, but you didn't. If we walked into a situation in a minute, knowing something might be the difference in living or dying."

Sam stopped and waited for Nathan to look at him. "Oh, and before I forget, exactly where do you think enemies of the state usually hang out?"

Nathan looked properly chagrined then grinned sheepishly at Sam. "I guess I see what you mean. Well, I might as well ask the question now. What are we doing here?"

Sam looked off, eyeing the trees and houses outside the window, before answering. In a matter of fact voice, he said, "We've got to go ask a recluse ham operator why his call sign ended up stuck on the front camera of a Mars rover during a live broadcast at NASA."

Nathan laughed and looked back at Sam. "Hey, I heard about that. Some kind of channel mix-up. So, what are we really doing here?"

Nathan continued to chuckle until Sam said quietly, "Pull the car over, Nathan." Nathan looked at Sam but couldn't tell what was wrong. Sam was staring out the front windshield as if nothing was wrong. Still, Nathan had just received a direct order from a superior officer, so he dutifully pulled over to the side of the road, stopped, and waited for whatever was next.

Sam leisurely looked out the front windshield, then the back windshield, making sure they were out of the traffic. Satisfied, he turned his considerable bulk sideways in the front seat until he was facing Nathan. He waited until Nathan took a deep gulp and looked back at him. The young agent was confused, and probably a little scared, so he spoke softly.

"Nathan, there are just a few things they probably did not teach you at the academy, so I won't hold it against you because you don't know shit from shinola, but you're going to have to understand a few things if we're going to work together. Now, are you ready to listen?"

Sam's tone of voice and manner was about the same as Mr. Rodgers on PBS asking an eight-year-old if he could do something. Nathan's reaction, wide-eyed, was similar. He just nodded for "Yes."

"Good. Okay, now here it is." Sam had Nathan's full attention, sure that he was fixing to get some real wisdom. "Did you ever watch the *Wizard of Oz*? You know, Judy Garland, Toto, the yellow brick road?" Sam's demeanor made it clear the question was serious.

Nathan nodded "Yes" again.

Sam continued, "Okay, right now, you're Dorothy, and you're in Oz, not Kansas. And when you're in Oz, all kinds of strange people are around, and all kinds of strange things happen. Do you understand what I'm trying to say, Nathan?"

Nathan nodded, and Sam nodded back that he was satisfied with the response before continuing, "And there are even witches and wizards and other people out to hurt you and me. You understand that concept, don't you?"

Again, Nathan nodded "Yes."

"So, with that background in mind, here are the ground rules. First, I never, never, ever joke about agency business. So when I told you we were going to see a ham operator about a postcard on Mars, I meant just that. Second, that was not some kind of channel mix-up. There really was a postcard from Tejas Hill on that Mar's rover, and it got there somehow. Third, the call sign belongs to one John Elvin Wright of Tejas Hill, and that's who we're going to see to find out how that happened." Sam continued in the same methodical voice, "Now, if you find that too hilarious, or simply ridiculous, you probably need to go back to A&M and get a teaching certificate. But if you're ready to believe that there are many strange things in this world, and you're lucky enough to have a job where you're going to get to see more than your share, you can start the car and head up the hill to the second right, and stop at the house on the left at the end of the lane by the city park. Now, which is it?"

Nathan looked out the windshield, started the car, and slowly began to accelerate up the hill. Sam was impressed at the way Nathan handled the situation, and relaxed on his side of the seat. Nathan could tell Sam was impressed with his handling of the situation. Everything was co-pacetic, and the cosmos was in balance as the LTD II topped the hill and made the second right turn, stopping in front of Elvin's house.

Elvin watched the plain black Ford pull up in front of the house. He had been waiting for someone to come ever since the debacle at NASA on Cable News Nationwide. He smiled to himself as he watched the two agents get out of the car and glance suspiciously up and down the vacant block. All Elvin could see was Mrs. Abram's fourteen-year-old Collie, Chelsea, laying in the sun next door. Maybe they thought it was going to attack.

Elvin chuckled to himself as he remembered the fear he felt when he realized that the postcard was going to lead right back to him. "Oh, my God," he remembered asking. "What am I going to tell them when they come? You know they are going to come and question me."

Klatoo had seemed unconcerned. In fact, Elvin could have sworn he saw a slight smile crease the edges of Klatoo's black lips. "Mr. Wright, it really doesn't matter what you tell them. You can tell them that you had some cards stolen. You can tell them that you've mailed those cards all over the world, as I'm sure you have. In fact, you can tell them the truth if you want. They won't believe it, so it really doesn't matter."

Klatoo seemed to float over next to Elvin and patted him on the shoulder with his little gray hand and long, thin fingers. "You are a very lucky man, Mr. Wright. You now possess knowledge that only a handful of humans possess, and you have experienced a trip no other human voluntarily has."

Klatoo paused. "All we ask in return is a little help from you in lo-cating an anomaly in town we're very interested in." This time, the little sucker actually smiled at Elvin. "Why don't you and Yasha go back to your house and visit after we get back, and she'll fill you in on what we need."

Elvin remembered how he couldn't believe his luck. Yasha at his house! By the time she left that evening, he would have robbed graves for her if she had asked.

Mars was all right, but three hours alone with Yasha was better. He would do anything to keep in contact with his new friend. Oh, yeah, and Klatoo and the saucer, too.

Back in the present, the doorbell rang. Elvin let it ring a second time before he leisurely opened the front door and looked at the two men. Although they were dressed the same, they could not have looked more different. The young one, eager and expectant, the older one bored and jaded. Assuming what he hoped was the right mix of curiosity and fear, he asked, "Can I help you?" He looked from one to the other with false concern. "Is something wrong?"

The older one took the lead. "Mr. Wright, I'm Agent Nikosia, FBI," he said, flashing a badge about the size of Oklahoma, holding it in the air long enough for Elvin to examine it through the screen. When he felt Elvin should be satisfied, he whipped the badge back into his coat pocket in one smooth move.

"This is my partner, Agent Henry." Nathan smiled at Sam first, happy to have been referred to as partner, then, remembering his manners, smiled and nodded at Elvin. "We just have a few questions. Do you mind if we come in?"

Sam was already opening the door, so Elvin had to back up as he held his arm out to the living room. "Of course, come on in." Sam was already by him, heading down the hall, so he turned his attention to the young agent.

"Have a seat anywhere you like." Elvin gestured toward the only couch in the room, sitting in the only chair so there would be enough room for the three of them. Nathan dutifully sat down on the couch, uncomfortably waiting for Sam to finish his impromptu survey of the house.

Sam, on the other hand seemed in no hurry; he was scanning every inch of the house, had even walked past the living room down the hall, as if he were confused, so he could check out the back of the house. Elvin and Nathan waited in embarrassed silence as Sam slowly made his way around the back of the den, coming back into the living room from the back of the couch.

"Oh, sorry, I guess I missed a right turn, didn't I?" Sam chuckled.

Although no one was fooled, Elvin laughed as he remarked, "Probably my mistake. It's easy to miss the door," while thinking to himself, *Yeah, if you're mentally retarded and legally blind.*

"It's not every day I get a visit from the FBI, so what can I do for you?" Elvin waited for a response.

Sam took his time; he had already reached into one coat pocket and pulled out a dog-eared notebook. Now he was fumbling around his shirt pockets for a pen. Finding none, he looked at Nathan. "You got a pen, Nathan?" Instantly, Nathan whipped out a silver cross and handed it to Sam.

The skinny little pen looked like a straw in Sam's big paw. He moved his hand back and forth, looking at the pen as if it were an alien gun. "You know, I never could get used to an expensive pen like this. It just doesn't fit the hand like a good "gimme" pen, does it?"

Elvin was aware that all the time he had been rummaging around, as if in confusion, Sam was using the opportunity to study him. Despite that knowledge, Elvin seemed amazingly calm. Somehow, he now felt superior to his peers, confident that he would be safe, no matter what.

The two men continued to study each other for the split second it took Elvin to realize it was his turn to reply. "Oh, yeah, I grew up in a store where every salesman left a free pen. Those big round pens really fit a hand, don't they? Anyway, I always lose the expensive ones, don't you?"

Sam slapped his knee in agreement. "Hell, yes; I'm lucky if they last past the first day." The two men laughed easily, but Nathan was ill at ease with the casual banter. He thought they were here for a reason, and these two were yucking it up like two old friends from high school.

"What kind of store did you grow up in?" Sam seemed really interested, and Elvin found himself liking the older agent more by the second. "It was a local store my parents owned, the kind with hardware, electronics, toys, a little of everything."

Sam was obviously impressed. "Get out of town! There was a store like that where I grew up. I used to about live down there. They had everything—bikes, camping stuff, radios and TVs. Hell, I wish we had a store like that now that didn't cover eight city blocks, like Wal-Mart."

Elvin nodded in agreement. "Tell me about it. Half the time I go to the mall, I have to walk around the store three times to remember the entrance I came in so I can find my car."

The two laughed easily for a few seconds, lost in their own memories. Sam finally seemed ready to get down to business. "Well, Mr. Wright, as much as I like reminiscing about the past, I guess you know that's not why we're here, don't you?" He looked dead into Elvin's eyes, and all the humor and camaraderie was gone.

Elvin paused and swallowed. "Well, I would expect it's about my call sign card showing up on that channel mix-up with the president at NASA." Elvin was careful to parrot the laughable excuse that the White House had put out.

Sam held his hands up in the air for a second, as if Elvin was arresting him. "Well, you've got us figured out, but you know how it is—we have to follow up all the leads to try to find out how that happened." Sam smiled another self-deprecating smile. "You understand, don't you?"

"Of course. You can ask me anything you want." Elvin appeared the model of cooperation, complete with an expectant look on his face as he waited for the questions.

"Well, Mr. Wright, let's assume for just a second that what happened wasn't an accident at the station. Let's assume that it was exactly what it appeared to be—your call sign card on a Martian rover." Sam paused to see what effect he was having.

"You mean for real?" Elvin tried to look suitably surprised. "You mean my call sign card was really on that Mars rover?"

Sam looked back, again seeming bored. "Well, we're not exactly saying it was or it wasn't, but let's just say for the purposes of our visit with you today, it was. Exactly how could that be, given that particular Mars rover was launched several years before you got those call sign cards printed? And yes, we did check with Pound Printing in Houston and confirmed the date of your order with the new college logo." Sam smiled, leaned forward, and looked into Elvin's eyes. With the room that small and Sam that big, his face was less than two feet from Elvin's face, and that was no accident. "Tell us Mr. Wright, how could that happen?"

"Good Lord, I don't have a clue how that could happen." Elvin hoped he looked dutifully surprised. "Surely you guys don't think I flew to Mars and put it there for a joke? Astronomy is one of my hobbies, so I know it would take several years to get there and back, and they can tell you out at the campus that I haven't been off more than two weeks in years."

Elvin laughed nervously. He was down to chattering to fill the silence left by Sam, who was not speaking and had never taken his eyes off Elvin. "Maybe somebody sent it FEDEX. You know they say they deliver anywhere in twenty-four hours." Elvin laughed again, partly out of nerves, but mostly at the absurdity of the situation.

When he looked back, all he saw was Sam measuring him with a stare. "Well, Mr. Wright, one thing I've learned in this business is that there is a lot I don't know, and a lot more I don't understand. So as far as I'm concerned, you may well have flown to Mars and put that postcard out on that Martian rover for a joke."

Sam wasn't laughing. In fact, to Nathan, Sam's voice was sounding a whole lot like Mr. Rodgers again when he asked Elvin, "Did you do that, Mr. Wright? Did you fly to Mars and leave your ham radio call sign card on that Martian rover?"

This wasn't going as Elvin had expected; this guy was serious. Sensing anything but the truth would sound worse, he decided to hang it all out and tell them the truth. "Okay, you got me; I was here alone late one night when a little gray alien named Klatoo invited me to go to Mars and asked me to bring a couple of my cards. When we got there, he put one on the rover before we came back." Elvin paused, looking from Nathan to Sam.

Nathan looked like he was watching *Jeopardy* in Russian, and didn't understand Russian. Sam was just taking it all in, obviously enjoying Elvin and Nathan's discomfort.

"It only took an hour to get there and back." This time, Elvin looked at both of them without a smile, and then started laughing. "I'm kidding, I'm just kidding. You can't possibly believe that's the truth. I just don't have any other explanation for how it could happen. I didn't mean to make fun; I just didn't know what else to say. You both seemed so serious."

Nathan began to chuckle as if he had finally gotten the joke. Sam looked at Nathan like he had just farted out loud in church and waited until he quit chuckling, then said, "Mr. Wright, only you know for sure if you're telling the truth or not." Sam's tone was very matter of fact. "From my point of view, your version is about as believable as any other explanation I could come up with." He paused. "Since it was your call sign card up there, I guess I'm going to have to say I believe you." Sam took his time and glanced around the room again, as if admiring the twenty-year-old worn furniture. "Is there anything else about the trip you need to tell us? Maybe a sexy girl who is half-human, half-alien?" This time Sam's face had just a hint of a smile.

Elvin was freaked out. Totally freaked out. His face turned red at the thought of Yasha. This agent not only seemed to really believe him, he either knew about Yasha or was guessing. Maybe he was just guessing. "Well, if that's the game we're playing, no, I don't remember any beautiful aliens. Just the little gray guy."

Sam nodded as if he was satisfied and began to put his notebook up. Looking off as if he were already thinking about lunch, he spoke casually again. "Well, thanks for your time, Mr. Wright. If you get another invite like that, I sure would appreciate it if you would give me a call." Sam handed Elvin his card and looked down at Nathan, who had not moved an inch.

"You about ready, Nathan, or do you have any questions for Mr. Wright?" Nathan looked like he seriously had no idea whether to jump or run. Instead, he bobbed up off the couch as if he had just seen a copperhead between the cushions. "No, I guess you covered all my questions."

As Elvin started to get up, Sam held his arm out as if to stop him. "Don't bother getting up. We'll show ourselves out." He got about halfway to the door and stopped, then turned around, "Say, you wouldn't happen to know where a fellow could get a real lunch, do you?"

Still too astonished to be surprised anymore, Elvin answered without thinking. "I'd try Connie's café up on the square. It's real good."

Sam appeared grateful. "I'm sure it is, and thanks for the tip." Sam started out the door, and then stopped and turned again, "By the way, please give my regards to Klatoo; we haven't heard from him in quite some time."

Elvin almost said, "I will," before he caught himself.

Sam almost laughed aloud, watching Elvin stifle the response that almost escaped his lips. With that, Sam turned and went out the front door behind Nathan, making sure he stopped the screen before it banged and eased it closed, smiling at Elvin as he turned and headed down the sidewalk. Then they were gone, and Elvin was left standing in the middle of the hall with more questions than answers.

Nathan didn't say anything as they drove away. As they turned back onto the main street, Sam seemed intent on peering out the passenger window, as if interested in the succession of plain, small town houses going by. Nathan couldn't tell if he was looking at the houses, the kids in the yard, the dogs in the street, or the trash and equipment in many of the front yards.

He was surprised when Sam casually asked, "Well, Nathan, what did you think about our Mr. Wright's story?" Sam looked around at Nathan, giving away nothing, waiting for his response. Nathan went over the encounter with Wright in his mind, wanting to get it right.

He was perceptive enough to understand that Sam was more interested in the quality of his response, rather than the speed, so he took a page from Sam's playbook and pretended to take in the scenery on his side as he drove up the hill toward town.

He did not look directly at Sam when he answered, but kept driving. "Well, I thought he seemed real sincere and was telling the truth until he went off on that wild story about going to Mars. What a crock of shit." Nathan shook his head from side to side, smiling in disgust.

"I'm just curious; why do you think that?" Sam's face gave away nothing as Nathan glanced at him.

"Well, he sounded concerned when we got there, and he sounded like he wanted to be helpful. I just couldn't believe it when he went off on that insane story, and I can't understand why you just left it at that. Why you didn't ask more questions?"

Sam was glad the boy showed enough spunk to risk angering a superior. Nathan finished with, "What did you think?"

In his laid-back manner, which was becoming more comfortable to both of them, Sam paused before answering, "Well, I reached the complete opposite conclusion from the interview than you. I thought his concern at the front door was a total act. He seemed entirely too comfortable. Most people would have been scared shitless after waiting a week, knowing we would be showing up sooner or later, even if they were innocent. Second, I don't think he was a bit worried about what he was going to tell us and figured we would accept his confession for a joke. After all, who would think we might believe a story as strange as that, even if it was true. When we did, he really got upset and confused. By the time I hit him with the half-alien girl, he was almost panicked, and by the way, Nathan—" Sam made sure Nathan was looking at him. "There was a half-alien girl involved in this deal. You can bet on that."

Sam seemed to be in a mood to lecture. "The first thing you're going to have to learn is to watch how people act when they say things to you as much as you listen to what they say to you. If you watched our

148

friend back there, he was too relaxed, too accommodating, and too polished for a recluse like him—almost superior in his demeanor. He was having fun with us at the start, and he actually looked relieved when he told us about his trip to Mars, because that was the literal truth, and the truth is always more easy and comfortable to tell when you think you're immune from the consequences." Sam looked at Nathan to see if he was getting the point. "Did you happen to notice how upset and frenetic he got, almost passively hostile, when I didn't react in disbelief? Did you remember he said something like, 'Well, if that's the game we're playing'?" Sam enjoyed this type of informal debriefing. "That's an admission that he knew we knew he was playing a game. He was actually disappointed and confused when I didn't question him further, and you can bet he's really upset and confused right now. As to why I didn't ask any more questions, he told me what happened. I wanted to leave him off-base so he has a lot of time to think before I come back."

Nathan was amazed. "You mean you think he was telling the truth? Why would you believe a story like that?" As they pulled up in front of Connie's, Nathan pulled the car into one of the three parking spaces and waited for Sam to answer.

"Four reasons, Nathan. First, I know that card was actually on Mars independent from his story. Second, the card is connected to him. Third, he made the mistake of mentioning a name, Klatoo, when he told his story. And fourth, the same instincts that have saved my life and broke cases for twenty years tell me he was telling the truth, except he lied about there not being an alien woman. Instincts, Nathan—the hair on the back of your neck. You had better listen to the hair on the back of your neck. It'll save your ass more times than not. If you never trust me on anything else, trust me on this; always follow your instincts, especially when the objective facts support your hunch."

Nathan was especially curious about one exchange. "What's the deal on Klatoo? I heard you tell him to give Klatoo your regards. Do you know something about Klatoo?"

Sam finally smiled at Nathan. "Not a damn thing, son. That's called a hunch, and it costs nothing to play a hunch in a case like this. I never heard of Klatoo outside of an old 1950s movie, but it's unusual to make up a name in a story you're making up on the spot. Did you see the color drain from his face when I said that? He almost passed out. I can tell you one thing. There is a Klatoo, and he knows him. When we get back, we'll run some traps and try to find out if there's any file on Klatoo. Until then, we'll just let Mr. Wright stew about it."

Sam smiled and thumped Nathan playfully on the shoulder. "Hey, we gonna sit in this damn car all morning, or we gonna eat?" Sam was halfway out of the car before Nathan got his door open.

Chapter Twenty

"I CAN SEE CLEARLY NOW"

"Twash, twash, twash, evewy whewc you look in this town, theys twash!" Leon was on one of his social tirades, and when Leon was on a social tirade, about all you could do was agree.

"Yeah, trash everywhere." Larry almost groaned his agreement as he shifted the new Dodge 3500 dually into fourth gear, automatically glancing in the mirrors at the big gooseneck trailer hauling the D-6 dozer, to make sure everything was still tied down right.

There might have been some advantages to working with a halfwit like Leon. He clearly idolized Larry and would do anything he was told. There were disadvantages to the deal, too, and today was a prime example. Leon had a bad habit of getting his pea brain fixated on something. It might be a show he saw on TV. It might be Rush Limbaugh on the radio. It might be anything. Today, it happened to be the trash problem in Tejas Hill.

Honoring a twenty-year-old oral agreement that no one could really remember, the city only had trash pickup every two weeks. Two weeks worth of loaded diapers during August in Texas is a smell that few communities are subjected to. Tejas Hill was one of those few communities. People actually welcomed winter so the trash would stop stinking so bad. Adding to the problem was that innate instinct to keep any kind of broken-down junk car, motorcycle, equipment, or anything that might have some value later in this life or the next. Unlike other parts of the country, or even other parts of Texas, a lot of people who didn't have to felt the need to rathole anything that was broke and too darn big to lift or move easily. Some people thought it was just a white trash, redneck trait. The truth was it was a survival instinct, honed by reconstruction, war, the Depression, another war, and the hard times in-between. It had gone on so long that now it was in the genetic code of

151

most rural Texas males from modest backgrounds. Today, it was unfortunately occupying a large part of Leon's modest genetic code.

"You evew been to San Antonio, Lawwy?" Leon was wound up, so Larry didn't even get the chance to groan an answer. "They got that rivew that wuns thew the city, and how about Salado? They got that cweek. If evewyone in Tejas Hill wasn't so damn twashy, we could do that heaw. You know what I mean, Lawwy?" For emphasis, Leon punched Larry in the knee with his one-liter Pepsi.

"Yeah, I guess so; a regular Salado here in Tejas Hill." Larry entoned just loud enough so Leon could hear him. He knew that if he tried to stop Leon, or change the subject, he would just piss him off. Then Leon would sulk all day and maybe all week, and that wasn't any more fun.

As much as he hated to admit it, Larry actually enjoyed being around Leon on a good day, when he wasn't on a tear. This just wasn't going to be one of those days. He had started to mention the official-looking black Ford with the two guys in suits he saw a while back going up the hill toward town, but knew it was useless to try to change the subject. On a normal day, that one strange car would have been the source for a morning of entertaining conversation and speculation. Just not this morning.

"Look theyw, Lawwy—twash in that yawd." Leon pointed to a front yard dotted with rusted motorcycles. "And that yawd, too, see that twash? Twash, twash, twash—even the college is beginning to look twashy. Just look at that statue on top of the college. It even looks twashy, like someone shootin' the finger at the woeld." Leon was really getting wound up as they drove by the college.

Larry was down to parroting whatever Leon said until he wore the subject out. "Yeah, darn statue shootin' the finger at the world." Larry groaned again, reached into the console, pulled out the Tums, got two, and put them in his mouth. Something tickled the back of his mind. Something Leon had said. What the hell had Leon just said? Yeah, something about the statue on the college shootin' the finger to the world.

"I wish I lived in a woeld with no twash, no twash at all." Leon was fixing to gear up on the next yard as Larry slowly brought the big Dodge to a deliberate stop in the middle of the block in front of the college. Leon looked around in surprise. He couldn't see why they were stopping. Everything was still on the trailer.

Finally, Leon looked over at Larry. Larry was dead serious when he looked at Leon and said, "Leon, there ain't no statue on the college; there's only a lightning rod." Larry turned back to stare up at the college. Both of them looked at the top of the college on the front of the big gable above the four huge limestone columns, where the big dome had once stood like a silver beacon in a desolate country.

There on top was what appeared to be a life-sized figure, left arm extended out and up, as if there might have once been a sword in the hand. Instead, the hand appeared frozen in the universal symbol for defiance, the middle finger extended in an eternal insult to the world.

"I got a bad feeling about this, Leon." Larry was already getting out of the truck, heading for the college building, oblivious to several cars pulling up and stopping behind him. Leon did what he always did. He followed Larry.

Back at the diner, Sam and Connie were bull shitting each other in the eternal exchange between a waitress and a career traveler. Sam wound up to the occasion. "You know, Connie, you don't mind if I call you, Connie, do you? You got a real nice little town here. With a little cleanup, this place could be another Salado or Jefferson."

Connie acted like this was the most interesting conversation she had ever had and the idea was original. Actually, about every third person from out of town opined how the beautiful geography of the place would lend itself to another bed and breakfast, antique shop weekend get-a-way destination, like Salado, Jefferson, or Fredericksburg.

"For instance, take that statue on top of the college there; it must have had a sword or something at one time. Now it just looks like a guy giving an obscene gesture to the entire town." Sam watched as Connie's face went from polite agreement, then glanced across the street and went blank in total surprise, her mouth open. Her order tablet slipped out of her hand to the floor.

"Hey, Connie, it doesn't look that bad. It was just a joke." Sam watched with increasing alarm as he faintly heard Connie say something under her breath. Sam touched her arm gently. "What did you say?"

Connie never took her eyes off the college as she said in a monotone, "The college doesn't have a statue on top of it."

By that time, Sam realized several men were running up the front steps, a small but growing group of citizens gathering on the front lawn, pointing and gawking. "Let's go, Nathan." Sam was already up, pulling his coat back so his holster was clear.

Nathan didn't know what was happening, but ran to catch up as they crossed the street toward the big front staircase. Sam was already yelling back, "Get the digital camera, and bring the crime scene tape." Nathan changed direction and ran back toward the LTD.

Ahead, Sam saw the two men running closest to the entrance of the college, one normal size, the other almost a giant. Under more normal circumstances, and with more time to reflect, Sam would have probably likened the two men to Dr. Frankenstein and the monster. Under these circumstances, Sam did what he did best, make a quick decision, and act on it.

"FBI. Stop, you two." Those three initials stopped Leon and Larry cold. Sam saw the giant one stop and spin around, his face going from concern to amazement, changing emotions quickly, much like a child. "FBI? Awe you fow weal?"

Sam caught up to them, puffing from the exertion. "You bet I'm for real, and I need some help, right now!" Sam made sure both were looking at him. Up close, he could tell the smaller man was the leader. "Quickly, what are your names?"

The smaller man measured Sam up and down for a long moment. Satisfied, he replied in a measured tone that instantly impressed Sam. "I'm Larry Clakey, and this is my partner, Leon Nealy. You can trust him."

With that, Larry put his hand on Leon's shoulder. Leon was still gawking at Sam's gun shining out from under his coat in the shoulder holster. It was unspoken that Larry was assuring Sam he could trust Leon despite his looks.

This time, Sam measured Larry for a long moment. "Okay, Leon, I need someone to help secure this scene before it gets all tore up. So you stand here in the front door until my partner Nathan gets back, and tell anyone who tries to get by here that there's an FBI agent upstairs that's going to arrest them if they go past this point. When Nathan gets here, you tell him Sam said tape off the doors then bring the camera up. Then you keep everyone out of the building."

Sam turned back to the door. "Larry, you go with me and show me how to get up on that roof." They started through the door as Connie ran up. Larry stopped Sam with an arm on the shoulder. "You might want to let Connie through. Her dad was a professor here, and she used to play all over this building. She knows it better than anyone."

Sam smiled at Connie. New friends happen fast in a crisis. "Fine, come with us, Connie. We need to get to the roof." It had been over a decade since Sam had been anywhere near in good shape, so running up three flights of stairs after running across the street and up the steps took about all he had.

When they reached the top floor, Connie stopped, looking at the wall as if searching for something. "There used to be a closet landing that had the stairway to the roof, but they've remodeled this floor since I was little." She paused. "The door was hidden to look just like the rest of the paneling. You had to know just the right spot to find it."

Sam was already walking down the long hall. "Which side was it on?"

Connie paused, as if thinking. "On the left; it was on the left and near the far end. I remember the afternoon sun shone on the spot in the winter. I used to sit in that warm spot after school waiting for my father to get through in the evening. Look for a gap between the baseboard and the floor. That was the only giveaway."

Sam was already down the hall, pulling a pair of plastic gloves out of his pocket and putting them on as he felt along the bottom of the hall baseboard. "I found it. Larry, you stay here and keep anyone other than Nathan out until Connie and I come back, and don't touch anything, okay? Connie, come with me and don't touch anything on your way up." With that, they were gone, leaving Larry alone.

Sitting down to wait, Larry got a cigar out of his chest pocket and rolled it with his tongue. He didn't smoke; he just chewed the cigar to relax when he was nervous. Chuckling, he thought, *Well, Mama always wanted me to go to a university.*

Sam, having gone through the hidden door behind Connie, paused and allowed his eyes to adjust so he could take in the scene. The landing was small, with raw milled wood in twelve-inch widths on the wall. The staircase was stone, with some kind of old, brown linoleum set in the footpath. The flooring was worn by decades of sporadic traffic. Sam punched the button on the light switch, mentally noting he had not seen switches with two buttons except in ancient houses and buildings.

A clear, bare light bulb came on at the top of the stairs. Surprisingly, there was virtually no dust anywhere. Sam made a mental note to check on cleaning in this area. There were no obvious tracks on the floor as he and Connie slowly walked up thirteen steep stairs, which opened onto the crawl space under the roof.

At the top, a wooden floor covered the ceiling tresses, creating a path three feet wide leading to the horizontal metal door that opened onto the roof. Sam had to duck at the top, since there was only about five feet of crawlspace headroom. Although he made his way to the opening as quickly as possible, he pointed out details to Connie out of habit as he went. "Look at this headroom; you would have to be a strong son of a bitch to carry a body hunched over with your legs bent."

Connie nodded, "Yeah, if you were carrying the body." Sam looked back at her as he asked, "What do you mean 'if' you were carrying the body?"

"Well," Connie followed Sam across the narrow wood path to the door. "Maybe whoever is up there met someone in the bell tower."

Sam stopped cold and turned, hunched over to look into Connie's face. "What bell tower? We're fixing to be on the roof, aren't we?"

Connie nodded. "Yes, but once we're on the roof, there's a catwalk over to the bell tower. You can't reach it from inside, only from the roof."

Sam turned and made the last few steps to the metal door to the roof. "Connie, I've got gloves on, so let me open the door, and please, please don't touch the door when you follow me through. There may be prints."

Connie nodded her understanding and agreement as Sam turned the doorknob, amazed at the balance of the heavy door and the ease with which it swung open. The morning sunlight was a welcome relief after the dim crawlspace.

"Which way? I've lost my sense of direction." When Connie came up into the sunlight, she pointed to the east side of the roof. "Over there, on the other side of the bell tower."

At first, the figure looked almost like a statue, the surreal pose of the left arm, extended up and out in a final gesture of contempt. The closer they got, the easier it became to see that the figure was not a statue, but a dead body.

Carefully, Sam and Connie negotiated the narrow metal catwalk along the ridge of the gable to the spot three feet from the edge where the body was suspended on an oversized curlicued lightning rod, two inches in diameter, shaped like a seven-foot cross in the Victorian style.

The body was held upright by what looked like ¾-inch reinforcement rod, the kind you put in a concrete slab, wrapped in a continuing spiral around the body, then up the neck to the left arm, holding it in position.

The reinforcement rod was wrapped around the lightning rod and even crossed under the crotch to keep the body from sliding down. Connie stayed back several feet, seemingly happy to let Sam get close to the body.

Having worked construction in college, Sam was amazed at the smooth shape of the spirals that kept the body in place. He knew reinforcement rod was difficult to bend in a smooth curve, especially small-diameter smooth curves. Someone would have to be Superman, or have a pipe bender on hand. Either way, Sam just couldn't see how it was done on site on this roof in the dark.

Careful not to touch the body, Sam turned to Connie. "I really could use your help to see if you know who this is. If you don't mind, could you come over where you can see the face?"

Connie didn't move; her face was slightly ashen. Sam thought she was in shock and started to repeat the question. Connie stopped him. "I heard you the first time. I don't have to come over there; I know who it is. It's Kinnerd Irvin, and someone really has a sick sense of humor."

"How do you know? You can't see his face from there." Sam looked out at the gathering crowd below and turned back to Connie.

"It's not difficult; Kinnerd is the only person in town that wears that color of coveralls everyday, and I can recognize his hatchet head from any angle. He's the town gas man, and everyone here would know his profile from the back because we've seen his back working on gas lines as much as we've seen his face. Half the town has accused Kinnerd of shooting them the finger. That's what I meant about the sick sense of humor." Connie leaned in closer, staring at the body. "How did he die? I don't see any blood."

"Bingo, little lady, you get the brass ring for being quick because I don't see any blood, either. In fact, I can't see any obvious sign as to why he's dead, but he is dead." Kinnerd's face was almost as gray as his coverall. Eyes closed, his body swayed slightly with the wind as it moved the lightning rod at its base.

Sam walked back over to Connie, took a deep breath, and looked around as if there might be something else to look at on the roof, and then he put his arm around Connie's shoulder in a fatherly way. "Tell you what, Connie, why don't you go back down, being very careful not to touch anything, and tell Nathan to call the nearest field office and have them send a full forensic team down here with the truck and all the equipment, and I'll stay up here and see what else I can see." Sam turned away then thought of something else. "Oh, tell him to designate one local officer to come up here when they get here. I don't want the keystone cops up here. Can you do that for me?"

It may have been the condescending tone in Sam's voice, or it may have been the arm around the shoulder. Whatever it was, Connie seemed to wake up out of her daze. Moving out from under Sam's arm, she said, "Look, I've seen dead people before, and I'm not going to break down or anything, so you can dispense with the condescending grandfather impersonation." She started walking back toward the door, stopped and turned with a grin on her face. "Unless you want oatmeal with milk in it for supper." Sam laughed quietly to himself as she disappeared down the stairway and he turned back to the body. Damn, he liked that woman—all spunk and no charm. That combination was hard for a man like Sam not to like.

Leaning over the edge, he waved to the crowd gathered below, hoping they could hear him. "It's okay, folks; we've got help on the way, so all of you need to stay out of the building. The best thing to do is to go back to work." No one moved, but maybe they wouldn't try to rush Leon, who was still guarding the door like Chester trying to cover for Matt Dillon.

Then, out of the blue, came a voice. "I don't think you could move those folks with a Sherman tank; at least not before you bring the body down."

Sam spun around to see who was on the roof, only to see a small, wizened man in a pair of Levi's and boots and striped denim shirt with suspenders walking back along the catwalk toward the body. Sam spoke forcefully to the back of the straw cowboy hat. "Sir, sir, I don't know how you got up here, but if you don't leave immediately, I'm going to call the sheriff to arrest you."

The words seemed to have no effect, and the old cowboy kept heading straight for the body. Sam wondered if the old guy might be deaf and cursed himself inside for leaving a halfwit like Leon in charge of security as he tried to reach the body first. The old cowboy was already there, looking around the shoulder to see the face.

Sam was about to speak again when he heard a clear, ringing voice. "Well, well—Kinnerd Irvin. I guess the stupid son of a bitch finally shot the bird at the wrong old lady." He chuckled, "Boy, you are sure going to have your hands full figuring this one out."

Sam's patience was gone. Placing himself directly behind the old cowboy, he spoke quietly and clearly and held his badge out so the old man would see it when he turned around. "FBI, Mr. This is my last warning. If you don't leave this roof immediately, I'm going to make sure your next stop is the jail. Do you understand me?"

Once again, the old cowboy acted as if he had not heard a word. "Son, you got any idea how he died? I can't see a mark on him, can you?" This time, the old cowboy turned around and looked first at the badge in the leather folder and then into Sam's eyes. The old man's face was lined and grooved from years in the weather. He appeared to be about seventy, and the eyes were clear blue and amazingly probing as they took in Sam's face.

Just as quickly, the old man ducked under Sam's outstretched arm without missing a beat, leaving the badge and Sam's arm dangling stupidly in thin air. "That is one hell of a badge, son. That thing must have cost a hundred dollars. I bet it sure weighs you down on a hot day."

He was already halfway to the bell tower on the catwalk when Sam caught up to him and spun him around. Enough was enough. "Mister, I don't know who you are, but as of right now, you're under arrest for interfering with a federal crime scene, and I'm going to call someone to carry you to jail."

The old man stood quietly, making sure not to move. He had a wry smile on his face as he waited patiently for Sam to stop speaking. "Now, son, don't go gettin' your shorts in a wad; no one's gonna arrest me if you call." Sam rarely was thrown off balance, but he was definitely missing something here. To make matters worse, Connie was back, leaning against the stairwell railing with her arms crossed, stifling a laugh, and seeming to enjoy the confrontation.

"What exactly do you mean that no one's gonna arrest you? Are you threatening me?" Sam was fixing to get real serious, even if this was an old man.

"Easy, son." The old cowboy didn't move a muscle, but his eyes were still amused. "You could call the governor, but he ain't gonna arrest me because he wouldn't have anywhere to deer hunt this fall. You could call the Texas Rangers, but they ain't gonna arrest me unless the governor tells them to, and we already talked about him. You could even call the president, but he ain't gonna arrest me 'cause I'm on the task force that oversees security at his ranch. So, son, who you gonna call?" The old man was already laughing as he looked back up at Sam. "Ghostbusters?"

"Who the hell are you?" Sam was past ready for this little charade to be over.

The old man seemed relieved, having stopped laughing at his own joke. "Glad you finally asked, son. Wayland Woodland; I'm county sheriff here." With that revelation, Wayland stuck his hand out with a big smile while Connie broke up laughing against the staircase.

Sam knew the name. Every law officer of any note in Texas knew who Wayland was. Quiet and unassuming, Woodland was the kind of officer who had built a reputation that almost approached legend status over fifty years, while habitually shunning all publicity. Be that as it may, Sam had been on the wrong end of the joke too long to let the sheriff know he knew he was somebody special in the business.

"Sam Nikosia, FBI, Dallas. Glad to meet you, sheriff." Sam shook the outstretched hand, surprised at the firm grip and roughness. This man obviously worked outside every day. "It might have been a little easier if you had just told me who you were up front."

The sheriff, laughing to cover embarrassment, replied, "Oh, hell, Sam, I'm so used to everyone knowing me around here that I occasionally have a senior moment and forget that other people don't. My apologies."

It was time to get back down to business. "Well, sheriff, I appreciate you checking in with me, but I want to be clear that the FBI has federal jurisdiction over this crime scene since I discovered it in the course of an FBI investigation." Sam paused to make sure he had been understood and added, "I intend to direct this investigation myself."

Sam knew how jealous local authorities could be in protecting their turf, and he was prepared for whatever argument he got in response. He was going to be disappointed if that was what he was expecting.

"Oh, hell, son, you don't have to worry about me. The way I see it is you got a body crucified here on this roof that was walking around less than twelve hours ago, with no obvious cause of death and wrapped in reinforcing rods bent cleaner than a machine shop could do in a week. To be honest, I'd probably have you arrested if you tried to dump this one off on me. On top of that, half the town and about a fourth of the county won't be sorry to see Kinnerd dead. Whoever did it won't have to come up with much of a defense to be found not guilty.

To emphasize the thought, Wayland shook his head, laughing as he looked back at Sam, "No, sir, you couldn't pawn this piece of shit off on me if you tried."

Sam was somewhat stunned at both the attitude and the candor. "Well, as long as we understand each other."

The sheriff was already heading for the staircase. "Don't you worry, Sam, we understand each other real well." The voice got thinner as he disappeared down the staircase. "I'll make sure my boys don't get in your way, and you can return the favor by keeping me informed as much as you can." With that, Sheriff Woodland was gone, and Sam realized he had forgotten to ask how the sheriff already knew the victim was still alive less than twelve hours ago.

Sam looked around at Connie, who was trying to stifle a laugh. "You could have told me who he was before I made an ass out of myself."

Connie's rebuff was good natured and quick. "Well, I might have if you hadn't been so busy flashing that big ol' badge of yours and trying to intimidate a helpless old man."

Sam looked at Connie for a minute and grinned. "Yeah, I guess I did kind of jump the gun." Sam saw a few county squad cars pulling up. "If you're all done laughing at me, would you mind going back down and seeing if one of the county officers could take over for Larry and Leon and keep everyone out until the forensic team gets here? And please ask Nathan to cordon off the entrances and keep everyone and I mean those officers, too, from coming inside the building and to come up once he has some help."

Connie stood, yawned, and stretched her arms, looking bored, and then saluted in mock seriousness. "Yes, sir." With that, she turned to head down the staircase.

"Hey, Connie," Sam called as she started to leave. Connie turned around, expecting more orders. "Thanks for the help; I know this isn't everyday stuff for you."

Connie smiled, obviously happy that he had noticed. "You're welcome, Sam." Then she was gone.

Chapter Twenty-One

"MEANWHILE, BACK AT THE CEMETERY"

Abra felt like she was back in high school as Dennis's Saab eased by the college at midnight with the lights off. The moon was almost full and the wind was blowing the clouds by like ethereal horses on a celestial racetrack, sometimes hiding the moon, only to return with an unearthly glow that sent shadows fleeing from the ancient shrubs that lined the college grounds.

There was a quiver in the pit of her stomach that she hadn't felt in years. Somehow, it was almost like that night when she was a freshman and she and her friends, flush with the heady freedom that a new driver's license gives you, had driven to the local cemetery to hold a séance.

The real reason the boys went was to get the girls scared so they might be willing to park instead. It worked. Abra got her first French kiss that night, and a whole new set of feelings in a whole new set of places. You just don't forget that kind of thing.

Back on Tejas Hill, she couldn't help feeling a little ridiculous stacked in the small front seat of the small convertible with Dennis and Skippy and a bunch of tools and flashlights in the small back seat.

This was ridiculous; they were all grown. What would happen if the police came? She laughed to herself. "Oh, yeah, there aren't any police other than the two FBI agents investigating the murder, and they were spending every night at the Hilton in the nearest big city. Abra felt Skippy's hand, seeming to accidentally fall on her leg about three inches from ground zero.

It was funny. If he were a contemporary from her city world, she would have slapped him. Somehow, she couldn't bring herself to be mad at Skippy. He had a bad dog way about him that made you want to put up with whatever he did, even when you knew he wasn't innocent and sure wasn't a pitiful puppy dog. Abra did have feelings, just not for Skippy.

Anyway, it had been a long time since a man had been interested enough to try to breach the old defenses, and his hand actually felt pretty good. Abra shifted in the seat, and Skippy's hand ended up about an inch from ground zero. Even Skippy was too surprised to move on that one.

As the Saab came to a quiet stop in front of the cemetery gate, Dennis looked around, and in a conspiratorial voice, said, "Okay, everyone be quiet."

Skippy got out, stretched, and spoke loud enough for Dennis to cringe. "No, shit, Shurlock, I was thinking of pulling out the bagpipes and breaking out with my personal version of "Amazing Grace." What do you think?"

Dennis didn't qualify the jab with an answer as he started handing out shovels, ropes, tools, and lights. "Come on, guys, this is serious. Quit screwing around. Goliath told me I'm off the payroll in a week if I don't come up with something. Well, I intend to come up with something before I leave, but they're not going to get it."

Abra was impressed that Dennis was learning to look out for himself. He was beginning to get the big picture. Skippy was impressed, too. "I'm impressed, Dennis; if you get much smarter, you're gonna figure out how much of your beer I'm stealing every day."

Trouping up the hill to the cemetery entrance, Dennis wasn't going to let that go by. "Don't worry, dumbass; I know exactly how much of my beer you steal, and I'm planning to get it all back in manual labor tonight!"

"Man, why do we have to lug all this shit through the cemetery? Why can't we just drive up to the park where we don't have to walk so far?"

Dennis kept walking as he answered Skippy's question. "Simple. No one will be driving by the cemetery entrance this time of night, but half the town might drive by the park gate. We just need to get behind that big red rock wall, and no one will see us. The best way in is through an old gate I found in the back of the cemetery."

Actually, Dennis was quite proud of his reconnoiter of the city park and cemetery. Under the pretense of strolling through the cemetery, looking at the old epitaphs, he had chanced upon the small gate at the back of the park overgrown with vines, no doubt installed by a past city employee moving from one property to the other to mow. A ten-foot red rock wall, constructed in the thirties by a civilian conservation corps, when the city still had dreams of grandeur, bound the front of the park.

Once behind the wall, Dennis had experimented on several nights making various levels of noise to see if he would be noticed, knowing he could retreat through the back gate before being discovered. He had discovered that the huge wall effectively muffled almost any sound he could make.

Just as the small entourage was making its way through the middle of the cemetery, the moon went behind the clouds, and the local pack of coyotes decided that night was officially on. For those not from the country, a pack of coyotes celebrate the night by leaving their daytime dens and churning into a chorus of howls fit for a Bella Lugosi movie. As if thinking that very thing, Dennis paused, waiting 'til the others stopped, and intoned in a thick Transylvanian accent, "Listen, my little friends, to the children of the night."

The coyotes sounded like they were about twenty feet away, and Skippy and Abra instinctively huddled a little closer together. "Cut it out, man; you're creeping me out with that vampire talk!" Dennis saw Skippy actually shiver in the wind, and he liked that, given the way Skippy was hogging all the quality time with Abra.

Dennis decided to have a little more fun as they walked toward the back of the cemetery. "Hey, Skippy, in that eight years of college you went through, did you ever read *The Dunwitch Horror* by H. P. Love-craft?"

Skippy wasn't having any of it. "It wasn't eight years, you little creep, it was seven, and no, I never heard of *The Dunwitch Horror* or anybody named Lovecraft. Hey! Wait a minute, wasn't he the villain in a James Bond movie?"

Dennis ignored him. "Man, I sure do remember that—green goo and a portal to another dimension in a dark cemetery with a horrible creature waiting for the gate to open to devour humanity. Damn, that was a creepy book. Even now, it's kind of scary." Dennis stopped a second, looking at the moon glowing through the clouds. "Especially here."

Now Abra scooted up next to Dennis, tucking under his arm. Dennis had enough instincts to put his arm around her. Abra spoke in a low voice. "Kind of cool out here, isn't it?" It wasn't that cool, but Abra and Dennis didn't care. Skippy damn sure did. "Hey, Abra, don't go getting the Beaver riled up, or he'll have wet dreams for a week."

Ignoring Skippy, Dennis, and Abra stayed hugged up as they made their way to the back of the cemetery and the gate. Once there, they made their way through the overgrown gate, handing each other the tools and lights as they passed. Once on the other side, everyone sighed in relief. You could rationalize it any way you wanted, but there were many reasons why people avoided the places of the dead.

It was instinct. It came from a time when people did not have houses to hide in and doors to lock. It came from a time when people were more in tune with nature and the night. When people did not have to wonder about gods, spirits, and curses, because they were real—in the animals, in the weather, in the rocks, and especially in the dark just beyond the firelight, an everyday part of life.

In that time, they knew what we only feel as a chill in the back or the hair on the back of the neck standing on end—that uncertain feeling that there really is something waiting out there in the dark, just beyond the light. Something unseen and dangerous. The same feeling that makes a young child huddle a little deeper under the covers on a cold, dark night. The certain knowledge that evil and danger are real, and yes, they do lurk in the dark.

In a perverse way, it was that knowledge, that certainty that death waited in a thousand guises out there, that made life exciting. The comfort in which we live now, the feeling that there is a cure and an answer for every threat, has robbed us of the true excitement that comes with uncertainty, leaving us to watch scary movies and take adventure vacations to try to find a little of what has been lost. Life is better on the razor's edge, but we don't even know where the razor is anymore.

As Abra, Skippy, and Dennis made their way away from the gate into the park, their excitement and that tickle in the pit of the stomach grew. Each of them felt very, very alive. "Hey, Einstein, what's the plan now?" As usual, it was Skippy who broke the silence.

"Well, Beto Boy, my little machine tracks a void in the structure of the hill all the way to the western edge. I would say it was a natural cave, but the path is too straight."

Skippy took a minute to digest that and seemed satisfied. Abra wasn't. "Where does this void seem to go?" she asked as she shifted the pick ax and rope from one shoulder to the other. In college, she had rock climbed in Colorado with her roommate a few times. It felt good to have a shoulder full of equipment again.

"I knew someone would ask me that, and that's the one thing I don't know. It heads back toward town from the bluff in a straight line, but it gets deeper as it goes into the hill. The one thing I can tell you is the direction. It goes straight under the college, but I lose it right after that."

It was a cool night with a cold front approaching. Once he finished talking, Dennis had the distinct feeling of being watched and shivered involuntarily. Still tucked under his arm, Abra felt the movement. Before she caught herself, she hugged in a little closer and whispered, "Are you okay, honey?"

If Dennis had died right then, he would have died happy. He read the sincerity and transparent intimacy the statement carried with it. Like the cyborg in *Bladerunner* responding to the advances of a very human Harrison Ford, Dennis felt warm and happy to the core. "Yeah." He squeezed her hand back. "I just had a feeling we're being watched, that's all." He laughed to himself. "Silly, huh?"

"Yeah." Abra squeezed his hand again. Hand squeezing was reaching a whole new level on Tejas Hill.

Skippy, watching the two, was thinking of throwing up. "Hey, you two, if you want to keep up this junior high hug fest bullshit, why don't you take it back to the car?"

Dennis could not resist a rare moment with the drop on Skippy. "Jealous, Beto Boy?"

No comment.

Dennis's hunch was absolutely correct. They were being watched. The drone was a triangle three inches across, and it hovered at a constant 3500 feet, the optimum height to survey the spot from which the strange readings came. The drone utilized the same alien anti-gravity technology that Klatoo's ship used.

It was a small, but incredibly sophisticated security system programmed to notify Klatoo when any suspicious activity occurred on the hill. Regardless of where he was, Klatoo had instant access if an alert went out, and three people sneaking through the back of the cemetery at midnight on a full moon with digging tools was the kind of alert that was routed directly to him.

He was in his rest cycle. Klatoo, like all of his kind, had long since abandoned sleep in their dim world. Cycadian cycles and rhythms all but disappeared when their sun became too weak to sustain the cycle. Still, it was nice to have down time, so the aliens kept the sleep time, amusing themselves in their own ways. They could dream without sleeping, which was much more satisfying when you could remember whatever you dreamed and control the content to some degree.

Klatoo was reliving a conquest off the edge of the Kurr galaxy when the alert came in. The experience was as satisfying as a Viking reliving the rape, pillage, and plunder of a village. Actual rape and pillage were beneath an alien, unless done under the guise of scientific research, but the thrill of victory and the humiliation of defeat were not. In human terms, Klatoo was most akin to a Japanese shogun—manipulative, dangerous, and cruel, but fiercely loyal.

Instantly awake, he digested the drone report in nanosecond data speed. Instantly, facts were measured, options considered, and a decision made. Floating weightlessly in his ship halfway to the moon, Klatoo communicated silently with the first mate.

"Hand me my Cingular cell phone, will you?" The question was really a direct order, and the response was near instantaneous. The phone appeared in his hand. Klatoo chuckled as he dialed the instrument as if he were a human dialing a rotary phone.

He could have communicated with Elvin in ways the CIA could never imagine, but in doing so, there was the danger of discovery. Better to use a normal and accepted method of communication. Klatoo liked Cingular best. The little number pad on the new phones fit his delicate gray fingers perfectly as he dialed Elvin's home number.

He waited for the answer. "Elvin, Klatoo here." The greeting was less than unnecessary given the squawk in the background before the translator added voice. Still, formalities must be observed. "I hope I'm not interrupting anything between you and Yasha on your, what do you call it? Oh, yes, a date. Anyway, I hope I'm not disturbing you."

Elvin was trying to put on his pants as he talked, hoping Klatoo could not hear or sense his frustration. Klatoo knew exactly what he was doing by reading Yasha through the phone and was struggling not to laugh.

"Not at all, Klatoo; what can I do for you at this time of night?" Elvin turned to the bed where Yasha lay naked, totally unaware of her raw beauty, looking like an exotic Venus in a French impressionist painting. Languishing like a satisfied cat, she stretched, smiling in satisfaction at Elvin.

Yes, it had started out in the most foul and manipulative way, with Yasha just following orders from Klatoo. To Klatoo, she was a half-breed novelty and much like a poor niece in the manor house of a rich uncle in nineteenth-century England, she was never quite allowed to forget her place. To her complete surprise, once she broke through the stone wall that was Elvin's heart, steeled by years of neglect and his cold family and strained childhood, she found herself captured by the one thing the aliens could not give her. Love—simple, carnal, painful, but always incredibly real.

Elvin would have dove off a cliff to be with her, and it was getting to the point she wasn't far behind him. It had taken her weeks to seduce Elvin, and now, two months later, they lay in bed, drinking hot chocolate and eating Ritz cheese crackers after a long evening of lovemaking, planning her escape and how they would tell Klatoo.

Knowing Klatoo's abilities, Yasha filled her mind with mild contempt and humor for Elvin, sending just the right mix of aversion and condescension through the phone. Klatoo, having engaged in more human chitchat than he could normally stand, got right to the point. "It seems that our young scientist and his alcoholic sidekick have united with the white-haired archeologist and are at this moment in the park preparing to dig something up. I would appreciate it if you could find out what the hell is going on, and remember, Elvin, we must have the prize if they find it." He paused. "I would hate for them to recover what we seek and leave Yasha and I with no choice but to leave."

The threat was clear and hung in the air like a thick acid, burning Elvin inside. "Don't worry, I'm almost gone. I'll find out what they're up to."

Klatoo seemed satisfied with the instant response. Seeing no reason to carry the conversation further, he replied, "Fine, and please tell Yasha hello for me." He hung up without waiting for a response.

"Trouble on the hill?" Yasha yawned, stretching her taunt body so that every muscle rippled as if highlighted.

Elvin almost forgot what he was about to say. "Yes, looks like Dennis, Abra Avant, and that Skippy guy are about to dig something up in the park. I've got to check it out. Want to go?"

Yasha was feeling freer every day. She realized she did not give a tinker's damn what Klatoo would think. "Sure, let me just get a little something on."

Elvin continued to stare as she got out of the new sheets and bed-spread he had bought at Bed, Bath and Beyond for her. "Make it as little a something as possible, okay?"

Chapter Twenty-Two

"Now I Know Why Men Go to Deer Camps"

S am and Nathan had been at the "deer camp" for approximately three days when Klatoo made that fateful call to Elvin. Nathan had expected to work undercover from time to time when he signed on with the agency. He had daydreamed that he might have to go under deep cover as a drug dealer, mafia financier, or some other underworld figure. He had not ever thought that his first undercover assignment would involve imitating Bubba at the deer camp.

His first inkling that all was not going to be black suits and plain Fords with tuna-can hubcaps had come approximately two weeks into the murder/Mars postcard investigation. Sam and Nathan were eating the buffet breakfast at the Waco Hilton. Well, actually, Sam was grazing the buffet like a hippo in a large pool of lotus and water lilies while Nathan, mindful of his physical fitness, was trying to stretch his one fruit bowl and raisin bran for the hour and a half it usually took Sam to meet his quota of 5,000 calories to make it to the next buffet at 11:30 a.m.

Without looking up from his plate, somewhere between a double bite of fried eggs and link sausage followed by a bite of pancakes brimming in butter and syrup, Sam asked, "Hey, Nathan, you got any western clothes? I mean old western clothes?"

Nathan thought for a minute as he savored the slice of extra fresh honeydew melon and answered, "Well, I bought a pair of burgundy Justin Ropers for a party I got invited to, and I've got a new pair of Levi jeans. That's about it." Having grown up in a number of metropolitan areas, Nathan was a little unsure what Sam meant by "western."

Sam kept eating. Really, how could someone put that much food in their body? "Let me guess," Sam said as he mopped a biscuit in left-over butter and syrup. "Zip-up fly?" Nathan's blush gave away the answer. Sam let that one slide on by, and continued without a pause. "No sweat; we'll just make a little trip by the undercover clothes agency and get you fixed up."

Hey, a new office he had never heard of. "Cool! The undercover clothes agency? They didn't tell us about that at the academy. Is there one for every major office?"

Sam seemed amused as he got up. "Hey, don't let the waitress take that pancake; I ain't through with it yet." Nathan nodded, thinking his old tomcat would have never tormented a mouse as much as Sam had already tormented that poor pancake.

When Sam returned with what could only be described as a meat-lover's orgasm plate, he continued as if Nathan had just asked the question. "Yeah, they got an undercover clothes agency in almost every city we have an office, but it's really super secret. Not everyone has access. Hell, I shouldn't even be telling you about it. If we go there, just be quiet and act like it's no big deal, okay?" Sam stopped eating and looked at Nathan with the look he reserved for serious questions, waiting for a response.

"You can count on me Sam; I won't say a word unless I have to." Nathan was really pleased with his progress with Sam. He had learned a lot about what Sam liked and did not like and had made it his goal to get through each day without getting one of Sam's "Are you mentally retarded, or just acting stupid?" looks. He was batting about 50/50 so far, but that was better than at the beginning.

Surprisingly, Sam was actually beginning to enjoy having Nathan around. After years of partners who didn't give a damn about anything but climbing one more step up the pay ladder on Sam's shoulders, it was nice to have a partner that: a) thought he was smart; b) believed anything he was told; and c) hung on every scrap of advice he could put out, no matter how much of it was pure bullshit.

Nathan was so pleased with the prospect of the secret undercover clothes rendezvous, he didn't notice that Sam had finally quit eating and was watching him nurse his next to last piece of melon. "Hurry up, Nathan; we don't have all day for you to eat breakfast."

Before Nathan could get his jaw off the table, Sam was already up, yelling at the waitress, "Hey, Wanda, you got a check? I'm gonna leave a twenty and a ten and you keep the change, okay?" Sure, it was okay, since the tip was going to be ten dollars on a twenty-dollar check.

Outside, Sam got in the passenger's side. "You drive."

Nathan stopped at the entrance to the hotel. "Which way?"

"Left," was all Sam said, picking his teeth with a toothpick. "Then take a right at the Auto Zone."

After a few blocks, Sam had more directions. "Take a left at the second red light, and turn into the first parking lot."

Nathan was on high alert. What kind of cover would the place have? It couldn't be obvious, so it had to have some kind of front. Nathan wondered what the front business would be. He so concentrated on following the directions that he didn't look up until he stopped in the parking lot behind the building on the corner after turning left.

The back of the one-story building was plain, and that was being charitable. *Man, they really wanted this place hid*, he thought. Talk about local color—there was a large dumpster with a guy who looked slightly retarded putting something in or taking something out, Nathan couldn't tell for sure.

On the other end, there was a tractor-trailer with a large sign on the side. "Donations welcome. No mattresses accepted. Do not leave items when trailer is full or closed." Obviously, the customers could not read because there was a pile of stuff around the trailer and at least two mattresses that looked old enough to have come out of Al Capone's hotel room.

Sam sat quietly, watching Nathan survey the place. Slowly, Nathan's gaze left the trailer and settled on the sign in front. "Salvation Army Resale Store." Sam watched Nathan's expression as he realized the joke was on him, and turned to Sam. "Man, you are a real turd, you know that?"

Sam just grinned as he got out of the car. "You ready?"

Inside, everyone they saw greeted Sam like a long-lost friend. The first guy inside the door was obviously a recovering addict. His emaciated arms and standout arteries gave the game away. "Hey, Danny." Sam slapped him on the back as he went by. "How you been doing?"

Danny winced at the slap on the back, but was obviously proud to be noticed. "Sober for six months, Sam. My old lady even told me she'll take me back if I stay straight a couple of more months."

"You hang in there, Danny. You'll be back in the saddle before you know it." Sam kept walking, talking under his breath as Nathan struggled to keep up. "That's Danny. He was a small-time dealer, got busted and copped four years at Big Springs. Seems to be doing okay."

Near the back of the store, Sam stopped behind an older lady in her middle seventies, her bleach-blond hair in a bun, lots of cheap costume jewelry, and an outfit that looked like Cher's mother. She was helping a washed-out, waif of a girl about sixteen pick out what appeared to be a prom dress.

As authoritative as a New York fashion designer, she surveyed the blue formal the girl was trying on. "It's a little loose in the back, but the color is dead on. You wear that, and the boys are going to run over each other trying to dance with you." The girl looked at her, searching her eyes to see if she was telling the truth. It was pitifully obvious that she had been lied to most of her life.

The old lady didn't blink. "I meant what I said, honey. You're a knockout in that dress."

Blushing, the girl seemed happy until a frown crossed her face. "How much is it? Granny gave me ten dollars, and that's all I've got. I hope it isn't more." She was stricken at the thought. But before the thought could ruin the moment completely, the older woman laughed, "Ten dollars? Heck, you can get the dress and a pair of shoes, too. Why don't you go over to that rack and see if we've got any formal shoes to match, while I see what these handsome guys want, okay?"

The girl beamed with pleasure. Life had not given her many moments like this. She looked like queen for a day as she headed for the shoes. The lady smiled at the girl until she turned the corner then she grabbed Sam in a bear hug. "Sam, you old son of a bitch, you're a sight for sore eyes." She let go and backed up, taking in all of Sam's large body. "Looks like you been eating good, huh?"

Sam winced, blushed, and smiled all at the same time.

"Now, what brings gentlemen like you to the Neiman Marcus for the poor and inconspicuous?"

"How's tricks, Evelyn?" Sam and the lady were holding hands and grinning like two young lovers that hadn't seen each other all summer.

"You know, Sam—the same parade of addicts, mental cases, and child abusers." Her face went serious. "Some make it, some don't, but we keep trying, don't we?" She asked the question as if she really needed some assurance.

Sam's face clouded up a little. "Yeah, we sure do. We keep trying to make it better." They squeezed each other's hands one more time, then let go as if any more emotion and affection would be too much for both of them. Looking for an out, Sam turned to Nathan. "Evelyn, meet my newest partner, Nathan. He's so fresh out of the academy that I learn about twenty things from him every day!"

Nathan, ever the gentleman, stood up straight and stuck his hand out. Evelyn ignored the hand and hugged Nathan as if he was a long lost nephew. Temporarily without oxygen from the dizzying combination of "old lady" foundation makeup and Chanel No. 5, Nathan damn near passed out before she released him, holding him out for a close examination.

"You better listen to me, young man; this guy has forgot more than most agents ever know. You'd do well to watch and listen, and I mean that." Her face was suddenly stone cold sober, and Nathan could see she did really mean it.

"I know" was all he could manage, hoping it was enough. It was. She released him and looked back at Sam with the old smile. "Now, what kind of cover do we need today?"

"I don't need anything, but my young friend here needs some deer camp clothes, low-rent deer camp clothes." For emphasis, Sam paused. "1978 Ford-type deer camp clothes."

Evelyn's eyes rolled up as if she were reviewing the entire inventory of the store in her mind. In fact, she was. After a few long seconds, she looked at Nathan, grabbing the seat of his slacks before he could jump. "Let's see; looks like about a 32X34 jean and a medium shirt, right?"

Nathan swallowed hard, still feeling her fistful of wadded up slacks against his butt. "Exactly right."

Evelyn let go, slapping him lightly on the butt as she turned. "Damn straight I'm right. I'm always right." She headed down the aisle, Sam and Nathan following. The rest was kind of a blur. Before he knew it, Nathan had five pairs of old Levis, button fly, four cowboy shirts, one welding shirt, a package of fruit of the loom underwear, an old leather belt with a Harley buckle, and a pair of work boots that had really been worked in.

Evelyn looked pleased, and Sam looked amazed. "Lose the hair mousse and grow a little stubble, and he'll fit right in down at the cattle auction barn."

Sam hugged Evelyn one last time as they paid out. "You're the best, Evelyn. Sometime you and me are going to get that rib eye steak, okay?"

Evelyn slapped him on the arm. "Don't bullshit me, you old Romeo; I've been waiting for that steak for ten years. I'd settle for a chicken fried steak at Ma Goodson's place instead."

Sam waved over his shoulder as he opened the door to leave. "You got it, Evelyn." The door closed. Pretty soon, they were in the car and out on the highway, and Sam seemed lost in thought.

Finally, curiosity got the best of Nathan. "You known Evelyn long?" He looked back at the highway, in case the question hit a nerve.

To the contrary, the question seemed to bring Sam back from wherever he had gone in his mind. "Yeah, about twenty-five years." He continued, apparently needing to tell the story. "Yeah, Evelyn was a real socialite when I first met her. Came from a farm in Crockett, but had higher aspirations. She married the guy that owned the first mall in this city and lived in a big house on Franklin Avenue. You know the kind— 5000 square feet, a porte cochere on the side, and a real big pool in the back." He paused, lost in thought for a block or so, before continuing. "She had a daughter. She looked like Vivian Leah in *Gone with the Wind*. Too damn beautiful and too damn smart to be sixteen. Got mixed up with a local drug dealer about thirty years old—cocaine and then heroin. I was on the task force back then and busted her a few times. At first, Evelyn and her husband didn't believe it and hated my guts. After a while, they began to see the effects, and then Evelyn came to me and wanted help. We tried everything—counseling, private care, even Betty Ford.

"I'll tell you something Nathan." Sam focused on Nathan driving. "You can't save someone that's hell-bent on dying, and that girl was hell-bent on dying. I found her behind the old Safeway in Bellmead— beat up, raped, and dead. She had needle tracks all up her arm. Eighteen years old, ninety pounds, and used up. I had to tell Evelyn and her husband. He never recovered. He was older and died about a year later. Most people would have grieved and that would be it. Not Evelyn. She blamed it on spoiling the girl, too much freedom, and too much money. She blamed herself mostly, and I guess she decided to do something about it. She sold the big house, cashed in the stocks, bought herself enough of an annuity to guarantee she could eat, and put the rest in a foundation for wayward young girls. You probably heard of it. 'Polly's Ranch'?" Sam looked at Nathan to see if he had.

"Yeah, I have heard of that. I thought it was some national deal."

"It is national, and you just met the sole benefactor."

Nathan couldn't make it all fit. "If she's the benefactor, what is she doing in Waco at the Salvation Army?"

Sam pointed to the corner. "Take a right. She's doing what she loves, what she was born to do—helping people that haven't got much of a chance one on one. Those people know the difference between Evelyn and a nine–to–five social worker at human services. She could walk down the darkest alley in Belmead in the middle of the night, and no one would touch her. She's that loved around here." Sam looked around and smiled at Nathan. "That's another thing I want you to learn, Nathan—the difference between most people and real people. Most people aren't real people. When you're lucky enough to meet a real person, try to see if they fit anywhere in your life. Try to make it so they would help you if you needed it. I'd take one Evelyn for fifty agency people in a pinch if I really needed help. There isn't much she wouldn't do for me, or for you, now that she knows you're with me. Don't you forget that. You might need her some day."

Nathan couldn't really see how that would happen unless he needed more bad clothes, but he knew enough to nod at Sam and try to take the advice to heart. Sam sat back in the seat, burped big, reached inside his coat pocket, and popped two Tums into his mouth. He spoke to no one in particular. "Damn, that heartburn is eating me up. I just can't figure why I get it so bad."

Nathan looked over at Sam to see if he was serious. He couldn't be serious, could he? He had just polished off about two pounds of eggs, pancakes, link sausage, sausage patties, bacon, grits, and four cups of coffee with three spoons of sugar each and a lot of cream. Had Sam bothered to return Nathan's glance, he would have seen Nathan's eyes wide open in disbelief. Nathan looked back to the road going by, thinking, *Heartburn! He's lucky it isn't heart failure.*

"Have you ever thought of going on some kind of a diet?" Nathan floated the idea in a tentative voice, unsure how Sam would take what the simple question implied. He didn't have to wait long.

Sam stopped eyeing the manicured yards going by, turned full around in the seat to face Nathan, waited an impossibly long moment, staring straight and hard at the side of Nathan's face, and asked in a firm, quiet voice, "Why, Nathan, do you think I'm fat?"

Nathan could feel the eyes burning a hole in the side of his face and chose to get very interested in turning left at the next corner. When

Sam didn't look away, he knew he better say something. "No, well, not exactly fat. You know—maybe a little extra weight. I mean, I was just kinda worrying about your health, seeing the way you eat at breakfast, and well, at lunch and dinner, too, for that matter." This was not going well. "Don't take me wrong; I just thought maybe it might help that heartburn if you ate a little lighter." Nathan finally turned around, smiling hopefully. Sam was not looking amused.

Little pissant, Sam thought. *Thinks I don't realize I'm forty pounds overweight and couldn't come near to passing the agency physical exam.* That brought Sam back to when he was Nathan's age—thin, buff, stomach full of abs, able to eat anything that moved and not gain an ounce. Time took care of that, big time. After his wife died, Sam had buried himself in his work. At home, he ate too much, and sometimes, drank too much to fill the empty void.

Seeing the way Nathan's face sunk with his consternation and the way his Adam's apple shook when he swallowed hard, Sam suddenly remembered his own boy and felt bad for jacking with Nathan. Heck, the boy was right, and he probably was just thinking about what was best for him. Sam looked back out the other side of the car. "Yeah, maybe you're right. I probably ought to hit that fruit and cereal bar with you tomorrow morning. You got some pretty good ideas sometimes for a rookie." He slapped Nathan on the shoulder with a big bear fist. Things were fine again.

Back at the deer camp, Nathan sat in his folding chair, a fresh cold Coors in the Koozie, and the irresistible smell of a medium-rare rib eye cooking over an open fire, next to a skillet full of Worcestershire, butter, steak seasoning, shrimp, onions, bell peppers, and fresh mushrooms sizzling over the fire.

From the next camp chair, Sam called over, "Hey, Nathan, do me a favor and turn those baked potatoes in the coals before they burn on that side."

"Sure thing." After three days, Nathan was getting to be an old hand at camp cooking, flicking the foil wrapped potatoes over without a glove, quick enough not to burn his hands.

To the side, the dessert du jour lay hidden in the Dutch oven, but Nathan knew the apple and cherry pie filling was simmering away with a crispy butter crust just under the lid covered with exactly twelve coals.

He had learned the first night—not ten, not fourteen—exactly twelve coals for exactly thirty-five minutes, and the cobbler was done perfectly. Nathan was beginning to understand why Sam was forty pounds overweight. From the way his Levis were fitting, he was about five pounds heavier in the last three days alone.

"You know something, Sam; I used to hear about friends going hunting and camping, and I just didn't get it." Nathan paused, taking in the thirty-mile ring of horizon that led gently off the hill—a red sunset with pink and scarlet clouds fading slowly into a sky that went from blue, to deep green, to indigo.

A young red-tail hawk shrilled his call, alerting the small rodent population that death was coming for anything careless enough to be seen. Other than the occasional bird, the quiet was deafening. Nathan took a long, slow drag off the longneck, feeling the same click that Paul Newman was looking for in *Cat on a Hot Tin Roof.*

Out here, not much seemed to matter beyond another beer, the steak, the potato, the veggies, the cobbler, another steak, maybe another beer, and, oh, yeah, another beer. Time expanded, and long silences around the campfire became as welcome as the hectic, accelerated bar talk of which his generation seemed so fond.

At first, Nathan wondered what they were really doing as they checked out the old Ford pickup from the agency pound. It looked like shit, but under the hood, it had a fresh Ford 390 police interceptor engine with a big Holly four-barrel carb. The four-speed stick shift was a Hurst shifter with a horizontal nickel shift knob that conformed to your fingers. It got about eight miles to the gallon, and Sam, uncharacteristically, wanted to drive most of the time.

Compared to Nathan's personal car, a new Audi A-6, it was prehistoric, but Nathan quickly figured out that big V8 would pull a stump out of the ground. He found himself wondering what a 390 conversion would cost for a used truck.

Listening to Sam on the cell phone, he was able to piece together that the land they were on was owned by a college professor from the political science department at SMU. The professor, with long white hair and baggy clothes that vaguely reminded Nathan of the outfits he saw his dad and mom wearing in the sixties in all those old family pictures, was actually a minor operative for the agency who fancied himself an important double agent reporting on the minor anarchist and leftist tendencies of his colleagues. He was tickled pink to help when Sam called.

After a quick $400.00 run through Super Wal-Mart for tents, chairs, mattresses, pillows, propane lanterns, flashlights, fire starter, matches, toilet tissue, plastic utensils, pans, pots, ice chests, cups, coffee pot, can openers, and a whole lot of other stuff, Nathan stood dumbfounded at the mound of necessities in the back of the truck. He was wondering to himself how the pioneers ever made it and how they could get one more thing in the truck when Sam came back from putting up the two shopping baskets, slapped him on the back, and said, "Hey, you ready to hit HEB? I hear they got rib eyes and Coors on sale this week."

Before they left HEB, Nathan had learned two important things: one, how much an old Ford truck can really hold after you think it's full, and two, how "real men" really eat. The first afternoon was a blur of colorful rip-stop nylon tents with fiberglass connecting poles that were harder to put together than a model of DNA, gathering dead wood for the fire and learning that supper cooked by Sam was a glorious event to be savored at leisure.

Later, after midnight, a cold breeze blew in from the northwest. While surveying the belt of Orion, closer and brighter in an ink-black sky so clear the Milky Way looked like a milk stain across the sky, Nathan finally asked the question he had been wondering about all day.

"Hey, Sam?" Slow sip on the Coors, long silence.

"What, Nathan?" Long sip of Coors by Sam.

Nathan spoke without looking away from the beautiful sky. "What exactly are we doing out here?"

After a minute, Sam seemed to rouse in the reclining aluminum lounge chair. "Have you ever seen a sky with stars that sharp and clear?" Sam asked, ignoring the previous question.

Nathan's reply was unhurried. "No, I don't ever think I have." Long silence, long sips.

"Oh, yeah." Sam caught his train of thought again. "What are we doing here?" Another pause. "You see that multi-band radio receiver on the camp table hooked up to that whip antenna?" He didn't wait for an answer. "Well, I've narrowed the murder and the Martian postcard investigation down to three parties of interest. Our friend Elvin Wright, town visitors Abra Avant, and her two friends, Skippy Beto, who, by the way, is the only son of the Beto Broadcasting empire, and the local resident engineering genius, Dennis Smith, from Goliath."

Sam got up, stirred the fire with a stick they kept for that one purpose, knowing not to put it on the fire. "Okay, I'll bite," said Nathan. "So what has that got to do with the receiver over there?"

"Well," Sam seemed pleased with what he was about to say. "Now that the judge has signed the wiretaps, we're going to be privy to every conversation to or from any of them on their cell or land lines." Sam warmed to the subject. "It may take a few weeks for something to happen, but I think we can weather it fine out here. I'm even thinking of getting a travel trailer if it goes on long enough."

It was tonight, the third night, after two days of mundane communications having nothing to do with the investigation, when the receiver came to life with the call that would change everything. Sam was midsteak when he heard that otherworldly static for the first time, followed by the measured, simulated alien voice. "Elvin, Klatoo here."

Nathan could not believe his ears, having never quite bought Sam's unwavering belief that aliens and half-breed alien women were involved. In that short two minutes, he realized that he better start paying a lot more attention to what Sam said. As soon as the phone clicked off, Sam purposefully got up, yawned, and started for the truck, reluctantly leaving the half-eaten steak on the plate on the table. "Come on, chief, we got a little show to go to."

Nathan finished his beer in two swigs, and without thinking, thought, *Damn, I think I'm really gonna like this job.*

Chapter Twenty-Three

"DROP, DUCK, AND COVER"

Back on the hill, Dennis and crew had reached the end of the bluff. Skippy looked gingerly over the edge, yawned, and opined, "Okay, Einstein—looks like the edge of the world. What do we do now? Fly?"

Dennis ignored the jab as he patiently began to unload the rope, tools, and bags he was carrying. After a suitable pause to show his disdain, he replied casually, "You can fly if you want to, but I would recommend you fall." With that, Dennis simply disappeared over the side.

Startled, Abra's breath froze in her chest. Skippy let the event filter through the six-pack he had polished off at the house. Satisfied with the understanding a few extra seconds can bring at such times, he looked gingerly over the edge, and asked in a soft, intentionally feminine voice, "Hey, honey, you okay?"

Before she could catch herself, Abra slugged Skippy in the arm hard enough to bring a wounded, "Hey, that hurt!"

From below the edge, the response drifted up. "If you two are through abusing each other, you can start handing down some tools." Dennis's head appeared over the edge with a large grin. This time, both Abra and Skippy wanted to kick him and dumped their load on him at once. The head disappeared under the avalanche of stuff.

Anticipating they might be interested, Dennis explained as he started picking up ropes and equipment. "If you want to know, there is a ledge over the edge that's large enough to stand on. It slopes down to about fifteen feet below the bluff to the spot we need to work on."

After easing over the edge, Skippy reached up and helped Abra down. Using their lights, they followed Dennis down the ledge, which was mostly obscured by weeds. As she went along, Abra's hand trailed the wall of the bluff, feeling the rough limestone layers deposited by millions of years of advancing and receding shallow seas. Fossils from numerous epochs littered the layers, giving evidence of a time before man, when mollusks, trilobites, and hard-shelled fish ruled the universe.

Unconsciously, the tips of her fingertips recorded the gradual change as the layers gave way to a rough sandpaper feel, much like a shark's skin. Then the rough edge gradually changed to a smooth, uniform texture. The change in texture was enough to reach through Abra's concentration on her flashlight and her next step.

Stopping, she shined the big Mag-lite back over the path. She saw the layered limestone give way to a sandblasted surface that looked infused with small grains of polished sand that reflected tiny bursts of multi-colored light. Finally, as she turned the light to illuminate the wall next to her, she realized the surface looked like frozen, molten lava that had been sprayed with midnight blue metal-flake paint from a '65 Impala.

"Dennis, I'm no geologist, but this is downright strange." The feel was so odd; she could not stop running her fingers over the combination of velvet and sand that reflected a distorted image of her hand in the light.

Dennis was nonplused, having long since gotten used to the effect. "Yeah, it is unique, but you might want to turn the light out and see the strangest part."

Abra was beginning to sense a joke at her expense. "Yeah, what are you going to throw on me when I turn off the light?"

Dennis was offended. "Hey, what do you think I am—an eighth-grader?" The response was for once an identical and unanimous "Yes!" from both Abra and Skippy.

"Okay, you non-believers, just turn off your lights and prepare to be amazed." As they turned off the lights, both looked around, trying to see the great event. Nothing. Skippy and Abra looked out from the bluff from horizon to horizon and back to the wall, seeing nothing.

Skippy yawned. "Hey, Mr. Wizard, when are we supposed to get it?"

Dennis yawned back. "Just look back down the path and let your eyes adjust."

Abra looked back where they had climbed down and saw the light of the small towns nearby stop abruptly at the edge of the vertical bluff.

Her eyes slowly began to follow the path down to where they were. It took her a minute to realize there was light guiding the way, faint at first, then plainly visible in an ever-increasing opal gleam.

It was like each small grain of sand on the wall above the path was lit from within, flashing a weak light into the night. Abra touched the wall to see if it would rub off. Skippy, having finally figuratively "seen the light" said, "Man, either I've drank too much Bud, or this wall is glowing."

"It's almost like when you were a kid and squished a firefly and rubbed its tail on your fingers. They would glow green for minutes." Abra was still amazed. "Is it a reflection, or what?"

Dennis sat on the ledge, his feet dangling over the sloping edge. "I guess I'd have to say 'or what.'" He paused. "The one thing I am sure of is that it is not a reflection. I've covered it with material to shield out all extraneous light, and it still glows, fluctuating as if something were running over the source like water, shielding the power. Each grain is its own tiny generator, and it never seems to run out of fuel. Whatever it is, it's part of the same phenomenon you saw with the water. There is great radiation here, but it is as harmless as the water."

Abra couldn't take her eyes or hands off the glowing surface. "Why hasn't someone found it before?"

Dennis was still sitting on the edge, taking in the thirty-mile view from horizon to horizon. "I suspect they have in ancient times. This place has always been special to indigenous people. As for modern man, how many people do you suspect have walked this path in the dark during this century, and how many of those would have turned off their light long enough to see the glow?"

"Why hasn't someone seen it from far away?" Abra asked.

"Simply put, the illumination is too low to be visible beyond a few yards, although it plays hell with night vision goggles." Dennis got up and slapped Skippy, who was sitting in the path playing with a bug, on the shoulder, "Time to go to work, chief. Hold your light on this spot right here." Dennis marked the spot with his hand.

"What are you going to do?" Skippy was already on the spot as he asked.

"Well, the Interocetor says this wall is only a few inches thick at this point, so I'm going to drill some pilot holes, and if all goes well, a masonry saw will connect the holes to make an entrance."

Abra and Skippy looked at each other. "Entrance to what?" came the joint reply, more or less in unison.

That brought a rare joke from Dennis. "You two have got to quit doing that. You sound like the Double-Mint twins. I really don't know what this is going to be an entrance to. That's why we're heavy on rock climbing supplies—but I can tell you what I think." Dennis paused, waiting to be asked to proceed.

Abra looked at Skippy, who looked at Dennis. "Oh, pleasssse, Mr. Dennis, pleasssse tell us what you think. You know us manual labor helpers can't figure out this complicated stuff withoutin you tell us," chirped Skippy in his best Uncle Remus voice.

Dennis looked at Skippy with his best Jack Benny deadpan, and said quietly, "You know something, Skippy; I used to have a stray dog I got at the pound that amused the hell of me. You do, too, but you drink a lot more money up in beer than that dog ate in Gravy Train."

Skippy took a minute to digest that deep thought and analyzed it in his best Budweiser style. Somewhat comfortable that he had made the right analysis of the meaning of the statement, replied, "Thanks, I appreciate that, and I like you, too."

Abra turned away so Skippy wouldn't see her rolling her eyes in disbelief. Satisfied, Skippy slapped his hands together as if he were ready to go to work. "Hey, we gonna dig something up, or what?" With that, he shined his light back on the spot with a look of sheer concentration, as if the job were incredibly tedious and difficult. Dennis obliged the effort by starting to drill the first pilot hole. Sparks flew as the bit sheared off the spot, unable to bite into the shining rock.

"Man, these bits are coated with diamonds, the best you can buy. Hand me that punch." After hammering a small impression, the drilling bit took hold, and the hole slowly increased in depth as the sparks flew in a steady stream. As the hole broke through, Dennis couldn't help note that it was more as if he was drilling glass than stone. Three more holes followed in an orderly succession.

"Skippy, hand me that masonry saw and plug it in that battery pack." Skippy had done a brief stint as a tool salesman at Lowes. He hadn't learned much during the week he worked before they realized he was smoking pot in the break room, but he knew he had never seen a saw like this one that didn't plug into a wall. "Man, where did you get this thing? It looks like a Harbor Freight Sawsall on steroids."

Dennis was pleased anytime his handiwork was noticed. "I modified a stock AC saw and built this battery pack from lab parts. I can run it longer than we're gonna need tonight."

Skippy examined the saw with a newfound respect. "Cool," he said, and gave it to Dennis.

Abra groaned under her breath at the revolting combination of male bragging and male bonding. She half expected them to break into gorilla sounds and thump their chests.

"Abra, I need you to pump up that sprayer and spray water on the blade at a real slow, steady rate. Can you do that?"

Abra picked up the sprayer, pumped it up deliberately, and then pointed the tip at Dennis and mashed the handle, spraying a steady mist in Dennis's face. "Like this?" She smiled, stopping the spray, but not in a hurry.

"Yea, Abra, just like that, only there, okay?"

"Sure boss," came a calm and satisfied reply.

Like an oversized game of connect the dots, Dennis gradually began cutting the legs of the puzzle. The hole would be large enough for any of the three to pass through. Gradually, the frivolity and joking stopped. It was as if each person began to realize that whatever was on the other side, it was gonna be special. Special began to turn to dangerous as they neared the last of the last cuts. As if an unspoken message had been passed telepathically, Dennis stopped three inches from the end of the last cut on the top.

Standing, Dennis wiped his brow, and sat down on the edge, dangling his feet, and looking out at the expanse of dark punctuated by occasional town lights in the distance, mirrored with the sparkling overlay of stars. Skippy and Abra stayed where they were, unsure of what was happening. With the lights out and the sound of the saw gone, they became aware of a cool gentle breeze, and the faint highway sounds from five miles away.

Dennis did not look back as he spoke. "I don't know if the two of you know it, but we're fixing to make some history here. I don't know what we're going to find, but it's going to be something big. I think I understand how Howard Carter felt when he punched that hole in King Tut's tomb." Dennis surveyed the horizon slowly. No one said anything.

This time, Skippy knew enough not to laugh. Abra felt a chill. That fear in the dark was close tonight, very close. No matter how she tried to shake it, the vision of her sitting in the chair, Linton's hands around her neck, had become more vivid as the saw came closer to the end of the cut. She did not want to admit it, but in a perverse way, she wanted to feel that way again.

Abra realized that Dennis was talking to them again. "I just want you to know, I never had many friends. Whatever happens, I wouldn't want it to happen with anyone other than the two of you."

Abra reached down and hugged Dennis, then turned his head around and kissed him square on the mouth.

Skippy looked like he just watched someone eat a cockroach. "Ah, shit, you two are grossing me out." He stood up, yawned, and said to no one in general, "Okay, shall we kick some ass or what?"

Lights came on. Water began to spray, and the saw cut the last three inches. Leaving the last quarter inch, Dennis stopped the saw and stood up. "Hand me that rubber hammer, Skippy."

Skippy handed him the hammer, backing up the trail as if expecting an explosion. Abra stood her ground beside Dennis.

Dennis looked at them and said, "Here goes." With that, he gently tapped the center of the cut. The last quarter-inch split along the saw line and for a minute nothing happened. Then, as if hit by an unseen hand, the square of rock literally jumped out of the hole, falling to the ground on the edge of the ledge.

Skippy had the presence of mind to grab it before it fell over the side. "Man, did you see that? It shot out of that hole like it was pushed."

Dennis was nonplussed. "It was pushed. I've been measuring a reduction in gravity around this hill for months. I'm not surprised."

Abra wasn't catching the science. "I don't understand. How could that make it shoot out like that?"

Dennis began to throw a loop of rope over his shoulder. "Simple—it's just like an airplane wing or the sail on a sailboat. When the pressure is lower on one side than the other, you get lift. You just saw that plug fly out of that wall—only gravity was the wind."

Skippy's mouth hung wide open. "Man, they sure didn't teach any of that shit at the high school I went to."

Hanging around Skippy, Dennis was turning into a regular little comedian. "Yeah, I guess science wasn't big at the alternative school, was it?"

Skippy had climbed up the rocks near the top of the ridge. Looking over the top, he spoke a little lower. "Maybe not, but knowing when someone's about to crawl up your ass sure was, and someone's fixing to crawl up our ass if we don't find somewhere to go fairly quick from the flashlights I see coming in the front gate."

Scrambling up behind Skippy, Dennis barely got, "Yeah, sure," out of his mouth when he saw flashlights go out just inside the park gate. "Uh-oh, we've got to come up with something quick. Any suggestions?"

Having spent a good deal of his short adult life dodging irate dads and husbands, Skippy knew a thing or two about thinking fast. "Yeah, I do. They really did teach thinking fast at the alternative school." He made sure he had Dennis and Abra's full attention.

"Here's the deal. Dennis, you throw all the equipment into that hole you just opened. Abra, find a bush or rock, or anything you can put over that hole, and then the two of you shine that light into the hole and see how far you're gonna fall when you climb in head first, and I suggest you start falling into that hole in the next fifteen seconds unless you want a block party with whoever is coming."

Abra was already on her knees, shining the light in. "It looks like a tunnel about five feet around, going down at a gentle slope, just like Dennis said it would, but I can't see the end."

Skippy rubbed his hands together as if he might be fixing to actually work. Savoring the pure fear on both of their faces, he looked around and said in an unhurried voice, "Why don't the two of you hit that hole while I make sure we don't leave anything to give us away."

Abra and Dennis almost ran into each other trying to get to the hole first. Embarrassed, they stood up, each motioning for the other to go. Skippy shook his head. "Okay, I'm the hall monitor, now, just like I'm sure you both were in grammar school, so you go first, Abra; Dennis, go second, and I'll be behind you in about a minute. So go, now!" Abra was gone in the blink of an eye, Dennis right behind her.

Alone, Skippy pulled another longneck out of his backpack, opened it, threw the cap off the bluff, and climbed back up the gently sloping ledge until he could just stick his head over the grass like a World War I soldier peeking over the edge of a foxhole. Gauging the distance, Skippy saw two people approaching in the distance, about two hundred feet away, but very slowly, with no light.

"They know we're here, or they wouldn't bother sneaking up," he thought to himself. "Now how the hell do they know we're here, and why are they after us?" An adrenalin rush was nothing new to Skippy.

Not as good as going out a bedroom window in a sheet, but pretty damn close.

In no particular hurry, he felt like a mountain lion hidden in the brush, watching a hunter. At least, that's what he felt like until he realized the newcomers were heading straight as an arrow to the spot where the ledge trail was closest to the top of the bluff.

Skippy turned the Bud up, drinking half the bottle but never taking his eyes off the slowly advancing duo. The quicksilver clouds, backlit by the full moon, cleared at that moment, giving Skippy just enough time to duck down below the grass, and just enough time to tell that the duo was a man and a woman. A very, very long-legged woman.

Skippy finished off the beer as he ducked back down the trail, turning toward the drop off. He reared his arm back to throw the bottle as far out as possible, knowing the sound, when it hit two hundred feet down, would not carry, when a strange sound stopped him cold. It was almost imperceptible, but just loud enough for him to hear it literally zoom in from far away. The closest thing he could think of was the high-pitched whine the turbo on Skippy's Saab made when they blasted off the hill onto the highway at sunset.

Skippy peered in front of him intently, tying to focus on the exact spot the sound had stopped and now was a gentle whirring. In front of him, he saw the horizon, lit by the small towns. Above, the sky had cleared, the moon was huge, and the larger stars twinkled like bright, brittle diamonds, except for right in front of him.

There, just there, about twenty feet out, the air seemed to shimmer, just as heat off hot asphalt makes images appear to shimmer. Tiny flashes of light randomly exploded in the air, almost like the static on a TV with no signal. *Yeah, okay, I know where you are now*, Skippy mouthed to himself.

Pretending to turn away, Skippy suddenly turned back, throwing the bottle as hard as he could at the shimmering area. What happened next happened so fast that Skippy could barely perceive it. In the split second it took the bottle to cover twenty feet, the air coalesced, and for the briefest instant, almost imperceptibly, he saw the craft in all its platinum glory, lit by the plasma units at the top, bottom, and around the side, seething in a rainbow of color, like liquid fire.

Just as the bottle reached the edge of the craft, it disappeared with the slightest whoosh, as if the air had rushed in where the craft had been. The longneck never paused, continuing to tumble end over end out of sight.

Skippy stood, transfixed and dumbfounded, until the sound of the couple slowly approaching reminded him of where he needed to be, and quickly. Sliding to his knees, Skippy crawled into the hole backward like a crab into a shell, pulling the small bush Abra had left against the opening.

He had a good idea that whoever was coming would know where he had gone, so he wasted no time turning around, lighting the way with the small LED headlamp Dennis had insisted he carry. Moving as fast as he could on his knees, he could just make out Abra and Dennis, now able to stand upright, as if there was not much hurry. They must have heard him, too, because they stopped, waiting for him.

By the time Skippy reached them, he had added two more bits of knowledge to his rather small repertoire. First, he had a mild case of claustrophobia. Second, crawling on your knees was a lot harder than he remembered as a child.

Sensing the tunnel was getting taller, if not wider, Skippy quickly caught up, wasting no time between panting for breath. "Turn that big light off." They did, sensing the panic in his voice. "I've got good news and bad news." Another gasp for air. "The bad news is we got a lot stranger company than the two people coming up the hill." Another gasp for air.

Dennis was used to exaggeration from Skippy. "So, what's the good news?" he asked.

If looks could kill, Skippy's might have done him in. "The good news is I don't think that hole you made is big enough for a flying saucer to get through."

Dennis and Abra looked at him, then at each other, and might have laughed, except for the wide, dilated eyes and animal panic emanating from every inch of Skippy's body. He looked like he was fixing to run. "Listen, I don't have time to explain, but we need to get on down to wherever this tunnel goes as quick as we can. Use this; the light is harder to see." He handed the LED light to Abra.

She turned without a word, and Dennis and Skippy followed. At first, the three were intent on making their way down the tunnel, which seemed to go on forever as they made steady progress downward. The angle got steeper as it went down, requiring they keep all their attention on the rippled rock floor to keep from falling as the light from the small beam created ever changing shadows.

Gradually, Dennis discerned a dim light in the distance. Not light like the moonlight outside—rather, a dim glow. The glow grew until he could tell it came from an opening. "Abra," was all he said at first.

"What?" The reply was short, and Abra's voice still contained a hint of panic.

"Turn out the light."

Abra stopped, turned to face him, and snapped, "Are you crazy? We're not going to be any better off if we fall and break a leg." It was a side of Abra that Dennis hadn't seen before.

Skippy edged by on the side, mumbling in his ear as he passed, "That's the ball and chain voice of a future wife if I ever heard one."

Dennis stayed calm, using a firm voice he had never used on any woman. "Just do it, Abra. Trust me and turn off the light."

She did. At first, the dark was deafening. "Okay, the light is off; so what now?"

"Just wait a minute. Let your eyes adjust."

"Look, Dennis, this isn't another one of those glowing—" She paused for a long second, as her night vision returned. "Walls." The word came trailing out, already thought, and too late to stop.

Skippy was nonplussed. "Okay, we're in some kind of cave, with glowing blue-green walls and a flying saucer waiting outside." He shook his head. "This may just be the best Saturday night I ever had." Turning, Skippy headed for the opening and the brighter glow beyond. Abra followed, with Dennis in tow after a quick look behind to see if lights were following. They weren't, at least not yet.

As they passed through the rough opening, they saw the walls open into a large oval cavern, roughly two hundred feet across. It looked much like one of the caverns open to the public in south Texas, except the walls seemed lit from within, casting a cold blue-green light the exact shade of a lightning bug.

In the center, what looked like a small pool of water twenty feet across seemed lit from within. The three stumbled into the cavern, amazed at the scene. Dennis realized he was holding his breath and needed to breathe. Abra gingerly stepped toward the pool, drawn by the shimmering glow below the surface.

"Be careful," Dennis warned her in a whisper. Something about the place made you feel you shouldn't make any more sound than possible. The cavern had the feel of a holy place, much like a sanctuary in a European cathedral.

"Don't worry," Abra said as she made her way to the edge of the pool. "It's only a few feet deep." She leaned over the edge to look. The pool was a perfect turquoise, crystal clear, but with a surface in flux, shimmering with bubbles rising to the top in a constant stream, like a pot boiling on a stove.

The bottom of the pool was pure white sand, with thousands of small springs bubbling up. On one side, the edge of the limestone pool was broken off, creating a waterfall into a dark hole where the water disappeared, as if returning from wherever it had come.

Appearing to end a few feet below the pool surface, Abra saw a tall pillar of black stone, reaching from deep in the pool toward the surface. It looked like some kind of altar, but you could tell it was completely natural. The top of the pillar was cupped and appeared about three feet across. The pillar looked harder than the limestone around it, as if it had been thrust up from a different stratum. In the cup in the center lay the most amazing piece of rock Abra had ever seen.

As she leaned over to see better, Abra realized she was too far over. Just as she was about to fall in, Dennis caught her waist and pulled her back. "I said, be careful, Abra. That pool may be a hundred feet deep."

"It can't be, Dennis. Look, you can see the bottom just a few feet down."

"Watch." Dennis leaned down, picking up a small rock. Sitting on his heels, he held the rock out over the water. "Count the seconds when I let it go." With that, he gently let it drop at the surface.

By now, Skippy was leaning over the pool with his hands on his knees. Under his breath, he counted off the seconds as the stone fell, as if in honey. "One thousand one, one thousand two, one thousand three," and so on, expecting the stone to hit the bottom that shimmered just a few feet below at any time. It didn't.

After many seconds, he lost sight of the stone as it continued toward the black stone altar and the bright white sand bottom glistening just beyond his reach.

Skippy shook his head, "Man, that's really creepy. What's wrong with that water? It must be as thick as syrup."

"No, the water's fine; it's just very deep." Dennis explained to Skippy. "A rock falls in feet per second in water. I figure that rock fell close to a hundred feet before it reached the top of the pillar, and another hundred feet until I lost sight of it." They all stared, spellbound, as the stone in the top of the pillar continued to simmer.

"Hey. Einstein," Skippy called, without taking his eyes off the pool.

"What?" Dennis answered in the same hushed voice.

"What is that rock laying on the pillar? I never saw anything like that in the mineral section of the natural museum in the sixth grade." Expecting the usual well-thought-out and factually correct explanation, Skippy waited patiently.

After a long pause, Dennis spoke without looking up. "Naw, I don't think I did, either, Skippy." Skippy looked up in amazement. Einstein stumped was not something he was used to. After a life of running on instinct with little factual knowledge, he had become accustomed to having the virtual encyclopedia on all subjects that was Dennis on hand to answer all mysteries, big or small.

Dennis felt the raw edge of excitement and fear rise in his stomach and found that he liked the feeling. "What do you think it is?" This time, Dennis was asking the question.

The stone in question lay quietly simmering. It appeared to be several feet in diameter, which meant it was probably three to four times that large at the depth it lay. It was roughly circular. So far, pretty normal. It wasn't the shape or size; it was what it was doing that made it amazing.

The surface was jet black, like onyx, but with no reflection, and it was covered with a million dots of brilliant light, as if it had diamonds embedded everywhere. Each point of light pulsed from within, sometimes bright, sometimes less, coming in waves, as if fueled by a flickering atomic furnace. Every time the pinpoints pulsed with light, the water boiled and seethed around it, releasing bubbles that roiled to the surface. As their eyes adjusted to the light, they each saw that the water pulsed in time with the strange rock; the walls of the cavern did as well.

Suddenly, Dennis drew in his breath. "Wait a minute, I've seen it before. I know what it is." Abra and Skippy turned to face him, waiting for an explanation. "Think! You've seen the films of nuclear reactors? You know the ones that show the core?"

Now Abra got it. "Of course. The core simmering in heavy water. It looks just like this. Jesus, do you know what we're watching? It's got to be the real thing, or we would be dead." Abra touched the water gingerly. "It's cold fusion, isn't it?"

Dennis nodded. "Got to be, or something close to it. All those billions of dollars, and the answer was simmering right here under a limestone bluff in Texas." Dennis was excited, talking fast, as if he were dictating technical notes for a scientific journal. "The natural design is perfect. The reactor stone sits in the middle of a natural pool fed by pure cold spring water percolated up from the white sand bottom of the pool. After cooling the stone and damping whatever type of radiation it emits, the used cooling water cascades back into the earth through a large hole. Now I understand about the radiation in the water I showed you at the house. It makes perfect sense.

"The water leaves the pool, falls back into the rock, where the city water wells pick it up further down in the strata. Once the water is exposed to air, the radiation dissipates. Whatever effect the water has on humans affects everyone who drinks from the Tejas Hill Water System. That explains why the place is so odd and the people so strange."

Skippy nodded as if he finally got it. "Well, that explains why all the locals are so odd, so what's your excuse, Einstein?"

Dennis thought to himself that Skippy would probably crack a joke sitting in the electric chair in Huntsville.

"Seriously, guys, I hate to break up this episode of *Nova*, but we've still got two people and probably a little gray alien on our ass, so let's find a way out of here."

Sometimes, a joke is too close to the truth. Just as he turned to look for a way out, Skippy saw something floating even with him. A dull gray instrument with a decidedly menacing look connected to slender gray fingers was pointed at him. "Aw, shit. A little gray alien!"

"Yeah, we got it, Skippy—a little gray alien." Abra didn't look around.

Dennis was still examining the pool and spoke without looking. "Quit joking around, Skippy; go find a way out while I finish checking this out."

"I ain't joking, Dennis; you might want to turn around." It was the use of the name Dennis, not Einstein, not Genius; Skippy never used Dennis' given name unless it was bad. Dennis started to turn around when he heard the telltale static before the translation.

"By all means, Mr. Smith, keep on describing the phenomenon; so far, I believe you've just about nailed it."

Dennis and Abra turned slowly. In the pale glow, Klatoo hovered purposefully at eye level.

Abra dropped her flashlight without realizing it.

"Please, Mrs. Avant, there really is no need to gawk. Aliens have feelings, too. They tell me green actually highlights my gray skin." Klatoo laughed quietly at his little joke, and the translator obligingly brought forth a light chuckle. Abra would have fainted if Dennis hadn't caught her.

"Please, pardon my rudeness. A few introductions are in order." From his tone, they could have been in the drawing room of a Jane Austin novel. "My name is Klatoo. Well, not really, but you wouldn't understand the pronunciation of my full name, so that is my name here. I am the fifth general of the Mogollon Squadron of the Imperial Fleet in charge of galaxy Luna—your galaxy."

Klatoo then performed what appeared to be a second-class Boy Scout salute with military crispness, using his reedy, thin, gray fingers. "That is my assistant, Yasha, in the corner, accompanied by Mr. Elvin Wright, whom I believe you already know."

Until then, Dennis, Abra, and Skippy had been so engrossed with Klatoo that they had failed to notice the entrance of Yasha and Elvin. Elvin nodded, "Hey," and waved the same small, low wave he would have given at the front door of Connie's store. Yasha did her best Audrey Hepburn, looking gaunt and suave.

Skippy was blown away by Yasha. He couldn't take his eyes off her, until Klatoo, rather annoyed, waved whatever was in his hand. "Yes, Mr. Beto, she is beautiful, but we have more pressing business at hand." Klatoo looked back at Dennis. "I want to commend you, Mr. Smith. We have monitored your protracted and clandestine investigation of the hill. You have done a job that would pass muster and earn you respect in any civilization I know of, and that is more than a few. What a regret."

Dennis liked the first part, but didn't like the sound of the last part. Klatoo's voice was full of disappointment at something valuable about to be lost. "Normally, we could use someone with your talent."

Skippy couldn't resist. "Don't tell me—they just quit hiring down at the mine in Mogollon." Skippy laughed, looking around at Abra and

Dennis. "Aw, shucks, guys, there goes that good union job we were hoping for."

Dennis and Abra looked at him as if he was crazy. It took Klatoo a moment to get the joke then the translator issued another soft chuckle.

"Very amusing, Mr. Beto. Believe it or not, we have been watching you, as well. You might be surprised to learn that we have young men like you on our world as well."

"Let me guess—" Skippy smoothed his hair back as if he was getting ready for a scene in a movie. "Handsome and good with the women?"

Klatoo shook his head in the universal sign for a negative answer. "No, rich, addicted, and generally worthless. We call them juniors. In fact, one of my sons may well be your counterpart. I believe he is in his eighth year at university."

That stung Skippy. "Hey, I got out in seven." He looked genuinely offended. "You know, extended degree plan, changed majors a few times. It just takes time."

When Klatoo turned his attention back, his demeanor turned serious. "We really would like to stay and visit, maybe discuss our little find for a while. Unfortunately, I can't take earth's polluted atmosphere and pressure for very long, so we need to get on with it."

Dennis hoped he was right when he said, "Let me guess—you want us to get the rock out for you." Everyone knew which rock he was talking about.

Klatoo looked truly disappointed. "I wish that were the case, then I could delay the inevitable a little while longer. Unfortunately, Yasha and Elvin can do that for me with a little help." The statement sunk in on Dennis, Abra, and Skippy, and they gradually realized what he meant.

Skippy seemed nonplused, but really was just trying to buy a little time. "Well, I don't know about the rest of you, but my dance card ain't full, and I'm a hell of a swimmer. Certified life guard, with four years experience at the Highland Park Country Club Pool." Skippy smiled hopefully. "Surely, Elvin could use a little help, Mr. Klatoo." Skippy hoped kissing ass worked the same with aliens as it did in Highland Park.

Elvin bought it, nodding his thanks. "Thanks Skippy; I really don't swim that well, to tell you the truth."

Abra was silent, thinking this all seemed like a bad Ed Wood, Jr. movie script. But it was becoming more and more obvious that they were expendable, and in the not-too distant future. The Avant family had always been high strung, and she had just found the family gene for pissed off. She took a step forward, and Klatoo involuntarily floated backward a step. "I don't want to be rude, Klatoo, but from where I stand, you appear to be about four feet long, anorexic, and weigh about forty pounds. I don't see why I can't just wring your little gray neck and go on down the road."

"Bravo, Mrs. Avant, and you would be correct in assuming you could do just that, if it weren't for one small detail." With that, Klatoo raised the object again, pointing it at her. "This is a very politically correct instrument. It recycles your body in the blink of an eye. Ashes to ashes, dust to dust. I believe that's how it goes in your quaint little book." Klatoo smiled a dead, doll-eyed smile. Like a shark, his eyes did not blink, unless threatened. That gave him the appearance of menace at all times. A smile only magnified the menace.

While Klatoo talked, Skippy had been looking around for a back door to the place, thinking he would take his chances running. Better to be shot in the back than stand there and take it. At first, he thought his eyes were playing tricks on him when he saw two shadows emerge from the tunnel without making a sound, blending into the shadows among the rocks. He could have sworn that one of them was the FBI agent that had been snooping around town ever since Kinnerd Irvin was murdered. Making sure not to look directly at them and give them away, he watched hopefully as they flanked Klatoo, Yasha, and Elvin on two sides from the rear.

"I really must apologize in advance for what will come next. I would enjoy discussing this further, especially with you, Mr. Smith, but we have a busy night, and the three of you have a meeting with whatever God you pray to." Klatoo turned to Elvin. "Elvin, I'm afraid you must join your friends; you have served your purpose well, and please don't think I don't appreciate your amusing Yasha."

Elvin looked at Yasha, horrified. Surely, she would stand up for him. Instead, she stood ramrod straight and turned only her neck to face him. Suddenly, her eyes did not blink, just like Klatoo. In that instance, Elvin realized that the elongated features and eyes that made her so mysterious were what evidenced the alien side of her. "Please, Elvin, you didn't think I really cared for you, did you?"

Elvin was broken. In an instant, his life was meaningless. He thought about the night his life changed. The trip to Mars. He thought about how naive he had been—making sure he had a twenty in his billfold to go to Mars. What else did a loser like him expect? How could he have thought this beautiful creature, this Venus, could love him?

Just as suddenly, he realized it didn't matter that much. He had his fling at life. The last few months had shown him how empty and futile everything before had been, and it would only have gotten worse. He still wouldn't change the last few months. Elvin had one thing he was going to say and he was going to say it before Klatoo did whatever he was going to do.

"Yasha, look at me." She did, more cold and alien than he had ever seen her. "I may not have meant a thing to you, and I don't know one thing about the rest of the universe, but I bet wherever there is life, there is love, and I bet that there is no one, anywhere else in the universe that ever loved anyone as much as I love you. If I die tonight, it doesn't matter that you don't love me, because I love you enough for both of us. Don't ever forget that. That kind of love means something wherever you are. Wherever you go."

Her eyes flickered for an instant as Klatoo watched her, searching for some indication of her emotions, but her cold gaze never wavered.

Without another word, Elvin walked over and stood next to Skippy. He was a human, no longer just a Texan, not just an American, not even just a citizen of the world, but a human, and tonight, that meant everything.

Sarcasm seemed to be a trait of the aliens. "How touching. I'm sure Yasha will put that in her scrapbook." His mood turned serious. "Now, enough is enough. You will all go to the edge of the pool and face the other way. I promise you will not feel pain."

No one moved.

Surprisingly, it was Skippy who spoke for them, and even he had no idea where the sudden jolt of courage and defiance came from. "Look, Klatoo, in Texas we don't turn and run, and we never abandon our women. I may not be John Wayne, but I damn sure remember the Alamo. So you can kiss my furry ass and shoot us to our face."

Klatoo shivered slightly at the mental picture that statement gave him. "As you wish, Mr. Beto. You can die where you stand."

Skippy was just fixing to charge, hoping he could buy Abra and Dennis time to jump Klatoo, when a calm voice came from behind.

"I wouldn't do that, Klatoo, unless you want to join your ancestors as well." Klatoo and everyone else froze as Sam walked out of the shadows. His service pistol was aimed at Klatoo's head. "I'm sure this pistol is barbaric to you, but it will kill you dead for any graveyard anywhere, and I assure you, it will hurt like hell. Nathan, I want you over there—" He pointed with his gun without taking his eyes off Klatoo. "So you have a clear shot at Klatoo. Now, Klatoo, hand your weapon to Skippy."

Klatoo analyzed the situation with his superior intellect in a nanosecond, seeking weakness, advantage, or a new strategy. Unfortunately, a stalemate was the same wherever you were in the universe. "Agent Nikosia, we seem to find ourselves at a draw. You can kill me, but my reflexes are fast enough to kill Ms. Avant and likely one more of her friends before I die. I am a soldier, and I will not give up. So we can play this game until you get tired and give in because my sleep cycle is much longer than yours." Klatoo stated the obvious without emotion. "I guess the next move is yours because I'm not putting anything down, and if you move, Abra dies first."

The game was on now. No one knew what to do next. No one could move. Nathan's brain was running overtime. What would Sam do? How long could a person hold a gun on someone before something gave and someone was killed?

Sam wasn't going to show fear, but he was thinking about the same thing that Nathan was. Abra, Dennis, and Skippy didn't know what to think, except Skippy thought he would probably end up doing something real stupid. Right now, he just couldn't decide which stupid thing to do. Everyone knew that sooner or later, probably sooner, something would happen to break the uneasy and unnatural equilibrium that was keeping them all alive for the moment.

"Well, who is going to die first, Agent Nikosia?" Klatoo taunted Sam, but Sam wasn't taking the bait. His eyes and gun didn't move off Klatoo.

"You can shoot him, Sam. He can't kill anyone." Yasha knew now was her time to act. She could not betray Klatoo before the arrival of the two FBI agents because the humans did not have any real defense to his weapon. Now, she understood the balance of power was even only so long as Sam thought Klatoo could kill with his weapon.

Klatoo heard the words and cursed the day he had taken the halfbreed under his wing. Sam wasn't about to be tricked. "What did you say?"

Yasha spoke slowly, in a clear and deliberate voice, so as not to be misunderstood. "I said, you can shoot Klatoo. He cannot kill anyone. His weapon cannot kill, only burn and stun on the setting on which he has it, and he will have to drop his aim to change the setting."

With that, she deliberately strolled over to stand beside Elvin with the rest of the humans. Her walk was so sensuous and so unhurried, it was obvious she was mocking Klatoo, knowing he could not take his weapon off Abra without fear of Sam drilling a hole in his large gray head.

Sam spoke again without looking at her. "Why should I believe you?" Sam had a healthy distrust of Greeks bearing gifts, and this Greek wasn't about to fall for a Trojan horse.

Yasha never missed a beat. "Two reasons. First, Klatoo will die if you believe me and fire either way. Why would I lie if doing so will only get him killed? Second, you don't have a choice. He may get uncomfortable, but he can hold this position long after your arms and brain give out. He may be small, but little aliens are formidable opponents. So, I would suggest you shoot him now. Abra or Skippy may get knocked unconscious or scarred from a burn, but that will be about all that happens."

Sam weighed the options and logic. She certainly had a point. Still, he was trained to protect citizens at almost any cost, and right now, he couldn't see a good reason to risk Abra. Skippy would have been a decent risk, but not Abra. Yasha did not wait for an answer, but slowly reached and took Elvin's hand in hers. The words that came out of Klatoo's speaker next would have turned a rap star red.

That might have been it. Sam might have shot Klatoo. Klatoo might have shot Abra. Skippy might have charged Klatoo. Skippy might have gotten his butt permanently scarred with burns. Any of those things might have happened, but they didn't. Instead, just as everyone was fixing to do whatever he or she was going to do, an odd sound broke the deafening silence.

From the dark rear of the cave came the sound of a door, an extremely heavy, well-hung door opening—its massive hinges whining in complaint as if they had not been coaxed to move in decades.

After what seemed like an eternity, there came a pause, then the sound of hard shoes, deliberately walking toward the assembled group in the gloom. No one could risk taking his or her eyes off the enemy, though the new intruder had the attention of every ear.

Gradually, a tall shadow seemed to grow in the gloom. What at first was simply a silhouette gradually gave way to the familiar outline of an impeccably tailored sport coat and an emerald ascot.

Linton Eggleston strode into the center of the opening, placing himself directly between Sam and Klatoo. He spoke without preamble or introduction, but in a civilized greeting reserved for family members that would mean nothing to all but one in the room. "Klatoo, what a long time it has been. I trust the gods still attend our mother's table?"

In Klatoo's culture, there were certain niceties and manners of speech that could not be ignored or sidestepped. "Yes, brother, she still enjoys their bounty to this day." With that, they both bowed their head ever so slightly in the required greeting of mutual deference.

Required courtesies having been met, Klatoo wasted no time getting to the point. "Linton, every time we meet, I wonder again why I did not kill you when you were a child and I had the chance. You may speak well now, but I will always remember the savage child on this hill, throwing stones at my ship. That is exactly what you will always be to me—a savage with a stone."

The contempt in Linton's eyes was clear as he replied, "The feeling is mutual. No matter how well you mask your true deviant nature with knowledge and technology, you will always be the bully kidnapping my people for your experiments. You may regard me as an inferior, but you caused me to be." Linton's glare was unwavering.

Klatoo's eyes blinked one time, leaving the nictitating white film over the dark pupils, as if he were going to attack. Doing so was the ultimate insult, similar to someone telling you to talk to the hand. "If you feel that way, you must also hate our mother." Klatoo intended the words to anger. "No one forced her to bear you; they only forced her to try to raise you. That was the mistake, to assume that you could be anything other than a freak in both worlds. You never quite fit, do you, Linton? You didn't in ours, and you don't in yours. A freak." With that insult, the nictitating membrane slowly opened.

It was rare that an alien ever let emotion affect his judgment. However, the need to insult Linton, based on sibling rivalry of the worst kind, had clouded Klatoo's judgment, making him forget he did not know all of the abilities Linton possessed. That had been the point of the failed experiment which ended with Linton being unceremoniously dumped back on the hill at the age of twelve, after spending eight years on the home planet as an equal in Klatoo's house, albeit an unwelcome equal.

As with a shark, by closing the protective membrane over his eyes, Klatoo had clouded his vision. Years later, the people in the cave would replay what happened next and even discuss it on odd occasions, but their memories would never quite match. Of all those present, Abra was the only one with enough experience around Linton to grasp what happened.

Just as the membrane began to open, Linton seemed to move the twelve-foot distance to Klatoo in the blink of an eye. At the same time, a large black object on a short stick appeared in his right hand, poised over Klatoo's neck. The other arm was now around Klatoo's neck, holding him in position to slit his throat.

Only Abra recognized the black object for what it was—a ceremonial obsidian knife of the type common in the cayokeon mounds in Missouri to the bloodstained alters of the Toltecs in Central America.

"As always, Klatoo, you are too close to the truth. A savage with a rock. That is what I am. A savage with a rock. Do you feel it?"

Abra saw Linton move the blade with the slightest of pressures and the razor thin line of green blood that followed. The edge was sharper than any razor, capable of cutting through ribs to bring out a live, beating heart, a scenario that had been played out in ancient America thousands of times.

To his credit, Klatoo did not flinch, instead brazenly taunting Linton, "Can you do it, Linton? I bet you can't. I bet you can't do to me what I would already have done to you in the same position."

If the taunt was intended to affect Linton, it didn't. "Let's see if you're right, Klatoo. Here is the test. You can drop the stun rod, or I will finish the job, and you will drop the stun rod. Either way, you will drop it. Now, what is your pleasure, brother?"

Abra saw the pressure on Klatoo's throat began to grow, and she knew it would keep increasing until all else was blotted out of Klatoo's mind. For the briefest second, she almost felt sorry for the little gray alien. Regardless, her relief was instant as the odd weapon fell from Klatoo's hand. Sam picked the weapon up quickly, putting it in his coat pocket.

Satisfied and moving in a blur, Linton was suddenly back where he had been, leaving Klatoo floating in place, feeling naked, inferior, and slightly ridiculous. Eight beings let out a combined sigh of relief, one a sigh of disgust.

"You may have won for now, brother, but I have all the time in the world. I will be back for the stone. You can't stop me."

Linton smiled slightly, understatement in word and expression apparently a mark of the alien psyche. "As always, you are correct as far as it goes. Yet, like most aliens, you often miss the forest for the trees. I won't be able to stop you, but the stone will. Ask yourself a question, Klatoo." His manner was that of a professor in charge of a class. "You and Mr. Smith should know the answer. What keeps the radiation in check? What keeps the tremendous power you both know is there from exploding and taking this whole planet with it?"

Klatoo's response was instant. "The water—obviously, the water. So what? Water is plentiful."

Dennis realized the obvious first. "It's not the water that keeps the stone from being moved. I bet it's more than simple water. It's the amount of water, the depth of the water, the fact it's not recycled, and possibly the mineral content of the water."

Linton clapped in a steady, measured mock applause. "Bravo, Mr. Smith. You are, true to your reputation, absolutely correct. Anyone who tries to move the rock from its present location will find that the harmless, beneficial radiation that has brought us all here, directly or indirectly, will burn them to a crisp. Unfortunately, it will also incinerate everything in this end of the solar system."

Linton turned back to Klatoo, strolling toward him until Klatoo instinctively floated backwards. "So, brother, bring your thrusters. Blow a hole in the hill. Marshall all the engineering expertise that you possess and prepare to meet your maker." Linton smiled to himself, as if enjoying his next thought before speaking it. "I would appreciate a polite warning before you do, so I can join Mother and mourn your passing." Still smiling courteously, Linton bowed slightly and said in a measured tone, "Now, it seems we have no more business at this time, so please, brother, don't let the door hit you on the way out." Never mind there was no door—everyone got the message.

Sam and Nathan had been dumbstruck by the drama that played out before them, but Sam sprung into action as Klatoo turned in midair, obviously intent on whatever he could do to salvage a graceful retreat.

"Wait a minute. No one is going anywhere." Klatoo stopped, hovering. He did not face Sam. "Someone is fixing to be under arrest, starting with that damn little alien." Nathan amused himself wondering how Sam would cuff the little sucker and get him into the Ford truck.

Linton turned to Sam. "Agent Nikosia, I fully understand about the heat of the moment, but please," he paused, moving slowly until he was in front of Sam, who was not looking at all certain as to what he should do next. "Think about it. What are you going to do? You could arrest Klatoo. I would certainly enjoy that. However, do you recall what happened to all the people who met the aliens at Roswell? Do you remember the ridicule and wasted careers, the scapegoats that never made it to retirement over that incident?" Linton held Sam's eyes with his. "How long do you think it would take you and young Nathan to go from heroes to jokes and ridicule as soon as the agency and government cover-up began? A week? Maybe two? I'd say three at the most before you find yourself out of a job, left to tell your story in the *Enquirer*." Linton smiled, shaking his head slightly. "Believe me; the two of you are far too honest to come off as anything other than complete idiots. After that, you could make a living on the flying saucer convention circuit for a few years. After that, it would be all over.

"You know the deal, better than anyone here. The government can't tell the truth on this. They never could, and they probably never will." Linton let Sam mull it over. "The decision is simple. Holster your gun, let Klatoo leave, and then leave yourself. The only crime I've seen so far that can be proven is trespass on my private property, and the last time I looked, that's a misdemeanor, of which you are as guilty as Klatoo. Tell the agency what you want and live to retire to that cabin on Mangus Pass."

First, Sam thought, *Does everyone in the world know about Mangus Pass and the cabin?* Second, he thought a long minute about what Linton had said and he knew in his heart that every word Linton had spoken was right. He knew the cover up would be immediate, and he would be the scapegoat. He and Nathan. He might have done it for truth and honesty to himself, but he couldn't do it on principal and ruin Nathan's career and life.

Decision made, he holstered the gun and turned to Klatoo. "Get out of here, you little son of a bitch, and if I ever see you again, I'll kill you." Klatoo began to float away. Seconds after the static, the translator started laughing a quiet, amused laugh then spoke one word as he slipped out of sight down the dark tunnel. "Suckers!"

Sam watched the tunnel until Klatoo was clearly gone, then he turned back as if nothing had happened, yawned, stretched, and nodded to Nathan. "You about ready to go?" Without waiting for an answer, he turned to leave.

Nathan paused. "What about everybody else?"

Sam paused, turned, and addressed the small group still standing rather defiantly by the shimmering aqua pool, "Oh, yeah, anybody want to leave with us? I've got a good light." Sam held up a huge Mag-lite and grinned.

As if released from a spell, Elvin looked around, realizing he no longer had his flashlight. "Gee, Yasha, what do you think? Maybe we ought to go back with them. I mean, the car's that way anyway."

Yasha hesitated. "Elvin, I don't know what Agent Nikosia will have in store for me now that he knows about my little problem."

Sam seemed slightly insulted. "Hell, lady, do I look like Immigration? I wouldn't give a shit if you came from Transylvania and your name was Dracula after what you tried to do for me tonight. I never forget a favor. As far as I'm concerned, you're jake with me. In fact, I think I might just be able to arrange some nice citizenship papers showing you're a domestic from Nicaragua." Sam held his arm out in the universal gesture of invitation and smiled. "So, ya'll all about ready to go?"

Elvin and Yasha exchanged one of the domestic glances that pass for a full conversation among couples, and without a word followed Sam and Nathan into the dark tunnel.

Nothing was said on the walk back. At the cemetery gate, the group paused, and Sam stuck his hand out. "Well, I guess this is where we part company."

Elvin shook his hand. "I can't tell you how much this means to me."

Sam looked down for a minute, remembering his wife, more than he really needed to if he was going to stay sane. When he looked back up, he spoke from the heart. "You don't have to; I had somebody like Yasha once myself." With that, he turned, leaving Nathan to follow.

Back in the truck, Nathan's heart was still beating double time. He couldn't stop talking. "Damn, was that something or what? Can you believe that? A real live alien general? Nobody, I mean nobody at the academy would ever believe this!"

Sam didn't say much, nodding occasionally. Finally, he patted Nathan on the shoulder. "Ease it down a little, son. It's just one night, and you're going to have a lot of nights. Trust me, a lot of nights." Studying the countryside going by in the headlights as they turned into the gate at the pasture, he said, "Okay, maybe not a whole lot of nights just exactly as strange as tonight, but a lot of nights all the same."

Sam stopped at the pasture gate. Nathan was still in a fog, replaying every moment. Finally, he realized they weren't going anywhere, and Sam was sitting at an idle, just looking at him. "Hey, Nathan."

Nathan looked at Sam. "What?"

Sam looked just a little perturbed. "Get the gate, gate boy."

"Oh, yeah, sure. I forgot." Feeling stupid, Nathan got out of the car, opened the gate, and got back in after Sam drove through. Soon they were back at camp.

Sam stopped the truck, got out, and headed for the fire. Reaching for the fire stick, he stirred the coals to life, throwing on several large logs. "Hey, Nathan, we got anymore rib eyes? These are cold."

Nathan rummaged through the ice chest, finding a Styrofoam tray with four huge rib eyes over an inch thick. "Yeah, a whole package."

Sam was at the card table, pouring Pepsi over Crown Royal and ice. He made two, handing one to Nathan. He held his up as if to toast. "Here's to an interesting night, partner. You did a hell of a job keeping cool in there."

Graduation had been good, but Nathan had never felt like a real agent until he heard the word "partner," and this time, he could tell Sam meant it. Nathan toasted Sam's clear plastic cup with his own, an equal at last. Later that night, after several rib eyes, cobbler, and more drinks, Nathan finally was calm enough to analyze the night.

They were in the Walmart reclining lounges, and the night breeze was turning cold. "Hey, Sam."

Sam looked away from the fleeing clouds reluctantly and faced Nathan. "What, Nathan?"

Nathan looked back at the sky. "It's a shame we don't have some proof of what happened. Nobody will ever believe it, will they?"

Nathan had noticed that when Sam was relaxed, responses sometimes took a few seconds.

Sam seemed unperturbed. "Oh, I wouldn't say we don't have any proof that it happened." With that, he pulled the dull nickel rod that he had taken from Klatoo out of his pocket, aimed at the tea jug on the card table, and pulled the trigger. A white-hot beam of plasma spanned the distance instantly and the jug seared as the liquid boiled through the gash in the side.

"Don't worry, Nathan; you're in for half of whatever I can get for this little gadget when we sell it to the skunkworks of one of the major defense contractors."

Nathan's blood ran cold. Any property recovered on an assignment was government property. "Sam, we've got to turn it in, don't we? It belongs to the department."

Sam looked back at Nathan as if he was an insect again. "Son, don't go dense on me now. What would we tell them? Where would we say we got it? Do you know what they could do to us on a story like this? Didn't you hear Eggleston? He nailed it cold." Sam waited a second so Nathan could take it in. "Anyway, the unspoken rule is that it's okay to make an honest buck, as long as it winds up on our side. Hell, what do you think the bureaucrats we would give this to at the agency would do with it? Exactly what we're going to do with it." It was important to Sam that Nathan learn about the real world. "Understand one thing, Nathan; never trust the boss too much. In this business, all you have is your instincts, and to the department, we're just another tool. If you don't look after yourself, you won't make it too long."

Sam made sure he caught Nathan's eyes in the fire. "There's only one exception to that rule. You never cross the line to the other side. It's okay to make a little profit on this side. Never, never on the other side. Understand?"

Nathan gave Sam a grin and a thumbs up. "Damn straight." His learning curve was getting better by the minute.

Chapter Twenty-Four

"MEANWHILE, BACK AT THE CAVE"

As Sam, Nathan, Elvin, and Yasha slowly disappeared into the dim recesses of the tunnel, Abra, Skippy, and Dennis realized they were still in one piece and the standoff was over. Under his breath, Skippy intoned, "Folks, I've had my butt whipped, I've been chased on foot, in cars, even once in a plane. Hell, I've even been shot at, but I don't think I ever came that close to dying. That felt like high noon at the OK Corral."

No one said anything for a few seconds, then from Dennis, "Ditto."

Skippy couldn't resist. Turning to Dennis, he slapped him on the shoulder with the back of his hand. "Get out of here! You mean an irate husband has shot at you, too? I didn't know you had it in you, you old dog you."

Dennis just glared back. "No more Bud for you, Skippy."

Gradually, Abra realized they were not yet exactly free, they were still in Linton's territory, and Linton was still standing there motionless, as if waiting for the three of them to realize this drama still had a little life yet. Abra hoped her unease was uncalled for. Where Linton had been a friend moments ago, she was not sure what he was now.

Without facing Linton, she started for the tunnel in a slow but purposeful walk. "Come on, guys, I think we need to leave."

Dennis seemed surprised and started to object. "Abra, hold up, I want to—"

He was cut off as she firmly grasped his shoulder on the way by. "Now, Dennis. We leave now." Her voice was quiet, just loud enough for Dennis to realize the determination or fear that he heard. Skippy was, as usual, happy to tag along, bringing up the rear. They almost made it to the tunnel.

Life is full of almost. You almost scored a touchdown. You almost won the lottery. You almost graduated from college. That is the nature of almost—little turning points that change your life for better or worse, or maybe that don't change your life at all. You never really know until later. And so it was with this "almost."

Somehow, by the time Abra drew near to the tunnel entrance, Linton was suddenly there, suddenly being the operative word. First, he wasn't there, and then he was. There was a blur—that was all. Unlike Abra, who had seen this phenomenon at a much slower speed in the shop, Skippy and Dennis nearly plowed into Linton before they realized he was there, blocking their exit.

Perception is a funny thing, and one of the emotions humans perceive quickly is danger. On the surface, the situation was not threatening. An older gentleman was blocking the exit. Nothing dangerous there. Sport coat and all, Linton would have appeared someone you could simply approach and ask politely to move. And that would have been the correct perception, except for the eyes. This seemed to be a night for dead shark eyes. Gone was the urban smile of an aging charmer. Instead, the face held no expression, making his half-alien eyes that much more menacing.

Abra's blood ran cold as she remembered the last time she had seen that dead stare and heard the words. "I'm going to ask you a question, and the answer will determine if you leave here alive."

Skippy saw the eyes, but even lower, saw the arms tense, the ancient weapon at ready. He was already thinking as he stopped, *This guy is too old to be real tough. Maybe I've got a chance.* That is when he got a demonstration of what Sam had already found out earlier. Linton could smell thoughts. Yes, smell, not read.

Linton used a sense present in humans to some degree—some more than others—but magnified in the alien makeup. The sense was not as exact as reading. It truly was more like smelling an aroma to Linton. "Yes, Mr. Beto, you might have a chance. Unfortunately, it might be a chance to die needlessly after being incredibly lucky so far this evening." Skippy's mouth fell open. Linton continued calmly. "Please don't take that as an invitation. I'm not Clint Eastwood, and that statement wasn't meant to be the equivalent of 'Make my day.' I simply need to ask the three of you a few questions." He seemed in no hurry. If done for effect, the intended result was clear. He had the undivided attention of all three. "If the answers are satisfactory, this may still turn out to be an interesting evening for all concerned."

Skippy almost thought, *Yeah, and what if the answers aren't satis-factory?* but he remembered Linton's power before the words were completely formed in his mind. A slight, cold smile crossed Linton's features for a second. "Well done, Mr. Beto. Your survival and learning instincts are better developed than most."

No one else knew why Linton had said that, but Skippy sure did. He began to play the Beatle's "Hey, Jude" in his mind—the long version, complete with music and vocals. Linton grimaced slightly.

Dennis looked confused. Abra touched his hand and spoke quietly. "Dennis, Mr. Eggleston is not quite what he seems, so please, please don't do anything foolish."

"You mean aside from being half-alien, there's something else about Mr. Eggleston that isn't what it seems?" Under different circumstances, Skippy and Abra would have broken down laughing at this side of Dennis. Not now.

The situation was beginning to feel like another standoff. Linton seemed as uncomfortable as they did. "I would appreciate it if the three of you would accompany me back to the passage from which I came." With that, he held the long, slender, manicured hand that did not hold the obsidian axe toward the other passage and dipped his head slightly, as if he were inviting them into his drawing room for after dinner drinks.

As they turned and began to walk, Linton in the rear, all weighed their options, except for Skippy, who was thinking, *Hey, Jude, don't be afraid. Take a sad song, and make it better.* Man, how about that Paul McCartney? He made a mental note to update his CD collection with some old Beatles.

Linton seemed intent on conversation. "Mr. Smith, would your talents include any expertise in anthropology, ancient biology—anything of that sort?" Dennis instinctively dropped back so that he could talk to Linton, and amazingly, Linton allowed him to walk almost beside him.

"Well, no, sir, not formal training. However, I was very interested in archeology, evolution, and anthropology early on. I always was interested why Cro-Magnon man disappeared, about the Ice Age animals, that sort of thing. Physics and physical science turned out to be where I studied, but I never lost interest."

Linton seemed pleased. "In that case, you are really in for a treat." Having just finished the long version with Paul screaming, *Yeah, yeah,* like a crazed black man, and Ringo singing, *Nah-nah-nah-nah-nah-*

nah-nah in the background, Skippy was thinking, *Yeah, and what are the rest of us in for*? Abra was numb, fully aware that Linton's cordial mood could change in an instant.

As they walked slowly, Linton continued, as if giving a guided lecture. "This cave has been feared, revered, and used continuously for many thousands of years—a sacred place, a spiritual place with special powers, Mr. Smith." Linton spoke in a casual, almost friendly tone as they walked. "You already know why, and so did the ancients in a general way. To you, the power is science; to them, the power was mystical. Don't be too sure your science will explain everything you've seen. It might, and then again, it might not."

Linton suddenly walked to the front of the group, apparently comfortable they were too far from the exit to make a run for it. "Let me show you something." He turned slightly to look back at them. "And please, don't try to run or do something else we will all regret." The hand with the stone axe stayed in his pocket. He led them around a natural stone column to another area lit by the soft glow of the walls. "Have you seen the cave paintings of Lascaux in France?"

"No," replied Dennis. "But I saw a replica that made the museum circuit."

Linton nodded. "Do you recall how the people used the light background and painted in dark colors to outline the animals so they could be seen when lit from below?" He seemed more excited, animated. "Here, the people used the glow, outlining and defining the animals with dark paint to shield the glow, allowing the animals to be backlit, almost like a photographic negative. He stopped before a wall, holding his hands up to illustrate the point.

Each person stared in awe, except for Skippy, who stared with mild curiosity and little more. The wall was semi-circular, fifteen feet tall, with large niches in the lower areas at spaced intervals. Each niche seemed occupied by something, but it was the border of the ceiling that held their eyes.

The wall was a giant procession of ancient animals galloping in great herds. They were done in perspective, so that they seemed smaller at the left edge of the wall and grew in size as they neared the natural viewing point at which they stood.

It was obvious that the artists who created the scene understood the elements of drama, theater, and presentation. Each animal appeared carved in bas-relief, with paint used only for outline and detail, such as muscles and features, with open areas left to glow, and a small area around each animal blacked out. The effect was of a long procession of mammoth, mastodon, horse, deer, sloth, dire wolves, saber-tooth cats, giant elk, and giant buffalo careening down the wall. In places, and near the edges, there were separate vignettes with hunters and spears, ambushes and blood—hunting scenes depicted in detail, the people captured for eternity in the exact climax of the hunt, some gored, injured or trampled, some victorious, with the prey felled and slaughtered. The entire scene, executed with primitive, but timeless talent, and backlit by the soft green glow, was a masterpiece.

To Abra, it was much like being shown the ceiling of the Sistine Chapel. She knew virtually every important piece of ancient art and this was beyond anything she had ever seen. Her apprehension was, for the moment, forgotten in the sheer magnificence of the work before her.

Even Skippy seemed finally to be affected by the scene.

Dennis spoke first. "This is unbelievable. If the world knew this were here, Tejas Hill would be changed forever."

Linton nodded. "As usual, Mr. Smith, you have cut to the heart of the matter. The world would beat a path to this place for that priceless piece of universe in the pool and for the historical and artistic significance of this cavern. Either one would make this place important on a global basis, and that is something I cannot let happen." Linton waited before continuing as if weighing whatever he was going to say or do next carefully. "As amazing as this all may seem, there is more." With that, he moved toward the nearest of the niches carved in the side of the cave under the glowing tableau. He waited for them to catch up and stood aside without saying a word.

The niche, like the rest of the cave, was lit by the soft luminescence. It was large, large enough to walk into, with a slab of rock carved like an altar against the back wall. On the slab, Abra, Skippy, and Dennis saw a dark, indistinct shape, almost like some type of huge animal had lain down and gone to sleep.

Dennis walked apprehensively into the niche and leaned slowly over the slab to see what the thing was. As his eyes adjusted, he realized the animal was some type of bear, but a size he had never seen. A front paw lay extended from the body. The paw would have covered Dennis's chest. Each claw was approximately six inches long. The bear looked so natural that Dennis would have thought it was simply asleep, as it appeared as fresh as if it had just fallen, had he not seen the spear.

The spear was short and approximately an inch in diameter—the type an archeologist would recognize as having been thrown from an aztal, or throwing stick. The hilt was buried deep in the bear's chest and must have struck the heart, causing instant death.

The others stared in amazement, having followed Dennis inside to see the mystery. As if reading his thoughts, Linton agreed with Dennis. "Yes, he does appear as if he died today." Dennis knew what the beast was—a cave bear, a giant and ancient version of the modern grizzly.

Cave bears had been a part of the pantheon of giant mammals that characterized the Pleistocene age during the last ice age and disappeared about the time modern man began to assert his presence. In that time, bigger was better. Dennis also knew this animal became extinct somewhere between eight and twelve thousand years ago.

Linton seemed pleased at their amazement. "Please, look in the rest. Each contains a different treasure." From that point on, Abra, Skippy, and Dennis slowly made their way from one niche to the next.

Each contained a different animal. In stunned silence, they made their way through what almost appeared to be a morbid zoo of long-extinct, dead animals. Each had been killed cleanly, the means of death still apparent. A dire wolf, a saber-tooth tiger, a giant sloth, a giant plains buffalo, twice the size of its current form, and others he recognized only vaguely from the resemblance to modern animals. There were giant birds, condors with bodies as large as a man and huge folded wings. There was even a crocodile, gigantic by any modern standard.

Little was spoken, except for Dennis, occasionally naming an animal as they viewed it. After the initial shock wore off, Abra became brave enough to carefully touch some of the animals. Their fur and bodies were soft and supple, not hard like mounted specimens. She could feel the structure of bone and muscle under the fur. It was obvious that the bodies were not replicas or mounts, but the full, complete bodies. There was no odor, other than whatever natural odor the animal's fur would normally impart.

Finally, the group, with Linton close behind, observing, made their way to the last niche. On closer inspection, it was not carved like the rest, but a side cavern created with the rest of the cave. Inside were two huge animals. Dennis knew what they were before he entered.

The two ancient elephants were similar in size and stood approximately twelve feet tall when living, with tusks almost that long. One was covered in the deep fur of the Ice Age era. The other was short-haired, like modern elephants. Both had the characteristic Frankenstein forehead of extinct elephants. Both had been felled by multiple spears, still embedded in their body.

Even Skippy was taken back. Somewhere in his body, the genes of a long line of entrepreneurs began to assert themselves. "Good God, this is like the *Lost World*. Mammoths and mastodons haven't been around since the last ice age. Even I learned that in college. They've been trying to find viable DNA to clone these things for years. This is amazing. You could make millions of dollars with these things as specimens alone, much less their value to science and for the DNA."

Abra and Dennis stopped and stared at Skippy, momentarily astounded that something that was not only correct, but fairly insightful had finally come out of his mouth.

Dennis turned to Linton. "It's the stone in the pool, isn't it? It must be a meteor, but not like any I've ever seen or heard of. Can you tell us how this place can exist?"

Abra winced, remembering what Linton had told her he would do if she threatened him or his existence. She had a good idea that the current situation fit that bill exactly. No matter. Linton, having kept the secret for so long, seemed almost eager to tell Dennis what he knew. "It is a meteor, Mr. Smith, and as you said, not like any other."

"It hit this hill before known history and bored its way inside to the place it rests now. Under any other circumstance, if it had not struck the underground river and the basalt column where it rests, it would have blown the earth to oblivion. As you already know, if the rumors of your comments at Connie's store can be believed, it is highly radioactive, but not with radiation as we know it. Otherwise, simple spring water would not damp it or neutralize it. I have not been able to identify what it is about the water that shields and neutralizes what I can only assume would otherwise be deadly, but I know it does." Linton had been moving closer to the wooly mammoth as he spoke and finally laid his hand on the huge shoulder, stroking the fur gently at the point where a large spear entered. "These great animals are one example of the amazing effect the rock has on everything it comes into contact with, but not the only example. Have you ever wondered why the people on the hill are so odd, so talented, so eclectic? Just different? Have you ever wondered why the place seems to have such an attraction to all that stay long enough to be hooked?"

He was impassioned, as if asking the questions for the first time. "This place has power that would make Stonehenge pale. The People always recognized this cave as a place of tremendous power, a place where mastery over all living things could not only be shown, but perpetuated. By accident, they found out that whatever they brought down here would not decay. In their minds, by bringing an example of each animal that was important to them, they insured not only a successful hunt, but the continued success of the animal as well. Unlike now, the People revered the animals they hunted. They understood their life was contingent on the welfare of each species. They understood the creator was alive everywhere, in everything. It was only later that tribal leaders learned that when you could compartmentalize God in specified sacred places and control access to that power, you could control the people. That was a sad day.

"Gradually, the People disappeared through the effects of disease, weather changes, migration, intermingling with other cultures, and finally, the Europeans. All the usual reasons. But some stayed. Some here on the hill, me included, are descended from the People. They may not know it consciously, but they carry bits of the secret and majesty of this place in their very fiber. They cannot leave for long. I've seen them leave, but they always return. If they don't, their children do, drawn by the same magnet that binds me to this place. I leave, but never for long."

Abra watched Linton, spellbound by his words. It was clear he was speaking now as much to himself as to them, almost as if he felt the need to explain his existence to himself.

"I have to return to the hill, to that wind that never quite ceases, to the waves in the grass, and the view. I've seen that view so long, but never long enough to tire of it. Somehow, I still expect to see a huge herd rising from the west as I did so long ago. Maybe buffalo, maybe mammoth, with the hunters and predators waiting. Picking off the weak, the old." He turned to face them. "You cannot imagine the sheer majesty that unbridled nature can provide. Nothing left now comes close. Life is a pale existence of what it once was." Linton surprised even himself with the intensity of his words. "You have absolutely no idea how empty our lives are in a world where every pleasure is moderated, every danger controlled, every impulse inhibited. If you could only see what I have seen, you would understand what life was like before the world and nature were tamed and sanitized.

"My God, even the weather has been damped, as if the smog and pollution has slowed it to a crawl. They tell us what next week will be like. It is the struggle, the uneasy balance between the known and unknown that used to exist naturally that has been upset. I long to see it return. I long to put things right as much as I can before it is too late, but I cannot do it alone."

Abra and Dennis were spellbound by the speech. Abra understood Linton enough to realize how foreign it was to his makeup to reveal that much about himself. Skippy had his own take on the speech. "Hey, did you grow up in the sixties or something? My old man used to talk like that when I was a kid. Always talking about getting back to nature—that kind of stuff. I always thought it was just an excuse to smoke pot, but looking back, I think he really believed it back then." Skippy seemed caught in a rare moment of reflection. "You know, he almost never brings that kind of stuff up now, but I can tell he isn't real happy. Sometimes he talks about how he has to make an appointment to have fun, how he used to be able to take off, and go camping, or fishing anytime the mood hit him. How all the money in the world isn't worth losing your freedom." Skippy looked serious for once, contemplating his next statement carefully. "I guess I understand that. I've been running from his life as hard as I could ever since I was old enough to see how—" He stopped, as if trying to remember something. "What's that word I saw in an old novel? Oh, yeah. Vapid. That's the word I was looking for. How vapid his life is."

Linton turned to Skippy with new respect. "That is the exact word, Mr. Beto. I could not have thought of a better one."

Dennis waited for his turn to speak. "Mr. Eggleston, if you really want to change the world, you have the building blocks of a great start right here. That stone holds secrets about energy I could only begin to guess. It needs to be studied, understood. Maybe whatever secret drives it can't be recreated, but if it could, it could revolutionize life. It has the potential to end reliance on fossil fuel. Any scientist would sell his soul to have a career to work on solving the riddles that rock holds. People all over the world could have cheap, portable energy, and billions of dollars would be freed up. That is, if the energy companies didn't get to it first. If they did, you wouldn't ever see it until it could be controlled by the handful of energy and utility companies that control the world. Well, almost control the world. I forgot about Wal-Mart for a minute."

Skippy was caught up in Dennis's idea. "Man, you wouldn't believe how pissed off people like my dad and his crowd would be if there was some major industry they couldn't control. They talk about cutting taxes for the little guy at the political rallies, but I know what they really say when the doors close and the real business is done. 'Trickle down' is just a catch phrase. It means you drop a bucket of money at the top of the tree and maybe a few pennies trickle down to the average guy on the ground. If they cut your taxes $1000, they cut theirs by millions, and that assumes they pay taxes. Most of the time, they don't. When you can afford top of the line accountants, you usually don't. They know that, too. They laugh at the rednecks that support their candidates. They even have a name for it. They call it the "Bubba in the Dodge Truck vote.""

Suddenly Dennis didn't seem quite as excited. "Hey, Skippy, there's only one problem. Research like this would cost a fortune. You'd have to have a first-rate lab, scientists in a number of disciplines, and a boatload of equipment. You'd never be able to finance anything close to what it would take to study that rock without selling out to a major research company." The air seemed to have left Dennis's balloon.

"Not necessarily, Einstein. I got a trust fund." Skippy goosed Dennis in the arm and winked at him at the same time. "We could use my trust fund."

Dennis wasn't convinced. "You don't understand, Skippy. I'm not talking about Highland Park, new Porsche-type money. I'm talking about General Electric-type money."

Skippy put an arm around Dennis and spoke low and clear for once. "Hey, Einstein, I ain't talking about Highland Park, new Porsche-money either. I'm talking about General Electric-type money. My grandfather set it up fifty years ago with blue chips for the grandchildren. Well, I'm it, and it's just been sitting there compounding all this time. Dad's been trying to figure how to screw me out of it ever since I turned fourteen and decided not to buy my clothes at Brooks Brothers, but Granddad had some foresight. The trust fund comes with a lawyer out of LA who has one job—to protect my interests, and he doesn't give a damn what anybody in Dallas thinks about him. So far, he has, and if I make it to thirty years old, I control it, lock stock and barrel. I may look stupid, but you don't grow up being a Beto and not understand the art of the deal. I know how you set things up. I know where to hire the people that cover your back, and I know which lawyers can draw a contract so you don't ever lose."

Skippy had their attention for once. "When I was a kid, before things got screwed up, Dad used to carry me everywhere, to the boardroom, to the lawyers, in meetings. After it was over, he would ask me what I thought about certain people and what I thought about something he did or didn't do. Then he would tell me if I was right or wrong about the people or the deal and why. Looking back, he was teaching me the family business. I just didn't know it then." Now Skippy was talking to himself more than to them. "I guess I've just been marking time, knowing the day would come when I could do what I wanted." He looked at Dennis. "Up until I met you, I didn't know what I wanted. I know one thing now. My old man would hire you in a second. He wouldn't worry about what he was going to do with you. He'd hire you understanding he could find something that would fit your skills, and you would make him a whole, whole lot of money. He's a lot smarter than those clowns at Goliath and I am, too. With your talent and my money, we could burn the house down."

In the shadows, Linton had backed up, standing quietly by Abra, who was as intent as he was, listening to the two young men, lost in their dreams, caught up in the excitement of the idea. It wasn't until he stepped closer that they realized he was still there. "That's all very well and good, gentlemen, except for one thing. I own this cave and everything in it, including that rock. I have good lawyers as well and other means to protect my property that you've only sampled tonight."

He saw the disappointment on Skippy and Dennis's face, but continued. "I knew when I first met Abra and watched the alliance the three of you put together that this moment would come. I knew Mr. Smith would not leave this hill until he found out where the power came from. You're not the first to come sniffing around this hill, and I knew I would have to make up my mind if you were going to end up the same way the rest did." Everyone knew what that meant, and no one was smiling at that prospect. "I have lived a long time. At first, I did not understand what was here anymore than anyone else would have. I simply knew it was here, where it came from, and to some degree, some of what it did. In the last century, science exploded. In the last seventy years, I read and began to understand what the rock might represent. I am a rich man. When you live long, you learn by trial and error what works. But, even as rich as I am, I do not have the knowledge to answer the questions without having to give up control, as Mr. Smith realized a minute ago. I needed a combination of intellect and money I simply did not possess.

"Earlier, I told you I was going to ask you some questions. The answers to those questions would determine if you left this cave or became the same as the animals in the niches. I only have one question now." Linton paused. He really, really liked drama. "Can the two of you do business with an aging alien half-breed with very definite ideas?" The grin on his face was both startling and a relief to Dennis and Skippy.

Without missing a beat, Skippy stood up to his full six-foot, four-inch height, stuck out his hand like a Dallas banker, and said, "Damn straight I can."

Linton looked at the hand as if he were going to take it, but instead, turned to Dennis. "How about it, Mr. Smith? I believe it is time to either fish or cut bait. Are you in?"

Dennis nodded. "Yes. Yes I am." With that, Linton shook Skippy's hand. "Do the two of you mind if we dispense with last names?"

It was obvious from the smiles of relief going back and forth between Dennis and Skippy that it was fine by them.

Linton clasped his hands together. "Tell you what; I had intended we all leave the way I came in. However, that would leave your car and equipment for anyone to find, and that would not be smart. Why don't the two of you go and get the car, cover the entrance you made with very heavy rocks, and meet Abra and I at my shop?"

Apprehension and concern swept over Dennis's face. As he began to turn to Abra with the obvious question, she stopped him. "It's okay, Dennis. Mr. Eggleston won't hurt me. Go with Skippy. I have unfinished business with him as well."

When no one moved, Abra shook the back of her hand at them with a grin. "Go, get out of here." All tension was gone at that point, and Dennis and Skippy were already heading for the tunnel, discussing plans in animated voices.

Linton let them almost get to the tunnel then stopped them with his voice. "There is just one thing, gentlemen." He waited until they stopped and turned around. Slowly, he brought his hand out of his pocket with the obsidian axe and laid it in his other hand. His face was stone again, and he did not blink. "If either of you ever, ever tell a soul where this place is, or what it holds, I will cut your heart out and send it to God. And I don't mean the one down at the church." A long second went by. "Do we understand each other?"

Skippy looked astonished, holding his hands out in mock insult. "Are you kidding, Linton? That would be like giving away the goose that laid the golden egg, wouldn't it?" It seemed Skippy was learning the value of a good question as well. Dennis nodded his agreement with Skippy, and the two of them turned and disappeared into the tunnel.

To no one in particular, Linton said quietly, "Those two are going to go far; very, very far." Satisfied, he turned to Abra. "Well, I guess that just leaves the two of us to conclude our business. What exactly can I do for you tonight, Ms. Avant?"

Abra turned to face Linton, speaking calmly. "Well, there are two things you can do for me. The first is this." With that, she slapped Linton across the face, bringing blood to the corner of his mouth. His gaze never wavered, and his voice was as calm and quiet as hers had been. "All right, and what is the second thing I can do for you tonight?"

Abra turned and headed down the path that Linton had come. "Is this the way?" she asked.

"Yes, just follow the path to the door." Again, he asked, "Now, what else can I do for you tonight?"

Abra stopped and turned to face him in the center of the path. "Simply tell me the truth. You told me before there was a greater mystery, and you would tell me if I asked again. I'm asking now. I want the whole story, more than I ever wanted anything in my life. If you don't tell me, I don't know what I'm going to do." She was almost breathless and still angry.

"Will you promise me one thing?" Linton's face was serious.

Abra waited a long second to answer. "What?"

Linton smiled the enigmatic smile she had come to love and hate at the same time. "Will you promise never to slap me again?" With that, he wiped the small amount of blood off his lip with a fresh handkerchief.

Abra's face softened, as if she had just realized what she had done. She touched his lip gently. "I hurt you. I'm sorry; I didn't mean to hurt you. It's just that you've scared me too many times. One minute, you're Dracula, the next you're someone's kindly great-uncle. Which is it?"

Linton's face was amused. "It's both, my dear. I'm actually both. But then again, so is everyone. It's just that most people don't live long enough to have to face their dark side." He turned, stepped to her side, offering her his hand as if they were on a Sunday walk. "Walk with me, and I'll tell you everything I know." He turned to face her as they walked. "I want you to know something. What I tell you now I have never told anyone and will never tell anyone else, as long as I live."

She could tell he meant what he said, and nodded, sensing he needed a sign of her understanding of the magnitude of what he was about to do. Linton smiled slightly in appreciation, turned with her hand on his arm, and walked slowly.

"Do you remember when I told you I was the man in the photographs, but that I was not the man at the meeting with the Indians in the woodcut, but I knew who was there and exactly what happened?"

"Yes, I do," she answered. He seemed satisfied and continued.

"The great mystery is not how old I am. I am very, very old and will probably outlive you and maybe your children. That is not the great mystery. The great mystery is what I hold in my brain."

Abra looked up at him. "What do you mean?"

"When the meteor you saw tonight fell on the hill, there was a man on the top of the bluff, just above where you entered the cavern tonight. His name, in today's tongue, was Little Eagle. He is the only person who ever came into direct contact with the whole rock outside of the pool it sits in now. It has been in that pool since the night it fell, with the same underground river flowing over it for many thousands of years."

Linton was lost in the story, no longer looking at Abra. "Somehow, the meteor altered his DNA in a way that continues to this day." He stopped for a minute, trying to line up his thoughts to tell the tale in a way she would understand. "In all living beings, there are things like instinct that automatically pass from generation to generation. They are 'hardwired,' to use the computer generation's term. Other mental processes, like memories of events and emotions, are 'softwired' and die with that person. Somehow, the meteor hardwired Little Eagle's memory, and beyond that, the memory of one child, usually male, from each generation forward."

Linton looked into Abra's eyes to emphasize what he was saying. "From Little Eagle on, the memories and emotions of each generation passed down, as elemental a part of the DNA as the ability to walk and learn. I can see Little Eagle in my mind, squatting on the top of the hill, in the cold, waiting for the meteors without even knowing what they were. More than that, I can feel his emotions and remember his language, his words, and his thoughts."

Linton stopped and turned to Abra. "I can do that for every generation since he climbed to the top of this hill, over ten thousand years ago. I know history first-hand. I know places and things historians have never heard of. I know hundreds of languages and sign, and I know religions that have not existed for thousands of years." He turned and started walking again. "It is almost like having lived that long. I have seen history from the end of the Ice Age. I have knowledge that only one person in each generation has. Knowledge that has never been written down for obvious reasons. Up until now, anyone who told the truth would have been branded a witch, heretic, or lunatic. Even today, I would be ridiculed and very likely placed in an institution. I wouldn't blame you if you didn't believe me." Linton's face had a haunted look. "If you don't believe me, tell me now, and you can leave, and neither of us will be hurt." He looked down, as if unable to see her answer.

Abra held both his hands firmly and made sure their eyes met again. "I believe you. I knew you were not like any other man the first time I met you. I almost began to question if you were mortal. Now I have a question. Why are you telling me this? Why are you trusting three people tonight after keeping your secrets for centuries?"

Linton turned away from her. For once, he did not appear to be in total control. "I am tired, and more than that, I can sense things are going badly, and quickly. Up until now, I have been able to reinvent myself every twenty years or so by simply disappearing long enough to come back as a relative. But DNA, fingerprints, and Social Security have made it more difficult than ever to protect the truth. I want to share what I know in a way that will not threaten me. Yes, I still have a long life ahead. I am tired, but not tired enough to threaten my own existence." Again, he turned to face her, taking both her hands in his. "I wish you were older or I was younger. You are the woman I have been looking

221

for." Then his face turned sad, sad and resigned. "Yet, I know you and I are not meant for each other. Close, but no brass ring." Abra tried to hide her amazement that he was voicing what she had thought so early on. "I've watched you with Dennis. As unlikely as it seems, you are close to falling in love with him, if my experience means anything."

Abra looked away, having refused to face the growing feelings she herself had been surprised at. They were at a large steel door on huge hinges. Linton pulled a handle that looked like the ones she had seen in banks, and the huge door groaned again slightly as it slid open into a dimly lit hallway lined with roughly dressed blocks of stone, similar to those covering the college.

They passed through the door and began walking, this time holding hands. Linton went on, "No matter, you can never control a heart; sadly, not even your own." He smiled at her as if to say that subject had been discussed enough. "The reason I tell you these things is because I cannot tell them myself to anyone else. But you can tell them for me, under the guise of archeology and research. I can tell you where to look. I can tell you where places and things are that will amaze the world, and I can tell you exactly what they mean and how to prove it. I can make you the most famous historian and archeologist in the history of the world and you can do a great favor to mankind." Linton eyes were on fire with excitement. "Even more important, with Dennis and Skippy, we can bring the animals in the cave back to life. We can re-store a world that should not have gone away. We can shine a light on ecology and nature in a way that no one has ever been able to do. I have lived long enough for science to catch up to my dreams, but I need your help. I need all of you, and in return, you will all reach heights you never dreamed of." Linton stopped and turned to face Abra as if he were going to propose. "If you are the woman I know you are, you cannot walk away from this. If you do, everything I've learned and know will be for nothing."

Abra walked away from Linton, just far enough to be out of reach. "And what will you do if I say I won't?" Her gaze never wavered from his eyes. "Will you send my heart to God? Will you watch the fear in my body, contemplating the possibility of my own death with pleasure like you did before?"

Linton, for the first time she ever saw, visibly crumbled. Suddenly, he looked as old as he probably was, and not omnipotent—far from omnipotent. "No, even if you walk out of here and tell the world what I have told you, I will never hurt you. You are as near to love as I will ever get, and I've realized that means more at this point than everything else." He smiled wistfully. "You are truly free, Abra. Do what you will with immunity. If you help me, it must not be out of fear. Respect, maybe, but never fear."

Abra faced Linton, and then she walked in close to him and, holding his head in her hands, kissed him gently on the lips. "Thank you; that is the most beautiful gesture a man ever made to me, and, yes, I will help you."

With that, they continued down the hall to a blank wall. Linton touched a spot where nothing seemed to be, and a door opened onto a stairway that led up. At the top, Linton again touched a spot where nothing seemed to be, and suddenly, a panel opened, and they were in an upstairs hall in the college.

As if on an afternoon promenade, they made their way out the front door, down the steps, and down the street to Linton's shop, where the Saab sat with Skippy and Dennis inside, waiting for her.

Once there, Linton yawned. "I don't know about you, but there is only so much a human can do in one night."

Skippy nodded. "That may be true, Linton, but you're not exactly a typical human, are you?" He was smiling.

"No, Skippy, I'm not, but I try not to rub it into anyone's face. Kind of like you don't try to rub Highland Park in anyone's face."

Skippy got back into the car after letting Abra in. "Touché, boss."

Linton started to turn, then, as if having a last minute thought, turned back. "Why don't we meet at Connie's for lunch tomorrow at the back table? You know, the one with "the Table of Knowledge" under the varnish. It's private, and we can discuss the future."

Linton started to walk away, then stopped and turned back to face the car. "Our future and everyone else's." With that, he unlocked the shop door and disappeared into the dark interior. For a second, it was almost as if the whole night had been a dream.

Chapter Twenty-Five

"Now You've Heard My Story"

T he rest is history. These press releases will give you an idea of
what happened after that:

DALLAS MORNING NEWS "BUSINESS PAGES"

Beto heir, Byron "Skippy" Beto announced the formation of a new
company, named Abragen, with co-founder and rising scientist, Dennis
Smith, and well-respected auction appraiser, Linton Eggleston as a
backer. The two intend to conduct basic research in alternative, clean,
and non-polluting energy sources. Industry insiders, including the father of co-founder Beto, predict the company will have little effect on
conventional energy companies and lament the waste of Smith's talents, who has been widely respected to this point in scientific circles.

ARCHEOLOGY MAGAZINE

Well-respected artifact collector and appraiser, Linton Eggleston,
and historian and archeologist Abra Avant, announced the formation of
the Little Eagle Foundation, a non-profit group formed for discovering
previously unknown artifacts and history and for research into the biology of extinct animals. Like other groups, the foundation hopes to
investigate the cloning of extinct species.

Then, five years later:

ENERGY MONTHLY

Abragen announced today that it has solved the Holy Grail of cold
fusion, which has long eluded the scientific world. Even more shock-

ing, the company announced plans to make the technology available to the world at a reasonable cost, which they predict will be far less than conventional energy sources.

The word on the street is that every major energy company and most utility companies have made overtures to Abragen to purchase the technology, to no avail. In a statement today, co-founders Smith and Beto stated their goal from the beginning was to help the world, plain and simple. If true, this development could shake the energy industry to its core.

Then, two years later:

SCIENTIFIC AMERICAN

The Little Eagle Foundation has successfully cloned a species of buffalo that has been extinct for thousands of years and made the animal available for scientific inspection. Once common, the huge beast is twice the size of its modern relative, the American bison.

Researchers have been given access to the animal and report that it's DNA is distinctly different from that of a modern bison and appears to be as claimed. The foundation further announced that problems with a limited gene supply have been overcome by small manipulations in the DNA, which mimic natural selection and hopes to create a viable herd of the animals to be released back into a portion of their former natural habitat.

Of even greater interest, the foundation claims that other species, including both a longhair and shorthair version of the mammoth will soon be available for inspection, which indicates the possibility that the animals may already exist. The Little Eagle Foundation has consistently astounded the scientific community since its inception with a series of previously undiscovered sites and the recovery of artifacts of a quality and quantity that has amazed the archeology community.

Of even greater potential significance are the advances in ancient languages and religions that have come from the work of the foundation, which now includes some of the most talented minds available under the capable hands of director, Abra Avant, whose insight and knowledge virtually defy logic.

Then, fifteen years later:

WORLD ECOLOGY

Huge parks have been designated in Central Africa, Central America, and West Texas for the introduction of viable populations of previously extinct animals, including dire wolves, saber-tooth tigers, cave bears, wooly mammoth, and shorthaired mammoth. With the worldwide push to limit population so successful and an unexpected drop in births worldwide, large tracts of land are once again available to be returned to a natural state. A debate that had raged as to the choice to either protect existing or previously extinct species has largely been rendered pointless as natural areas continue to grow in the face of ever-decreasing populations of humans. Eco-tourism continues to grow as more and more people have funds to travel because of the availability of near cost-free and clean energy to industry and individuals all over the world.

Then, sixty years later:

THE NORTH AMERICAN TIMES

Leaders of Canamerimex met at a summit conference in the capitol today to discuss concerns over the increasing and bizarre changes in climate that have plagued the continent in recent decades. The inability to predict the seasons or their severity and the increasing occurrence of extreme and violent weather, have rendered conventional agriculture almost impossible, making the development of dependable food sources paramount to the continued existence of the continent as a viable society.

Finally, twenty years later:

THE NORTH AMERICAN TIMES

It is with deep regret that the publishers of the *North American Times*, the last operating source of daily news in the hemisphere, are ceasing operations effective Friday. The current chaos, advancing ice sheets, and failure of the government, coupled with the shortages of food and reliable distribution channels make it impossible to continue to operate. On behalf of the publisher, editors, and reporters, we wish you all well. May God bless Canamerimex, and may God bless you and your families.

Somewhere in North America, a man sits alone, cold, in a limestone cave, at an ageless wooden table, writing with an ancient pencil.

Well, dear reader, that is my story. I don't know if you will believe it, but I have written it on paper, with antique pencils that I got from my mother.

I told you the story just as she told me so many, many decades ago. But I could have told it without her, because I carry it inside, just as my father did. It is cold, very cold here, and I have no idea what will happen to this manuscript.

No one knows what will happen anymore and the small group I live with lives like everyone else in the part of the world we know—day-to-day. I sign this manuscript with my name, and I tell you who I am so you will understand how I know these things.

I am Linton Avant. My mother was Abra Avant, and she was married to the man who raised me, Dennis Smith, the great scientist. I always knew he was not my father, although I loved him like a father. When my mother explained to me as a child that Dennis could not father children, and that a dear friend named Linton helped her father me, I understood all, because I already knew who Linton was, and I knew who everyone else before him was.

I am probably the last of my kind, unless some miracle happens. I continue to hope, as my memory tells me that life has a way of surviving anything.

Above all, I believe in life.

Linton Avant, 2258

"Epilogue"

The big limestone hill was so old, even time did not remember how it came to be there when the boy climbed the limestone bluff to the top. He squatted on his heels and looked out over the horizon as the swollen red sun went down. The ever-present wind blew warm from the south this day, making the grass in the cracks in the rock weave in rhythmic waves as if by some unseen hand.

The sun was setting in the west, making its daily journey through the dark cave only to arise again reborn in the morning in the east to light the way for the People. Its pale yellow light cast horizontal rays across the immense bank of thunderheads that stretched as far as the eye could see to the east, making the approaching storm appear even darker and more ominous as the sheet lightning played on the edge of the clouds, as if they were a great screen.

The boy scanned the northern horizon from west to east. The big hill sat like an island between three distinct landscapes. To the north stretched the narrow bridge of land the People called the Great Way. All things came and went along the Great Way—predator and prey, hunter and hunted, making it a place with incredible plenty and incredible danger.

On both sides of the Great Way, the two competing ice sheets the people called the Big West Cold and the Big East Cold stood immovable, gray with a thousand years of silt, sand, dirt, and rock picked up as it made its way inch by inch to the great shallow sea that lay to the south of the bluff.

The bluff was land's end, like a lighthouse on the shore of the sea, where all the elements that controlled the people's lives met. When the wind blew from the north, the people were cold and huddled in their skin-covered tents or under the hole on the west side of the bluff. When the wind blew from the south, the people languished in the warm, content to watch the big ice sheets shatter as they shed huge chunks of ice at the shore of the sea, throwing water and foam hundreds of feet in the air.

The boy did not think in groups of words and sentences. His thoughts were complex, a mixture of those things his senses told him—sight, sound, the feel of the wind, warm, cold, emotions. At the same time, his world was colored by memory—the stories the people told around the fires at night. The stories of when the Big Cold covered all and the people huddled in caves.

These shared memories were reenacted in simple words and symbols and told by the storytellers to entertain the people and scare the children at night. The people did not remember those things the stories told about, but they knew the stories were true and happened a long time ago.

Unlike the other people, this boy was different. He had memories that did not come from his own experience or the campfire stories. He came to the bluff often to be alone, where he could play the strange pictures and feelings in his mind. Understanding was a concept unknown to him, but one that he sought without knowing why. As the sun sank, and the evening turned dark, the boy would close his eyes and run the pictures in his mind's eye. He could see unknown animals with great shaggy trunks and white tusks crossing the space where the Big West Cold now was. He could see great expanses of green grass, so lush and thick a man could not see over it, making the smaller stone outcroppings in the distance seem like islands in a vast swaying green sea. He could see vast herds of shaggy beasts with horns coming out of their great heads tearing up the grass in a solid, moving, seething mass that stretched for miles. He could see strange men in strange dress, all different, but all the same in many ways, stretching in an unbroken line to him. He knew he came from these men.

He would sense words and sounds, spoken together in long groups in a way the people did not do anymore. The sounds were somehow familiar, he could put pictures to the sounds, and yet, he did not understand what many of the pictures were. There were great colored things with people in them that rolled and even flew without any person or animal pulling them. There were great smooth caves with openings and decorations, with people coming in and out and light in openings at night as if lit from a fire. There were pieces of ice with life-size images in them on every side that moved and made sounds, and even a small box that you could touch to change the pictures. If he stayed long enough, he could remember the bad times coming and then, the great chaos. Changes in the weather, the great floods, droughts, storms, winters, and the way the seasons became confused and unpredictable.

He remembered how the warm places and easy food gradually disappeared, the world became ever colder, and the people became sick and began to fight and break up into small groups. He could sense when the people began to lose the meanings of the words and sounds, and life through the great cold became a never-ending struggle for survival. Finally, hours later, as morning approached, he would remember when the Great Cold retreated and the warm sea came behind it bringing the fish, and the great way opened up from the north, bringing the animals and other people from other places and life became good again. The campfire stories replaced the ice with pictures in it that he saw in his mind.

On nights when he could stand it, he would stay on the bluff all the way to the end of the memory, until he could see his own father, lost in the southern sea on a small raft, far from land and feel the hopelessness his father felt, blown too far south by the wind to ever return, only to be rescued by a sudden southern squall.

Each time he came, the memories became dimmer, as if the act of remembering was slowly eating them away. The genetic trail that made him special had run its course—once strong and potent, now thin and weakened by a thousand generations. The boy knew inside that the seasons would only pass a few more times before he would be unable to play the memories in his mind, and then he would not be special anymore.

This night, as the storm approached from the east, the lightning lit the sky. The boy could hear the waves crash against the back of the bluff and see the great ice sheets lit from above by the flashing bolts. Storm clouds scudded low across the dark sky as the white stars of the Dipper twinkled. The boy was used to such a raw display of nature in all its fury, but a 21st century man, used to a world slowed by eons and smog and contamination would have been amazed by the raw display and frightened for his life.

It was almost as if the Big Cold had cleansed the world like a great flood and recharged all the natural forces. The world was young again, powerful and untamed, with new fires alive in the volcanoes along the equator and other fault lines. The people on the bluff, like the people in Noah's Ark, were as new as a clean slate as well, strangers in a strange new land, learning by trial and error, untouched by the old knowledge and memories, all except the boy with his faint memories and flickering bits of understanding. The old memories were like an ancient bridge to the past, worn by time and long use, bound to collapse upon itself with just a few more crossings.

Suddenly, the boy saw new fires in the sky, different from the lightning. A few at first, and then a torrent, blazing overhead from the northern sky heading south, only to go out before reaching the ground. A thousand generations had passed since the cold black hole and the nova with a heart of fire had passed over Little Eagle. In that time, it had traveled in its long, lonely, elliptical orbit across half the galaxy, seeing stars born and stars die. As it neared earth again, smaller fragments were again pulled away by earth's gravity, destined to burn up before reaching the ground, all except one.

This one ball of flame, bigger than the others, came burning across the sky, ever lower as it aimed for the bluff. The boy became fearful as he saw it looming ever larger and turned to run as the ball crashed into the side of the bluff below him, throwing him to the ground and showering him with sparks like glittering coals from a fire, but strangely cold at the same time.

Amazed to be alive, the boy got up, looking around, and saw the glowing black rock that would change his life, a part of the same rock that still lay lodged inside the bluff and would change the lives of all the people who lived there. He knew the rock was special and carefully touched it to see if it would burn him. Scanning the windswept horizon, lit by the almost constant flash of lightning from the storm, he hid the rock in his fur knapsack as the cold rain began to fall.

He kept the rock hidden to himself for the rest of his long life, always aware of the cold fire inside that never went out, even when they buried him in a small cleft on the west side of the bluff, and his son, without knowing why, knew to take the rock from his knapsack as they covered his body with a dire bear skin, then with rocks.

His son carried the memories inside him, strong and clear once again, and became a great leader and gave the people many innovations that no one could have imagined. And so it went, on and on in a repeating cycle with an end that even time does not know.

THE END

www.ingramcontent.com/pod-product-compliance
Lightning Source LLC
Chambersburg PA
CBHW030254200626
46816CB00002BA/636